THE LOW LIFE

For the
readers at
Beaconsfield!

Brian Doyle

THE LOW LIFE

FIVE GREAT TALES FROM
UP AND DOWN THE RIVER

Brian Doyle

UNCLE RONALD

ANGEL SQUARE

EASY AVENUE

COVERED BRIDGE

UP TO LOW

A GROUNDWOOD BOOK

DOUGLAS & McINTYRE

TORONTO   VANCOUVER   BERKELEY

To my granddaughter
Michaela Ashley Doyle
and to my grandson
Willem Seamus Brian Ray

Collection copyright © 1999 by Brian Doyle
Up to Low copyright © 1982 by Brian Doyle
Angel Square copyright © 1984 by Brian Doyle
Easy Avenue copyright © 1988 by Brian Doyle
Covered Bridge copyright © 1990 by Brian Doyle
Uncle Ronald copyright © 1996 by Brian Doyle
All published by Groundwood Books
First paperback edition 2002
First published in the USA 2002

Groundwood Books / Douglas and McIntyre
720 Bathurst Street, Suite 500
Toronto, Ontario M5S 2R4

Distributed in the USA by Publishers Group West
1700 Fourth Street, Berkeley, CA 94710

We acknowledge for their financial support of our publishing program the Canada Council for the Arts, the Ontario Arts Council and the Government of Canada through the Book Publishing Industry Development Program (BPIDP)

ONTARIO ARTS COUNCIL
CONSEIL DES ARTS DE L'ONTARIO

National Library of Canada Cataloguing in Publication
Doyle, Brian
The Low life : five great tales from up and down the river / Brian Doyle."A Groundwood book."
Contents: Uncle Ronald — Angel square — Easy Avenue — Covered bridge — Up to Low.
ISBN 0-88899-383-8 (bound).–
ISBN 0-88899-498-2 (pbk.)1. Children's stories, Canadian (English). I. Title.PS8557.O87L68 1999
jC813'.54   C99-932407-1
PZ7

Library of Congress Control Number:
2002111721

Printed and bound in Canada by Friesens

Index

UNCLE RONALD
WHERE *they found us in 1895*
7

ANGEL SQUARE
WHO *we were when the war was over in 1945*
95

EASY AVENUE
WHEN *we tried to climb up in 1948*
179

COVERED BRIDGE
HOW *we almost tore it all down in 1949*
263

UP TO LOW
WHY *we clung to the magic from 1950 on...*
339

UNCLE RONALD

To my grandson Aidan Jeffrey Ray
A.K.A. "A.J."

A curled-up dead maple leaf, one of the last, limps down the cold, clay path like an old, crippled spider.

I remember that so clear.

I was going for two pails of water.

It was late fall.

Late fall, a hundred years ago.

I'm a hundred and twelve years old and I can't remember what I had for lunch today and I can't remember the name of the nurse who looks after me and I can't tell you the name of the place it is where they've got me living and I can never remember the name of the old geezer I play chess with here every day, but I can remember everything, in vivid detail, about November, 1895, when the army came up from Ottawa to attack the people around the little town of Low.

And I remember that dead leaf blowing down the path.

1. HE LIKED ME BETTER THAN HER

My father beat my mother with his belt. And when I tried to grab him one time, stop him, he beat me with the belt, too. Now he was beating both of us all the time.

When he beat my mother he would beat her with the buckle end of the belt. But when he beat me he would turn the belt around and hold the other end so that he'd be beating me with the end that didn't have the buckle on.

My mother told me that he did that because he liked me better.

"He uses the buckle end on me because he doesn't like me as much as he likes you," my mother used to say.

When my father decided it was time for one of our beatings he would undo his belt buckle and then pull the belt as hard as he could from around his pants through the belt loops. The tail of the belt would make a loud flapping sound as it came around through the loops. Then it would fly out, coiling in the air like a hateful snake, high up over my mother, high up over me.

Sometimes we'd be lucky and his pants would fall down and he'd have to stop beating us to pull them up and we'd get away—run outside and down the alley.

My father worked on the square timber rafts. The lumber barons tied the huge timber together and floated them down the Ottawa River to Montreal and then down the St. Lawrence River to Quebec City. The men would live on the raft and be gone for weeks at a time.

"There's a raft leavin' in a couple of days," my mother would say. "Let's hope he's on it!" Or she'd say, "Maybe the raft will break up on them and part of it will float out to sea with him on it, please, God!"

But then one day my mother was shaking and crying and she told me that he was fired off the rafts for fighting and now he was going to be home more. That's about when she started her plan for us to run away.

But then she changed her mind. She decided to give him another chance. He was going to change. Everything was going to be different. She said he was once a very sweet man. I didn't believe her. Even when he would sing to her in his so-called beautiful voice. He'd sing a song with her name in it. My mother's name was Nora.

There was a new steam mill opened up over in Hull by the Gilmours and he got a new job over there dumping waste wood, like sawdust and knots and bark and log-ends, into the huge furnace that burned all day and all night to boil the water to make the steam to drive the saws to cut the logs into lumber.

My father would be home more now. Everything would be different. But it wasn't.

My father worked up on top where the conveyor belts dumped the waste wood into the red-hot, white-hot firepit. His job was to make sure everything went into the flames. Nothing got stuck, nothing escaped. And neither did we. The beating started again.

And my mother changed her mind again.

"Good training for him," my mother said, "because in the next world he's going to be engaged in a similar kind of position, only this time, he'll be *on* the conveyor belt!"

One night my father came home and went right to sleep with all his clothes on. My mother's plan was to get his belt off while he was still asleep and tie his hands behind his back with it. Then, when he woke up he wouldn't be able to whip it off and start beating us with it.

He was snoring so loud the windows of our little shack were rattling.

We stood beside him for a long while to see how asleep he was.

"If it wasn't a mortal sin," my mother whispered hoarsely, "I'd take up the axe right now, this minute, and chop his cursed throat!"

My mother undid his belt and we started trying to haul it from around his huge belly. As we pulled together, counting one, two, three each time, he started rolling back and forward. You could hear him sloshing while he rolled. The harder we pulled the more he rolled, but the belt was still caught underneath him.

When he fell off the bed and crashed onto the floor, my mother and I ran and hid.

He was quiet for a while. Then the snoring again.

His opening snore was like an explosion.

The cat stood on tiptoes and arched her back and tried to get rid of all her fur.

My father was on his stomach now. Lying on the buckle. It was not possible to get that belt off him. It was hopeless.

And he'd be up sooner or later. And then we were for it.

We went to bed. I curled up in my mother's arms and we slept for a couple of hours.

I dreamed my mother's eyes burned like hot coals inside their dark rings.

I dreamed we stood beside my sloshing father.

"Get me the axe!" I dreamed she whispered loud.

I dreamt I felt the feel of my father's hot blood squirting across my cheek.

2. WAYS NOT TO WET THE BED

My mother woke me up early. She knew I hated waking up, knew I was afraid of waking up, knew that the idea of waking up in the morning filled me with shame and with dread.

The reason for this was I was wetting the bed, pissing the bed every night. I couldn't help it. I couldn't do anything about it. I hated to go to sleep at night because I knew I'd wake up soaking wet and smelling bad. And the mattress all soggy. I was so ashamed. And afraid. Afraid that people would find out. Ashamed and afraid because when you are as old as I was then, you shouldn't be pissing in your bed.

I'd sometimes dream that I was standing over the pot and that everything was all right. Then I'd let go and as soon as I'd let go I'd realize that I wasn't standing over the pot at all, I was dreaming I was standing over the pot and actually I was still in bed and then I'd wake up and it would be too late. And I'd feel the warm on my stomach and my legs.

My mother and I tried everything to get me to quit.

Tried not drinking any liquid after four o'clock in the afternoon. But then I couldn't get to sleep because I was so thirsty. By midnight I couldn't stand it any more and I'd get up and drink about a gallon of water and then go to bed and right to sleep. The next morning I'd be swimming.

Or I'd lie right on the edge of the bed, tight against the wall. Pressed up against where the mattress met the wall. Fall asleep like that if you can. Piss down the wall and the side of the mattress. They'd never know. Wallpaper was all stained from the leak in the roof anyway. But that didn't work because most of the time after I'd fall asleep I'd roll back over onto the deep middle of the bed and be back in the same old fix all over again.

"Oh, poor Mickey," my mother would say in the morning. "What are we going to do with you?"

She'd be ripping the sheet off the bed, turning over the mattress which already had stains on the other side from the times before.

"We've tried everything," she'd say. "We'll have to get the doctor over, see what he says about it!" And then she'd sigh.

She was right when she said we tried everything.

My mother was always reading, and in a story she read to me once by Charles Dickens called *A Christmas Carol*, a famous story, the hero, Scrooge, had bad dreams because of some cheese he ate before he went to sleep.

We thought that if I ate a lot of cheese before I went to sleep I'd have nightmares all night which would take my mind off wetting the bed. The cheese gave me nightmares all right but they were nightmares about wetting the bed. So that didn't work.

I tried tying an empty bean can under the bed to the spring with a wire and digging a hole in my mattress and lying on my stomach over the hole. Didn't work. Wound up with my foot stuck in the hole and the bed soaking wet again.

Tried a clothes pin on my "spigot" as my mother called it but it just caused a lot of pain and one night I nearly exploded.

A nice lady in the next shack who my mother said was a witch told me to try tying cloves of garlic around my waist and my thighs but that just made things worse because urine mixed with garlic smells worse than just plain urine.

The stupidest plan was attaching a hose to myself and hanging it out the window.

There were so many thieves in Lowertown that you couldn't even leave your clothes on the line at night or you'd come out in the morning and they'd be gone.

My father had stolen a hose from the mill where he worked. Brought it home, he said, to beat us with it.

I attached the hose to my spigot with string and a strong, nickel-plated tie clip I found outside Roger the Embalmer's shop in the snow one spring on Bank Street. Then I hung the hose out the window.

Anyway, in the middle of the night, a thief going by saw the valuable hose hanging out the window, grabbed it and ran.

I was sore for about a week after.

I wasn't going to school that year. The year 1895. I passed everything the year before but when I started back in September something strange started happening to me.

Every time I sat in my desk and the teacher said good morning, I'd lose my breath and I'd faint. I'd flop down on the desk like a dead fish and they'd have to haul me out and put me in the cloakroom on some coats on the floor and then get somebody to go to my place and get my mother to come and take me home.

This happened so many times that the school told my mother to keep me at home until the doctor figured out what to do with me. When the doctor finally came over to Lowertown and over to our shack, he decided I'd better stay home from school for the rest of the year and rest up as best I could.

That's what he said.

"Keep him home from school. Let him get rested up."

My mother just looked at him. "Doctors!" she said.

Not too long after that I started wetting the bed.

3. WISHING SOMEBODY ELSE WAS YOUR FATHER

My mother woke me up gentle, soothing, saying she had a plan, hurry, quietly, your father's still on the floor, we have a plan. It was a plan she'd had for weeks.

It was now or never.

She pulled up a board from the floor under my bed and took out a box. In the box there was a new pair of denim overalls, with bib. There was a tag on the overalls: "Half price sale—50 cents. O'Reilly's." There was also a set of woollen combination long underwear, with trap door. The tag on this beautiful underwear said: "Half price sale—60 cents. O'Reilly's." And a little sign: "If O'Reilly made them, they fit."

"I wonder how O'Reilly knows what size you take, Mickey," my mother said.

I rubbed the new woollen underwear into my face. It felt so smooth and smelled so new. It was the nicest piece of clothing I'd ever felt.

My mother had a sack packed for me for a trip. There was a pencil and a pad. A cake of soap and a towel. Socks. A shirt, mitts, scarf, a toque. A bottle of Skiel Cod Liver Oil "for plump cheeks."

There was an envelope with seventy-five cents in. There was a copy of the book *Beautiful Joe* by Margaret Marshall Saunders. There was a packet of tea and a small bag of sugar. And a little paper sack of hard candy.

"You're goin' to stay at the farm with me brother for the winter. You're goin' to get out of this. This is no place for a child."

She broke a loaf of bread in half, wrapped it in newspaper, squeezed it gently into the sack.

"I've been stealing money from your father's pants for weeks now, preparing for this moment in our unfortunate existence!" she was saying as she helped me into my new clothes and put her finger to her lips.

No more talking.

My mother sat at the table and scribbled a note. She scribbled it in a planned kind of way—a note that she wanted to look scribbled in a hurry. She actually was very careful about the scribbling. The note said, "CPR depot—7:00 A.M."

She looked at it to see if it looked right and then she pushed it gently off the edge of the table and watched it flutter naturally under the chair.

She looked at me and winked.

My father would find it there. She hoped.

It was a false clue.

I said a silent goodbye to the cat, rubbing her furry head and touching her cold, wet nose to my lips.

We stepped past my father's body on the floor. I leaned down, looked down in the gloom to see if his throat was axed. But I knew it wasn't. I knew it was just a dream. He was rolled over on his back now. Rolled over during the night. He was half under the bed.

The look on his face—his eyes half open, his mouth gaping, the blood heaving and pumping in the veins in his neck, his flapping cheeks, his caked lips—all these filled me with fear.

We slipped quiet out the broken entrance of our shack. While I was pulling the door shut he let out a roar that made my heart stop. The whole building seemed to shake.

But he wasn't awake. He was just choking on an extra big snore.

We picked our way through the mud between the crooked shacks and went up the dark path to the street.

There were quite a few people in the street. It wasn't even 6:00 A.M. but people were already on their way to their jobs in the mills. The electric streetcars were a new thing then, in Ottawa. They made the street look joyful, and the sound of the bell and the crackling of the wires and the warm glow of the lights gave you a happy feeling, a safe feeling.

The sign on the electric streetcar said Chaudiere Falls. We'd go as far as the turn over to Hull, then get off and walk the rest of the way to the CPR depot.

My mother was going to put me on the train to Low, Quebec, to my Uncle Ronald O'Rourke.

"But not until tonight," she explained. "The real train you'll be on leaves Union Depot at 5:30 tonight. We're going to the CPR depot this morning, pretending to take a train there. West or south or east—he'll never figure it out. We could be headed for Toronto or Halifax or New York as far as he'll ever be able to tell!"

Under one of the new electric streetlights on Rideau Street I saw a small crowd gathered around. The crowd was watching six policemen lined up at attention. They weren't Ottawa policemen. Ottawa police didn't wear knee-length boots so shiny that the new electric streetlight reflected off them, glittered off them. And Ottawa police didn't have spotless blue uniforms with twinkling gold buttons. And Ottawa policemen definitely didn't wear those tall, fancy, strange-looking hats with the feather plumes and chin straps with tassels.

Ottawa police were usually covered with mud from rolling around in the streets all the time trying to arrest people day and night.

The streetcar was delayed because somebody's pig was on the track and wouldn't move and there was a wagon upset up the street and there were Thanksgiving turkeys running all over the place.

The fancy policemen were being checked over by their captain. They were all tall and handsome in their outfits. And they wore revolvers in shiny black-leather holsters on their broad belts.

"They're not from around here," a man who was standing beside my mother and me on the streetcar said in a loud voice. "Nossir," he said. After he thought for a while about what he just said, he said, "Nossir, they be's from someplace else for sure. Not from around these parts. Definitely from away somewhere else…"

My mother was rolling her eyes. "I suppose if they weren't from around here, they pretty well *have* to be from someplace else!" she said, and everybody on the streetcar laughed.

My mother had no patience with people who said obvious things.

The streetcar got moving again.

"Now, in your sack," my mother was saying, "you have yourself a pad and pencil, and you'll write me a letter every Sunday, tell me how you're making out. Here's the postal box number written on the back of the pad where you'll send it. I won't be where we just left or anywhere near where your father is. But I'll have the mail picked up at the main post office every Monday. And I'll expect a letter there from you, me bucko, without fail, each Sunday! You'll pay the stamps out of the seventy-five cents you've got in the envelope..."

"Seventy-five cents is pretty near a dollar. And a dollar's quite a sum for a young lad to be goin' around with," the man beside us said.

My mother turned on him, her eyes flashing.

"Would it be askin' too much, sir, for you to keep your gob shut and your ugly face out of our affairs!"

Everybody on the streetcar laughed again.

My mother had no patience with people who couldn't mind their own business.

We moved down to the back of the car and my mother continued her instructions.

"Now, you have a cake of soap there. Use it every morning when you get up first thing, no matter how cold it is in your room. And take a spoonful of cod liver oil before you go to bed at night. When that bottle runs out, me second cousins once removed, the O'Malley girls, will supply you with another.

"Now, the tea and the sugar is a gift for me cousins the O'Malley girls. The candy, that's a little treat for the O'Malley girls, too. Have a piece of it from time to time yourself and think of your mother..."

My mother looked at her own reflection in the dark back window of the electric streetcar, and I looked at both our reflections, and while the trolley above us threw sparks into the air and made our reflections flash, we cried a little bit together.

A woman got on the streetcar selling ripe plums. My mother got two for one cent. We ate the plums and by chewing and sucking on the plums, forgot our tears.

The streetcar headed over Sappers' Bridge and up Wellington Street.

We were getting to the Parliament Buildings. I loved looking at the Parliament Buildings. They were so strong and solid and beautiful now with the electric light. And they made you feel proud and safe.

While I shaded my eyes against the streetcar window I saw a beautiful man striding very straight and smooth wearing a tall silk hat and carrying a walking stick and gliding under a streetlamp in front of the Parliament Buildings.

He had on a tall white collar and a long black coat and white gloves.

I was looking at him, wondering what it would be like to have a father like him instead of the one I had.

My mother saw me looking and told me that the man was Wilfrid Laurier. He would someday be called *Sir* Wilfrid Laurier and would be Canada's first French Canadian prime minister, but nobody knew that then.

"There's a kind, good man," my mother said with a sigh. "There's a gentleman. I'll wager my soul he doesn't strike his wife and young ones with his belt!"

Mr. Wilfrid Laurier turned through the iron gates and walked toward the Parliament Buildings.

I wanted with all my heart to have someone like him for a father.

Suddenly a fire wagon clanked by. It was pulled by four wild-acting horses. The wagon was jangling its bells like mad and the firemen were hanging on for dear life as the wagon nearly upset while it passed around the streetcar. Waves of mud were sloshing off the wagon wheels and hoses were flying and buckets and tools were bouncing into the air. People pushed to the front and sides of the streetcar to see what there was to see.

In the distance, west on Wellington Street, the sky was a red glow.

Two more reels went by and people on the street were running.

As the streetcar got closer to the Chaudiere Falls where it would turn to take the passengers over to the mills to work, the sky got redder to the west and it was full of flying showers of flame.

The news came back to us at the back of the electric streetcar.

The CPR train depot was on fire.

4. A FUN FIRE

The bone-dry cedar shingles, red-hot, were flying up and away from the roof of the CPR depot like shooting stars and raining trails of beautiful red and yellow sparks over the Chaudiere Falls. Sheets of red and blue flame were splashing up the tall wood walls of the depot.

Windows were exploding. The crowd was going *ooh!* and *aah!* A lot of people were going to be late for work at the mills over the river that day.

It was hopeless to try and save the building. The firemen were hosing the other sheds around to keep them from going up in flames.

And people further away were gathering pails of water around their little houses and shacks, just in case.

Travellers were trying to save suitcases, boxes, packages. Two men and a bunch of kids were rolling a smouldering wagon full of baggage into a big puddle of mud along the tracks. A man was running with a suitcase on fire, kicking it, hitting it on the ground, dragging it through puddles trying to put it out.

Steam engines were groaning and roaring, banging and shunting boxcars further down the tracks away from the depot, away from the flames.

The platform was now on fire. Yellow tongues licked the planks. Down the way an open coal car had taken too many burning shingles. The coal in the car had ignited. The firemen trained their hoses on the coal. Blue flames and steam exploded into the sky and the crowd cheered.

The water pressure from the new city hydrants was as powerful as they said it would be. The firemen were happy, excited. Look how high the water goes, their faces were saying.

A man wanted to get his luggage off the end of the platform as the flames reached out for it. The police held him back.

"The last shirt I own in this world is in that top box," he was yelling.

"Looks like you'll be goin' to church shirtless!" shouted a man with a voice I'd heard recently. It was the pest from the streetcar who my mother had told to shut his gob.

"Maybe you'll be able to get a real good shirt this time with the insurance money!" another guy in the crowd shouted.

"And have a mind to get the shirt made by O'Reilly. That way it'll be sure to fit ya!" shouted the pest from the streetcar.

"Unless it's the wrong size!" the other answered and the crowd let out a big laugh.

"Wrong size or not, at least it won't be on fire!" shouted the pest.

"Unless O'Reilly has a fire. What'll he do then?" was the answer.

"Why, I suppose he'll wind up the way he is now—shirtless!"

"Unless they up and have a FIRE SALE at O'Reilly's!" shouts the pest's partner. The crowd was moaning because the jokes were so bad.

"Why don't you two go and get a job on the stage up at the Grand Opera House and give us a rest!" my mother shouted and the whole crowd roared with laughter.

"Do you think it's possible," my mother said quiet to me, "to be born without a brain at all?"

I knew why my mother was speaking out and drawing attention the way she did on the streetcar and then there at the fire. She knew my father would be asking people if they'd seen his wife and kid. She was making sure they didn't miss us. People would tell my father they saw us.

He'd make them tell. Everybody was afraid of him.

The trains west and east were late leaving, of course, but they left Ottawa all the same, and we hoped that my father would believe we were on one of them.

My mother and I moved slow back to the back of the crowd, pretending to go to the trains but then pulled our collars up around our faces and circled quick back toward town and Parliament Hill.

We left the glow of the burning depot behind us. We walked past the iron gates where I saw Wilfrid Laurier go in. The sky started to lighten and we headed across Sappers' Bridge.

My mother pulled my arm and we backed up against the side of one of the bridge pillars. I followed her eyes where they stared wide at a streetcar moving past.

There were only a few people on this one, now that the rush hour was over.

It wasn't hard to spot my father sitting there in one of the centre seats, staring straight ahead.

His face was twisted in rage.

He was heading for the CPR depot.

Looking for us.

Did I say I was well over a hundred years of age? I forget. I think I did.

Sometimes, when you're my age, your body feels so light you feel like you're going to disappear. Or you feel kind of transparent. I feel sometimes afraid that when the nurse comes in to check on me she'll be able to see right through me. I feel papery, like the skin of a long-gone bug. But I don't really think about my body most of the time. I ignore it as much as I can. I mean, what's the sense? I've spent decades feeding it, watering it, satisfying it and enough is enough.

They can come in and suck me up their vacuum cleaners for all I care.

No, now it's my mind and my mind only that I care about.

And my memory. My memory, which is like an ancient painting on the wall of a deep cave. If I carry the flaming torch into the cave, get the light shining just right, flickering just nice there in the shadows, and if I recognize and remember the symbols and the letters, the pictures and the words, well then, I can read and interpret exactly what's there.

There was the fire at the CPR depot. My mother and I pretended to get on one of the trains early that morning. Then we slipped away, spent the rest of the day hiding around town in places where we were sure we wouldn't run into my father.

Like church, for instance.

We went to morning mass at St. Brigit's and then went down to the Sisters of Charity to see if we could pick out a big warm sweater for me and maybe an extra flannel shirt out of the clothing-for-the-poor bin. We got a nice sweater and a shirt and later walked up St. Patrick Street and met Father Fortier, the priest who had baptized me. My mother and Father Fortier had a chat in private. I knew what they were talking about. My mother was telling him where she was sending me to get away from my father. And she probably told him where she was going, too, but I wasn't sure. Father Fortier knew all about our troubles. And more, probably.

I didn't like Father Fortier much because of what he did when I was baptized. See, I wasn't baptized for some reason until I was around five years old. Usually you get baptized when you're just a tiny baby about the length of your father's forearm, but for some reason I wasn't available.

But, when I finally did get baptized, Father Fortier was mad that I was so old, so he pulled my hair until I cried and told me he was doing this so I'd never forget this moment. He had a fistful of my curly hair, and was squeezing it while he put the holy water on me. The water running down my face was holy water and tears.

"I'm pulling your hair, lad, so's you'll never forget this sacred moment," he said, and then just to make sure I'd never forget that sacred moment, he banged my forehead five times against the side of the stone basin. Once for The Father. Once for The Son. Once for The Holy Ghost. And twice for *Amen*! (Once for Ah. Once for men.)

He was right.

I never did forget that sacred moment.

My mother had more money than I ever saw. She had been stealing a little bit out of my father's pants every chance she got for the last couple of months. She had almost nine dollars in coins in her bag.

We went into a drugstore on Sussex Street and looked around in there. The guy behind the counter was writing out a big ad on a piece of cardboard.

"Odorama Tooth Powder," the sign said. "A New Thing—25 cents!"

"What's that?" my mother said.

"It's a new thing," the clerk said.

"I know that," my mother said. "I can read. But what does it do?"

"You sprinkle it on a brush and scrub your teeth with it," the clerk said. "Your breath'll turn out smelling like the first rose of summer!"

"I'll take one," my mother said.

The clerk gave her a big smile and wrapped the can of tooth powder and shoved his face up close to hers, breathing all over her when she paid him the money.

"You could use a dose of it yourself!" my mother said, fanning her hand in front of her face.

My mother was what you call outspoken.

We walked up to the Oriental Cafe on the corner of Bank and Sparks. Meal tickets were seven for a dollar or fifteen cents each. "Fried oysters served with every meal!" the sign said.

We each had meat and potatoes and bread and butter and tea.

When we were finished, my mother said to the cook, "Did you forget the fried oysters, or are we havin' them for our dessert?"

When the cook started apologizing, my mother interrupted him. "Never mind," she said. "Give us an extra chunk of bread instead, and I'll put it in the boy's sack. He's goin' on a trip."

When I looked at her, wondering why she was bringing so much attention to herself when we were supposed to be on a train miles from here by now she said, "Don't worry, your father never comes near a place like this. Look around you. Do you see a sign anywhere that says 'Beer For Sale'?"

Later on that afternoon, in the Union Depot, my mother gave me the expensive tooth powder and helped me pack it and the bread in my sack. While we were stuffing the sack a porter came over to see what we were up to. My mother waved him off and we moved into a corner that was more private.

"The tooth powder is for your Uncle Ronald. There's instructions on the bottle. He's in love with the Hickey girl down the road. This will help him court her."

She hugged me and made me promise to write to her. She had tears in her eyes and hugged me again.

"You'll hear from me as soon as I figure out what we're goin' to do," she said. "Now, get on the train, get yourself a seat and wave to me out the window."

And I did that.

6. LOTS OF McCOOEYS

On the train I took the book out of the sack that my mother had packed for me. The book was *Beautiful Joe: The Autobiography of a Dog*. The dog, Joe, telling the story of his life. The book was hard to concentrate on because you kept trying to forget about the fact that the dog could write a book. The story would be going along fine and then a little voice would interrupt your mind and say, "Just a minute. How can a dog think this stuff, say this stuff?"

In the story, a violent milkman named Jenkins slaughters a whole litter of baby pups except one. This one he cuts off the tail and the ears. I guess that's the one he liked the best. The dog's name is Beautiful Joe and gets adopted by this nice Protestant minister and his kind family. It's a story that almost makes you cry except you can't because every now and then you say to yourself, did the dog get somebody to write this for him? Then you don't feel like crying, you feel like laughing.

It was also hard to concentrate reading because of the loud conversations going on in the seats around me.

Two old guys sitting across from me were talking about a family that lived somewhere around Brennan's Hill and Low. The family's name was McCooey. The two old guys trading stories about the family of McCooeys had their window open and a lot of soot from the smokestack of the steam engine was blowing in the window. The reason they had the window open was so they could spit their tobacco juice through the window instead of on the floor.

When the train left Ottawa, they were spitting on the floor. They spit on the floor while we stopped in Hull, and then Ironside and then Farmer's Rapids and then pulling into Chelsea. While the train was taking on water at the station at Chelsea, a conductor came along and told the two old guys to quit spitting on the floor.

"Where do you think you are, at home?" he told the two old guys.

"We don't spit on the floor at home," one of the old guys said. The one with hardly any teeth.

"Well, don't do it here then," the conductor told them, "or you'll be put off the train and you can try walkin' for a while."

"Walkin' might be faster 'n you're going along, anyway," the other old guy with the big hairy ears said.

"Open the window and spit out there," the conductor said. "And try not to hit any innocent bystanders!"

So the two old guys were spitting tobacco juice out the window. But sometimes a gust of wind would take what they spit and blow it back in and give me a bit of a shower.

Me and my book by the dog, Beautiful Joe.

By the time the train pulled into Tenaga they were still talking about the McCooey family.

"Oh, they were a big gang, the McCooeys were," the guy with the hairy ears said.

"And there's lots of them left, I suppose," the guy with only a few teeth said.

"There's a few of them left," said the other old guy, squirting a big slurp of tobacco juice out the window into the wind and right back in onto the seat beside me.

"There's Walkabout McCooey, who all he does is walk all over the place all the time, winter and summer, spring and fall, rain or shine."

"And there's Peek-a-boo McCooey, who's always looking out from behind trees or rocks or posts or buildings."

"And there's Turnaround McCooey who can't take a half a dozen steps without turning completely around. If he's walking down the road to church, for instance, he'll walk for a little bit, stop, turn completely around, then continue on his way until pretty soon he'll have to stop and turn himself around again."

They were talking like this off and on while the train stopped at all the little places on the way up to Low.

Gleneagle, Kirk's Ferry, Larrimac.

Before each stop a second conductor, one with a voice like a cannon, would walk through the car, yelling out the name of each place.

"Burnet! Next stop Burnet!" he came through again, booming out the name of the next stop. Some of the passengers would tease him, saying, "Didn't we just go through Burnet back there?" This would make the huge conductor bend down and look out the windows of the train to see where we were. Then he'd yell out again, even louder this time, just to show he was right all along, "BURNET! NEXT STOP BURNET!" and make everybody screw up their faces from the pain of the noise of his awful voice.

At each stop there was a lot of shouting and blowing of steam and grinding of metal and slamming of doors. At each stop, empty metal milk cans would be thrown off and piled onto wagons along the train. And when the cars clanged together, the flesh of the horses hitched to the wagons would quiver and their tails would switch.

And there were lots of people on the platform at each station, there to meet the train. It was exciting. They would go and stand on the platform and watch. See who was coming to town, who was leaving, what kind of parcels were dropped off from Eaton's and other places.

It was exciting to meet the train every evening. You didn't need a reason. You didn't have to be picking up a parcel or meeting somebody or saying goodbye to somebody. It was just exciting to go and watch.

Sometimes you'd see people open up packs of the *Ottawa Citizen* or the *Evening Journal* and maybe look for something in the paper they wanted to see.

Sometimes you'd see somebody open up the paper and read something to a couple of other people.

After Burnet there was Chemin-des-Pins and Cascades. Often the train would run right along the Gatineau River, making the lamps sparkle and run in the darkened water.

The two old guys across from me were still trading gossip about the McCooey family.

"And then there's Shirt-tail McCooey, who wears all the shirts he owns at the same time. He has about ten shirts and in the morning he gets up and puts all of them on! And they say each day he rotates them."

"Rotates them?"

"Yes, you see the one he wore on the outside yesterday, he puts on the inside today. That way he always has a different shirt next to his skin each day and a different one on the outside each day, so he never has to wash them!"

"Patterson! Patterson, next stop!" the huge conductor boomed.

"Didn't we just leave Patterson?" somebody shouted. The conductor, who was shaped like a barrel, bent down and checked out the windows at the shadows of trees and fields sliding slowly by, just to make sure.

"PATTERSON! NEXT STOP PATTERSON!" he bellowed, and everybody in the car held their hands over their ears and laughed.

I was getting tired of hearing about the McCooeys, and I tried to get back to my book about the mutilated dog, Beautiful Joe. We stopped at Farm Point and then Rockhurst, and came into Wakefield, which was a pretty big town right on the water.

Until two years before, Wakefield was the end of the line, but now the train went all the way up to Gracefield, past Low. A brand new track.

People in Wakefield were pretty excited when the train came up from

Ottawa every night because the train ran right up the main street of town. It was so close to the houses that you could see into the rooms—maybe see them having their tea or almost shake hands with them from the train window while they sat and rocked on their little verandahs after supper.

It was a mild evening for November. But this evening there was something else in Wakefield getting almost as much attention as the train.

In a large express wagon pulled by four horses there were six policemen and some other men following in another big express wagon also being pulled by two teams of powerful horses. As they passed under the streetlamps I could see it was the same six policemen my mother and I saw that morning on the street in Ottawa. The sides of the express wagons were down so everybody could see the shiny, knee-length boots, the spotless blue uniforms and the twinkling gold buttons.

And the tall, fancy, strange-looking hats with the feather plumes and chin straps with tassels.

And their revolvers in the shiny black holsters on their broad belts.

You could tell the way people were watching the two teams of four trotting by, hauling these strange-looking policemen and other official-looking gents, that nobody knew who they were or where they were going.

One thing was sure, they weren't staying in Wakefield. They were heading north.

"They won't be doing any trotting once they leave Wakefield," one man who was passing up the aisle was saying. "The roads above here are knee-deep in mud!"

After Wakefield things got a lot quieter and darker. The little stations at Alcove and Lordsvale had hardly any light.

The two across from me were still talking about the McCooeys.

"And there's still lots of others. Whistle McCooey, who whistles all the time, even in his sleep, they say; and Barnyard McCooey, who can imitate all the animals on the farm; and Mean Bone McCooey, who fights all the time."

And then the other one: "And Mouthwash McCooey, who swears all the time, even though his old mother washes his mouth out with homemade soap every night; and Sobbing McCooey, who cries all the time, even when he's laughing; and Nosey McCooey, who smells everything (he'll smell your shoulder if you stop to talk to him on the road); and Ahem McCooey (she says 'Ahem' after every second or third word); and Boner McCooey, well, we don't have to point out how *he* goes around all the time!"

They were running out of McCooey stories and one of the men, the one without very many teeth, was dozing off. The one with the hairy ears was trying to explain about Tommy Twelve Toes McCooey, who had six toes on each foot and could outrun a deer...

But there was another conversation further up the aisle that floated into my ears, blocking everything else out. I put my book back in my sack and acted like I was ready to get off the train.

I stood up and stretched and picked up my coat and sack and moved up toward the end of the coach and sat down again. There were quite a few empty seats since we left Wakefield. A man and a woman were talking. The man was eating an onion.

The train wheels clicked and the engine chuffed and the trees and rocks echoed by. We pulled in and out of Brennan's Hill hardly seeing anybody and only one light.

I listened to the gossips speaking quietly.

"Yes, and the two women, twins they are, identical, brought the bailiff into the kitchen, sat him down at the table with a cuppa tea and got around behind him and one of the identical twins—nobody knows which one of course because they're both so exactly the same—one of them brained him a good one with a porcelain pisspot on the back of the head and knocked him silly. Then the twins, they opened the trap to the cellar and rolled him down in there and he spent two days or more down there before they let him out and sent him down the road and told him not to come back...

"A bailiff named Flatters it was. Shot dead as a doornail outside his house in Aylmer only a few weeks later."

"Was it the twins that done it, that shot him?" said the man with the mouthful of onion.

"That's what they say," said the woman. "That's what they say."

"The O'Malley girls, is it? Is that what they're called?" asked the onion man.

"I believe it is," said the woman. "Yes, the O'Malley girls is what they call them, I believe. Shot him dead outside his own house."

"Quite the girls they must be, them O'Malley girls."

"Yes, they must, they must indeed!"

Could that be right? I thought. My mother's second cousins once removed, the O'Malley girls? The cousins I had the sugar and tea and candy in my sack for? Murderers? Couldn't be. Must be some other people with the same name. But identical twins? How many identical twins could there be around named O'Malley?

"LOW! NEXT STOP LOW!" the huge conductor roared right behind me, making the hair on the back of my neck stand straight out while the train let out a bellowing, lonely cry that echoed again and again from the oldest mountains in the world.

7. A BED OF THISTLES

The headlamps of the steam engine tried to stab into the dark forest but they couldn't. There was no moon but the sky was clear and if you shaded your eyes with your hands you could see some stars.

There were lanterns at each end of the platform and other lights moving around in the gloom. Parcels and mailbags and cream cans were being loaded onto wagons and some men were throwing short logs into the car behind the engine.

There were smells of burning wood, sawdust, spruce gum, horses, leather, milk, plums.

It was a nice night for November, not cold, but you could feel, every little while, a small burst of Arctic air, just a warning that it was coming. Winter. First Thanksgiving, then winter.

Shadow shapes were working, moving around, laughing, shouting in the half light of the Low station.

The train let go a giant sneeze and started moving with a grinding shudder.

Conversations were going back and forward.

"Lovely and mild?" somebody said.

"It is that," said somebody else.

"Little wetter than last fall," somebody added.

"Quite a bit wetter," another agreed.

"You know it's going to snow any day now!" shouted a man from the other end of the platform.

"We know that!" another one said from on top of a wagon.

"Then it will be winter for sure!" yelled the first.

"We know that, too!" roared the other.

"And then, spring!" the first kept on.

"We know all this. Why are you telling us these things that we already know?"

"Just reminding you is all. Just to make sure you're up to date!"

Soon the train howled away up the track into the bush and around a bend, and the little light on the caboose twinkled into the trees and disappeared.

The station was sudden quiet. Most of the people seemed to fade into the night as fast as the train did. The train left and sucked the life right out of the station with it.

Except for one shape, standing off to the side in the flickering light of the lantern at the end of the platform. In the shadows beside him, his horse and rig.

It was the first time I ever met my Uncle Ronald. And the first word I ever heard my Uncle Ronald say was my name.

"Mickey," he said, the name rumbling deep out of his broad chest. "I've come to meet ya." I loved the sound of my name, the way it came out from inside him.

He took my bag from me with two fingers. At first he looked to be about as tall as my father but then I realized he was standing down on the second step up to the platform. When I stepped down beside him I was standing beside a giant.

In the mostly darkness he was there.

He helped me up into the little rig and then got in himself. When he put his weight on it the springs sagged and groaned. There was a little dark-lamp on a hook behind him.

"This is Second Chance Lance," he said gently, introducing me to his horse. "He's very intelligent. Aren't you, Lance?" Lance's left ear twitched as he began pulling us out of the station yard. Soon we were in the complete dark. Uncle Ronald closed the shutter on the dark-lamp and cut off the shaft of light.

"See more with that out," he said, and Lance broke into a trot. "Once your eyes get used to the dark."

The stars showed the line of trees, and Lance's hooves thudded soft on the grassy road.

"The main road is mainly mud," said Uncle Ronald, "but these side roads are fine."

We passed slow some open fields and a winking farmhouse light or two.

We rounded a bend along a fence and Lance slowed down to a walk while Uncle Ronald whispered to him, "Sh, sh, sh." We stopped without a sound and Uncle Ronald put his huge hand on top of my head and turned it to the side and pointed with his other arm where I should look.

"Look there!" he whispered. I looked down his arm where he was pointing. All I could make out was a fence and a clearing. Uncle Ronald snapped the shutter of the dark-lamp open and sent a shaft of light toward where we were looking.

Two big round yellow eyes.

A complete white feather coat covering everything, feet and all.

A snowy owl.

"Arrived yesterday," Uncle Ronald said and slid shut the lantern. "He's early. Beautiful creature. Powerful. Won't say a word, though. Will he, Lance? We tried on our way over to meet you to get him to talk. Not a word out of him."

Lance seemed to know that there was no use hanging around to hear the snowy owl say "hoo," so we took off again, thumping softly up the road. The rig swinging smooth along.

"I had a letter from me sister. You'll stay with us for a while." A long pause. "Or longer, we'll see." I hadn't yet seen Uncle Ronald's face. It was mostly his voice that made me feel so safe.

I wondered what she told him in the letter. Did she tell him she was stealing money from my father's pants? Did she say she thought of axing his throat? Did she tell about the belt and the fear? Did she say about me and my problem with beds? Did she say in the letter my father wanted to kill us?

"I know your father," he said.

I waited. Waited for him to say more. But he didn't.

The soft thudding of Lance's hooves on the grass stirred something along the road, making a loud buzzing whirring clatter. Lance answered with a short whinny of his own.

"Never mind those partridge, Lance. You leave them alone. They need their rest."

One farmhouse we passed had a flickering lamp on in an upstairs window. The curtain was drawn but I saw the shadow of a figure moving several times.

Uncle Ronald looked up at the window as soon as it came into view and kept his eyes on it until he was twisted almost right around in his seat.

I wondered who lived there who he was so interested in.

A stream bubbled alongside us in the dark as we drove.

We turned into a side road that was even softer and quieter. We stopped. We were at a closed gate. Lance lifted the wooden latch with his nose. He bunted the gate with his head and pulled us through. Behind us, I heard the gate swing shut and heard the wooden latch fall back into the notch.

"That top hinge needs a little oil, doesn't it, Lance?"

The next gate was the same.

We slid quiet past some buildings looming alongside and then pulled up to a stop. Lance let out a pleasant little sigh and a short neigh in his throat. Glad to be home.

The door opened and a woman in a long dress and an apron raised a lamp for us.

"Come in, young Mickey, ya poor thing. You'll come in and sit down and have a plate and a cup..."

Uncle Ronald disappeared with Lance and I went into the kitchen. At the stove was another woman, in the same long dress and the same apron.

"Come in, young Mickey, ya poor thing. Sit down there and there'll be a plate and a cup in front of ya quick as a wink!"

It was the O'Malley girls!

Uncle Ronald came in. "This is Edith and Mildred O'Malley, Mickey," he said, but he didn't say which was which or who was who. This was the first look at him I had in the light.

His eyes were big and dark and his hair was black and curly and hung over his broad forehead and partly over his ears. He was as tall as the door, and his shoulders were broad and sloping from his muscled neck. He wore a great belt round his middle with a tail hanging down on each side. When he took off his jacket his chest pulled and strained the buttons of his shirt. His wrists were wide and his hands strong and veined. His thighs filled out his pants and his boots were round in the toe and wide in the heel.

He was big and powerful but looked soft and gentle at the same time.

After a little snack of fried pork and bread and butter and tea and a lot of fuss, I unpacked my bag.

While I placed the things from my bag on the table, the O'Malley girls stood behind me. I was pretty tense at first, sitting there at the table. Was this where the bailiff was sitting when he got knocked silly with the porcelain pot?

I put the pencil and pad out.

"I'm to write my mother a letter every Sunday," I said.

"We'll remind you," the O'Malley girls said, both at the same time.

I put out the cake of soap and the towel and the O'Malley girls showed me where the washstand with the basin and the jug was.

To each item I put on the table—the socks, the mitts, the shirt, scarf, toque—the O'Malley girls said "mmm" or "good" or "grand."

To the clinking envelope with the seventy-five cents in it they said, "He has his own money," and to the bottle of Skiel Cod Liver Oil they read the label, "For plump cheeks," both together like a little song.

To the book, *Beautiful Joe* by Margaret Marshall Saunders but really told by the dog, they said, "Hard to believe, a dog writing a book!"

To the tea and the sugar and the candy, they said, "How thoughtful of your mother, she didn't need to..."

But the hit of the unpacking was the can of Odorama Tooth Powder. Uncle Ronald was sitting with his chair leaned back against the wall next to the chimney.

I echoed my mother's words.

"This tooth powder is for Uncle Ronald to help him court the Hickey girl down the road," I said.

"Indeed!" said one of the O'Malley girls and then they both laughed quietly the very same way. Uncle Ronald's chair hit the floor with a thud. He was laughing too but his face was a little red.

Time to sleep.

They put me in a little narrow bed in the space under the stairs. They sent Uncle Ronald out to the barn to make my mattress.

"He'll have the trundle bed under the stairs," one of the O'Malley girls said. "Fill that sack with fresh straw, Ronald, and he'll be as snug as a bug in a rug, as they say!"

The sack was sewn out of unstitched flour bags and then filled with straw and hay.

"Put some clover in, too, Ronald, so's it will smell real nice," the other O'Malley girl called softly as Uncle Ronald left with the big sack.

"And try not, Ronald, to put too many thistles in with it!" one of them said, and they both gave me a big wink at the same time.

"Thistles sticking in your back, Mickey, have a way of keeping you awake all night!" one of them said.

"That's the truth, Mickey," said the other one.

Maybe it would be a good idea to be awake all night, I thought, filling up with disgust for myself.

"Maybe you should fill it up just with thistles," I said, feeling pretty sorry for myself.

They both gave me a question-mark smile. The same, exact same little smile. I wondered if they knew what I meant.

The O'Malley girls had curly red hair, freckles, brown eyes. They spoke their words very clearly. They always said your name when they said anything to you. They would often touch you when they talked to you. Always had a sweet smile for you. Small, even teeth. Pudgy arms. Small hard hands. Walked and worked around the house making almost no noise. Very neat. Everything in the right place.

Each wore a small crucifix cross on a little chain around her throat.

I went to bed and lay squeezed as close to the wall as I could.

The lamp moved up the stairs over me and shadows danced and light slid and ran and winked and then it was dark.

I dreaded going to sleep.

But I went, anyway.

8. UNCLE RONALD BEATS THE ROOSTER

It took me a long time to figure out where I was.

I knew one thing for sure. There was something sharp sticking in my back.

And the sloping structure above me was creaking and stretching and sagging and through the cracks a shimmering flame moved down.

And there were heavy tiptoed footsteps.

And something enormous was on its way down from somewhere to harm me. Something raging and dangerous descending to me, going to smash me flat.

Half asleep still.

I was buried alive under something somewhere and my father was coming down to finish me off.

But then, what was sticking in my back was cleaning out my brain and blowing away the fog of terror.

I was in my Uncle Ronald's farmhouse sleeping under his stairs and the thing sticking in my back was probably one of his thistles. And the bag of rage coming down was only Uncle Ronald making his way as quiet as he could down the staircase.

Then the dancing flame of another gliding coal-oil lamp showed two shadows, two figures exactly the same shape along the wall. The O'Malley girls.

I heard Uncle Ronald go out the door and the O'Malley girls moving around the kitchen, clanking metal. Then I heard Second Chance Lance outside snorting and then Uncle Ronald came back in and then the O'Malley girls went out and got in the rig and Lance thumped away.

Then Uncle Ronald crept by me and went back up to bed without using a lamp, as quiet as he could, making the stairs groan in pain from his weight.

And then I heard the spring of his bed grind down, heard him sigh. A big sigh and then silence.

My mattress was dry so I thought I couldn't have been asleep that long.

I began planning how I would get up in a minute without banging my head on the stairs. I planned how to find my way in the dark to the door.

I felt warm and safe while making these plans because Uncle Ronald was there in the house right above me.

I planned how to open the door and slip out onto the cold grass in my bare feet. I planned to piss, come back, find the bed, get back in, move the thistle.

While I was making all these careful, big plans I fell asleep again.

When you wake up on a farm, it's supposed to be the rooster who wakes you up. It wasn't the rooster, though, this time, on my first morning on this farm. It was Uncle Ronald. Uncle Ronald was up long before the rooster ever even took it into his tiny brain to open one of his sharp little eyes and give a cock-a-doodle-do.

The first thing a person does in the morning is listen. Some people hear birds, some hear bombs, some hear alarm-clock radios, some hear thunder, some hear the breathing of somebody loved, some hear silence. But my sound, the sound that I heard that morning, was Uncle Ronald. Of all the sounds I ever loved from any time of the day or night—the sound of a fly buzzing on the dining-room window on Sunday afternoon, the sound the metal would make when you clipped Lance's harness to the ring or his trace to his whippletree, the sound a calf makes when its nose is halfway into a pail of milk, the sound of the knives of the mower over on the next field, the sound the workhorse makes when she's headed for the well after a long hot day, the sound of the whip-poor-will at night, the sound of sleet against the kitchen window when you're warm inside the house, the sound of lightning and the sound of thunder, the sound of the axe splitting a stick of hard ash, the sound of the ticking clock, the sound of the dog snoring behind the stove, the sound of the ice breaking up on the river in the spring, the sound of the summer breeze in the white pines, the sound of the rooster and the bull, the heat bug in August, the gooseberries hitting the bottom of the pail, the sound of blowing out the lamp—of all these sounds I've loved, I love best the memory of the sound of Uncle Ronald in the morning.

First he'd go downstairs in his sock feet so as not to wake anybody up. When Uncle Ronald put on his first boot he'd stamp it and stomp it on the kitchen floor. He'd be making sure that his foot was at the very bottom of the boot, making sure that the bottom of his foot and his boot were tight together for the rest of the day. He'd slam the heel of the boot into the kitchen floor right on top of the trap door that went into the cellar where he always stood. The cellar where the O'Malley girls once put the tax collector. Then he'd slam the ball of his foot onto the trap door that went into the cellar to make sure his toes were well fixed into the toe of his boot. Then he'd bang the whole boot, thundering his full weight into the boot on top of the cellar door, turning the whole house into a huge drum.

Then he'd do his other boot.

Then, once my Uncle Ronald had his boots well on, he'd start to get ready to wash his face. You could hear him clanging the dipper against the water pail and then you knew he was filling the basin with just the right amount.

Then you could hear Uncle Ronald begin to growl and you knew he had his hands in the icy water in the basin and you knew that any second now you'd hear him howling in pain when he cupped the water in his hands and drove it into his face. He would force the icy water into his face like a crazy man smashing himself in the face with a board. Once he got by the first water shock, Uncle Ronald would grab the bar of soap and begin trying to rub his whole face off with both his hands. While he was doing this he would make blubbering, spitting, slobbering, bubbling, coughing, snorting, sucking, choking sounds—sounds like you would hear if you were hearing a man drowning in something thick, like pudding.

After Uncle Ronald was done with his face he'd unbutton his long underwear to the waist and grab the face rag and do his neck and his chest and then under his arms, which was the worst, coldest part. While he was doing this part of himself he would make a sound like you hear today ambulances and police cars making. *Woop! Woop! Woop! Woop! Woop!*

Now Uncle Ronald was finished washing and was putting his underwear top back on and his big shirt, sighing the whole time, sighing and grunting and clearing his throat and making other sounds that he made when he was happy like sniffing and coughing and growling and smacking his lips and blowing puffs of breath out his nose with a grunt, like boxers do when getting in shape for a fight, punching a large bag in a gym.

Now Uncle Ronald was ready to put the kettle on.

First he cut kindling.

Beside the stove was a woodbox.

Beside the woodbox a small block.

Uncle Ronald had a short piece of rough lumber maybe left over from when he built the new barn the year before, in 1894.

Around the time the track was finished and the first train came up to Low.

Uncle Ronald cut kindling the way you see cooks on TV cut celery or mushrooms. He would have that piece of lumber end cut into about a dozen strips exactly the same width in less time than it would take one of those cooks on TV to slice up a bunch of celery. The second last strip to be cut would spring away right beside Uncle Ronald's big finger that was holding up what was to be the last strip.

Then Uncle Ronald would sink the small axe back into the block with one lightning-strong flip of his wrist and the blade of the axe so deep that he was the only one who would be able to pull it out again.

Then Uncle Ronald would start banging and clanging and ringing the stove. He'd shake the grate, slam the crank back on the hook, hit the draft back and forward, lift the iron lids and bang them down, open the door, kick it closed, pick wood out of the box, throw it back, pick other wood, open the door again, kick it shut, ring the metal ashes shovel, kick closed the ash box, drop the lifter onto the floor, rattle the poker, twist and squeal the rusty spring of the damper, ding and ring and dong the iron frying pan and smash the kettle onto the stove top three times, just to make sure it knew who was the boss.

And it was somewhere during all this friendly racket that lying there I made a discovery that filled me with wonder and joy.

My mattress was dry.

I had not pissed the bed!

Then I heard the rooster crow.

Too late, mister rooster!

Uncle Ronald beat you to it!

9. POLICEMEN'S NUTS

The fire in the stove sounded like clothes snapping and whooshing on a clothesline in a big wind.

"The O'Malley girls won't be down for breakfast this morning," Uncle Ronald told me as he buttered a hot thick piece of almost burnt toast for me. "They had to go out in the middle of the night to do some work and they're pretty played out."

"I heard them," I said. "I heard them go out." I waited to see if he was going to tell me where they went, what they were doing.

Uncle Ronald poured me a cup of hot tea and moved the heavy pitcher of cream over closer to me, pushing it across the table with one finger.

I waited a little longer.

Uncle Ronald plopped a ladle of porridge in a bowl in front of me and gave me a spoon and showed me that the brown sugar was in a big tin on the table.

"The sugar's hard in the tin. You'll have to hit it on the side of the table a few times to loosen some up fer yerself."

He wasn't going to tell me.

"Where were the O'Malley girls going?" I said.

"Yep," said Uncle Ronald. "Pretty tired they were when they got back. I checked on them a while ago. Sound asleep the two of them in their bed together. Just as quiet as two spoons in a drawer."

Uncle Ronald flipped over two pancakes in a pan on the stove and shoved some more wood in and kicked the hot iron door shut. He went to the pantry and got out a big sticky jar of maple syrup. Not telling me.

"Good year last spring for the syrup," he said softly, as though it was some kind of a secret. "I've got twenty of the best maples in the Gatineau. Just look at them and they'll offer up their sap to ya."

I wondered if he bothered to tap the trees to get the syrup, or did he just pet them and whisper to them and squeeze them?

"What were the O'Malley girls doing last night?" I asked. Uncle Ronald poured thick cream on my porridge from a white jug.

"Do you like cream on your porridge?" he asked.

Not going to tell me.

He filled a big kettle from a pail and set it on the back of the stove.

"After breakfast I'll show you how we get water," he said.

"Some men on the train said stuff about the O'Malley girls," I said.

"The well is at the bottom of the cliff out there. We have a winch so you can get the pail of water up without havin' to go down there yourself. I'll show you how to work it after your breakfast."

I was about to give up when Uncle Ronald whispered in my face while shoving a plate of pancakes in front of me, dousing them with butter and covering them with syrup.

"Can you keep a secret?" he whispered.

"Yes," I whispered back. "Yes I can."

"Well, here it is, then. The O'Malley girls, they were out late last night removing some policemen's nuts!"

10. SECOND CHANCE FOR LANCE

There was no more talk about the O'Malley girls.

Uncle Ronald showed me how to get water.

From the house a clay path led through a small potato field to the edge of a cliff about three stories high.

There was a short wood pier at the top of the cliff, held there by heavy rocks eleven hundred million years old.

A heavy tight wire ran from the pier down the cliff into the clear sparkling well water. There was a crank that turned a drum that wound up a long rope that was attached to a little pulley wheel and a snap hook.

You snapped the pail to the hook, let the pail run down the wire on the pulley wheel until it hit the well water. Then you waited until the pail filled up with water and sank out of sight.

Then you started to turn the crank, pulling the pail up the wire to where you were. Then you unhooked the full pail—careful don't spill any—and set it down.

Now you did it all over again with the second pail.

Now you had two full pails of beautiful water to carry back to the house. Two pails were better to carry than one because you were balanced and it was easier to walk.

Uncle Ronald carried two.

I carried two.

Back in the house, Uncle Ronald piled all the breakfast dishes into a tub and was pouring boiling water over them when there was a heavy pounding on the door.

"That'll be Even Steven," Uncle Ronald said. "Open the door for him before he breaks it down!"

I opened the door and a short man as wide as a stove took my hand and shook it.

"This is me sister's boy," Uncle Ronald told him. "Come to stay with us for a while. You sit down, Steven, and talk to him, while I go out and milk the cows. The O'Malley girls are tired and won't be down until later. The tea's still warm in the pot."

Even Steven's hand felt like a big knot in a pine log.

He started talking as he poured his tea.

"Big doin's in town," he said. "Policemen in funny-looking hats. Here for the taxes no doubt. Big wagons. Stayed overnight at Brooks' Hotel. Came in late. Sneaked in. Didn't take the train you were on. Came in like thieves in the stealth of the night!"

I wanted to tell him that only yesterday I saw policemen something like that—once in Ottawa, once in Wakefield—but Even Steven kept talking.

"Did Ronnie tell you what happened to the last tax collectors that came around here? He didn't? Get one of the O'Malley girls to tell you what happened. Edith or Mildred, it wouldn't matter which one. They both tell it well.

"One of them was alone in the house that day. Her sister was out in the chicken coop and her cousin Ronald was in the far field and at the door is this bailiff calling himself Bailiff Flatters. Shows her his badge. She brings him in and sits him at the table and him polite as anything— an average-size fella, clean shaven, wearing a suit, lot of papers in a satchel—puts on his spectacles, gets out a pencil, goin' down a list of names, tellin' her all the while what the O'Malleys owe and how much in arrears and how many years back it's been, and now he's not as polite as he was but she's being very polite, puttin' on the tea for him and tellin' him about how her father came over in '47 without a shirt on his back, leavin' the old country because he was hounded by the likes of this and what were taxes for anyway, what did the government ever do for us up here when we wanted decent roads and a school? While she was explain-in' this to him he says that her father had no business settling on this land and that they didn't even have any legal title to it and that her father was only what they called a squatter. A squatter! That made her blood boil! Insulting the name of her poor ol' father, God Rest His Soul in Heaven, callin' him a squatter if you please! Just then, her eyes fell on the piss pot which was sittin' on the bench beside the stove (she'd just emptied it when he came knockin'), and she grabbed it by the handle (it was their best one, the heavy one, the porcelain with the big roses embossed around the rim), and she swung it round and she brained him with it, hit him a dandy across the side of the head just as her sister, Edith, or was it Mildred, came in with the eggs. Then they pulled up the cellar door—that one right there—and the two of them they rolled your Mister Bailiff Flatters down into the darkness down there! You could say she *flattened* your Mister Flatters. Squatter! You can squat down there for a while, Mr. Taxman! they told him.

"Everybody loves hearing the story, specially the part about the roses around the rim of the pot," Even Steven said.

"I'll bet his head was ringing for a week after that!" he laughed. "Kept him there two days! A year or so later somebody shot the man in front of his house way over in Aylmer. Wasn't the O'Malley girls though. They've never been to Aylmer. Low is as far as they've ever been in their whole lives. Everybody says they did it though. That's good, don't you think? To have a reputation like that? I wish they'd all say that I went and shot him!"

It was hard to see where Even Steven stopped to take a breath. He could store a lot of volume of air in that stove of a chest of his. Good for talking for a long time without taking a breath!

"Soon your Uncle Ronnie will be back in and we'll hitch up Second Chance Lance and skip into town and see what the soldiers in the funny hats are going to try to do to us. Lance'll get us there in no time flat. Did your uncle tell you about Lance? How he got him. He didn't? How old Mean Bone McCooey was skidding a big stick of square timber up his steep road on Dizzy Peak with little Lance there—Lance a way too small for that job. Every time poor little Lance'd get the weight partway up the slope it'd get too much for him and back down he'd slide. This was a big joke to Ol' Mean Bone. Ol' Mean Bone was sayin', 'This is your last chance, Lance,' and started callin' him Last Chance Lance just to get a big laugh from all the lads standin' around watchin'. And your Uncle Ronald, he was there, and he got to feelin' real sorry for the little horse so he offered to buy Lance right there on the spot—offered him a litter of piglets and a hardly used crosscut saw—but Ol' Mean Bone, he wouldn't hear of it. He wanted that little horse to pull that heavy piece of square timber up that steep slope or perish tryin'! Then, your Uncle Ronnie, he made a bet with Ol' Mean Bone. Bet him the price of the horse that he could get Lance up the hill with that load, first try. If he could, he'd get to keep the horse. If he couldn't, he'd give him the pigs and the saw and go home empty-handed. 'I'll take that chance,' says Mean Bone, and the bet was on. 'One condition,' says your Uncle Ronnie. 'You'll have to turn your back on us until it's over.' 'Why is that?' says Mean Bone. 'Because I think it's your ugly face that's keeping this horse from doing his best on this job,' says your Uncle Ronnie. Well, everybody laughed and Ol' Mean Bone laughed too and turned his back and said, 'Go ahead, do your best you two, for it won't be long that I'll have meself a nice litter of pigs and a crosscut saw hardly used, and you'll be goin' home empty-handed!'"

It was hard to concentrate on Even Steven's story because he didn't seem to be breathing. And the longer he didn't breathe, the higher his voice got.

"Well, it didn't take your Uncle Ronnie long to win the bet. With Mean Bone's back turned, Ronnie tied a strong rope round his *own* waist and cinched it to Lance's horse collar and dragged both horse and timber up the top of Dizzy Peak with everybody cheering and hanging on to Mean Bone so he couldn't turn around and see what was happening!"

As Even Steven was finishing the story about how Uncle Ronald called the horse Second Chance instead of Last Chance, I was thinking how lucky Lance was to have somebody like Uncle Ronald, so strong and yet so kind, to be his master.

Just then, while Even Steven at last took a breath, Uncle Ronald came in from the milking.

"Let's hitch up Second Chance Lance and go to town," he said softly. "See what those policemen in the funny hats are up to."

11. THIS WONDERFUL THING

It was still pretty early in the morning when Second Chance Lance and Even Steven and Uncle Ronald and I got to the first gate. Lance could only open the gates one way because they only swung one way. So on the way out the road a human had to open the gate and hold it open while the rig went through.

While Even Steven was opening the first gate Uncle Ronald started to tell me how Steven got his name.

"Steven talks a lot and knows just about everything about everybody, but now and then there are some things that are so secret that..."

We were through the gate now and Even Steven got back in the rig, so Uncle Ronald stopped what he was saying.

He finished it while Even Steven was off opening the second gate.

"...but now and then there are some things that are so secret that people around here often say, 'And Even Steven didn't know about that one!' For instance, what I said about the policemen's nuts? Even Steven doesn't know about that one! At least not yet, anyway!"

Even Steven climbed back in and we thumped on down the grassy road.

I was feeling kind of privileged.

I knew that the O'Malley girls probably weren't murderers. I knew how Second Chance Lance got his name and why everybody called Steven Even Steven. And I *practically* knew a secret that Even Steven didn't know, though I didn't know the whole thing just yet.

The second farmhouse on the left side of the road had curved railings around a big verandah and apple trees in the front yard with a few dead apples giving off the last smell of fall. The way Uncle Ronald was looking up at a second-floor window made me realize it was the same house last night he looked so long at.

He looked long again at the window.

Even Steven looked at me and winked a big wink. He knew something I didn't know. It was one of those big winks where you use your jaw, your cheek, your whole face. And you have to give your head a big nod downward as you do the wink.

Try it sometime. But be careful you don't hurt yourself!

Even Steven pointed off the road the other way to a little crooked house built on some rock in under the bare trees.

"That's where Jimmy Smith used to live. He's famous. First person ever to be killed by the Gatineau train! We're very proud of our Jimmy. Three or four have been killed since, but you never forget the first one. Track's only been through here two or three years now. Cut him up into twenty or more pieces! His name is known all the way from Ottawa to Gracefield."

I started to get the idea that Even Steven wanted to be famous. Wanted his own name to be known up and down the Gatineau Valley.

A little later, Uncle Ronald pointed to a big brown bird taking off with slow wing beat from a steep cliff. It screamed at Lance and us, *Ke-a, ke-a, ke-a!*

"Gyrfalcon," Uncle Ronald told me. "Makes its nest out of the bones of its prey."

In the town of Low, people were finishing their breakfast. There was smoke from every chimney and mist on every window. People were out pumping water and carrying wood and emptying pans.

Lance pulled us through the mud past the train station to Brooks' Hotel. There was a little crowd bunched around in front of the big hotel verandah.

The smell of breakfast was wrapped around the hotel like a fuzzy, thick scarf.

Some people in the crowd were teasing the two men hitching up teams of horses to the wagons.

"How much are they payin' you, Paddy?" says one farmer.

"Enough," says Paddy. "A free breakfast!"

"Enough to pay your taxes, Paddy?"

"If they'd like the breakfast back," says Paddy, "they can have it when I'm through with it, which won't be long now the way I'm feeling!"

Everybody laughed.

Each heavy horse was twice as big as Second Chance Lance and they had eight of them—four for each wagon.

They were getting ready to pull some pretty heavy loads.

All of a sudden the double doors to Brooks' Hotel opened and six policemen with shiny boots and funny hats and revolvers came out and lined up on Brooks' big wooden verandah. The same ones I'd seen early yesterday morning in Ottawa and last night in Wakefield.

The crowd was getting bigger and the rumours were going around.

"They're going to collect money," said one big farmer. "Money they say people owe in taxes. Well, they won't get any money at my place. There is no money at my place! You can't get blood out of a turnip!"

"No, but they can put your best cow into one of those big wagons there instead of the money and then what'll you do?" said another man wearing a hat that was pulled down over his ears.

"What if they can't find my best cow?" said the big farmer.

"Well, then, I suppose in a case like that they won't be able to put it in one of those fancy big wagons, will they?" said the man, pulling his hat off and bowing a big bow to the crowd, making everybody laugh.

"They won't find *my* very best cow," shouted another farmer with a voice like a goat, from the back of the crowd.

"Why is that, Johnny?" came the question from the man with the hat off.

"Because *all* my cows are my very best cows!" answered the goat voice, and the man with the hat bowed for him and got a big cheer.

I was thinking if my mother was there, she'd tell them all to go down to the nearest stage and open up a comedy show.

And shut your gobs!

Uncle Ronald wasn't laughing with the rest. He wasn't looking serious either. He looked like he was just taking it all in—understanding it all. Maybe thinking about something else, something deeper.

Soon the sergeant was done drilling his men and getting them all checked out and then they were ordered to march off the verandah and board their wagons.

They were looking pretty shiny and clean and had to be careful getting on board because the wagons were parked in an extra big pool of mud.

The bailiffs and the lawyers in their suits were already on the other wagon and things were ready to take off.

The chief bailiff was checking over a long sheet of paper where there was listed the names of all the people who owed taxes, which was everybody.

The wagons began to move.

The muscles of the haunches of the powerful horses bunched and moved under the smooth skin like engines.

What could the townspeople of Low do against such power?

The horses drew the express wagons, towing them easily and powerfully through the mud.

All of a sudden the front wheel of the second wagon took a crazy angle, then wobbled the opposite way, and the wagon dipped forward and dumped the bailiff headfirst into the road. When a wagon loses a wheel, horses don't like it, and they begin to panic. As the rear wheels folded in and dropped off, the teams shied violent to the side, whipping the wagon so the rest of the guys in the fancy clothes slid off the rear of the deck into the mud.

The same thing was happening to the policemen's wagon, only the opposite. One rear wheel went first, dumping the police against the back rack of the wagon. Then the front wheels fell right off, digging the front of the wagon deck deep into the clay and mud. The powerful horses were in a gallop, so when the front caught, the police were catapulted into the air and had quite a ride in space before they landed and slid along the road into the mucky ditch, the liquid mud.

The crowd was in a joyful mood. Singing and dancing and laughing. A free show!

The wheels fell off the wagons—somebody removed the nuts that held the wheels on! The policemen's nuts!

"I wonder was it the O'Malley girls?" said Even Steven to me and Uncle Ronald. I looked at Uncle Ronald. He showed nothing.

"I wonder if people will say it's the O'Malley girls who did this wonderful thing!" said Even Steven. His face glowed with excitement.

"Maybe people will start sayin' you did it, Steven!" Uncle Ronald said.

"Maybe they will!" Even Steven said, hoping.

12. WILD GEESE AND FALSE TEETH

For the rest of the morning the tax collectors were trying to get somebody to help them find new nuts for the wheels for their wagons, but nobody knew where you could find anything like that.

"Nuts? Nuts for wagon wheels? We don't think there's any nuts around this part of the country. Not for wagon wheels, anyway. There's other kinds of nuts around though!" the people were telling the bailiff and the lawyers and the policemen after they got out of the mud and got back up on the verandah at Brooks' Hotel.

"There was a nut come up around here a few years back but somebody shot him!" somebody shouted.

"The squirrels have hid all the nuts by now," shouted another funny farmer. "Come back in the spring. We'll get them to dig some up fer ya!"

Then the bailiff started asking everybody if anybody had a wagon they could lend to the tax collectors.

Nobody knew of anybody who would lend them a wagon.

Did anybody know of anybody who might *rent* the tax collectors a wagon or two for a couple of days?

Nobody did.

"I had a wagon once, but the wheels fell off!" shouted the guy with the hat over his ears, and everybody laughed.

Later, the tax collectors decided to walk around to some of the houses in the town and collect some taxes and they started asking people if they knew where so-and-so lived and where such-and-such lived. They were reading names from a list.

"Can anyone here lead us to the residence of Mr. John Egan?" the bailiff called out.

Silence.

"Can anybody here tell us where Patrick Hayes lives?"

Nobody could.

"Is there a Patrick Flynn residing in this area?"

Nobody ever heard of him.

"Does anyone here know a Michael Doyle?"

Nobody did.

"William Gleason?"

Silence.

After about ten more names, the bailiff lifted up his hands and looked up at the grey, dark sky. It was hopeless.

Then the guy with the goat voice shouted, "Maybe it would help if you went over the names again. Why don't you give it a try?"

The bailiff looked suspicious but then started the list over again. "John Egan?" Silence. "Patrick Hayes?" No answer. "Patrick Flynn? Michael Doyle?" Nothing. "William Gleason?"

"No," goat voice said. "I guess it doesn't help going over the names again after all!"

Everybody roared.

People were just starting to get bored with this game when along came Father Foley in his neat little rig.

He talked for a while to the head bailiff and made some kind of a deal with him. If they left the policemen on the verandah of Brooks' Hotel, he'd show the bailiff where some of the people lived.

The crowd got a little disgusted and broke up and drifted away.

We found out later that at the first place the bailiff knocked on the door, somebody poured boiling water on him from an upstairs window.

Even Steven stayed in town to see what was going to happen, and Uncle Ronald and Lance and I left for home.

On the way we stopped to watch a V of geese heading south.

"They've been practicing for about a month," Uncle Ronald said. "At first they did nothing but argue about how to get into the V and who was going to be the leader. Squawking and honking and crashing into each other, feathers flying."

He went quiet and we listened and watched. Uncle Ronald and I, both our faces to the sky. The V of geese was very high but you could hear them away up there, jabbering away, excited to be moving at last. Happy to be together at last.

It was a sad sound.

I was thinking of my mother. Missing my mother.

"How many do you say there are in that flock up there?" he said. He didn't take his eyes from the sky. The V formation was perfect except for a few extra on the end of the right leg of the V. If a couple of them would move over onto the end of the other leg of the V, it would be perfect.

"Not counting the last four on that long side, how many do you count?"

I figured if I counted one line and then doubled it, I'd have the answer. But as hard as I tried, I kept losing track. As the birds moved across the sky, they'd get ahead of my eyes and I'd be missing some or counting some twice. Each time, I'd have to start over at the lead goose. I tried using my arm in front of my eyes to block out the geese until I counted them. I tried using my hands as blinkers.I tried making a telescope out of my two fists. It didn't seem possible to count geese while they were flying.

"There's two hundred forty-four," Uncle Ronald said. "Two hundred forty-eight counting the four strays at the end."

We could hardly hear them now as they flew south, following the Gatineau River.

"They'll be over the Ottawa River in less than an hour," Uncle Ronald said.

I wondered if my mother would see them.

"It'll take those fancy policemen a lot longer than that to get home," Uncle Ronald chuckled. Then, back to the geese.

"Yessir, Lance," he said. "Two hundred and forty-eight geese. Imagine all those roasted up and set on a long, long table for Thanksgiving!"

Further up the road, where the creek ran along, Uncle Ronald nudged me and then out of his pocket he pulled the can of Odorama Tooth Powder. He got out of the rig and kneeled beside the creek, and snorting and whooping and gasping, did his mouth with the powder and the ice-cold creek water.

Back to the rig, he pulled out two short rods from the back, each with a line and a hook and a piece of red cloth for bait.

"Let's move up stream a ways," he said softly. "I might have frighted the fish a bit just now."

Might have.

In a quiet pool along a mossy log we floated our hooks with the red cloth and in the time it would take you to do a job on your teeth with Odorama Tooth Powder—a new thing—we had six sleek glistening little trout.

Uncle Ronald threaded a forked stick through the gills of each fish and laid them out on a cedar bough, like a fancy presentation in a store window.

"Let's make a visit, Lance," he said, and Lance knew just what to do.

He turned in without even being told to the house with the curved railings around the verandah and the apple trees. This horse was smart. He could probably write a book. Something like the dog, Beautiful Joe. Tell his life story. Story sort of the same. Going from a cruel master to a kind master.

The clouds were bruised blue, hanging low over the slanting black and gold field. Two crows called back and forward between two bare trees.

A pine grosbeak went *tew-tew!*

"Let's see if Cecelia Hickey likes these fish we brought," Uncle Ronald winked at me.

With the trout on the cedar bough cradled in one arm, Uncle Ronald knocked on the door and it opened while he was knocking. A man with a nose shaped like a sweet potato with a wart on the end of it the size of a big, ripe blueberry was already talking. He was glad to see us and would we come in for God's sake and stop standing out here in the chill.

There was a long black hair growing out of the wart on his nose.

He showed Uncle Ronald his teeth.

"Brand new," he said. "They just come in on the train last night from Toronto. Eaton's! The newest thing in false teeth. Sixty-day trial. If I don't like them after sixty days, I send them back!" He was saying he was glad to meet me and that he knew my mother and how long was I staying and a whole lot of other stuff when behind him came up his daughter Cecelia. Cecelia Hickey, the girl Uncle Ronald cleaned his teeth in the creek and brought the six trout on the cedar bough for.

"They're beauties. Thank you, Ronnie," she said and blushed and gave the fish to her father. "Put these in the cellar in the cool, Pa," she said, "while I take me two gentlemen callers into the parlour!"

Uncle Ronald nudged me. "She liked the fish," he whispered.

Mr. Hickey was still talking about his new teeth as he went out to the kitchen.

Cecelia had black hair, thin black eyebrows, black eyelashes, black pupils, white skin, white teeth, full red lips, red cheeks, a round head, a long back, a small nose, long fingers, a low voice.

"Wasn't it terrible about the policemen's nuts?" she said, laughing low in her throat and then blushing.

Then she told me she was glad I was there visiting because I'd be in the parlour with Ronnie and her and that would make it so her pa wouldn't have to come in and sit with them and spoil everything. I would be a kind of chaperone.

They'd just got the latest invention, a new talking and singing machine that you wound up with a crank—a gramophone—from Eaton's.

"Now that the train is so regular, you can get just about anything if you have the money—and Pa has the money—sent because of he was in the will of somebody dead back in Ireland—I don't know who it was and I don't care—and they've got electric streetcars now in Ottawa and I read in the paper two brothers in France invented a moving picture and ..."

Cecelia was putting on her favourite record as she talked: "The Bridal March from Lohengrin." She was pretty excited.

She and Ronnie played it over and over again until I got pretty sick of it.

She had three other records. One called "Just Because She Made Dem Goo-Goo Eyes!"—which was a dumb love song—and a funny talking story called "Casey and the Dude in the Street Car," and a song with a lot of whistling and laughing that made you laugh but you didn't know what you were laughing at called "The Laughing Fool."

They stopped playing "The Bridal March from Lohengrin" at last and let me play "The Laughing Fool" a few dozen times while they went and sat on the couch. While I was winding the crank of the gramophone again for about the fifth time, I looked up and saw Uncle Ronald kiss Cecelia on the nose and I saw her blush.

I guess the Odorama Tooth Powder was working pretty good.

We got invited for supper and Mr. Hickey all through supper was taking out his teeth and putting them back in and showing us where they pinched and where they pushed against his tongue. He could hardly talk with them in and when his mouth was full of potatoes it was even harder to understand him.

Cecelia said she didn't know how he was going to last the sixty-day free-trial period before he sent the teeth back, because this was only the second day and look at all the trouble he was having with them already.

They obviously didn't fit him because you could hear them clacking together when he was trying to eat and Cecelia was a little bit embarrassed and Uncle Ronnie looked up at me over his plate and said with his kind eyes that I'd better not laugh.

It was hard to eat while Mr. Hickey was doing those things with his teeth and while the hair growing out of the wart on his nose was springing and nodding around like a loose wire.

But none of us could help laughing when Mr. Hickey got into trouble with some tea that went down the wrong way and he coughed his teeth right out into the big bowl of boiled beets on the table.

He finally got the teeth out of the beet juice in the bowl and put them back in his mouth. The red beet juice was dripping off them and he looked a lot like a vampire that was just back from finishing a real nice snack someplace.

After supper Uncle Ronald and Cecelia and I decided to take a quick ride back to Low to meet the train to see what the latest gossip was about the tax collectors.

On the way we stopped a couple of times to talk to some farmers. They told us some rumours and gossip about what happened to the tax collectors.

"They say they were scalded by water over at Flynn's," one farmer told us.

"They say that Mrs. O'Connor hit one of the lawyers over the head with a big stick," another farmer said.

Other rumours were that the bailiff was attacked by a vicious Thanksgiving turkey over at Nosey McCooey's and that at another place along the road the tax collectors were chased off by a wild gang of women with pitchforks.

Some said that some said that they heard that somebody warned that there would be bloodshed.

Somebody else saw somebody's kid wearing one of the policemen's funny hats.

Some said the farmers were getting guns and forming a gang.

Strangers would be sent home in wooden boxes, some said they said.

When we got there there was quite a crowd. Everybody had the same idea. We were wondering if there was anything in the paper about what happened. People were saying they'd be surprised if it got in the paper that fast but maybe there'd be something.

The rumours were going around about how the bailiffs and the lawyers and the policemen would soon have to take off back to Ottawa. Walking.

Walk all the way down the road in the mud back to Ottawa.

Some people said that they'd probably get somebody to rent them a wagon or two in Wakefield.

"That'll teach them to come up here and bother us!" some people were saying.

"But they haven't left yet," somebody said.

"Tomorrow's another day," somebody else said.

"Tell us something we don't know," somebody else said.

The train was right on time and not too many people got off.

The last person to get off was a woman with a bandage around her head. It was dark and she was partly in the lantern light of the platform around where the people were cutting the strings on the bundles of the *Ottawa Citizen* and *Journal*.

I moved closer. The woman looked familiar.

I moved closer.

It was my mother.

Her face was black with bruises and one eye was closed. One of her coat sleeves was empty.

"Oh, Mickey!" she said.

Uncle Ronald moved in around me and caught her as her knees buckled and she sank toward the platform.

13. BARK OF THE PUSSYWILLOW

Second Chance Lance got us home in a hurry after we dropped off Cecelia. He was nervous and wide-eyed, his eyes flashing in the lamps. He seemed to know there was violence around. Violence and pain. There was cruelty in the air. Second Chance Lance knew all about cruelty.

We brought my mother into the house and the O'Malley girls took over.

"Get Willy Willis at once!" they both said. Uncle Ronald touched my arm.

"We're going to get Willy Willis. You have to come and open the gates. It'll be faster. The sooner we get him here the better."

I looked into my mother's broken face.

She nodded painfully and we left. As I shut the door I watched the O'Malley girls moving around the kitchen, making my mother comfortable. They were grim and serious. Their faces were tight.

Lance pointed his head and after only a few steps he was into a speeding trot that made the spokes of our wheels whirr in the night. At the first gate we slowed to a walk and I jumped off and ran ahead and lifted the latch, opened the gate and hopped back on while the rig was moving.

Same with the second gate.

Not too far past Cecelia Hickey's (Uncle Ronald only once looked up at her window and not for long) we swung to the right down a road I never noticed before, a narrow twisting lane through a thick stand of white pine, tall and straight and ghostly as we drove. It got darker and darker the deeper we moved until I wondered how Lance even stayed on the road.

"He has more than eyes," Uncle Ronald said. "He has an extra sense."

Some of the soft needles of the white pine trees along the road touched my coat as we whooshed by.

Soon, off in the trees there was a light showing and Lance headed in. The light was a lantern flickering in the stomach of a large statue of St. Joseph, his head tilted to one side and his hands out. Behind the statue was a tiny log cabin. It had a door and a small square window on the front and on one side another small square window showing a yellow warm glow.

The door squeaked open before we knocked. A little man with burning eyes and black teeth and a voice like burnt toast spoke to us.

"God bless you, Ronald. Who's the boy?"

"My sister's lad."

"What's happened? What brings you here?"

"My sister. She's been beaten."

"Where is she?"

"Over home."

"You'll take me." The little man turned and went into his cabin, the door closing squeaking shut.

"Who is he?" I whispered to Uncle Ronald.

"Faith healer," Uncle Ronald said. "And doctor."

There was a small water pump beside the statue of St. Joseph and hanging on a hook right next to the lantern in the stomach was a small pail. I filled the pail and gave Lance a drink. He thanked me by making a low, friendly sound deep in his throat. The cabin door opened and Willy Willis, faith healer and doctor, stood for a second in the light. He was checking the pockets of his short coat and feeling a big sack that he carried to see if he had everything he needed. He was very bow-legged and you could see a lot of the light that came from his cabin through the large opening between his legs.

Standing beside Uncle Ronald he looked like a little monkey.

Lance pulled us home like the wind.

The O'Malley girls had five kettles boiling on the stove.

They were bathing my mother's eyes with the whites of eggs.

Willy Willis got out a little bottle of holy water and sprinkled it around the room and crossed himself and blessed the room and my mother, and the O'Malley girls crossed themselves and we all kneeled down and said some prayers that Willy Willis chanted real quick.

"Now," said Willy, "let's get on with the other part."

"That'd be just fine with me," my mother said through her swollen lips.

Willy Willis started pulling cures out of his sack and placing them on the oil-clothed kitchen table.

Each medicine was in a different shape. Some were little boxes of powder, some were twisted-looking roots, some were bark, some were big ugly dry leaves, some were little bottles of coloured liquid, some were pieces of cloth soaked in something, some were seeds, some were oil, some were fat mixed with gum or wax.

Each time he placed a medicine on the table he blessed it with a tiny prayer and then said what each was to be used for.

The O'Malley girls nodded together each time, memorizing everything Willy Willis said, pressing their lips together, repeating after Willy Willis, making sure they memorized everything exactly right, pointing each time, each pointing with a short, tough, red finger.

"Spruce gum and lamb fat salve for infections..." Willy Willis said and hit the little glass jar hard onto the table, his burnt-toast voice rasping.

"Spruce gum and lamb fat salve for infections..." the O'Malley girls chanted after him, pointing close to the little, thick jar.

"Blessed be the Father, the Son and the Holy Ghost," Willy Willis muttered each time.

"Poppy tea for sleep," Willie Willis rasped and hammered his knuckles into the table where he placed the crushed-up dried leaves for the poppy tea.

The O'Malley girls repeated and pointed and waited for the next one.

"Cow lily pounded into a mash for swollen limbs and a solution for bathing..."

Blessed be the Father, the Son...

Repeat.

Hit the table.

Point.

"Horseradish root and a water solution to promote appetite…"

"Lambkill for swellings…"

"Skunk Cabbage—a piece of the root pressed against the gum to relieve toothache…"

"Bark of the pussywillow boiled to a thick paste—a poultice for bruises…"

"Holy Mary Mother of God…"

"Juniper gum for cuts and sprains…"

"Balsam sap for abrasions…"

"Cedar oil for swollen joints…"

"Parts of sumac tree steeped in blackberry juice for earache…"

By the time they were finished, the table looked like an apothecary's window display.

The O'Malley girls pushed a big copper tub out into the middle of the kitchen floor and began filling it with hot water from the kettles on the stove.

They began undressing my mother.

"Why didn't you run away?" Willy Willis asked my mother, sticking his face right in hers.

"I did," my mother said.

"Well?" said Willy.

"I went back," my mother said.

"Why?" Willy said.

"I remembered there was some money hidden in another place that slipped my mind."

"What happened?" Willy Willis asked. His voice was so raspy you wanted to clear your own throat while he was talking.

"You're very inquisitive, aren't you, Willy Willis?" my mother said, defiant, sticking her battered face up to his. "Maybe even a bit nosy!"

"Never mind that, my girl," Willy wheezed. "What happened?" After a bit my mother answered.

"I went in the house and he came right in after me. He said a friend of his, a porter at the Union Depot, saw me put Mickey on the train. He said if I followed, he'd come up and get us. Then he beat me."

"When you went back for the money, did you think to give him one more chance at the same time?" Willy asked, gentle as he could.

My mother looked away from Willy Willis' face but said nothing. The answer was a silent yes.

There was a long pause.

"Take me home," Willy said to Uncle Ronald.

14. STAKED TO A MANURE PILE

While we took Willy Willis back he told us all about how years ago he visited the famous Brother Andre down at Cote-des Neiges under the western slope of Mont Royal, Montreal's highest mountain. Brother Andre was the doorman at the College of Notre Dame over there and although he was only a little, unimportant doorman and a messenger and a barber and a handyman and did all the odd jobs at this school for future priests, like doing the boys' laundry and fixing shoes and sweeping the floor and all that, he was also famous for curing the sick. He used oil from the lamp burning in front of St. Joseph's statue in the college chapel. He rubbed the oil on the sick who visited him.

And they got better. If they were crippled, they could walk. If they were blind, they could see.

Brother Andre, even though he was only a doorman at a school, was famous all over Canada for his cures and his St. Joseph's oil. Joseph was Jesus' dad and was the saint that all working, labouring poor people prayed to when they were sick or hurt. All the ordinary people.

And Brother Andre gave Willy Willis a little bottle of this magic St. Joseph's oil that time, that winter, when Willy went all the way down to the west slope of Mont Royal, Montreal's highest mountain, in the bitter winter weather to visit Brother Andre. And Willy brought the oil back to Low there to his little cabin. He didn't have much. He only used it sometimes. He had powers of his own.

He told us all this on the way home. He was pretty excited about it.

"And I'll use it on your mother tomorrow if she's worse," he said, as he climbed down from the rig. "St. Joseph would say she qualifies as a labouring person. She's labouring trying to make a silk purse out of a pig's arse!"

We let him off in front of the statue.

There was a bit of wind as he passed his light in the belly of the statue of St. Joseph outside his cabin and the flicker of the flame made Willy's shadow huge across his cabin and then small again. His legs made an "O" and then he was gone.

I asked Uncle Ronald what he meant.

"There's an old saying," Uncle Ronald explained as Lance came round and we left Willy's yard. "You can't make a silk purse out of a sow's ear. Willy changed it a bit. Your mother has tried for a long time to change your father from a mean man into a decent man—but Willy says it's hopeless. He says you might as well try to make a silk purse out of the south end of a pig," Uncle Ronald spoke in his soft, deep voice.

We were quiet all the way home. I was thinking it all over. Brother Andre and the mountain and Willy Willis and St. Joseph and the lamp oil and my mother and my father and a silk purse and a pig and the other end of a pig.

It made me smile and then I was ashamed of smiling, there in the dark, Lance and Uncle Ronald and I, whirring along in the dark.

When the warm yellow light from the farmhouse came round the turn, Lance did a throaty rumble.

At the stable Uncle Ronald undid the traces from the whippletree and eased Lance from between the shafts of the rig. He slung the leather traces over Lance's back gently. The traces, when they were in the air, frightened me, and when the metal hames clinked, Uncle Ronald noticed me raise my arm and pull back and turn my head away.

A look of great pity came over his face that I could see in the light of the stable lantern.

"Does your father beat you, too?"

I nodded, ashamed.

"Don't be ashamed," said Uncle Ronald.

He gave me Lance's reins, up short.

"You lead him into the stable. Just pull gently but confidently. He'll follow you."

I looked up into Lance's face. For a small horse he seemed pretty big from where I was. He was looking down his nose at me. His eyes were big and soft. He blinked them once.

"Well?" Second Chance's eyes said to me. "What kind of a person are you?"

I watched carefully while Uncle Ronald unbuckled Lance's bellyband and took off his harness and hung it up and rubbed Lance's back and neck where the collar and the bellyband had been. I paid close attention how the collar came off, how the breeching was unbuckled, how the reins unclipped from the bit, how the throat latch undid the bridle. How the steel bit came out of Lance's mouth across his teeth. How he seemed to enjoy it being gone. How he licked and chomped his teeth. He reminded me of Mr. Hickey trying to eat his supper.

We checked Lance's water, threw down some hay, rubbed Lance's nose, said goodbye to Lance, blew out Lance's lamps, locked the door quiet to Lance's stable.

Before we went into the house, Uncle Ronald told me something.

"When your father was your age," he said, "his father used to tie him to a stake on the manure pile and whip him with his horse whip. That's the way your father was brought up. I know. I was hiding once. I saw."

Inside, the kitchen was a mess. Water all over the floor, herbs and medicines and jars and powders and gum all over the table, soap on the stove. Rags and towels and clothes and bandages thrown around.

"They're upstairs," Ronald said, and we went up.

The O'Malley girls were standing on each side of my mother with their arms folded and smiling.

My mother was sitting up in bed surrounded by pillows and quilts. There were pots and bottles and dishes and vials and compresses on the two tables beside the bed. Four coal-oil lamps burned. The room was cheerful and bright and clean and smelled of flowers and starch and soap and mint and rhubarb and whiskey.

"We added some of our own cures," said the O'Malley girls. "That Willy Willis, he knows a lot, but he doesn't know everything! He doesn't know much about whiskey!"

After some talking, some laughing, some fussing, they blew out three of the lamps and left me alone with my mother.

She snuggled down into her luscious bed.

I had planned what I was going to say.

But I got it wrong.

"You can't make a pig's purse out of a silk south end," I said, knowing I had it all wrong.

My mother looked blank for a bit and then burst out laughing.

"Where did you get that, my darling boy?" she said.

"Willy Willis," I said. "But I think I said it wrong."

"That's all right, my boy, my boy, that's all right..." Then she cried some. And laughed again. "Oh, Mickey, what's to become of us?"

We hugged for a while until I noticed I was breathing in a horrible smell.

"It must be the skunk cabbage," my mother said when she saw my nose wrinkled up. "Don't worry, we'll get out of this. But we'll have to prepare. We'll have to get ready for him. Because he's comin'. As sure as the winter follows fall, he'll be here."

At home, in Ottawa, when we were sad and I couldn't get to sleep, my mother used to talk about picking berries and that way I'd get drowsy and...

"Tell about the berries," she said. "You remember how."

I did remember. I knew it all off by heart.

"The first berries are in the spring," I started. "The strawberries. They grow near the ground and they're shy and they hide behind their leaves and they're shaped like a tiny raccoon's nose and you pick them and put them in your mouth one at a time and they're so sweet and wild they surprise your mouth and you know you'll never forget the taste. Then comes, a few weeks later, the raspberries and they grow high off the ground and you tie a pail to your waist and tickle the berries off the vine with both hands so the berries go ping into your empty pail and be careful, watch the thorns, move slow through the canes so the thorns don't grab you. Then your pail is filling up and there's no more ping just a little plop each time and the sun is in each berry and the pail gets hotter and hotter from the sun-filled berries so that you can feel the heat on your face if you stick your head into the pail and the smell of the berries in there might make you faint..."

I was ready to tell the rest. Thimbleberry, blackberry, blueberry, gooseberry...then into the chokecherries and the plums and the black currants but she didn't need any more. She was peaceful asleep.

I breathed out her lamp and pulled her door soft shut.

15. A DRY BED

Even Steven was over bright and early. Uncle Ronald was finished growling into his icy basin of water and going *"Woop!Woop!Woop!"* and cutting the kindling and banging the stove and showing the kettle who was boss.

Then, the rooster.

And me with the best feeling in the world: a dry bed!

And then the sound of Even Steven, excited, telling what he knew.

I went up and looked in my mother's room. She was sleeping as calm and quiet and safe as a spoiled cat. I went back down to the kitchen.

Yesterday, Even Steven did something he couldn't wait to tell us about.

"You shoulda seen me yesterday, Ronald and Mickey! I took the wagon up the road and picked up two of the McCooeys. I picked up Whistle McCooey and Mouthwash McCooey. Whistle has an old deer gun there with no bolt in it and I had along that rusty old Napoleon one-ball musket I have with the bayonet attached. I had that and we whittled up a board to look like the shape of a double-barrel shotgun for Mouth-wash McCooey to hold and we drove by Brooks' Hotel in the wagon and the police sittin' right there on the verandah after their lunch gettin' ready to go back out harassin' innocent citizens…"

Uncle Ronald was getting the toast and the porridge onto the table while he listened. He had on a little smile while Even Steven was telling his story.

"Would the O'Malley girls be coming down to breakfast? Maybe they'd like to hear this…" Even Steven said, hope in his voice.

"No, they won't," said Ronald, mysterious. "They were up pretty late last night, working on a bit of a project…"

"A project? What kind of a project?"

"Oh, I wouldn't know," said Uncle Ronald. "Mickey and I, we were asleep, weren't we, Mickey?" Even Steven searched my face but I showed him nothing. Even Steven wanted to know everything and Uncle Ronald loved to keep him in the dark. Tell him nothing. Just to tease him a bit.

"People are all sayin' that it was them after all who took the nuts from the policemen's wagons..." Even Steven said, his face full of hope.

"Oh, we wouldn't know anything about that, now. The O'Malley girls, they don't say much, do they, Mickey?"

I shook my head.

"It's a mystery," said Even Steven, his eyes narrow. Then he brightened up. "Well, anyway," he took up his yarn again, "me and the two McCooeys—Mouthwash and Whistle—sail right past their verandah, right past their noses in our wagon with our guns pointing toward the sky. You shoulda seen them soldiers gawkin' at us! And Mouthwash, cursin' and swearing better 'n I've ever heard him. He uttered some swearin' there Ronald I swear I've never in my life heard before. He's the best. And I've worked in the shanties in the bush and don't you think I haven't heard more than my share of professional, top-of-the-line cursin'! And all the while there's Whistle McCooey, sittin' there with his gun, whistlin' a jig of some kind, whistlin' away, and Mouthwash cursin' away and the policemen on the verandah gawkin'. Oh, it was grand, Ronald and young Mickey. You shoulda been there for it!"

"We heard some rumours about guns, didn't we, Mickey, yesterday evening..."

"The only trouble with it was we couldn't get Mouthwash to face the policemen on the verandah as we drove by. He was swearin' real good, like I said, but he would only face straight ahead the whole time. We drove past more than a few times but he'd only face straight ahead, he wouldn't look at the police, so it lost a little bit of impact, you might say, him swearing straight ahead like that each time. But Whistle—that was a different thing altogether! Whistle whistled that jig right at them police, them paid assassins, each time we passed, right at them, bold as you please! Oh, it was grand! I wish you coulda been there, the two of ya!

"And another thing," Even Steven went on. "They say that there's a reporter got off the train last night at Brennan's Hill and he's been sending reports by telegraph and courier down to Ottawa!"

"Might be something in the papers tonight, then," Uncle Ronald said.

"Then we'll find out everything that's been goin' on!" Even Steven said.

"You think the paper will know more than we ourselves know, Steven?" Uncle Ronald asked.

"Sure enough! The papers, they know it all eventually!"

You could tell Uncle Ronald didn't believe this for a minute but he didn't say so. He was not the type to argue.

"Maybe," he said, giving me a look, "they'll tell us who removed the nuts from the policemen's wagons."

"Maybe they will," said Even Steven.

"Maybe they'll say *you* did it," said Uncle Ronald to Even Steven.

"Maybe they will," said Even Steven, blushing. You could tell he would love to get his name in the paper. He had the look of a lad who would love to be a little bit famous for a while, maybe.

"Maybe you're the one murdered that Bailiff Flatters some while back," said Uncle Ronald, teasing.

Even Steven started wiggling in his chair and getting a deeper colour and half laughing and half frowning.

He had the look of a lad who'd never ever murder a bailiff but wouldn't mind if people *said* that he did.

Behind Even Steven I saw my mother slip past the stairs and disappear into the parlour.

Uncle Ronald was poaching an egg in a small pan while Even Steven was acting like he was getting ready to leave. Each time he'd be leaving for sure, he wouldn't leave.

It was like watching waves pretend to leave a sandy shore and then come right back again. He kept remembering new pieces of gossip, new rumours.

I slipped out into the parlour and sat with my mother.

"We'll be ready for him when he comes," she whispered. It was what she was saying before she went to sleep the night before. It was almost as though she'd been saying it all night long and was still saying it this morning.

"I want you to steal a sharp meat-cutting knife from the kitchen when the O'Malley girls and Ronnie aren't looking. Steal it and bring it up to my bedroom, hide it under the mattress. And don't breathe a word!"

I went back into the kitchen.

Uncle Ronald was holding Even Steven gentle but strong by the elbow and helping him out the door. He was still talking after the door was shut.

My mother came in and sat down.

We hugged her and kissed her and said she looked a lot better, which was a lie.

"I know that's not true," she said. "I don't look better, I look worse, but I'll tell you something...I FEEL a whole lot better, I really do. Coming back up to Low was the right thing, the smart thing to do. And I'll tell you something else. I'll never go near that man again, so help me God!"

Then she ate her poached egg and asked for a couple more.

With thick toast, if you please.

And Uncle Ronald went back to showing the stove who was boss.

When he went out to do the chores I stole a long sharp knife out of the drawer and took it upstairs and hid it under my mother's mattress.

After the chores, Uncle Ronald gave me a lesson in harnessing Second Chance Lance and hitching him up to the rig.

First we put on Lance's collar. It made me laugh the way Lance pointed his head straight out so that it would be easy to slip the collar over his ears and onto his shoulders. He reminded me of a little kid putting up his arms so his mom could pull his sweater on for him.

Then Uncle Ronald smoothed Lance's back with a brush and threw the back pad over on him and moved it around a bit until it was comfortable. Then he cinched the bellyband tight. Uncle Ronald pulled the straps of the bellyband through the buckle quite hard—hard enough to make Lance step sideways to catch his balance.

Then the long leather traces got clipped to the metal hames on the collar.

Next was the leather breech straps around his rump which got hooked to the bellyband to keep the rig from running up on him from behind when he put on the brakes.

Then the crupper under his tail.

And last, the bridle around his head and the bit in his mouth.

He took the bit in his mouth like he didn't like the taste of the cold metal as he worked his tongue around it and while it thwocked against his teeth.

Then the reins got clipped onto the bit and the traces draped over his back.

Then I got to walk him over to the wagon. Gee. Haw.

Gee meant go to the right.

Haw meant go to the left.

Uncle Ronald backed Lance between the shafts of the rig and clipped the traces to the whippletree.

Ready to go.

But we didn't go anywhere.

"Now," Uncle Ronald looked at me, "to unhitch him we do the same only in reverse. Can you remember the order? It's easier to unhitch than to hitch. You tell me the steps and we'll see if you have it right."

"Right now?" I said.

"Right now," he said.

"Unclip the traces from the whippletree and lead Lance out from between the shafts," I said, hardly believing my own ears.

Uncle Ronald looked at me with deep affection in his face.

I got through the whole process with only a couple of mistakes.

We hung all the harness up on the proper pegs in the stable and patted Lance goodbye and shut the door.

"Now," said Uncle Ronald, "let's go in and you hitch him up this time!"

We went back in.

I took the collar down from the peg and held it up as high as I could. Uncle Ronald supported it a little higher for me and we waited to see if Lance would point his head for me.

See if he would accept me.

He looked at first a little impatient. "Didn't we just go through all this?" Lance's face seemed to say.

Then he pointed his head.

With Uncle Ronald's help, I ran the collar up over his head and onto his shoulders.

"You're on your way," Uncle Ronald said confidentially to me, as though he didn't want to embarrass Lance. "He's your friend. He's going to let you harness him."

Uncle Ronald had to help me with tightening the bellyband, but I did most of the rest of it pretty well by myself.

All those belts and buckles.

I never thought I would ever like the feel of belts and buckles.

When we were back hitched to the rig again, Lance was anxious to go this time. Uncle Ronald noticed a trace carrier was coming loose, and also some stitches on the breeching were coming undone, so he decided we'd take a trip over to Even Steven's place. Steven had a new outfit called the Farmer's Friend, a riveter that he got out of Eaton's catalogue a while back. You could repair harness with rivets instead of stitching.

On our way over to Even Steven's we came to an open, rocky clearing near the brow of a small hill.

As sudden as a clap of thunder, up over the hill from the other side a V of barking geese came roaring, flying low, gabbling and burbling and arguing.

They were so low you could hear their wings ploughing the air.

Lance pulled up.

"How many this time?" Uncle Ronald yelled out to me, even though I was sitting right beside him.

"How do you count them?" I called out, feeling I could reach up and pull one down by the feet.

"The way you learned to harness Lance!" Uncle Ronald shouted, laughing.

The way I learned to harness Lance.

Of course!

Backwards! From the back!

I jumped from the rig and started counting one arm of the V from the end.

How easy. The geese seemed motionless in the sky.

There were sixty-five geese counting the leader.

The other arm had one extra straggler.

"One hundred and thirty!" I shouted. "One hundred and thirty!"

"Exactly," said Ronald, more quiet now, and put his arm out to help me back on the rig and patted my shoulder and squeezed the back of my neck and pushed my hat down over my eyes and ruffled my hair.

"We'll pick up the Farmer's Friend at Stevens' and then head right into town to the station—see what's the latest," said Uncle Ronald, partly to Second Chance Lance, partly to me.

16. THE O'MALLEY GIRLS IS ONE

Rumours were flying around the station.

Even Steven and the two McCooeys had followed the police around in the afternoon after Father Foley found some new nuts for their wagons. The rules were if the people didn't have the money to pay the taxes that they owed, the police could take their stuff, their furniture, their animals, their tools. But they had to leave the people with two of everything. Two pigs, two horses, two cows, two chairs, two pitchforks, like that. Like in Noah's ark. They had a list of everybody and how much they owed. But they didn't get very far because people were hiding stuff. At one place somebody poured a full chamber pot on them. At another place they buttered the front steps and everybody fell down. At another place they chained the hay rake to the house and blocked the door. At another they put a team of horses in the kitchen...

The freight man was off the train before it even got stopped. He ran up and down the platform waving the *Evening Journal* and the *Daily Citizen*.

"It's all in the papers!" he was roaring to everybody. "It's all in the papers! Front page. We're on the front page. Everybody. It's all there!"

The bundles of papers tumbled out onto the platform and hardly any attention was paid to the regular baggage. The twine on the bundles was cut and the papers passed around while the cars of the train were still shuddering from the stop.

THEIR BLOOD UP!

was one big headline.

"Our blood is up!" shouted one farmer, his finger on the words, his paper raised high.

LOW MEN SAY THEY WILL FIGHT

BEFORE THEY WILL GIVE IN!

the smaller headline said.

"Yes, they will!" cheered another farmer, waving his hat in the air.

"You mean, 'Yes, WE will,'" shouted his friend and slapped him on the back so hard he fell against the side of the station.

"I mean, 'WE will,'" cheered the first one, slamming his hat back on his head so hard he had to take a step back.

MOB GATHERING

OFFICERS THREATENED

a smaller heading announced.

"A mob is gathering!" shouted Turnaround McCooey, running from group to group, turning and spinning with excitement.

"We are the mob, ya damn fool, ya!" somebody shouted and everybody laughed and cheered.

"Ya can't believe everything ya read in the papers!" somebody else shouted.

"WRONG!" another one said. "Everything you see in the papers is the honest to God TRUTH!" And everybody clapped and agreed.

THE POSSE TOO SMALL

TO COPE WITH THE MOB

a headline on another page said.

Nobody was paying any attention to the train or who was getting off.

People stood under the lamps in little groups.

One person would read some out loud then pass the paper to the next one to have a turn.

At the end of the platform a woman read a part about her neighbour who gave a big speech about Ireland to a tax collector—it was quite a speech, the paper said—and when the woman got to that part she burst out laughing and raised her fist in the air and cheered. Then she handed her spectacles and the paper on to the next person and that person read some more out loud.

Another group was reading about the police and a bailiff approaching the door of "delinquent ratepayer" John O'Rorke.

John O'Rorke himself was reading it out loud. Then he stopped.

"This is about *me*, for Gawd's sake!" he said. "This is about me!"

"Read it, John, read it in your best voice, like you've never read anything before. Give us your best, John!" people were pleading.

The train was leaving but nobody even noticed.

John O'Rorke cleared his throat and read in his best, serious voice, with a little bit of an accent, like an English actor on a stage:

The first of the delinquent ratepayers on the list was John O'Rorke. Arriving at the O'Rorke house, Constable Genest and a bailiff approached the door, which was opened by a daughter of Mr. O'Rorke.

"Is Mr. John O'Rorke at home?" asked Constable Genest.

"He's dead," replied the daughter.

"Well, who is in charge of this place?" asked the constable.

"I am. What do you want?" was the reply.

"His taxes are not paid, and I have come to collect them," said Constable Genest, as he advanced to walk into the house, followed by Sergeant Patry and Mr. Major. "Ye'll not git in here," was the reply of the young woman in the doorway, defiant. "I'll throw boiling water on ye if ye come any further," and suiting her action to her word she rushed toward the centre of the house where a pot of water was boiling on a cooking stove...

"Oh, Gawd help me I can't go on..." said O'Rorke and fell down on the platform holding his sides.

"We didn't know you were dead, John! When was the wake? Did we miss it altogether?" somebody asked and a wave of enjoyment went up and down the platform.

My mother and I and Uncle Ronald and Even Steven were reading our paper by the light of the dark-lamp on Lance's rig.

"Look here," said Steven, his eyes glowing. "Here's the part about the 'rebels' sabotaging the policemen's rigs. The paper calls us 'rebels'!"

"Us?" my mother said, turning to Steven. "Are you one of the 'rebels' who 'sabotaged' the policemen's rigs?"

"Well, no, I guess I wasn't, but I think I know who did!"

"Steven challenged the police, though, didn't you, Steven?" Uncle Ronald said. "Didn't you go by with the two McCooeys and the rusty guns in the wagon by Brooks' verandah while the police were sittin' out there after their lunch, pickin' their teeth?"

"I did that. That's for sure!" said Steven.

"Is that in the paper?" my mother said.

"Yes, it's right here." Uncle Ronald pointed to the paragraphs using the words "dangerous rebels" and "menacing" and "armed to the teeth," "threats of attack" and "apprehension of bloodshed."

"Do you believe what you read in the newspapers, Steven?" said my mother, who was feeling even better after being out in the fresh air. She felt good enough to want to tease Steven.

"The papers, they tell what they saw," said Steven, a serious look on his face.

"You and the two McCooeys, is this what the paper's referring to as 'dangerous, menacing rebels'? And it says here, 'hundreds who would just as soon fight as eat'?"

"I'll fight fer me rights," said Steven, sticking out his chin.

"You and the two McCooeys. That's three, not hundreds!"

"There's the O'Malley girls," said Uncle Ronald.

"Then that's five," said my mother.

"No, that's four," said one of the farmers who was listening in. "You see, the O'Malley girls is just ONE!" While the eavesdropping farmer was cackling away at his own joke, Uncle Ronald got serious for a minute.

He read from a small added part to the story at the bottom of the back page.

COUNTY SOLICITOR RETURNS

FOR REINFORCEMENTS

"What does that mean?" said Steven, looking a little uneasy.

"It means they're comin' back," said Uncle Ronald. "Bigger and better next time."

"Well, we'll be ready for them," said Steven, but not very loud.

While they were talking back and forward like this about what was in the paper, what they were saying faded further and further away until I couldn't hear them any more.

There was one thing and one thing only taking up all my attention right now.

And that was I thought I saw a familiar shape duck around behind the end of the station a minute before.

The shape was the shape of my father.

17. BURN LIKE ICE

The next morning I woke up in a pissed-in bed.

There was nobody around. I missed the rooster, I missed Uncle Ronald's morning racket. My mother wasn't in her room, the O'Malley girls were gone, breakfast was over, the dishes were done.

I filled a basin of warm warm water from the kettle on the stove and sponged myself down with a cloth.

I got dressed.

I carried the mattress out to the barn and emptied it out into the manger. The cows wouldn't know the difference. I rinsed out the mattress bag in the drinking trough and hung it up on two hooks on a beam to dry.

On my way back to the house I looked in on Second Chance Lance.

He was gone.

I was filled with dread.

I hadn't told anybody about what I'd seen at the station the night before.

I had gone to bed, silent, worrying about it. Maybe it wasn't him at all. And then again, maybe it was.

I went to sleep with horrible thoughts.

I dreamt.

Even Steven was at my window with one of the McCooey's heads on instead of his own head. Mr. Hickey was chewing off my leg with his new Eaton's catalogue teeth. My mother flew over, large and larger until her bruises turned into the colour of the bruised November sky. Willy Willis was screaming at the statue of St. Joseph until the fire in its belly reached out for him. Second Chance Lance was dead in a little dog basket, his ears cut off.

And in my dreams my father was nowhere, but he was everywhere. In everything, behind everything, under everything.

This morning, the house was silent. Creaked a bit. Then, only the clock in the parlour, ticking and tocking.

And the last house fly of the year, caught between the windows, trying every now and then to drill his way through the glass.

I put a stick of wood in the fire and picked up two pails and headed out to get some water (O'Malley girls' rule of the house, if you use water, go and get some more).

I picked my way down the clay path across the potato field, keeping my pails silent.

On a bare ironwood tree by the edge of the potato field a hairy woodpecker clutched and said *PIK!* and then did the noise of a green stick drawn along a picket fence.

One thousand one hundred million years ago, before the beginning of life, those Gatineau hills were formed.

Four hundred million years ago a great sea floated there.

Seventy-five million years ago the dinosaurs ran there.

Ten thousand years ago, another sea, the Champlain sea, dumped all that clay there.

Nine thousand years ago, human hunters from north and south met there, amazed.

One hundred years ago, I walked down that same clay to get two pails of water. I snapped the first pail on the hook and watched the pail ride down and hit the water. I watched it sink and fill.

I wound the full pail up and sent the second down.

While I cranked up the second pail I thought I saw my father again, standing at the bottom of the cliff by the well, looking up at me, waving, friendly.

I shut my eyes and when I opened them, he was gone.

I lifted the two pails and started back.

Ahead of me, limping along the cold clay path, was a curled-up maple leaf, struggling along like an old, crippled spider.

The sun was out, bright, and the breeze was icy.

My eyes filled.

The hot tears on my cheeks burned like ice.

All of a sudden, blind, I tripped and went down on my knees, dumping the pails.

The ancient clay became the sky, the bright sun turned and spun.

Then it was Uncle Ronald lifting me up and holding onto me, saying what's wrong, saying it's all right now, it's all right now...

Back in the house he said it didn't matter if I wet the bed, that he used to wet the bed and what did it matter, it's only straw or hay or clover or thistles or what and the cows will eat it, anyway, in fact they like it better that way and maybe we should all get together and piss in our beds regularly—the O'Malley girls, your mother, Even Steven and every-body—and haven't you noticed your friend Second Chance Lance, he doesn't care where he lets go, day or night...

And he went on like this to cheer me up until he made me laugh and then told me that this was the day, Saturday, that a couple of our down-the-road neighbours picked up the O'Malley girls and went down to the general store and they took your mother with them and she's not only feeling better but she's even lookin' better...and everything's going to be all right...

I didn't tell him what I thought I saw.

That afternoon (after Uncle Ronald helped me fill my mattress bag with fresh straw, hay and clover—no thistles for sure this time) my mother and the O'Malley girls came home and we all went over to the Hickeys' for a short visit.

Second Chance Lance liked it when the rig was full of people. There were five of us and I was squeezed in the back between my mother and one of the O'Malley girls.

Uncle Ronald was chanting a little jig under his breath...

> The horse is in the stable
> The pork is in the brine
> The dinner's on the table
> The washing's off the line...

Lance was speeding up on the turns, and when the O'Malley girls would squeal and say "Wheeee!" Lance would go even faster.

> The hay is in the hay mow
> The water's in the pail
> The beans are in the pot now
> Let it snow and hail...

After a few fast curves, Lance slowed down on a straight stretch.

Up behind us came a running man. He was calling something to us. We heard it as he raced past us.

"Soldiers comin'," he cried out. "Soldiers comin'!"

"That's Twelve Toes McCooey!" Uncle Ronald told us. "He's spreading a rumour he heard. Somebody told him to run up and down the road and tell everybody. I wouldn't be at all surprised if he was right. You know, he can run almost as fast as Lance can!"

"That should be exciting," my mother said. "Soldiers. Soldiers to come and collect a few dollars in taxes? How much do you owe in taxes, Ronald, do you know?"

"I owe six dollars and thirty cents."

"Are ye goin' to pay it?"

"Sure, I'll pay it, if they fix the roads and build us a local school."

"What's the most somebody would owe?"

"Oh, about ten or twelve dollars or so," said Uncle Ronald.

"I have some money I can give to ya," my mother said, and I looked up at her. I knew where she got the money.

She drew me close and whispered, pressing her lips to my ear. "I got the knife. I sewed a sling for it on the inside of my left sleeve. I've got the knife there now. Can you feel it? All I have to do is have my right hand up my sleeve, and when he comes at me, I'll whip it out and stick him with it."

She was whispering in a normal whisper.

I could hardly believe what she was saying.

What she was saying, what she was whispering, filled me with fear.

Up ahead, a man came running toward us at top speed.

"Here comes Twelve Toes again!" said the O'Malley girls.

He passed by us so fast we couldn't hear what he said. We couldn't make it out.

"What was he saying?" I asked.

"Soldiers comin', I guess," said Uncle Ronald. "Same as before!"

Then Uncle Ronald went back to his song.

Keep the butter churning
The sheep are in the pen
The year is quickly turning

And winter's here again.
The wood is in the woodbox
The fire's in the stove...
I'll go and catch a woodcock
And bring it to my love...

We pulled into the Hickeys' yard and piled out of the rig.

No sooner did we get into Hickeys' and hang our hats and coats behind the stove so they'd get warm than Mr. Hickey started showing everybody the new teeth he got from Eaton's catalogue.

Then Cecelia showed us her cats: one that had a moustache; one that caught at least six birds a day and had a little graveyard corner in the granary where it kept all the bones, beaks and claws and feathers; and another cat that she said that Willy Willis examined and said it had a bad heart.

Then later we all peeled apples for applesauce and Cecelia showed us what her dead mother showed her, which was how to peel an apple and leave the peel in only one long single curly piece and then she cried a little bit about her mother.

And my mother and the O'Malley girls cried a little bit, too, but very quiet.

Then later in the afternoon people got drowsy and Cecelia's two dogs lay down under the table so relaxed you could hear their bones knock on the floor.

Then, in from the parlour came the sound of a fiddle.

I went in and there was Uncle Ronald by the window, the fiddle under his chin, his big fingers so delicate on the strings, the long notes sad.

When his love song was over he lowered his bow and plucked some single notes on the strings with his fingers while he looked out the window at Cecelia's gnarled, bare apple trees.

Then he turned to me and winked and started a fast pounding beat on the floor with the heel of his boot that echoed through the house, turning the house into a thunder box.

"I asked her to marry me!" Uncle Ronald said and then began to sing:

Smoke goes up the chimney,
We dance around the room.

Songs of love within me
Snow be comin' soon!

And then everybody woke up again and Cecelia played on the new gramophone "The Bridal March from Lohengrin" a couple of times and then Uncle Ronald told me to wind up the gramophone again and they played "The Bridal March from Lohengrin" again and again until my mother and the O'Malley girls were rolling their eyes and Mr. Hickey was back asleep on the sofa and his teeth were out on the floor and the cat with the bad heart was pushing them quiet out into the hallway, playing with his sixty-day teeth.

After a big snack of bread and butter and sweet blueberry jam and tea we went home and I helped Uncle Ronald split some firewood, each piece almost exactly the same size.

"This is a Christmas present for Cecelia. I'm giving her a perfect cord of this beautiful ash for firewood. The finest in the country. To keep her warm this winter."

It was almost dark but the perfect triangles of the pieces of white split ash in the even pile at the side of the shed still shone.

My mother was going to bed early. I carried her coal-oil lamp upstairs for her and tucked her in.

"You were awful quiet today, Mickey, me son. Are you troubled?"

I lied to her that I wasn't and that I was just thinking about everything and wondering what was going to happen.

"What's going to happen?" I asked her, looking into her beautiful face there in the moving flame of the lamp, her bruises fading.

"We're not goin' back to him. Not in this world, me son, you can be rest assured of that," she sighed.

Then I told her.

"I saw him," I said. "Twice. Once at the station last night. Once at the well this morning. He's here."

"Well, then," she said, her face flushing red. "Blow out the lamp and we'll wait for him."

After a long silence in the dark, my mother said these words—words spoken one hundred years ago—and I can hear them still, this day, spoken in her strong soft whisper.

"There are two kinds of fire, my son. The fire of love and the fire of hate. He has changed the flames of love I once burned for him into a scorching, searing hate!

"And he'll get what's comin' to him!"

18. SIT DOWN AND SHUT UP

What Tommy Twelve Toes McCooey ran up and down announcing was true. The papers the train brought said it all:

TROOPS FOR LOW!

DETACHMENT OF 43RD RIFLES

ORDERED FOR DUTY!

DELINQUENT SETTLERS

IN A THREATENING MOOD!

A CALL TO ARMS!

MILITIA TO WADE IN MUD THROUGH LOW!

The next morning, Sunday, in church, Father Foley gave a sermon telling the people to pay their taxes. It's what God would want his flock to do. Then he called a meeting for right after mass.

At the meeting, Even Steven surprised everybody. He got up on his feet and asked Father Foley, bold as you please, what God cared about taxes, wasn't He more interested in our souls?

Father Foley told him to sit down and shut up. Everybody laughed except Uncle Ronald. He turned to me and said, "Steven is going to do something great one of these times. Something people will be proud of!"

Around noon, when the meeting was about over, we heard the train whistle.

Everybody piled out and down to the station.

Sure enough, a special train, with an army on board!

The station was buzzing.

Rumours were flying.

The train supposedly took longer than the regular train because they had to stop and check each bridge for dynamite. There was no dynamite. Only rumours of dynamite.

The papers had said that the mob was growing and getting uglier and uglier.

Barnyard McCooey was going around saying to everybody he met, "*You* might be gettin' uglier and uglier, but I'm stayin' just the same!" And then he'd imitate a goat or a cow.

The train had two carloads of men and four carloads of horses. And another carload of supplies.

It was the best train yet!

People were happy, cheering, laughing, clapping, pointing, commenting, as the soldiers and horses unloaded.

The soldiers were handsome and smart in their uniforms. The horses were strong and sleek. The smell of the polished harness and the squeak of the soldiers' boots and the clank of the ammunition boxes and the thudding of the rifles on the platform!

Peek-a-boo McCooey was everywhere you looked.

Boys were playing soldier.

Kids were wrestling.

Older girls were tying ribbons, brushing each other's hair. Women were feeling the bales of tent canvas, admiring the cases of canned meat. Men were shaking hands with the soldiers, patting them, smelling the oiled rifles.

There were over a hundred soldiers.

And over fifty horses!

What a show!

The next day, Monday, the soldiers started a house-to-house search for delinquent taxpayers. They had a huge wagon to take away your belongings if you had no money.

The O'Malley girls put a plan into action.

The family of the first house took everything they owned and went off and hid back in the bush with all of it. Cattle, furniture, clothes, pets, everything. Mildred (or was it Edith?) stationed herself in the empty house, dressed completely in clothes made of sugar bags to show how poor she was.

When the officials opened the door she invited them in for hot water because she didn't have any tea and would they like to sit down except there wasn't any chairs and what can I do for ya?

Since there was nothing there they could take and since she told them that the family that used to live here were all gone back to Ireland, all they could do was ask her to sign a paper and when she said she couldn't read or write, they just gave up and left.

They didn't know that when they got to the next house up the road, the other O'Malley girl was there playing the same trick.

And while she was doing exactly the same business with them, the first O'Malley girl left the first house and cut through the back fields behind the trees and set herself up in the *third* house.

The officials were mad and confused after visiting about half a dozen houses where in each house exactly the same woman was in charge of the exact same thing—nothing!

Meanwhile, the soldiers marched up and down the muddy road.

In the evening we talked about it all and laughed about how the O'Malley girls fooled the officials and confused them so.

I thought I might tell Uncle Ronald the next morning about my mother's plans with the meat-cutting knife but I remembered my mother's warning not to breathe a word.

Before I went to bed I thought I might tell one of the O'Malley girls—or both of them—but how can you tell a secret to somebody when you're not sure who that somebody is?

In the kitchen, one of the O'Malley girls must have been reading my mind.

"Now, Mickey, I suppose you're wondering how you're ever goin' to be able to figure out how to tell us apart, me and me sister. Whether I'm Edith or Mildred or what. Or Mildred or Edith or who."

"Which one are you?" I looked into her brown eyes while I asked the words, while I wondered what difference it was going to make, anyway, whatever she told me.

"I'm Mildred, you see, Mickey. But telling you this won't do you a bit of good. You see, pet, you're no further ahead now, are you?"

"No, I guess not," I said. "Mildred."

"Because, as you are well aware, the next time you see me come in the room you still won't have any way of knowin' if I'm me or me sister Edith. And if it happens to be Edith you next see you won't know whether it's her or me!" She was smiling the whole while she was telling me this, laughing a bit, too.

"What do I do when I see you both together?"

"You must watch us very carefully, Mickey," she said, sudden solemn. "Because we're very different in one way and one way only."

"Which way is that? Please tell me. I have to know," I said.

"Better if you watch carefully, Mickey. In the meantime, I'll give you a little riddle to help you along. Here's your riddle:

When I look in the mirror
and raise one hand
I see my sister."

Later, I watched both of the sisters together, working in the kitchen. They were talking about a big sharp meat-cutting knife that they couldn't seem to find anywhere no matter where they looked. I noticed that their clothes were exactly the same except for the aprons. Both aprons were sewn out of old sugar bags. You could still read the faded lettering that was almost washed out. The lettering was different. One apron said ATLANTIC SUGAR and the other one said REDPATH SUGAR. The Redpath Sugar letters were in faded red and the Atlantic was in blue.

All I had to do now was find out whose was whose or which was which.

While I was reading the aprons the clock in the other room donged eight times and the O'Malley girls took off their aprons and knelt down, one hand on the kitchen table and said their prayers. I knelt down, too, but I wasn't praying. I was watching them to see if there was any difference between the way they said their prayers.

And I kept my eye on their aprons. The O'Malley girl on the left had put her apron on the back of a chair and the other O'Malley girl had laid hers down across the basin on the wooden washstand.

When they were finished their prayers, the O'Malley girl on the left picked up the apron that was across the washbasin and the O'Malley girl on the right...

They'd switched aprons!

That night I put myself to sleep wondering what it was about the picture I had in my brain of the two O'Malley girls, kneeling, praying, one hand each on the kitchen table.

They were so the same.

Except for one thing.

But I couldn't see it.

And the little riddle.

The O'Malley girl looking in the mirror, one hand up. What does she see? Her sister?

A little riddle.

More like a big riddle it was to me then.

And then the morning, the wet, cold bed, the shame, the fear.

When was he coming?

Why didn't he come now, and get it over with?

19. STEVEN HERO

The next day, at one of Father Foley's meetings, Even Steven became a hero. And he is still known in some parts—even after a hundred years has passed—he is still known as the man who alone, single-handedly, all by himself, with help from nobody, defeated an army and sent them home!

Here's what happened.

Father Foley was having one of his meetings. He'd just finished telling another farmer to sit down and shut his mouth. Nobody knew what to do. The bailiffs wanted money. The farmers had no money. The soldiers were here to frighten the money out of the farmers.

"You can't get blood out of a turnip," one farmer said for the hundredth time.

"And even if you, ahem, frighten, ahem, a turnip," said Ahem McCooey, "it still won't give you, ahem, any of its, ahem, blood because as, ahem, everybody, ahem, knows a turnip hasn't got any, ahem, blood in it!"

Uncle Ronald had been thinking about this problem ever since the first bailiff got locked in the cellar a couple of years before.

That night at the meeting he had an idea that he was sure would work. He also had a plan. He would give this good idea to Even Steven and let him present it. That way Steven could get the attention that he always wanted.

Uncle Ronald stood up and Father Foley gave him the floor.

"Father," said Uncle Ronald, "Steven and I and some of us have been discussing an idea that we had and we've decided that the best person among us to present the idea would be Steven so here he is, Father, with what we think is the solution to our problems!"

Even Steven got up but nobody would listen at first until Uncle Ronald got up and asked Father Foley if Steven could have a bit of attention and Father Foley told everybody to shut up and listen to Steven and they did.

It didn't take Steven long to present the idea.

He told the crowd that since Thanksgiving was coming up in a few days that it would be safe to say that the lawyers and the bailiffs and the officials and the soldiers would very likely like to be home for Thanksgiving dinner and they would probably be happy to be offered anything so they could go home.

"But we haven't GOT anything!" shouted about fifty farmers.

"Ah, yes," said Steven, "but we could all PROMISE to pay, don't you see! We could all sign a big affydavy sayin' that we PROMISE to pay and get Father Foley to witness it and bless it and everything else!"

You could tell right away that it was a good idea because everybody started talking about it and forgot about everything else they'd been talking and arguing about for the last year or so.

In no time at all Father Foley got the whole thing going and elected a council to take a list of everybody's name to the officials—a list of promises to pay.

And Even Steven got elected to the committee.

And in the early hours of the next morning, the tax collectors agreed and the army started packing to go home!

Steven was the hero.

The man who, with a single idea, sent home an army!

Hurrah for Steven!

20. AND YOU SAID YOU LOVED ONLY ME

Around noon that day my mother was helping me harness Second Chance Lance. I told her all about how Lance got his name and how Uncle Ronald saved him and gave him a new life just like the dog in the book she gave me, *Beautiful Joe*.

"Except the book is hard to read," I said, "because the dog tells the story and you keep thinking how can a dog write a book!"

My mother had a nice look on her face and said, "It's only a book."

I was showing off how I knew how to harness Lance by myself and I told her how Uncle Ronald had showed me by first *un*harnessing Lance.

And that reminded me of how I learned to count geese in the air by counting from the back of the V instead of the front.

"That Ronnie," she said. "He's a smart good one, he is. You could do worse modeling yourself after that man and I'm not saying that just because he's me brother."

My mother knew how to harness a horse but she'd forgotten a lot of it.

When we got to tightening the bellyband, we both pulled as hard as we could but we knew it wasn't tight enough. The buckle had to be cinched up one more hole to be properly in place.

We were planning to go out for a little ride, just the two of us. I was going to try to talk her out of her plan to use the knife to stick in my father.

We hitched Second Chance Lance to the rig and left him there and then started walking back to the house to get Uncle Ronald to come and tighten Lance's bellyband properly for us.

As we rounded the house we saw my father standing there in the yard.

In the doorway, the O'Malley girls stood.

In front of the step, Uncle Ronald stood.

"Me wife and me son!" my father shouted, throwing wide his arms.

My mother's hand went slowly up her opposite sleeve.

She spoke to me without opening her mouth and without looking at me and without moving.

"Go and stand behind your Uncle Ronald!" she said. "Now!"

"Oh, Nora," my father started. "Please forgive me. I'll change, I promise I will. All that is behind us now. Honest to God, Nora, everything will be different from now on, if you and the boy will only come back to me. I can't live without you. You and young Mickey. You won't regret it. You'll see. I have a new job and the money's just pourin' in…oh, Nora!"

He stopped to take a breath and then put his hand to his heart and started to sing a song I'd often heard him sing. He had a beautiful singing voice.

> *The violets were scenting the woods, Nora,*
> *Displaying their charm to the bee,*
> *When I first said I loved only you, Nora*
> *And you said you loved only me.*

> *The chestnut blooms gleamed through the glade, Nora,*
> *A robin sang loud from a tree,*
> *When I first said I loved only you, Nora*
> *And you said you loved only me!*

His voice echoed around the farm buildings.

"The violets and the bees are long gone, me bucko! And nobody's seen a chestnut tree in years. And the last news of the robins I heard was that they're gone south fer the winter!" my mother said in her best sarcastic voice. She sounded brave but she was shaking. She was terrified. Her eyes were closed and her eyelids were trembling.

"Oh, Nora!" my father moaned. "Don't be so hard and cruel. Don't you know I've learned the error of me ways? I swear to you in the name of everything that's holy. I will never touch a drop of intoxicatin' liquor again the rest of me born days! I need you, me darlin', me little puddin', me little berry. You're everything to me. I'm a wandering raftsman with no raft, no anchor, I'm lost…a sorrowful, pitiful man alone…"

He was dabbing the tears from his eyes into the shoulder of his red plaid jacket…

> *The golden-robed daffodils shone, Nora*
> *And danced in the breeze on the lea*
> *When I first said I loved only you, Nora*
> *And you said you loved only me…*

His voice was trembling and sounding full of love.

"You can drop the singin', Michael, we're not goin' back with you..." my mother said.

Her voice was even and sounded strong. You could tell he knew she meant it.

"Young Mickey has learned more with this family in a few days than he ever did in twelve years under your tender-loving care..." my mother said, looking over at me.

A wood warbler gave us his four high thin notes.

There was long silence.

Then my father's face and his body made a sudden change. His face darkened with anger and his body tensed.

"You and the boy," he said. "You're mine. You belong to me!"

"We belong to nobody! We belong to ourselves!" my mother said stout, raising her face and puffing out her chest.

"You won't come home with me?" my father said.

"No, we will not!" my mother answered, squaring her shoulders, her hand up her sleeve.

"You stole from me!" my father glared, his face like a storm.

"I took what was mine!" my mother shouted, her eyes squeezed shut.

"Well, then, I'll take what is mine, one way or the other!" my father growled and stepped toward my mother. His hands went to his waist, his fingers working the belt.

My mother didn't move. I knew she was clutching the knife handle hidden up her sleeve.

She stood her ground, trembling, her chin stuck out at him.

He stopped right over her. He hesitated. He seemed surprised by her bravery. Why wasn't she turning her face away, protecting herself with her arms? Ducking down? Backing up?

Then everything moved at once.

His hands on his belt.

Me running into him.

My hands on his belt.

His hands cuffing me away.

My face onto the hard clay of the yard.

The O'Malley girls' hands on my mother.

Uncle Ronald's hand on my father's fingers, squeezing.

Uncle Ronald saying, "You'll take nothing from here, Michael!"

My father sinking in pain to his knees. Uncle Ronald crushing his fingers.

"You'll leave us alone and you'll be on your way off this property and you'll not come back!" Uncle Ronald said, squeezing like a vice my father's cracking fingers.

Uncle Ronald letting go.

My father rising, backing out of the yard, screaming, holding his hand.

"You pack of twisters! You filthy squatters! You don't even pay your taxes! They send soldiers to squeeze a few tax dollars out of your measly hides!" His face was purple with rage.

"Yous' are a pack of thieves. And now you're stealin' from me. That woman, your little sister, and that boy, they're *my* property.... Well, you'll pay for this, mister!" he snarled.

"Nobody, nobody steals from Mickey McGuire!"

Then he was turned and moving up the road, half running, leaning forward, holding his hand.

Beside my mother and at the feet of the O'Malley girls was their lost knife.

Everyone was frozen there, looking at the knife.

21. HEART OF LEAD

My mother was sitting at the kitchen table, half crying, half laughing.

"You stood up to him!" the O'Malley girls were saying. "He has new respect for you now! Did you see him hesitate? He saw your strength. He'll think twice about comin' back!" the O'Malley girls said.

"Maybe we're free, Mickey, my boy. Maybe we're actually shook of him now!" my mother laughed and cried. Then she pounded the table.

"Mother of God," my mother cried, her face in her hands. "When I saw the difference between him and you!" She looked up at Uncle Ronald and the O'Malley girls. "The difference! I'd rather die than go back!"

Her face was flushed with bravery.

While Uncle Ronald put some of Willy Willis's ointment on my forehead where I scraped it on the hard clay of the yard, Even Steven

came in the door to tell us he'd just been elected to another big-shot position, a special council to oversee the promises that everybody made.
Father Foley and other big shots were also on the council.

We tried to explain to Steven what happened with my father but he
was only half listening. His mind was on his new life as a big shot.

"What do you think he'll do?" Uncle Ronald asked my mother. "Will
he go back to Ottawa?"

"Oh, I don't know," my mother said. "He's stubborn and mean. He
may try to steal something from you. To get even."

"Lance!" I yelled.

"He can't take Lance," Uncle Ronald said. "Lance wouldn't let him.
He'd never get the harness on him. Lance would kick his head off before
he'd ever let him harness him!"

"Lance *is* harnessed!" I yelled. "And hitched!" I screamed and crashed
out the door.

I rounded the house and looked up to the stable with a sinking heart
of lead.

Lance was gone!

22. DIFFERENT-SIZED PIECES OF SOMETHING

Steven's team and wagon were ready. In no time we were pounding down
the road.

"He's a half hour ahead of us but he's not a horseman and he'll lose
time at the gates and on the turns. Lance won't cooperate. He'll have
trouble. And we can ask on the way. There's plenty of neighbours to help!"

Uncle Ronald was right. One of the gates was hanging open and the
other one had a broken latch. Second Chance Lance wasn't cooperating.

At the sharp turn we saw my father's hat in the mud on the road.

About a mile outside of Low, Boner McCooey yelled that "a man in
a hurry went by a while ago with your horse and rig! He was drinkin' out
of a little bottle of whiskey, acting crazy!"

In Low, nobody saw anything. Everybody was strolling away from the
station. They seemed a bit sad. The special train just left with the soldiers.

The fun was over.

In Brennan's Hill a woman with a pail at the pump in front of the store said the rig stopped for water a short while ago. She said the man was full of rage and the horse was frothing at the mouth and there seemed to be trouble with the rig or the harness or something.

About two miles down the road, just before Farrellton, we spotted them down a long curved turn.

Horse and rig and man didn't look quite right.

But they were moving at quite a clip.

My father was cutting Lance vicious with the whip. He snarled it up behind him and then over his head it coiled and writhed like a snapped steel cable. Then down with all the bulging of his shoulder and the hard thickness of his wrist onto the flanks of Second Chance Lance.

My father was an expert with a whip.

I knew then because of what Uncle Ronald had told me that my father had learned his lessons well. He learned the art of the whip from his own father. And now, he was teaching the belt and the whip to me. It wouldn't be long until I, too, knew it well and then passed the knowledge on to somebody else.

My unborn son, maybe.

And on and on.

But that never happened.

Because at that exact moment in my life, Second Chance Lance changed everything.

With his arm raised for another cut at Lance, my father hesitated. He heard something. So did we.

Then again. Clearer this time.

It was the sore-throat voice of the train. The train with razors in its throat.

The special train taking the soldiers back to Ottawa.

Down came the whip. Then, you could tell the way he all of a sudden moved that my father'd decided he'd beat the train to the level crossing ahead.

But then the next sad warning whistle was much closer. The voice of the train, again, something clawing at its throat. Angrier now.

Lance was doing a trot so fast his hooves were just a blur. Gobs of clay whizzed past my father's head.

Now my father for some reason changed his mind. Maybe it was the fierceness of the train whistle. And maybe the fact that he couldn't see the train at this point. You didn't see the train at this crossing until it was almost on top of you.

Whatever the reason, my father decided they weren't going to make the crossing in time. He lowered the whip and pulled the reins up short. Lance began to slow. They were coming up to the crossing.

"Whoa, whoa!" my father was roaring, although we couldn't hear him.

The breeching that Uncle Ronald had mended strained against Lance's rump.

My father, he was leaning back, pulling back the reins with all his weight, the bit in Lance's mouth ripping back, jerking back his head, dragging him up on his hind legs, screeching a high scream which we could almost hear, shaking his head and mane at the lead-coloured sky, as if he was crying, "My mouth! my mouth!" and trying to get rid of the choking bit that pulled into his throat.

My father loosened the pressure on the reins and Lance was back on four legs and braced, front legs locked, back legs almost sitting, sliding, skidding to a stop on the greasy ancient clay.

The train came roaring through the cut like a monstrous angry rhino and headed across the tiny field to the crossing.

I see that picture now, one hundred years later, as plain as I see this old spotted bony hand of mine in front of this, my wrinkled old face.

◆

Lance stopping, trying to pull up.

But now Lance's whole harness is collapsing. The bellyband has loosened and everything's giving way. The britches aren't holding and the rig runs up onto the backs of Lance's legs.

Lance kicks and bolts across the track.

His move is so quick, so surprising that my father is thrown from the seat and loses the reins when he grabs for the side of the rig to hang on.

With his head down, digging with all his strength, Lance bursts across the track.

The engine clips the rear of the rig and bounces it, tipping it and spinning it into the ditch on Lance's side.

The blow sends my father up into the air and tumbling and rolling onto the track in front of the engine.

While the whistle howls and shrieks like a wounded animal, my father is gobbled up by the wheels and disappears under screaming steel and hissing steam and thundering iron.

◆

The end of the train was past by the time it got stopped. Lance was struggling to get to his feet, in the ditch, tangled in the twisted harness, kicking the rig into splinters.

The freight car doors were sliding open, soldiers leaning out to see what happened.

People ran up and down the train looking underneath. Soldiers and trainmen bent down walking along looking under. Then one trainman, a conductor, came out from between two cars. He had on his face a look of horror. He pointed behind himself.

"Here's something!" he called out. "There's something here!" he said without looking back.

Then he walked away.

We won't say much more than that about it.

Maybe just mention that after a lot of fuss, they got to put quite a few different sized pieces of something into a wooden box and cover it quick with army blankets.

23. THROW THE FLOWER HARD

After the funeral I tried this:

I looked in the mirror and held up my right hand. The boy who looked out of the mirror at me was holding up his *left* hand.

The answer to the riddle was easy. One of the O'Malley girls was left-handed, the other one right-handed!

It was at the graveyard that I saw it.

Father Foley gave us each a paper flower to drop in the hole after the ceremony.

There weren't very many people there. Uncle Ronald, the O'Malley girls, me, Even Steven, the two gravediggers standing well back, Father Foley and, for some reason, Sobbing McCooey, who, I guess, went every day to the graveyard, anyway.

When it came to my turn, I threw my flower hard into the hole instead of dropping it like the others did.

Father Foley gave me a look.

My mother and Sobbing McCooey were the only ones crying.

The O'Malley girls were the last to drop their flowers in.

They did it together.

Exactly the same.

Except for one thing.

One used her right hand, the other her left.

24. CLEAR AS CRYSTAL

Second Chance Lance was recovering quick from his injuries. He had cuts and bruises and scrapes that Willy Willis did his magic on.

It was the afternoon before Thanksgiving and Lance and Uncle Ronald and I waited on Even Steven's road—Uncle Ronald with his double-barrel shotgun ready. He stood in the slanting gold sun, clear as crystal.

The geese came sudden, blasting over the hill from Even Steven's field by the river.

Their discussion was deafening. The barking and honking and yodeling was the only sound in the world. There were three hundred of them in the formation.

Uncle Ronald picked one about three quarters back on the right leg of the V and fired.

The goose crumpled and fell. He picked another one from the left leg of the V and just a bit further back and pulled the other trigger. The second goose was tumbling before the first one hit the ground.

The space left by each goose was filled immediately by the ones behind.

"You never take the leaders," Uncle Ronald said. "Two reasons. The formation needs the leaders to get them out of here and further south where there's food for them in the winter months. Also, the smaller and younger ones nearer the rear are not as muscular, more tender."

"Do we need two geese?"

"Cecelia and Mr. Hickey are invited. And we're going to ask Even Steven."

"That's nice," I said.

"And while I'm sayin' grace before the dinner, I'm goin' to announce the engagement of Cecelia Hickey and Ronald O'Rourke!"

We went into the bush and brought out the geese.

As we tossed them into the rig, a snowflake flashed in the angling sun.

Lance was still wide-eyed and tense from the gunblasts.

"Snow!" Uncle Ronald said, surprise in his voice.

"Catch one of the first ones on your tongue," he said. "It's good luck!"

We moved around with our heads back and our tongues out, Lance watching us.

By the time we were halfway home, the snow was coming down thick and soft.

"We always know it's going to snow but when it does we're always surprised," Uncle Ronald said. "I wonder why that is?"

"It's because something is starting," I said, surprising myself with an idea that I didn't know I had.

Uncle Ronald was surprised, too. He looked at me, startled, his face full of wonder and love.

THERE!

Yes, and I remember like it was just now, the big cheer that went up at the Thanksgiving dinner table when Uncle Ronald made his announcement!

That was one hundred years ago.

I'm a very old man now. In fact, I'm Canada's oldest citizen.

And I'm back wetting the bed again. But it's not so bad now.

Just about everybody around here where I am wets the bed.

In fact, if you don't wet the bed around here, they think there's something wrong with you.

You won't be hearing from me any more, by the way. I'm going to die soon.

At least, I hope I am.

I don't particularly want to live any longer.

A hundred and twelve years is enough, don't you think?

ANGEL SQUARE

To all my family, then and now.

Caution to those with Lowertown memory:
Many proper names have been altered to fit
the truth to my fiction.

1. LET ME TELL YOU

Let me tell you about last Christmas. The first Christmas after the war. And let me tell you about Sammy's father.

And Margot Lane.

When I heard what happened to Sammy's father I first thought Aunt Dottie said "assassinated" but it wasn't "assassinated," it was *assaulted*. Sammy's father was assaulted. Beat up. In the streetcar barns where he worked at night. Night watchman.

Dad said he saw it in the paper. A man in a hood went into the streetcar barns and beat up Sammy Rosenberg's father the night watchman for nothing. Mr. Rosenberg told the police what he saw. Then he went into a sleep.

"It wasn't for nothing," Aunt Dottie said. "It was because he's Jewish. Some people around here don't like you if you're Jewish."

It was coming up to the first Christmas after the war and everything was supposed to be nice from now on. And now this happened. Who would want to beat up a nice man like Sammy's father? A man in a hood. A hood made of a flour bag cut-off. The printing on the flour bag said, RITCHIE'S FEED AND SEED.

Ritchie's Feed and Seed is a store in the market next to Peter Devine's where we get our groceries. And near there is R. Hector Aubrey's where we get our meat. That's where Aunt Dottie stared so hard at Mr. Aubrey cutting the meat one time that he almost chopped his thumb off with the cleaver.

Sammy is my best school friend. We walk to school together. He lives on Cobourg Street, the same street as I live on. In Lowertown.

In Ottawa,
Ontario,
Canada,
Planet Earth,
The Universe.
December, 1945.

That was the address I put in my workbook at school. We were practising writing letters and addressing them. Letters to ourselves.

"Dear Tommy; How are you? I am fine," etc.

I asked the teacher if it would be all right if we wrote our letter to somebody else. He said no, the best way to practise was to write to yourself and then when you got that right you'd be allowed to write to somebody else and shut up and don't be impertinent.

Impertinent.

When he saw the address in my workbook he put a big X through it and tore the paper he pressed so hard. Then he said I was stupid.

His name was Mr. Blue Cheeks.

He was the worst teacher I ever had.

I said Sammy is my best school friend. We both have to cross Angel Square to get to York Street School where we go. It is a dangerous square to cross four times a day, so it is a good thing that we have each other for protection.

There are three schools on Angel Square.

On one side is The School of Brother Brébeuf where all the French Canadians go. But nobody calls them French Canadians. Everybody calls them Pea Soups.

On the second side of Angel Square is York Street School where Sammy and I go. Most of the people who go to York Street School are Jewish. I'm not.

I'm not anything.

But nobody calls them Jewish. Everybody calls them Jews.

On the third side of the square is St. Brigit's School of the Bleeding Thorns where all the Irish Catholics go. But nobody calls them that. Everybody calls them Dogans.

So four times a day most of the Pea Soups, Jews and Dogans try to cross Angel Square to get home or go to school.

Last year was the same.

Sammy would meet me on the comer of Papineau and Cobourg at eight-thirty and we'd walk down Papineau and then try and cross the square to get to school. At twelve o'clock Sammy would meet me at the schoolyard gate. We'd walk up York Street and then try and cross Angel Square to get home for dinner. At the one o'clock signal, the sound of the long dash on the radio, I would leave our house, meet Sammy and try the square again. After school at four o'clock Sammy would meet me and we'd try and cross the square one more time to get home. Quite a job.

All the streetcars come up Cobourg Street to go to the car barns for the night. When I am in bed at night I can feel the streetcars rumbling up Cobourg Street, one after another, going home to the barns to rest.

They shake my bed as they go by. In the summer, when we go up to Low to our cabin on the Gatineau River, I can't sleep very well because it is so quiet. There are just crickets and maybe a whip-poor-will. Not nice and soothing like the thundering of streetcars.

The barns where Sammy's father was night watchman have deep pits between the tracks with stairs going down each one so the mechanics can work underneath on the cars and fix them and grease them. Each pit is coated with a pad of grease and dust which makes it like a rug, and has a light in it that you can switch on and off.

Sammy and I would play cops and robbers down in those pits with our cap guns. There are a hundred pits in the barns. Sammy and I killed many cops and robbers there.

We don't do that any more. We're too old now.

I was half asleep when I heard about Sammy's father that morning. It was Tuesday morning and Aunt Dottie was waking me up to go to school. After she and Dad told me what happened I knew then why Sammy wasn't at school the day before. I had to do Angel Square four times by myself. That's why I was so tired Monday night.

Tired and full with dreams.

Dreams of Lowertown and movies and programs on the radio and Christmas. And Margot.

In one of my dreams I heard a long scream and I knew that something had dragged the lovely Margot Lane into the swamp. I went chasing into that evil darkness, gooey things pulling at me and mud sucking me down. I came to an old cabin and saw through the window that the evil professor in his white coat had the lovely Margot Lane tied to a chair. He was holding a red-hot poker near her lovely face. Her eyes were wide and mostly white and staring up to the side like the eyes of a scared horse. In my big black hat with the big brim and my cloak I turned invisible and went in the cabin and grabbed the professor's wrist as the poker came closer.

He had a German accent. He said this:

"Vat is it ZAT ISS holdink my arm? I cannot moof my arm!"

"Oh, Shadow," sighed the lovely Margot Lane, "you've come at last. I thought you'd never get here in time to save me!"

"Your ugly game is over, Herr Professor," I said in a very low voice. "This is your last innocent swamp victim! You can't escape The Shadow! Heh heh heh heh heh heh!"

I woke up and saw Aunt Dottie standing beside my bed.

"I heard some peculiar laughing in here," she said.

"I was dreaming I was The Shadow and was in a big swamp to save Margot Lane from the evil professor," I told her through the fog of waking up.

"I shouldn't let you listen to that awful radio program any more. It's so filthy. Roaming around in swamps! Go down the cellar and feel the tank. If there's any hot water you'd better take a bath before you go to school."

I think Aunt Dottie figured I'd get dirty even dreaming.

"Do I have to? I'm not even dirty."

"Hurry up. Of course you're dirty. Everybody's dirty after dreaming. Especially about swamps! Look, I think I see mud on your elbows."

"I wasn't *on* my elbows."

"Well, your knees then. Hurry up. The Quaker is almost ready."

The Quaker. Quick Quaker Oats. My favourite stuff. Specially with brown sugar. And we had brown sugar now. Brown sugar wasn't rationed any more. The war was over.

My favourite breakfast is to sit with the Quick Quaker Oats box in front of me while I eat the hot porridge with the milk and brown sugar. I eat and listen to Dad and Aunt Dottie talking. (My sister Pamela is already at her front window.) And while I eat and listen to Dad and Aunt Dottie talking I study the picture on the Quick Quaker Oats box. I can do those three things at once. Eat, listen and study the box.

On the box is a picture of a handsome Quaker in his Quaker outfit, standing there, smiling, looking out at me. No matter how I turn the box, his eyes are always on me.

That is one thing about the Quaker. He always looks at me no matter where the box is. If I can see the Quaker anywhere, on the table, over on the window sill, on the shelf above the stove, in the cupboard, he is looking at me.

The other thing about the Quaker is that he's holding a box of Quick Quaker Oats! And of course, on the box he's holding there's a picture of himself holding a box of Quick Quaker Oats. And on that little box there's the same picture. And if I had X-ray vision like Superman I would be able to see the next little Quaker and the next one and the next one.

"Get your nose off of that box, you'll get germs," Aunt Dottie said quietly as she pulled on her white gloves to serve Dad and me some toast.

"You never know where that box has been and who might have touched it," she said.

Dad gave me a wink. Then he said this:

"I read in the paper that these boxes are untouched by human hands. They're handled with tongs in the factory and sterilized robots take them off the trucks and put them on the shelves in the store. The only human hands that might have touched the box might be the hands of Toe-Jam Laframboise."

Toe-Jam Laframboise is the delivery man who drives the grocery truck. Toe-Jam never washes much. He drives Aunt Dottie mad. Dad said Toe-Jam never washes his feet because he can't get his socks off. The blue mould has scaled his socks right to his skin.

Aunt Dottie whisked the Quaker off the table and put him outside between the doors. Maybe the cold would freeze those germs off him. I saw him smiling at me as Aunt Dottie shut him out in the cold. Good-bye all you Quakers until tomorrow. How many Quakers were there? A million, I guess. If you had eyes like Superman.

I ate my Quaker, stood over the heat in the hall for a minute and took off for school. Outside, I waved at my sister Pamela in her window and headed up Cobourg Street.

A guy across the street I knew waved at me.

"Hi, Lamont!" he shouted.

Even though my name is Tommy, they all called me Lamont. Lamont Cranston.

It was the radio program everybody used to listen to called "The

Shadow," and on it, this guy, Lamont Cranston, used to make himself invisible and fight crime that way.

The program would start with The Shadow saying, "Who knows what evil LURKS in the hearts of men! *The Shadow* knows! Heh, heh, heh, heh...!" Then there'd be a lot of very scary organ music that would run all over the place then stop and then suddenly start again so sharp it would make you jump. I could just imagine the guy playing the organ, stabbing at the keys with his fingers to make me jump and hit my head on the radio. I'd hit my head because our radio didn't go up very loud sometimes because of some tubes that were burnt out or weak or something. I'd have to lie on the floor with my head stuck in between the legs of the radio so I could hear and sometimes the cat would be there with me. Sometimes the cat would purr too loud and I'd have to shove him away because I couldn't hear what was going on with The Shadow.

Then the announcer would say this:

"Years ago in the Orient, Cranston learned a strange and mysterious secret: the hypnotic power to cloud men's minds so they cannot see him.

"Cranston's friend and companion, the lovely Margot Lane, is the only person who knows to whom the voice of the invisible Shadow belongs. Today's drama: *The Devil takes a wife!*"

Organ music; bonk on the radio with my head.

Then, at the end of the program:

"Again next week, The Shadow will demonstrate that—the weed of crime bears bitter fruit. Crime does not pay. The Shadow knows! Heh heh heh heh heh....!"

Organ music.

Bonk!

The thing I haven't told you yet is this:

There was a girl I really liked in my class named Margot Lane. Everybody knew I liked her except one person.

That person was Margot Lane herself.

I turned down Papineau and looked at Angel Square. I had to cross that square to get to school.

I watched the groups of Jews running for their lives across Angel

Square. Who was chasing them this time? It looked like a vicious gang of Dogans.

In the distance, away across the other side of Angel Square, a terrified gang of Pea Soups was scattering. Moving in on them was a very serious-looking bunch of Jews.

In another place on the square two Dogans had a Pea Soup down and were beating him with their hats.

Over there, two Jews were tying a Dogan to a post.

Over here, two Pea Soups were trying to tear off a Jew's arm.

Over there, three Jews and a Dogan were torturing a Pea Soup with bats.

In the centre some Pea Soups were burying alive a Dogan in a deep hole in the snow.

Across there, a Pea Soup, a Jew and a Dogan had surrounded some-body they thought might be a Protestant.

Here, a Jew was beating up two other Jews.

There, six Dogans and five Pea Soups were discussing and pointing at somebody they had trapped, probably a Jew.

Over there, a Pea Soup, a Dogan and a Jew were all tangled up on the ground.

In another place on the square a group of Dogans was selling what looked like a stray Protestant to a group of Pea Soups. A Jew was acting as interpreter.

Somewhere else, two Jews were trying to unscrew a Pea Soup's head.

I started across the square. Alone—because Sammy wasn't with me. Because of his dad.

All over the square, Dogans, Pea Soups and Jews were tearing the sleeves out of one another's coats and trying to rip each other limb from limb.

Suddenly the bells from the three schools began to ring. I was lucky. I'd only had three fights. Lost two and won one. Not bad considering I was alone.

Priests and teachers were running, herding us all to our own buildings.

There was a lot of shouting and bawling. It was like runaway cattle in a movie.

Soon the square would be empty.

Only hundreds of mitts and hats and parts of coats would be left, dark patches in the white snow.

School was in.

School wasn't getting along with me very well lately. And I wasn't getting along very well with it.

It pretty well all started back when I was in Grade Five and Miss Strong just laughed at me when I said I wanted to be a writer when I grew up.

She didn't really laugh, I guess, she just made a kind of sound with her mouth like you would if you were blowing a little feather or a hunk of fluff off your upper lip just under your nose.

Or maybe it was way back in Grade Four when we had the I.Q. test. They gave all the grade fours an I.Q. test and I was the only one who had to go back the next day and do it over again. I saw Miss Frack and Miss Eck discussing mine. They were standing facing each other talking about my test. I knew because they looked over at me a couple of times. They both had huge chests and they were standing kind of far apart so their chests wouldn't bounce off each other.

They looked like two huge robins discussing a worm.

There was a lot of sighing and then they came and told me that I'd have to do the test again the next day. By the looks on their faces I figured they were saying that they knew I was stupid, sure, but could I possibly be that stupid? Could I be something subhuman? You'd have to be in a coma or something to score that low.

But Dad said that maybe I scored so high that the test couldn't record it—maybe I blew out all the tubes in the thing and they figured only a genius could score that high and they figured something went wrong with their test because even Albert Einstein couldn't score that high.

And they say he invented the atomic bomb.

That made me feel a little better.

But I didn't really blame Miss Strong for laughing when I said I wanted to be a writer.

After all, I was the second worst writer in the class.

Melody Bleach was the worst writer in the class. Her main problem was she never had a pencil and she couldn't write with a pen and a nib because she pressed too hard.

Dad said the reason was, she wasn't organized.

And she always put her tongue out when she tried to write after she borrowed a pencil or the teacher gave her one.

She'd stick her tongue between her teeth when she was trying to think of what to write. Some of the kids would laugh at her and make fun of her.

I laughed at her too but I also felt sort of sorry for her.

Specially when she wet herself. That was in Grade Three, I think. Melody wet herself. She was too scared of Miss Frack or Miss Eck, or whoever it was, to ask if she could leave the room.

So she just sat there and the water ran down off the seat into a pool on the floor under her desk. And the water ran down her cheeks from her eyes. There was water running out of her from both ends.

I think Dad was right. Her main problem was that she wasn't organized. Dad always says, get organized and you can't go wrong.

I was sitting there worrying about Sammy's father when suddenly I heard Blue Cheeks saying my name. Everybody was looking over at me. Even Margot. And Blue Cheeks was getting bluer. He was asking me about a grammar sentence. He was writing on the blackboard but he was looking at me.

Blue Cheeks could turn his head *right* around without moving his body. His head would start turning slowly and it would keep turning and turning until it was facing the other way. Then it would start back until it was back almost to the same spot. He could turn his head left and right so far that he could cover the whole 360 degrees without moving his shoulders. His head must have been on a swivel or something.

He would write grammar sentences on the board so that we could copy them out and then tell him what was wrong with them.

All the sentences he ever wrote on the board were wrong.

Every day we wrote down hundreds of sentences that were wrong.

Some of them were quite funny but if he heard anybody laughing or snorting, old Blue Cheeks's head would start coming around, slowly,

slowly. And we'd all sit there, hypnotized by how far his head could come round.

I used to think it would unscrew and tumble right off onto the floor.

But then, of course, if that happened he could catch it just before it hit because his hands hung down there near the floor anyway.

Somebody must have coughed or something and he looked around and couldn't catch anybody so he noticed I was in a trance and picked me as his victim.

I was thinking about Sammy's father, so I must have been staring into the blackboard like I was hypnotized. Dad said later that I must have looked like a cow watching a train go by.

"You! What is wrong with this sentence?"

He was pointing at the sentence he had just written on the board.

"Read the sentence, please," he said.

I read it. "Ralph edged closer as the moose sniffed suspiciously and snapped the picture," the sentence said.

"Well?" said Blue Cheeks.

I looked at the sentence again.

"Tell us, Mr. Daydreams, what is wrong with this sentence."

"It's something to do with the camera," I said.

"It's something to do with the camera, is it?" His head was right around facing me full-on now and his shoulders were still facing the blackboard. It seemed impossible.

"And the moose," I said, "and something to do with the moose."

"The camera and the moose," said Blue Cheeks, sarcasm dripping off his lips like syrup.

"And Ralph," I said, just to make sure, "there's something wrong with Ralph too."

"And what do you suppose it is that is wrong with Ralph?" said Blue Cheeks.

"He hasn't got the camera," I said.

"And who has the camera?"

"The moose seems to have the camera."

"And why has the moose got the camera instead of Ralph?"

"I don't know, sir. It seems strange, a moose with a camera."

"Why has the moose got the camera?"

"Maybe he took it from Ralph?"

"Why hasn't Ralph got his own camera?" Blue Cheeks's face was dark blue now.

"Maybe it *isn't* Ralph's camera!" I said, thinking I was on to something. "Maybe Ralph hasn't got a camera and the moose has a camera and Ralph's sneaking up on the moose to steal his camera!"

"Read the sentence again!"

"Ralph edged closer as the moose sniffed suspiciously and snapped the picture." I almost knew it off by heart by now.

"What is wrong with that sentence?"

Behind me sat Geranium Mayburger, the dumbest girl in the school. Geranium loved to whisper answers to people. Specially people in trouble.

"Hooves," she whispered behind me. "A moose can't take a picture because his hooves are too big for the button."

"Five seconds," said Blue Cheeks, "or you stay and write lines!" He sounded like he was choking. I was desperate.

"A moose could never hold a camera properly or snap a picture because of its large and clumsy hooves," I said, trying to make the best sentence I could.

I knew I was doomed, so I sat down.

Blue Cheeks gurgled, "One hundred lines—'I must learn my grammar!'"

A few minutes later the bell rang for recess and I was suddenly alone.

I had specially wanted to get out this recess and find CoCo Laframboise (nephew of Toe-Jam) on Angel Square and ask him what he thought of what happened to Sammy's father. CoCo is my best Pea Soup friend. He goes to Brother Brébeuf and their recess is the same time as ours. CoCo is smart and he is a good detective. He would be out there right now, fighting away, having a great time.

And I was stuck in here.

I wrote my lines like I always did, holding three pencils in my fingers so three lines would get written at once. I was the best line-writer in the class. I was so good and so fast, sometimes people would pay me to write their lines for them. I charged seven cents a hundred.

When I was finished I had time to write down what I had to get done before Christmas Day, which was exactly one week away.

1. Worry about what happened to Sammy's father.
2. See the eclipse of the moon tonight.
3. Get presents for Aunt Dottie, Dad, my sister Pamela, my friends and maybe one other, very special present.
4. Go to the show.
5. Work at home on the ashes.
6. Work at Talmud Torah.
7. Work at Woolworth's.
8. Be altar boy at St. Brigit's Dogan Church.
9. Sing at St. Albany's Protestant Church.
10. Get the lovely Margot Lane to notice me.

At noon I raced across Angel Square to go home for dinner.

On the square the war was raging.

I could see Killer Bodnoff, who, last year, was the toughest Jew, and my friend CoCo Laframboise, who was busy being the toughest Pea Soup; Manfred Mahoney, who was the toughest Dogan; not Denny Trail, the toughest Protestant, who had moved to New Edinburgh; Arnold Levinson, who was the sissiest Jew; Telesphore Bourgignon, who was the sissiest Pea Soup; Clary O'Mara, who was the sissiest Dogan; not Sherwood Ashbury, the sissiest Protestant, who had moved to Bank Street somewhere; Anita Pleet, who was the smartest girl; Martha Banting, who was the nicest girl; Geranium Mayburger, who was the dumbest girl; Fleurette Featherstone Fitchell, who was the dirtiest girl, even dirtier than Delbert Dilabio, and he was the dirtiest guy in Lowertown.

And Margot Lane, walking beautifully home to Whitepath Street.

And I was Lamont Cranston, invisible for now, racing home across Angel Square.

I don't know why, but as I was losing one small fight I was remembering something that happened with Fleurette Featherstone Fitchell in my laneway one time.

She drew an oval in the dirt with a stick. Then she cut it in half with another line. It looked like the side view of a hamburger bun.

She asked me if I knew what it was.

"It's a hamburger bun from the side," I said.

"No it isn't, silly!" she said. "It's something I've got that you haven't got." Then she drew what looked like a cigar in the dirt with her stick.

"Guess what that is," she said.

"A cigar," I said.

"No it isn't, silly!" she said.

Then she asked me if I wanted to see hers.

Our laneway is between two brick walls. The brick starts part way up and there is cement on the lower part. It is on the smooth lower part that we play alleys off the wall. In the summer the ground is mostly dirt with some weeds here and there. There are quite a few holes that have been dug for playing alleys and there are some shiny bits of glass around. And some small stones. When it rains there is a strong smell of cat piss.

I said no.

On the square, Delbert Dilabio and some guys were standing around saying things and listening to Fleurette Featherstone Fitchell saying worse things right back to them.

Killer Bodnoff and CoCo Laframboise were in a death grip in the corner of the yard.

Manfred Mahoney was looking for Denny Trail.

Anita Pleet was trying to explain something to Geranium Mayburger.

I left the square, ran up Papineau and down Cobourg to my house. I waved at my sister Pamela in her window and went in. Aunt Dottie gave me soup and peanut butter and homemade biscuits while we listened to "Big Sister" on the radio at twelve-fifteen. It was the same as yesterday. They were still arguing about whether Big Sister's sister should marry some soldier from somewhere. Halfway through the "Farm Broadcast" at twelve-thirty the radio tubes faded out again and I didn't hear a thing until the one o'clock signal came on.

At the sound of the long dash I left, while Aunt Dottie was reminding me about changing into my old breeks from my good breeks right after school before I went out again.

On the way back across Angel Square I had a chance to talk to CoCo, who wasn't too busy. He had just one guy down in the snow, throttling him with his own scarf. He'd let the scarf go loose a little and make the guy sing parts of this stupid song that was on the radio all the time.

Chickory Chick
Cha-la cha-la
Check a la romey in a
Bannana-ka
Wallika wallika
Can't you see?
Chickory chick
Is me!

We talked about Sammy's father.

"Maybe he's took somebody's job," CoCo said after we talked for a while between bits of "Chickory Chick." CoCo thought that maybe somebody was mad because Sammy's father got the job as night watchman and somebody else didn't and so they went and beat him up.

In a bannana-ka
Wallika wallika
Can't you see...?

said the guy being choked under the snow.

"He don't know dis song very good, eh Lamont?" commented CoCo.

"What about the Ritchie's Feed and Seed bag?" I said as CoCo tightened the scarf up a notch and the singer went quiet.

"Maybe somebody from da store," said CoCo, my favourite detective. "Somebody from da store who hates Jews."

Maybe he was right. It could have been somebody at the feed store. Would they be that dumb, though? Wearing a mask with the name written all over it? Maybe.

The five-minute bell rang at York Street School. I had to go. I said thanks and goodbye to CoCo.

"See you, Lamont," CoCo said, going back to his work on the singer. "'Ow's da lovely Margot Lane?"

"I'm going to buy her a Christmas present," I said.

"Bonne idée," called out CoCo, and I saw him start to pack his victim's mouth full of snow.

That afternoon we had science and our teacher, Mr. Maynard, was telling us again about the eclipse and how the earth stands between the sun and the moon and blocks out the light. And how you can see the shadow of the earth crossing the moon until the moon is completely dark.

Mr. Maynard, for homework, told us to watch it from nine o'clock to nine-thirty. The complete eclipse would be at exactly nine-twenty.

Killer Bodnoff said he could stay up all right but he couldn't watch the eclipse because "Gangbusters" was on the radio at nine.

Arnold Levinson said he'd try to watch it but he didn't know if he could last because he gets awful tired and anyway he's afraid of the dark.

Anita Pleet could watch it, yes, and as a matter of fact she had her own telescope and she'd do a project on it for Mr. Maynard if he'd like.

Martha Banting couldn't stay up because she was too nice.

Geranium Mayburger wanted to know where this whole thing was going to take place and would it be on her street too.

Fleurette Featherstone Fitchell asked all the boys in the seats around her if they wanted to come over and watch it in her back shed.

I said I could stay up and watch it.

Margot Lane said she would stay up and watch it from her bedroom window.

Then Mr. Maynard said a beautiful thing about the moon. He said this: "The lunar surface is fixed and unchanging while the Earth changes with each day, month and season. Let a single leaf fall from a tree on Earth and there will have been a greater change than may occur on the moon in a hundred autumns."

Mr. Maynard was the best teacher I ever had.

On my way home from school things were fairly quiet on the square and I only had one fight. I had some extra time so I cut up Heney Street and went into Sammy's place in the apartments beside the car barns.

I knocked on the door three or four times but nobody answered.

Then a lady came down the hall and told me that Sammy and his mother went to Toronto because Sammy's father had been taken there to a better hospital where he could have an operation on his head.

It was pretty serious.

After she went back down the hall I stood there for a while by myself and had a little conversation with Sammy's door.

"I lost one of my fights today because you weren't here, Sammy."

No answer, of course.

"Two Pea Soups jumped me from the rear on Angel Square. You weren't there in your usual lookout position."

The door didn't say a word.

"Who did this to your dad, Sammy? You don't know, do you? The only clues we have are that he was wearing that mask-bag with the seed store writing on it and that he hates Jews. That's all we know."

A silent, lonesome door.

"I'm going to get CoCo and Gerald to help me find out who did it."

I left Sammy's, passed by the car barns, and went home.

At my house I waved at my sister Pamela in her window. As soon as I got in the door she rushed to me and gave me a big squeeze. She always did that.

After Aunt Dottie inspected me I changed out of my good breeks and went down the cellar to shake the ashes. Our furnace burns wood and coal. You shake the furnace. Not the whole furnace (I used to think when Dad went down he'd put his big arms right around the red-hot furnace with all the octopus pipes crawling out over his head and he'd get really red in the face and he'd give the whole furnace a big shake, he was so strong) but just the grates of the furnace by attaching a crank handle to a steel rod and turning it (I used to pretend I was starting a car) and making the grate turn and the ashes fall into the bottom.

Then you shovel the ashes into the sifter and sift them because sometimes some coal that isn't burnt yet falls through and you have to pick those pieces off the screen and put them back in the furnace because coal is expensive.

The sifter is a kind of tub with rockers on the bottom and two handles and a screen and a lid. You grab it by the handles and shake it and rock it.

And the dust flies up into your face and chokes you.

Dad gave Aunt Dottie one for Christmas two years ago.

The furnace can be dangerous because if the coal is just starting to burn it makes poisonous gas, so you have to open up the drafts and make the gas go up the chimney instead of up the pipes and into your rooms where it will kill you.

Aunt Dottie often says "I smell gas" and runs down the cellar with her rubber apron on and opens up the drafts and lets all the expensive heat out over the low, small roofs of Lowertown.

"I don't smell gas," Dad said once when Aunt Dottie ran down the cellar. "She probably just let a little poop."

And I laughed for about twelve days every time I thought about what he said.

I laughed in school and everybody turned around and Blue Cheeks swung his eyes around onto me just like he was a searchlight at a prison looking for the escaping convict.

And people at recess would say I was crazy, laughing for nothing. And people on the streetcar when I would be going uptown would look over at me and shake their heads: imagine, a boy so young, and crazy already. "It must be the war," I heard one lady say to another.

"Maybe it's germs," I said under my breath and I started laughing all over again.

And here I was, shaking the ashes (I got ten cents each time for doing it) and thinking that Christmas was getting close but I didn't have any Christmas feeling yet. I was wondering when it was going to come. You couldn't make it come. It had to just happen.

But it better happen soon, I thought. Time was going on.

After supper at eight o'clock I listened to "Big Town" with Dad while Aunt Dottie put my sister on her rubber sheet with the talcum powder.

"Big Town," with Steve Wilson of the Illustrated Press and his secretary, the lovely Loreli Kilbourne.

At nine o'clock I got bundled up and went out into the beautiful clear and cold Lowertown winter night and looked up at the full moon.

The shadow of the earth was part way over it, taking a curved bite out of the side.

I could imagine standing there on the moon with this big smooth shadow coming over me. On the moon where nothing ever happens.

One leaf falls, Mr. Maynard said. A big event.

It was so peaceful I started to cry.

The shadow of my Earth moved slowly over the smooth moon.

If you looked right at it, you couldn't see it move but if you looked beside it, you could.

Soon it was completely covered. There was just a furry glow around the outside. Like the frost around my sister's face in her window.

I stood there on Cobourg Street for a while and watched some clouds blow over. I could sniff snow.

Then I could feel the Christmas feeling coming. It was coming over me. Coming up in me. Filling me up.

A feeling of bells and chocolate, hymns and carols, beautiful cold winter and warm rooms. Windows with snow and berries. And laughing and hugging.

In a little while it started to snow.

Big fat flakes.

Every one a big event, Mr. Maynard.

I turned around and went in the house and to bed, plotting about how to solve the mystery of Sammy's dad and letting Christmas come in and out.

2. CUL DE DEAD END

Sir John A. Macdonald was Canada's first prime minister. His birthday is on January 11. Last January when Margot Lane first came to our school (she wasn't in my class) I sent her a card. The card said: "Happy Sir John A. Macdonald's Birthday!" I signed it: "The Shadow."

I saw her every day in the schoolyard or on Angel Square but she never ran up to me and said thanks for the lovely card.

In February I sent her a card on Groundhog Day, Valentine's Day and Ash Wednesday.

That didn't do any good so in March she got a St. David's Day card, a St. Patrick's Day card and a First Day of Spring card from "Lamont

Cranston, The Shadow." Some of the cards I made myself and some I bought.

In April she got an Easter card and a St. George's Day card. In May a Mother's Day and a Victoria Day. In June Lamont sent her a Father's Day card and a First Day of Summer card.

From up at Low in July she got a Happy July card and in August a Congratulations on the Opening of the Ottawa Exhibition card.

When school started back in September (she was in my class now) I sent her a Yom Kippur card. In October a Thanksgiving card and a Halloween card. In November an All Saints' Day card and a St. Andrew's Day card.

Now it was December. It was almost a whole year since my first card and she still hadn't run up to me and said thanks for the lovely card. This month it was going to be a present. Not a card.

If that didn't work, I was going to give up.

CoCo Laframboise, my best Pea Soup friend, knew. Sammy, my best Jew friend, knew. Gerald, my best Dogan friend, knew. They also knew I couldn't just go up to her and tell her that I was Lamont Cranston, The Shadow, and that I was sending her all those cards. It would be too foolish. She would have to find out. She would have to want to find out on her own.

Gerald and Delbert Dilabio were standing outside my house when I came out the next morning to go to school. Delbert went to St. Brigit's of the Bleeding Thorns with my friend Gerald. I didn't like Delbert. And I had a good reason.

Delbert used to keep a frozen horseball or two in his hat in case of ambush. He surprised a lot of Jews and Pea Soups with those.

Gerald told me that when Father Francis came around to check Delbert's homework you could tell that Father didn't think that Delbert's head smelled very good. Lucky for Father, Gerald said, that he had very long arms. He could use his long arm to mark Delbert's homework all wrong while keeping his nose way up in the air near the ceiling.

But that wasn't why I didn't like Delbert.

Cobourg Street was pretty empty. Tons of snow floating down.

Just the odd streetcar going home to the barns.

I waved at my sister Pamela in her window.

"What does your sister think about?" Delbert said, as he packed a particularly big horse-snow-ball.

"I don't know what she thinks about," I said. "I know what she likes, though. She likes feeling Hello and she hates feeling Goodbye. When I come home she grabs me and hugs me so tight I can hardly breathe. She's pretty strong. Even if I just go to the store and come right back she hugs me like that. Just like I'd been gone for two years or something."

A streetcar came up Cobourg Street in a slow, quiet way. Around Christmas they were always like that. The snow made everything quiet. You'd just suddenly see one. Not like in the summer. In the summer you could hear them coming even before they turned onto Cobourg from St. Patrick.

We waved at the driver.

"This is what she thinks about. She thinks about Hello and Goodbye. The milkman and the breadman and the mailman get hugged pretty good too if they come in the door too far."

Cobourg Street was silent.

"What's wrong with her?" said Delbert.

"She's M.D.," Gerald said. Gerald knew nearly everything about my sister.

I didn't mind telling Delbert what he wanted to know. Even though he was so dirty. The more people who knew, the better.

And safer.

"What's M.D.?" Delbert asked.

"Mentally Deficient," I said. "She was born that way. Every time I go out the door she starts howling and crying a bit. Then she runs to her window and I wave at her and then she's all right."

"How old is she?" said Delbert.

"Two years older than me."

"Why doesn't she come out?"

"Can't," I said.

"Why?"

"Aunt Dottie can't let her out."

"Why?"

"Because she'd get lost," Gerald said.

"She used to be out in the summer," Delbert said. "I saw her."

"Yeah. Tied up so she wouldn't go away or get knocked down by a streetcar or something."

"Why can't she come out on her rope in the winter?"

"Has to have somebody guard her now."

"Why?"

"Because last summer some boys pulled her pants down. Didn't you know that?" I looked right into Delbert Dilabio's face.

"Who did?" said Gerald. He had mad in his voice.

"Arnie Sultzburger and some *guys*," I said, looking right at Delbert.

"What happened?"

"Aunt Dottie went out and slapped his face. Then Dad went over to Arnie's place and told Mr. Sultzburger that if Arnie ever came around here again he would kill him. That's the only time I ever saw Dad mad."

"Good," said Gerald. "That's good. I think I'll kill Arnie the next time I see him."

A Bourque's ice truck came down Cobourg Street in the quiet snow.

"She still wets the bed, you know. She wears napkins. She's like a little baby," I said. "I guess she's just like a little baby. Wave at her."

I knew Delbert had been with Arnie when that happened. And now Gerald knew too. I could tell by the look on his face.

Things would be a lot safer for my sister now. Gerald would help see to that.

Gerald said he'd walk part way over Angel Square with me since I didn't have Sammy. Three-quarters of the way over the square he would turn right and go to Bleeding Thorns and then I'd meet CoCo and he'd walk the rest of the way with me before he turned left to go to Brother Brébeuf. Then I didn't have far to go to York.

Gerald and I went down Papineau and onto the square. Because Gerald is a Dogan we'd only have to fight Jews and Pea Soups. If I was with Sammy I'd only have to fight Dogans and Pea Soups. If I was with CoCo I'd only have to fight Jews and Dogans. If I was with Sammy, CoCo and Gerald I wouldn't have to fight anybody.

And if I was alone...

Well, you know what would happen then.

I'd have to fight everybody.

Because I'm not anything.

While Gerald and I were strangling two Pea Soups with their own scarves, we were discussing the mystery of Sammy's father.

"Two clues," Gerald was saying as his Pea Soup's eyes started to bulge out pretty far, "two clues. He hates Jews and he has something to do with Ritchie's Feed and Seed."

"There are hundreds of people around here who hate Jews," I said as I released my Pea Soup's scarf a bit to give him a chance to breathe a couple of times because his face was getting a kind of purple colour.

"Well," said Gerald as his Pea Soup started to gurgle, "let's start with the feed and seed store."

"Right," I said. "We'll go today at lunch time. See what we can see."

"Get CoCo to come," said Gerald as he let his Pea Soup beg for mercy for a while before burying him in the snow.

"Good idea," I said.

After Gerald turned right to go to Bleeding Thorns, CoCo and I took on a small group of Dogans who didn't put up much of a fight. One of them had a yoyo with him and CoCo shoved it in his mouth to see if he could swallow it.

The two Jews we had to do were quite a bit tougher.

"Gerald thinks we should go to the seed store to check things out," I said to CoCo as my Jew tried to bite my ear off.

"Bonne idée," CoCo said as he tore the back out of his Jew's coat.

"Can you come with us at lunch time?" I said.

"Sure ting," CoCo said. "We can see if anybody dere 'ates Jews."

"We'll meet you on the corner of Friel and York," I said as my Jew ripped off my galosh and whipped me with it.

"See you dere," CoCo said.

The bell rang and our fight ended in a draw.

For some reason thinking about going to the feed store got my Christmas spirit back, so during Blue Cheeks's grammar class I figured out my shopping money.

The sentence we were supposed to be working on was this one: "I gave him a friendly slap as he left the room on his back."

I worked on my money instead.

Money Saved So Far

Shaking Ashes fifteen times—	1.50
Writing Lines for Killer Bodnoff,	
Fleurette Featherstone Fitchell and Geranium Mayburger	.21
Waxing Floors three times at Talmud Torah—	1.50
Singing Choir four Sundays at St. Albany's Church—	2.00
Altar Boying one funeral, one wedding at	
St. Brigit's Church—	1.00
Working two After-Schools at Woolworth's—	1.40
Four weeks' allowance—	1.00
Total So Far—	$8.61

"Well, Mr. Daydreams," I heard Blue cheeks saying, "do we know the answer today?"

"The words 'on his back' are in the wrong place," I said without looking up from my expense sheets.

"It should say, 'I gave him a friendly slap on the back as he left the room'."

Those wrong sentences were a lot easier if you didn't think about them.

I looked up and Blue Cheeks was staring at me with hatred in his face. He hated it when you got something right.

What a teacher.

That afternoon in Mr. Maynard's class we discussed the eclipse.

Killer Bodnoff said that last night on "Gangbusters" the moon was mentioned. Some crooks were stealing furs from a warehouse and the moon came out and the G-men shot all the crooks in the head.

Arnold Levinson said he was in bed with his eyes shut but he thought he *heard* the eclipse.

Anita Pleet had a huge project already finished, which she presented to Mr. Maynard with pictures pasted on it and printing and arrows explaining the whole thing. She said she read that a day on the moon was 708 hours long.

Martha Banting said, "Mr. Maynard, would you ever be *tired* after a long day like *that, wouldn't you*, Mr. Maynard!" She was so nice.

Geranium Mayburger said she couldn't find the eclipse.

Fleurette Featherstone Fitchell said she was discussing the eclipse in her back shed with some boys and by the time they let her out it was over.

I said that it reminded me of Christmas and then I felt kind of stupid for saying it.

Margot Lane said she watched it from her window and saw the whole thing. She said it made her think of all the other people around Lowertown who were probably watching it too. She said she was imagining what some of the other people in the class were thinking about when they were watching the same thing she was watching.

Or something like that.

Then she looked across the class at me.

At least I thought it was me.

Mr. Maynard had hung up some balsam and spruce and pine branches around the room.

It made the room smell like Christmas. The feeling was getting easy.

At lunch time I met CoCo and Gerald and we headed up York Street to the By Ward Market. Outside Devine's store there was a lot of activity. Sleighs piled with wreaths and branches and near them some stands with mistletoe and painted clumps of berries. And ladies selling cranberries. And Toe-Jam Laframboise loading up his delivery truck.

We went by R. Hector Aubrey's and there was a big crowd outside talking about the No Turkeys sign he had in the window.

We went into Ritchie's Feed and Seed store. Every bag in the store had those words printed on it. Everybody in the store was carrying one of those bags. Everybody leaving the store had one of those bags with those words.

"It's hopeless," Gerald said. "Everybody's got these bags."

"Maybe somebody who works at dis place 'ates Jews," CoCo said.

"Let's try to find out," I said and we moved deeper into the store, past the wire fencing and the fertilizer and the milk pails and the gardening tools.

Farther back in the store we could hear what sounded like an argument. I recognized Mr. Slipacoff, who owned the kosher butcher shop down the street, talking very loud to Mr. Ritchie in front of the seed counter.

CoCo and Gerald and I hid behind some sacks of feed and listened. After a while we could tell they weren't arguing. They were telling jokes and laughing. Then Mr. Slipacoff gave Mr. Ritchie a bag of fat meat and suet and they weighed it and had a pretend argument and then Mr. Ritchie weighed up a bag of broken seed bits and they traded the suet for the seeds.

And then they laughed and Mr. Ritchie pulled out a bottle from under the counter and they both had a drink and laughed and hugged each other and sang a little Pea Soup song about chickadees being a Canadian winter bird and Mr. Aubrey came in the back door in his bloody apron and Mr. Devine came in and they all had another drink or two and traded biscuits and suet and seeds and laughed and danced around.

"Here's to the chickadee! May he eat in the winter in peace, now that the war is over!" said Mr. Ritchie and they started telling jokes again.

They were trading food for their bird feeders.

"And it's your turn in the spring," said Mr. Devine, "to have the party!" He was talking to Mr. Slipacoff. "I'll bring the syrup. We'll have our hummingbird party!"

CoCo and Gerald and I were watching their bird party. Happy men. They didn't hate each other.

"What are you kids doing there?" Mr. Ritchie said, noticing us behind the bags.

"Nothing," I said, standing up, embarrassed. "We're doing a school project on birds."

The men all laughed and gave us some suet and broken biscuits and seeds for our birds and we went out of the store feeling very silly.

"Hopeless," Gerald said. "Nobody here hates anybody."

"A cul de dead end," said CoCo as we divided up the bird food and went back to Angel Square.

After school CoCo helped me across Angel Square and I ducked into Sammy's apartment to see if he was there yet. He wasn't, so I went home and changed my good breeks and took off to my job at Talmud Torah.

Talmud Torah is at 171 George Street back near the market. There are eleven wide wooden steps and solid wide wooden railings and two white pillars and two wooden panelled doors and a stone archway.

There are two windows, one on each side of the stairs. There are white kitchen curtains on the windows and a Star of David in each. The sign beside the doors says in English: Ottawa Talmud Torah. And underneath on the sign is some writing in Hebrew.

I felt the Hebrew writing with my fingers like I always did, trying to understand it.

The writing is like curly hairs, crooked wires, dots and half snowmen.

I felt the mystery with my fingers.

I tried to whisper the mystery but I couldn't.

Inside, I piled up the chairs of the schoolroom, swept the old hardwood floor, spread on the paste wax, polished the floor with the big mop with the cinder block on it for weight, and put the chairs back.

While I was doing that I looked at all the photographs around the walls of men with long beards and women in black dresses and groups of kids with their little caps and tried to read the curly hairs and crooked wires and dots and half snowmen written on the blackboard.

And I thought a lot about Sammy and his father.

It was a mystery.

That night at supper Aunt Dottie and Dad had a little argument about whether you call it supper or dinner.

Dad said they could compromise and call it "dipper" or maybe even "sunner" and Aunt Dottie said he was just being silly and that it was nothing to joke about.

Then Dad changed the subject and told us he couldn't get a turkey for Christmas because there was still a shortage of turkeys because of the war and Aunt Dottie said he should get two chickens instead.

"Yes," Dad said, "that sounds all right. We could have two nice chickens for Christmas dipper."

"Dinner," Aunt Dottie said.

"Sunner," Dad said.

"Why are there chickens but no turkeys?" I said.

"Because of the war," Aunt Dottie said.

"But why?" I said.

"Because they used them all in the war," Dad said.

"Don't listen to him," Aunt Dottie said.

"What did they use them for?" I said.

"They dropped them out of airplanes onto the Germans," Dad said.

"Lies," Aunt Dottie said.

"They also used them as camouflage."

"Why do you fill the boy's mind with lies?" Aunt Dottie said.

"They were also sent in as spies—espionage."

"Don't listen to him," Aunt Dottie said, and she covered up my ears.

At nine-thirty I listened to "The Shadow" with my head under the radio. Me and the cat.

The lovely Margot Lane was in a cave with a ghoul and Lamont Cranston turned into The Shadow and saved her.

The cat purred as The Shadow laughed and said "Crime does not pay!" and the organ got stabbed.

And I wondered if it was me she was looking at across the classroom when she said those things about the eclipse.

My Margot Lane. The real Margot Lane.

3. JUST A COMIC

The next morning, while I was standing on the heat getting ready to do Angel Square again without Sammy, the breadman opened the door and came in. He had Morrison-Lamothe on his cap and his basket was hooked over his arm. My sister Pamela nearly knocked him over giving him his hug. He smelled like horses and bread and cold winter air.

In his basket he had Christmas-wrapped cake and doughnuts and boxes with ribbons around them and jelly rolls with Santa stickers on them in crinkly transparent paper and gingersnaps that would be snappy even if it was a summer day. Gingersnaps in a row like huge brown pennies in long narrow boxes. And Aunt Dottie bought some gingersnaps and bread and Morrison-Lamothe smiled and gave her two small gingersnaps change (they were pennies this time) and (though it was pretty early) she gave him his little Christmas present all neatly wrapped and stuck. I knew it would take him hours to get it open once he got home.

Then my sister Pamela gave Morrison-Lamothe and me another big hug and I left for school.

On the way down Papineau, Gerald and I had a little talk with Chalmers Lonnigan, the Dogan who believed that God made the sidewalks and the streetcars and that Jews and Pea Soups went to hell when they died.

Gerald specially liked talking to Chalmers because of the crazy things he'd say.

"Aren't Pea Soups Dogans, Chalmers?" Gerald said.

"No they ain't. They're Pea Soups!" Chalmers said.

"Are Jews Pea Soups?" I said.

"No," said Chalmers, "they're Jews. They go to hell. And God made the streetcar tracks."

Gerald and I took turns talking to him, asking him things.

"What do Jews and Pea Soups do in hell when they get there?"

"They lie around with their tongues stuck to the streetcar tracks."

"Why?"

"Because they're Jews and Pea Soups."

"What happens to Dogans after they die?"

"Oh, they go to heaven."

"What do they do in heaven when they get there?"

"They eat pie and sing."

"What else?"

"Sometimes they get to go to the show. And you get a new cap gun whenever you want. And even a new bicycle maybe. And you don't have to take a bath unless you want to. And every week a man comes around and gives you ten dollars."

"Ten dollars! What for?"

"For candy, I guess."

"Is that heaven?"

"I guess so," said Chalmers, with a kind of sad look on his face. "I can't wait to go."

There was a long pause while we stood there listening to the snow fall down. Chalmers was thinking.

"Chalmers," I said. "What are you doing now?"

"Thinking," said Chalmers.

"What are you thinking about?"

"The atomic bomb," Chalmers said.

"The atomic bomb?" I said.

"What is the atomic bomb?" Chalmers asked, still looking down between his feet.

Gerald started telling Chalmers about the atomic bomb. He told him it was quite a small bomb but it could kill everybody in the world.

"The atomic bomb could kill everybody in the world!" I said.

"So?" said Chalmers.

"It's not like ordinary bombs that blow up buildings and factories and trains and hospitals and stuff," I said. "This is a little wee bomb about the size of a pea, I think, and it blows up everything and kills everybody!"

"So?" Chalmers said.

"And anybody who's left gets sick and swells up for about a month and bursts."

"So?"

"Think of it this way," Gerald said. "What if I told you that there was one of these bombs on its way down on us right now. What would you say?"

"I dunno."

"Okay Chalmers, there's one of those atomic bombs falling right down towards us right now, and when it hits here, everything is going to get blown up—everything—and everybody's going to be burnt to death and die!"

"Would it get all the Jews?"

"Remember last summer when they dropped one on the Japs and blew up Japan? Do you remember that, Chalmers?"

There was a long pause. The snow was piled up so high you couldn't see across the street. People would come down the sidewalk and go in their laneways and disappear, the snow was so high. The steel rungs up the wooden telephone poles were each stacked with snow. The wires were loaded with snow. The window sills were piled with snow. Every twig and branch of every tree was weighed down with snow. The sparrows and chickadees had to shovel little spaces for themselves so they could sit on the fences, there was so much snow. The cats were under the verandahs and steps, peeking out, crabby looks on their faces, wondering what to do about all the snow.

"I wish I was a Jap," said Chalmers.

"You're not very organized, Chalmers," I said. "You should try to get organized."

"If I was a Jap, I'd be dead now, because of the bomb, and I'd be in heaven. Heaven is nicer than Papineau, you know," said Chalmers.

Gerald and I looked at each other. Chalmers had never sounded like this before.

Then he said some more.

"My father says every time you see a Jew you should hit him and try to kill him!"

"Your father's crazy," I said.

After a few fights, Gerald and I met CoCo and we had a meeting.

CoCo said not to give up just because the feed store was a dead end. He said we should go to the car barns, the scene of the crime, and see what we could see.

After school I went right to my job at Woolworth's on Rideau Street.

Woolworth's. A Christmas madhouse. Perfume and candy and squeaky wooden floors. Records playing. The smell of perfume and chocolates mixed. Salesgirls with lipstick and earrings and long, curly hair. And pictures of Santa Claus everywhere. Long red and silver fuzzy streamers swinging and arching over the aisles. Wind-up trucks crackling away and the smell of hot dogs and fried eggs at the lunch counter. And toast. And the smell of damp fur and wet cloth and wet leather, the snow on people's clothes melting in Woolworth's. And people at the doors stamping their feet. The salesgirls and saleswomen laughing and talking to the people and to each other and the salesgirls' earrings sparkling and their long, curly hair bouncing and swinging over the perfume and around the chocolates and the toys and the toast and the pictures of Santa Claus.

Santa Clauses all over. Big ones hanging, laughing fat-faced, bulging eyes, big black boots, one foot up on a fake sleigh loaded with wrapped parcels of all sizes and shapes; smaller Santas standing on counters, holding radios or pointing at record players; Santas peeking out of mirrors, smiling and wishing everybody Merry Christmas; Santa being kissed by a beautiful movie star because of a dish of ice cream; Santa pasted on the walls eating chocolates; Santa, standing in the corner, peeking at people opening perfume; Santa modelling socks; Santa saying go to church; Santas sprayed on glass counters; Santas hanging and turning on threads; a record, somewhere, of Santa laughing and bells jingling; Salvation Army Santa, just outside the door, kicking his own boots, jangling his bells and hiding somewhere in clouds of his own breath, small icicles stiffening his white beard.

Red paper bells hanging from the lights making no sound at all.

And thousands of people carrying parcels and bags and dragging kids.

Dragging kids to go up and talk to the inside Santa on his throne.

It was Ozzie O'Driscoll again. Ozzie was a policeman who'd take his holidays around Christmas and get a part-time job playing Santa at Woolworth's. He used to pinch the kids and tickle them in the face with his beard and tell them a whole lot of stuff they never heard before about the North Pole. Like how Mrs. Claus used to hit him over the head with frying pans and pots if he didn't remember to bring every little kid in the world whatever he wanted. And he'd get them to feel the lumps on his head where she got him with a pan or a pot. And he'd tell them how sick he'd be after making his rounds and eating all that stuff everybody left out for him. Or how he could never remember the names of his reindeer and could they suggest some better names, names easier to remember. And some of the kids who weren't as shy as the others would suggest names like Uncle Jim or Captain Marvel for Santa's reindeer instead of Donner and Blitzen and those others. And often the kids would get so interested they'd forget to tell him what they wanted for Christmas and you'd see them going away afterwards with their parents trying to explain what happened.

Sometimes a parent would stop in the middle of the store and there'd be a little argument with the kid maybe, and maybe they'd both look back at Ozzie O'Driscoll, special Santa, at Woolworth's on Rideau.

My job at Woolworth's was bringing up stuff from the basement and putting it on the shelves. I'd come by Santa O'Driscoll each time, carrying the stuff. He'd always give me a big wink. You could almost believe in him, he was so good.

I wanted to go and ask him what to do about solving the crime. But I didn't. I felt silly about it. Maybe when I had at least a clue, then I could talk to him about it.

After supper Gerald and CoCo and I went up to the car barns to look around. The snow outside was black with grease from the streetcars. There are ten tracks leading into the blackness of the barns. Each entrance holds ten streetcars. When all the cars are in, sitting over the hundred grease pits, there are thousands of places to hide.

We slipped into Entrance Five between the cars, ran down the row and went carefully down the five slippery cement stairs into one of the pits and turned on the working light.

Looking up under the streetcar into the wheels and springs and steel, we could feel the weight above us. The grease and dust mixed under our feet into a soft mat. There were wrenches and bars lying around and heavy metal braces. Anything like this could be used for hitting a person over the head.

Suddenly we heard the new night watchman punch his time clock down the row and we switched out the light and stood flat against the wall of the pit, our heads almost touching the wheels of the streetcar above us. We heard him coming down the row, whistling softly to himself a little Christmas carol and soon his light flashed in our pit and out and over to the next one. Then he stopped whistling. He was listening.

We stopped breathing.

Then we heard some giggling and someone saying, "Sh!"

"Hey, what are you doin' in there?" the night watchman called, and we heard some scurrying of feet.

Then somebody ran by us.

"Let's go!" said Gerald and we ran quietly up the matted steps and down the row towards the entrance. We ducked behind the last car near the entrance to see what was happening.

The night watchman and another man with little eyes and a big mouth had turned on some lights and were looking under the cars.

"I think she's over there," said the man with the big mouth.

Then to our left, on the other side of the row, we saw a girl dart out and run into Cobourg Street. I recognized her.

It was Fleurette Featherstone Fitchell!

She slipped on the greasy snow and fell down and we caught up to her. She was puffing and laughing and crying at the same time.

"Fleurette, what are you doing here?" I asked her once we were safe down the street.

"Nothing. Just playing," Fleurette said, a really bold look in her eyes.

"Was there somebody else?" I said, thinking about the other running feet we had heard.

"Maybe," Fleurette said, her chin stuck out.

"Who was it?" Gerald said.

"You won't tell?" Fleurette said.

"No, we won't tell," I said. "Who was it?"

"It was Lester Lister," she said. "Lester Lister. We were looking for something. Something he lost when we were here before once. He's my boyfriend."

She was very proud when she said that last thing. I knew Lester. He was in St. Albany's choir with me. He didn't come from around Angel Square. He came from Rockcliffe. He went to Ashdown School.

He was rich.

"What do you do here in dis awful place wid Lester Lister?" CoCo said, nudging me.

"Oh, things. Talk. Things."

She was looking up into the falling Christmas snow. Then she said this:

"He lost his wallet. I was so scared. It was the night Sammy's father got beat up."

We were so surprised when she said this that we all started talking at once.

Suddenly she started to cry.

"I didn't see anything. I don't know anything." She was trying to rub the greasy snow off her legs where she fell down.

"You know someting," CoCo said. "What is it dat you know?"

"I don't know ANYTHING!" Fleurette screamed and ran down Cobourg Street into the night.

"It's none of your business!" she yelled out of the dark.

CoCo had to go home, so Gerald and I had to go over to Lester Lister's ourselves. If Fleurette wouldn't tell us anything, maybe Lester would.

I have to stop here a minute and tell you about Lester Lister and how I first met my best Dogan friend, Gerald Hickey.

Gerald moved in right near me on Cobourg Street last Christmas Day. That's when I met him.

Aunt Dottie had figured it would be a nice thing if I gave a guy named Lester Lister a present that Christmas Day because he was in the choir at St. Albany's and it was supposed to be nice to hang around with him because he was from Rockcliffe. I had to get on my good breeks and shine my rubber boots with floor wax and she helped me scrub my face until most of the skin was just about rubbed off.

Lester Lister was supposed to be a friend of mine.

Aunt Dottie said so.

We went over my own presents to see what one we thought we should give to Lester Lister. It would have to be a good one because of where Lester lived. They had a big verandah and a cellar you didn't have to duck your head in. And they had a car and they had a phone and their radio could be turned right up so you could hear it.

And they had rugs on their floors.

Aunt Dottie decided I should give Lester Lister my best present but I knew I couldn't do that because my best present was the tank with the rubber tracks that would crawl over anything once you wound it up (even a pillow on the floor) and that tank was now crushed flat as a penny run over by a streetcar because my Uncle Paddy had stepped on it by mistake with one of his big army boots.

I guess it was all right that Uncle Paddy had done that to my tank because he didn't do it on purpose and besides, he was the one who bought it for me in the first place.

Aunt Dottie helped me wrap the present for Lester Lister.

We had chosen the flying propeller that you twirled down a long spiral rod to the bottom, then with a little gadget you pushed it up the rod, hard, and sent it spinning into the air. I hadn't given it a good workout because of the deep snow. Maybe next summer when Lester Lister got sick of it he'd give it back to me.

Aunt Dottie got out the ironing board and ironed some wrapping paper flat and then she got out a ruler and a razor blade and cut the paper into a perfect square. Then she made some paste out of flour and water and pasted up a perfect package. She cut out a piece of cardboard from a box into the shape of a bell and coloured it with crayons.

Then she printed on the bell, "A special gift for my best friend, Lester. Merry Christmas."

"He's *not* my best friend," I said.

"Well, he's your *cleanest* friend," Aunt Dottie said, ignoring me.

"Why don't you put *that* then? 'To my cleanest friend, Lester'?"

"Don't be bold. It's Christmas," Aunt Dottie said. Then she put the package in a clean brown paper bag and folded the top of the bag over a few times so that it made a solid handle. Then she cut a hole in the handle for my four fingers to fit through.

I felt like Little Red Riding Hood or somebody being sent off to Granny's.

My Uncle Paddy and Dad were snoring in all the rooms. My sister Pamela was at her window.

I went out into the Christmas Day snow and from the sidewalk I gave Pamela a wave. The frost on the window was thick and made a beautiful pattern like fern leaves. In the middle of the fern leaves in the space where she had breathed away the frost, was Pamela's face.

It was like a holy painting.

I walked up Cobourg Street to the corner of Papineau. I was trying to figure out what I would say when Mr. Lister or Mrs. Lister opened the door. I knew Lester Lister wouldn't open the door. He didn't seem the type. I guess he wasn't allowed. It was always one of his parents. Mostly Mr. Lister. I often wondered if sometime it would be Mr. Lister's sister who answered the door. But I didn't even know whether Mr. Lister had a sister. It would have made things interesting, though.

"Tommy, I'd like to have you meet Mr. Lister's sister Esther." And maybe if another long-lost aunt or somebody came in and they were all happy to see each other and kissing and stuff, somebody might say "Mr. Lister's sister kissed her, she sure has missed her!"

I was trying to figure out how to put in blister and pissed her pants when suddenly out jumped Gerald Hickey from behind a huge snowbank. I was right in front of Gerald Hickey's house. It was the worst house on the whole street. It was even worse than ours.

"Where'ya going?" Gerald said and he spit in the snow.

"What's it to you?" I said.

"Never mind then," said Gerald, who was very proud.

"To Lester Lister's in Rockcliffe," I said, just to see what he'd say.

"What for?" He spit and got some on my waxed rubber boot.

"I have to give him this Christmas present."

Gerald Hickey hocked one clean over the snowbank. He was the best spitter around. The day was quiet with the few Christmas flakes coming down and no streetcars and only one dog way up around Heney Park probably barking.

Gerald Hickey and I were looking down Papineau Street towards Angel Square. I was wondering if we were going to have to fight. That was what you were supposed to do with new people who just moved in. Then, off the square and on up Papineau Street from the square, we saw two figures coming.

I knew they were Bodnoffs. Two tough Bodnoff brothers.

We waited and faced them as they got bigger and bigger coming up the empty silent Christmas street.

I hit the first Bodnoff across the side of the head with Lester Lister's present and knocked him down. Just when he hit the snowbank I scooped up a mittfull of snow and ground it into his face. I throttled him with his scarf for a while until I could see his eyes cross. I asked him politely if he wanted more and when he didn't I went to help Gerald with the other Bodnoff. We each took a leg and played wishbone with him until he asked us to stop. After a while we stopped and the two Bodnoffs went back down Papineau towards the square and got smaller and smaller. One of them was walking funny.

Gerald spit into the snowbanks and we went across the street to Provost's store and got one cent's worth of blackballs.

We opened the present the rest of the way and gave the propeller a few good spins.

Then Gerald sent it up so high over the low small roofs of Lowertown that it got lost against the grey Christmas clouds and if it came down at all we didn't see it and we didn't hear it.

Then Gerald Hickey and I went to Gerald Hickey's house and practised wrestling in Gerald Hickey's coalbin for about an hour.

Then I went home to try and explain to Aunt Dottie.

That was almost a year before.

Now we were going to Rockcliffe for real. A real reason.

To solve a crime.

It was snowing tons of snow. Snow floating down in beautiful tons.

We walked over the St. Patrick Street Bridge and up Springfield Road on to Acacia Drive and into Rockcliffe Village where everybody was rich.

All the streets in Rockcliffe are called Avenue and Way and Terrace and View and Place and Drive and Vista and names like that.

In Lowertown all the streets are called Street. Cobourg Street. Friel Street. Augusta Street. York Street. If a street was really in bad shape (houses all falling over and broken sheds and fences full of holes and broken windows and raggedy kids and older brothers back from the war always drunk) it wouldn't even be called a street. Like Papineau, for instance. Not Papineau Street, just Papineau. You ask Chalmers Lonnigan, "Where do you live, Chalmers?"

"I live on Papineau."

"Is that a street or an avenue?"

"I dunno."

Gerald and I had been together in Rockcliffe before.

We specially liked to go over right after supper when it was dark. We'd have our supper about five-thirty or six but the people in Rockcliffe had their supper about half past seven or eight. Rich people eat later for some reason.

Maybe it was because they weren't very hungry.

Lester Lister told me it wasn't called supper anyway. It was called dinner.

In Lowertown we ate our dinner at noon.

In Rockcliffe they'd have their dinner at suppertime and their lunch at dinner time.

Pretty confusing.

We'd gone over a couple of times when there wasn't much to do and looked in people's windows. We weren't looking in windows in Rockcliffe to see people taking their clothes off or anything like that. We'd look to see what they were having for supper (dinner) and try to guess what they were saying to each other by reading their lips.

It was hard to figure out what they were saying. Whatever it was, it didn't look very interesting. They weren't talking about germs, that's for sure, or turkeys.

Sometimes they wouldn't say anything for a long time. They'd just look at their fireplaces or their plates and not move their lips at all.

They were probably thinking about important matters concerning the world or Germans or something.

Or maybe they were all just thinking about money.

We arrived at Lester's fancy house and went up on the big verandah and rang the bell.

Gerald spit over the railing just as Mrs. Lister opened the door.

"Could I speak to Lester for a moment, please?" I said.

Mrs. Lister looked at Gerald and me like we were some kind of Martians or something.

"I'm afraid he's having dinner at the moment," she said. (It was about nine o'clock at night so of course they were having dinner.)

"It's about school," I said. "It's really very important."

"Just a moment then," she said, and left us standing out there in the cold.

Pretty soon Lester came out, slipping on a fur hat so he wouldn't get his brain exposed to the winter. As soon as he closed the door and stepped out on the verandah, Gerald crowded him up against the wall.

"Tonight you were in the car barns doing naughty things with Miss Fleurette Featherstone Fitchell and looking for your wallet which you lost the night somebody beat up Sammy Rosenberg's father. You and Miss Fitchell saw something that night that she won't tell us about but that you *will* tell us about because if you don't, we're going to spoil your dinner by telling Mummy and Daddy that you are studying hamburger buns and cigars with Miss Fitchell some nights instead of being where you're supposed to be, wherever that is."

It was so easy. For Gerald.

Yes, they were there, Lester said, in a whiny voice, they were there, but he's never going there again, honest, and that night they heard the yelling and they saw the man in the hood and they saw him hit Mr. Rosenberg and they saw him run away after Mr. Rosenberg fell down and they saw something fall out of the man's pocket and they were so scared but Fleurette picked it up and they ran out and when they reached the entrance a man stopped them and said that they'd better not say anything to anyone about this or they'd be awful sorry and then they ran home.

"What did she pick up, Lester? What was it?" I said.

"It was just a comic," said Lester. "Just a stupid comic book. It fell out of the man's pocket." Lester was fiddling with his fur hat.

"Okay, Lester," Gerald said, "go in and finish your dinner." Lester went in and shut the door quietly.

We stood on the St. Patrick Street Bridge for a while watching the ice and talking and then we went home.

A comic book.

Just a comic book.

But it was something.

It was a clue.

By Friday there was so much snow that every plough was out and the teams of men and the big sleighs were out all day and all night.

Each box sleigh is pulled by a team of horses and each sleigh has one driver and ten shovellers. The horses stand in a cloud of their own steam and their whiskers are frozen white and their manes hang down with gobs of ice. The ten shovellers shovel the snowbank into the sleigh and shout and swear and laugh and sing and play jokes on each other.

And that day the bells on all the harnesses were tinkling and jingling in Lowertown on the last day of school before Christmas, the first Christmas after the war.

Angel Square was raging; everybody was trying to get a good day of fighting in before the holiday.

All over the square the Jews and the Dogans and the Pea Soups were running headfirst into each other like mountain goats.

At school Blue Cheeks was in a very Christmassy mood and only gave out lines to Killer Bodnoff and Fleurette Featherstone Fitchell for passing pictures of hamburger buns and cigars back and forth.

I wrote a note to Fleurette and passed it to her when Blue Cheeks wasn't looking.

FFF.

Lester said you have the comic book the man dropped in the car barns that night.

I want it.

If you don't give it to me I'll tell Mrs. Lister about you and Lester and you'll never see him again.

Signed

Tommy

I watched her face as she read it. She was moving her lips.

When she was finished she looked over at me and nodded.

Her note to me said this:

Meet me after school gets out.
Signed
Fitchy

We were getting out at noon and so our last class was with Mr. Maynard. We sat around chatting and making cards. I made a card for him with a picture of a moon eclipse on it and some little noiseless bells.

I wrote this on it:

Merry Christmas, Mr. Maynard. I loved what you she said about the leaf on the moon.
Tommy

Then the bell rang and everybody ran out on Angel Square and tried to get home. The school was suddenly quiet.

I slipped into Blue Cheeks's room and wrote a Christmas message on his empty blackboard. It was a sentence he could have a lot of Christmas fun correcting over the holidays.

It said this:

The boy wrote Merry Christmas to his teacher and then quietly left the room on the blackboard.
Signed
The Shadow

It was his favourite kind of sentence. A wrong one.

I met "Fitchy" in the schoolyard and walked with her to her house on Friel Street.

"I don't like Lester Lister anymore, anyway," she said. "He ran away and left me. He's a coward."

I waited outside her back door while she went in to get the comic. There were a whole lot of cats under her back shed looking out at me standing there in the falling snow.

She came back out with the comic but she didn't give it to me right away.

"Do you want to come in the back shed with me?"

"I can't," I lied. "I've got to go to work."

"He was going to give me a watch for Christmas," she said.

"It's better this way," I said and I touched the hand that was holding the comic.

"I guess so," she said. "Lester Lister is a coward." She let go of the comic.

"You're not a coward, though," she said.

"Thank you," I said.

"It's okay if you call me Fitchy."

"Thank you, Fitchy."

On the way home I studied the comic book. It was a war comic with different pictures of Japs and Germans being stabbed and blown up.

Up on the corner somebody had written an initial.

The letter L.

The man who hit Sammy's father had written that letter there maybe.

L.

At home, while my sister Pamela was crushing me at the door, I could smell cake and fruit. Usually I didn't smell anything at our house. Funny how other people's houses smell like something but your own never does. Maybe it's because you're so used to your own house.

Gerald Hickey's house always smelled like onions and starch.

Sammy's house always smelled like incense and pickles and fish.

CoCo Laframboise's house smelled like beans and pie.

Lester Lister's house smelled like shellac.

Dad was home early too and he and Aunt Dottie were talking about turkeys and chickens again and this time Dad was saying he was having trouble getting *chickens* even and how Devine's and the other stores in the market were all out of them.

They were saying that it looked like we were going to have to have Mock Duck again.

Mock Duck is a big slab of meat piled up with dressing and then rolled up like a jelly roll and tied up with lots of thick string.

One Christmas my Uncle Paddy ate a piece of string from the Mock Duck about as long as his arm and Dad and I went out in the kitchen with him to help him pull it all out. It reminded me of a movie I once saw where Laurel and Hardy ate some wool socks and had to pull the long threads out of their mouths at a fancy dinner.

Aunt Dottie said Uncle Paddy ruined our whole dinner. I guess she was right. It wasn't very Christmassy watching a guy eat string for about fifteen minutes.

But I like my Uncle Paddy. He's a nice man. He's pretty cuddly. And big. Even bigger than Dad. He's in the Air Force Police. He is a very loud sneezer. Once he sneezed so loud that the cat ran headfirst into a wall.

Uncle Paddy has huge arms and wrists. One of his wrists is thicker than Gerald Hickey's neck. So is the other one.

Dad was putting on his coat and his scarf and was saying he had to go up to the Union Station to meet the soldiers coming in. One of his friends would be there. He was a Cameron Highlander.

His name was Frank. Back from the war.

I said I'd go with him because I had to go uptown to some stores to hunt for some Christmas presents.

We got off the streetcar and walked across Rideau Street into the Union Station. The *U* in the word *Union* was shaped like a *V*.

We went over to talk to a Red Cap in a red cap, a cousin of Dad's from up the Gatineau who stuttered. They talked and laughed for a few minutes and we talked about money then the Red Cap reached in his pouch where all his tips were and filled my hand with nickles.

"Merry Chri-Chri-Chri-Chri…" he said. "Come back to-to-to-tomorrow and I'll give you some more."

There were mobs of people all bundled up and stamping snow and we started down the long wide stairs to where all the thousands of soldiers were with their knapsacks and gear. Everybody was kissing and hugging and running and squealing and crying. Over the loud-speakers, Bing Crosby was singing "I'm Dreaming of a White Christmas." There was a huge Christmas tree twinkling in the middle of the floor and decorations and streamers crawled up the walls.

You had to lean way back to see the ceiling.

Steam floated in through the iron gates where the trains were.

We waited and watched for about a half an hour but there was no sign of Dad's friend Frank. Dad met one soldier he knew who said yes, Frank was on the train but he didn't know where he was now.

Dad said he'd go down to the market and look for him around there, so I said goodbye and went hunting for presents.

I went to Charles Ogilvy's, Murphy Gamble's, Bryson Graham's, Reitman's, Caplan's, Lindsay's, Orme's, Shaffer's, Stein's, Larocque's and Freiman's.

It was in Freiman's I saw it.

It was on the glass counter with a sign beside it. The sign said "For that girl of girls." Then there was a picture of Rita Hayworth.

Richard Hudnut's Three Flower Gift Set

Picture her rapture on finding this set
beneath the tree Christmas morn.
Soft green embossed gift box contains
Hudnut's lovely

FACE POWDER, ROUGE, LIPSTICK,
TOILET WATER, PERFUME, TALCUM,
VANISHING CREAM, BRILLIANTINE,
COLOGNE AND CLEANSING CREAM.

$7.50

I put two dollars down and asked the lady if she could hold the Richard Hudnut Three Flower Gift Set until Monday, the day before Christmas. Then I would bring in the rest of the money.

She said that I could.

She had a face like she was a sort of Virgin Mary. A little bit of a little smile, eyes looking up and to the right, head a bit on one side, and a halo sitting just over her head with nothing holding it up.

But it wasn't really a halo, it was some silver spray on a mirror right behind her.

In Freiman's I also found a duck for my sister Pamela. I always got her a little yellow duck made of rubber. You squeezed the duck and it went quack for you.

She really enjoyed the duck even though she got the same thing the year before. It was always like a new present because she didn't have very much of a memory. Every day she'd have to find out about squeezing the duck and making it do a quack. And she'd always laugh just like it never happened before. Every day she had a chance to be happy. Then the duck would be worn out by summer and Aunt Dottie would throw it away and she'd forget all about it.

Then the next Christmas, the duck, all over again, and happy, all over again.

She was lucky in a way, not knowing anything. She didn't have to know about Sammy's dad or a man named L or anything about the war or the fights on Angel Square or the Ritchie's Feed and Seed bags or Delbert Dilabio or Arnie Sultzburger.

Maybe she was lucky.

Or maybe not.

She also didn't know about Gerald or Sammy or CoCo or the lovely Margot Lane or Lamont Cranston or The Shadow or Mr. Maynard.

Maybe she wasn't lucky.

I don't know.

Then, in Freiman's, I saw Dad's present.

It was a Flat Fifty.

A Flat Fifty is a tin box (flat) with fifty cigarettes inside. You buy them for special occasions or if you have fancy tables in your house you can put one of these fancy flat tins out so that your guests can help themselves, don't mind if I do.

I buy Dad a Flat Fifty every Christmas. I always mean to change and get him something different but for some reason, just at the last minute, I wind up getting him another Flat Fifty. It's almost like being hypnotized. I'd be determined not to get him a Flat Fifty again but then I'd be in a store, Christmas shopping, and I'd see all the Flat Fifties stacked up with Christmas bows on them and I'd go over, pulled over there by some big magnet, and my mouth would open and I'd hear it say, "Flat Fifty, please."

I couldn't seem to help it.

And Christmas morning Dad would pick up his present from me and he'd weigh it in his hands and he'd feel the shape of it and he'd say, "I hope it's a Flat Fifty!" and then he'd rip the paper off.

"It is! It is a Flat Fifty! Just what I wanted. Thank you very much!" he would always say. And then when Aunt Dottie was opening hers from me (I always got her chocolates, I couldn't help it) Dad would say, "I wonder if it's chocolates." And then when Aunt Dottie would finally get it open (it took her about an hour to unwrap because she wouldn't tear the paper) Dad would yell, "It is! It is chocolates! Let's have a couple!"

"No, you're not having any, I'm saving these for *myself* for a change this year," Aunt Dottie would say and put them on the floor beside her.

(Uncle Paddy was there one Christmas Day and stepped in Aunt Dottie's chocolates by mistake—squashed every one of them.)

Then, after we helped Pamela open her duck and got her to squeeze it and make it quack a few times, Aunt Dottie would send me down the cellar to the cold storage to bring up some shortbread with the half cherry on each one and the Christmas cake wrapped in wax paper and we'd have a little snack.

So I went over to the counter with the Flat Fifties all stacked up with the Christmas bows on them and my mouth opened and I heard it say, "Flat Fifty, please!"

That was enough shopping.

I walked home through the gently falling snow. The lights from the people's windows along York Street were yellow and warm. Some cats picked their way into the laneways.

I passed the school and crossed Angel Square all alone. It was a beautiful square in the late winter afternoon.

All alone on Angel Square.

I came up Papineau and turned the corner onto Cobourg Street.

Dad and some soldiers were out in front of our house taking pictures of each other. One soldier, who seemed to be quite clumsy and off balance all the time, was trying to take a picture of Dad and the other two soldiers. Dad was in the middle. He had one arm around each soldier.

The soldier taking the picture was looking down into the camera, shading it with one hand and backing up, trying to get everybody in the picture. He had the camera down about at his waist and he had one eye closed while he backed up the side of the snowbank.

Quite a few people saw him when he fell backwards over the bank and did a complete backroll and got his head stuck in the deep snow. The camera flew out onto the streetcar tracks.

A streetcar with a driver and two inspectors was going slowly by, heading for the car barn; a lot of kids, making their snow forts, stopped and watched; three people pushing a car onto Desjardins Street saw; Chalmers Lonnigan peeking around Papineau saw; some Dogans looking out over their half-built snow fort up from St. Patrick Street saw; Aunt Dottie upstairs in her poem room, probably looking out, saw; Pamela, for sure, looking out her window through her frost frame saw.

It was Dad's friend Frank home from the war.

The streetcar quietly crushed the camera.

I took the comic over to Gerald's house and we studied it. We took it over to CoCo's house and we studied it.

L.

That night I went to my choir practice at St. Albany's Anglican Church.

I went up the hill on King Edward to the corner of Daly and followed in the deep footprints around the side of the church where some of the others in the choir had stepped. I went through the little green door and down the wooden stairs to the practice room.

It's a room like the room at Talmud Torah where I do the floors. There are even pictures on the walls caps; they have on black cassocks and white surplices.

Lester Lister was standing beside me, singing. In the middle of the hymn we had a conversation. It was easy. You sang what you wanted to say instead of the words in the Hymn Book.

Instead of:

> *Holy, Holy, Holy,*
> *Merciful and Mighty*
> *God in three persons*
> *Blessed Trinity*

I sang:

> *Got the comic from her*
> *Says she doesn't like you*

Says you are a coward
'cause you ran away.

When the hymn got to the second finish, instead of the real words, Lester sang:

I don't like her either
She's just a dirty slut
Now I can forget about
The watch I said I'd buy.

Lester Lister. What a slimy person.

I knew Gerald would meet me after practice because he always did on Fridays.

I walked slowly up Rideau Street waiting for him to surprise me like he always did. It was a game we played. If he got me, I would buy the drinks; if I saw him first, he would buy.

He was nowhere in sight.

Then I felt the gun in my back. I was about halfway home coming up Rideau Street on the north side right near Imbro's Restaurant.

Usually I would turn into Imbro's (and Gerald and I would have a cream soda), his gun still on me the whole time.

"Turn in here, copper," Gerald would say, "and don't look around or I'll drill ya!"

Inside the restaurant I'd have my hands up, not high but halfway up and wrists a little loose. Gerald would push me over into a booth for two near the door.

"Two cream sodas, doll, and be quick about it!" Gerald would say to the waitress. She would smile and be right back with the two bottles. I would pay the fourteen cents.

"Okay, sucker," Gerald would say, "drink up and let's scram, pigeon!"

Then, if the waitress came by again, Gerald might say: "You know, honey, you're much prettier when you're angry!"

The girl would just laugh because she was used to this. She'd heard it all before. It was the same every Friday night. Every time I got paid at choir.

"Stop that eternal pacing up and down!" Gerald might say to Louis, the owner, if he was around.

"A man like you could have an accident on the street, for instance. Hit and run driver maybe. You never know." They were things that people said in movies. Gerald would have his hat pulled down over his eyes and a fake cigarette hanging out of the corner of his mouth.

Louis would just laugh. He'd heard it all before. On Friday nights. My pay night at choir.

Outside, the Friday night was dressed up for Christmas on Rideau Street. The hydro poles were wrapped in boughs and the streetcars had a wreath in each front window. The shops had Coca Cola Santas hung up in the windows and some had small Christmas trees with flashing lights. Imbro's had some bells on the door and if you went out into the middle of Rideau Street and looked downtown, you could see a big tree on top of Freiman's and maybe a lot of other blue and red colours down there.

Gerald and I did part of our game with the waitress and Louis and then we discussed the comic.

Gerald said he thought that the L could stand for Lonnigan. Chalmers Lonnigan's father. He hated Jews. It might be him. It was worth a try. Gerald said he thought he worked at the museum.

I said goodbye to Gerald and went home.

Dad and I listened to part of the Friday night fights on the radio.

It was Tony Janero and Humberto Zavala. We didn't find out who won because the tubes got weak in the middle of round seven.

Finally all we could hear was the cat purring and now and then a streetcar going home to the barns, the rumbling muffled by the snow, shaking the house a little bit.

Aunt Dottie had hung some balsam boughs on the wall going upstairs. They smelled deep and fresh.

I went to sleep with Christmas in my nose and Margot Lane in my head.

Tomorrow Gerald and CoCo and I would have a talk with Chalmers Lonnigan and see if we could find out anything.

5. SOMETHING ICE COLD

Saturday morning I was sitting with my sister Pamela at her window trying to show her how to make shapes on the glass in the frost with her hands.

I made a moon shape and a sun and some stars but they weren't very good and she didn't understand. She wouldn't have understood anyway, even if I had made them better. She was having fun though, mostly because of how the frost made her fingers cold.

I made a shape of a duck on another part of the window just to see if she'd remember. She looked at it for a long time and pointed at it once and looked at me but then she forgot about it and started to hug me a little bit.

I think she was trying to remember but she couldn't.

Through the duck I could see Chalmers Lonnigan standing out there. He was standing on the snowbank, way up, his face up to the sky, his tongue out, catching snowflakes.

Since I didn't have enough money yet to finish my Christmas shopping and I had nothing to do until Gerald came over, I went out to have a little talk with him.

"Thinking about heaven, Chalmers?" I said.

"Do you want to go and hurt some Jews?" Chalmers said.

"No, I don't. No, I don't want to go and hurt some Jews, Chalmers," I said.

"Why not?" Chalmers said.

"Because," I said. "Why don't you go uptown or something or go to the show or read some comics or something?"

"I don't want to," Chalmers said.

"Well, I don't want to either," I said.

"Why don't you want to?" Chalmers said.

"Because my best friend Sammy is a Jew and he lends me his cap gun whenever I want and I lend him my cap gun every time he wants and I even sort of like his cousin Shirley from Toronto. I tried to kiss her once."

The last part was a lie but you had to tell Chalmers *something* to try and make him understand.

"Okay," Chalmers said, "let's go and get some Pea Soups then. There's some behind Brébeuf playing tunnel right now, I think."

"I don't feel like it," I said. Then I changed the subject.

I said: "How's your father?"

"Let's get some Protestants then," he said. Chalmers was really looking hard for something to do. I tried again.

"They're not easy to find," I said. "I don't even think there *are* any Protestants around here anymore." Poor Chalmers. How was he going to get to heaven this way? "Is it true your father works at the museum?"

He left a big silence. Then he started talking again.

"There used to be lots of them all over the place. My father told me that they used to kill them with streetcars." He had a sound in his voice like somebody was talking about their favourite cat that got lost or their brother who was kidnapped or something.

"There was only one or two," I said, "and I think they moved away."

"Where did they move to?"

"Uptown somewhere."

"There's lots of Dogans. Let's go get a few Dogans."

"Chalmers! *You're* a Dogan. And anyway, it's Christmas! You're supposed to be nice to people on Christmas!"

"Why?"

"Because Jesus said."

"No he didn't."

"Jesus was a Jew, you know," I said right to his eyes.

A look came on Chalmer's face like a streetcar had just run over his foot.

Just then Gerald Hickey popped up from behind the snowbank. I guess he had heard everything we said because he winked at me and started talking like on "The Green Hornet," a radio program we listened to.

Just to tease Chalmers.

"Word is out they found a Protestant down on Augusta Street. A bunch of Dogans is going over to interrogate him. Bodnoff and the Bodnoffs are getting a gang of their Jews together to invent some tortures for him and the Pea Soups are over there right now breaking down his snow fort. Want to go and watch?"

Chalmers was already running. He couldn't wait.

We met CoCo on the corner and went over to where the Protestant was supposed to be on Augusta Street but there was nobody there.

"Maybe it's a trap," Gerald said.

"Let's wait in the laneway for a while and see who shows up," Chalmers said.

Somebody had shovelled a path through the deep snow in the laneway and we started down the path but then we stopped. There was a big gang of Pea Soups in there arguing and fighting. They had one Pea Soup headfirst in a snow hole and they were shoving him farther down. We turned back.

We went two laneways down. There, the Bodnoffs and their Jews were plotting. They were discussing a snowman they had surrounded. It had a whole lot of sticks stuck in it and a sign around its neck. The sign said, Dogan or Pea Soup.

Behind the next garage a whole lot of Dogans were fighting each other, ripping each others' clothes.

There wasn't much to do on the Christmas holidays.

"I guess they're practising for when school goes back," Gerald said.

"Where's the Protestant?" said Chalmers, almost crying.

Then he turned around to go home.

Before he left he made a little speech.

"I'm going home. There's nothing to do. I wish I was dead and in heaven," he said. Then he left.

"Let's cut across Angel Square and go uptown," CoCo said. "What did he tell you? Anyting?"

"Nothing," I said.

We walked across Angel Square. It was very peaceful and white. There were no people fighting on the square because school was out. There weren't even any footprints in the perfect snow.

We walked up York Street right into the market and past Devine's and Ritchie's Feed and Seed and R. Hector Aubrey's meat store.

I saw Blue Cheeks coming out of Aubrey's with a bag of meat. He saw me but I got my eyes away just in time. I didn't want to spoil Christmas.

I saw CoCo Laframboise's uncle, Toe-Jam Laframboise, getting into his delivery truck. His boots were covered with snow and he was knocking them on the side of his truck. I knew that underneath his boots his socks were stuck to his feet forever.

We went up to the Chateau Laurier and slipped in the front door past the doorman and ran up the curving ruggy stairs with the gold polished railings all the way to the top floor.

We played Abbot and Costello on each floor with the fancy furniture on the landings. We pretended we were eating the furniture and that we were in a hypnotic trance that made us think we were termites. It was from a movie we saw once.

We slid all the way down the railings past the lobby and down into the floor where the swimming pool was and the entrance to the tunnel. The doors of the tunnel were hard to open because of the suction. We walked down the tunnel under Rideau Street like robots from a movie we saw once. We were coming from a lost underground city.

At the other end of the tunnel, in the Union Station, in the men's toilet, we twisted all the handles on the pay toilets like it was a big time machine. But it wasn't the same without Sammy.

I saw the Red Cap and he told me if I came back later he might have some more extra change for me.

We left the Union Station and headed for the museum. But first we sneaked through the Fire Escape door of the Capitol Theatre on Bank Street. The kids were starting to line up outside for the holiday show. It was "Captain Kidd," starring Charles Laughton. But we weren't going to stay.

We were upstairs above the main lobby. The red plush curtains were all around us. The theatre was still closed. It was like a palace for a Pharaoh.

There was marble and brass and copper shining all around us.

And big, curving stairs with marble railings curving up and the smell of popcorn and chocolate and the sound of feet on quiet rugs. I could see the box office down there and could remember the feel of the tickets—your little ticket in your hand that smelled like sweet cardboard when you were a little kid.

And the uniforms of the ushers like little soldiers. And their hats. And their white gloves, turned down. And their shiny black shoes and the exit signs in red and black and the paintings on the wall as you went down the wide winding stairs.

And the smell of dust and popcorn and darkness and the sound of the travelogue music maybe playing up the wide stairs, when you were a kid at your first show.

All this was making me sad.

All these things reminded me of Sammy.

It was time to go to the museum but instead we ran up to the Supreme Court and stood on the wide steps and played capital punishment. Gerald pronounced sentence on me:

"You will be taken from this place to another place where you will be hanged by the neck until you are dead and may God have mercy on your soul!" said Gerald in a sad, serious voice.

I bowed my head.

It was from many movies we once saw.

It was time to go to the museum. But we didn't. Scared maybe. Instead we went down Bank Street and we went into the U-Wanta Lunch restaurant and had some chips and gravy and the cook threw on some cranberries because it was Christmas and Gerald let the cranberries run out the side of his mouth and pretended he was shot until the waitress got worried and CoCo laughed and we left and went down Argyle Street to the museum and went through the heavy doors. Here at last. Suddenly the huge silence was on us.

Looking for Mr. Lonnigan.

Inside it smelled like rug dust, preserves, dried rose leaves inside a Bible. There were oak railings and brass knobs and marble stairs, marble walls and glass cases. I felt the buffalo's glass eyes. You feel them with your thumb and fingers when the Commissionaire isn't looking.

The silence was humming quietly and then a little kid's voice went all the way to the ceiling from somewhere with the sound of the paintings just hanging there and the sound of dinosaurs standing there, just in their bones; maybe the sound of bubbling water, soft, in the fish tanks; maybe a quiet Commissionaire in his dark blue uniform talking loudly because he was sort of old and a bit deaf maybe.

And we played movie around the elevator cables and cement gargoyles and long staircases, doors covered with padding, people holding hands, a scarf lying in a big marble room, faces looking through railings.

Three floors up in a big glass room an Eskimo stood beside his hole in the ice beside his dead fish with blood on it. We stood still there and watched him for a while. We stood the way he was standing, waiting to see if he'd move before we did. But he didn't. He was never going to move. Sammy and I had often been here.

And on the art gallery floor I saw a guy looking at a huge painting that was covered in glass. He was right up close to the painting and I thought he must really know a lot about paintings to be standing that close.

But then he wiped his hand over his hair and I realized he was looking at his own reflection in the glass. He wasn't looking at the painting at all. He was checking his hair.

We asked the Commissionaire if he knew Mr. Lonnigan.

Sure he did, but Mr. Lonnigan didn't work there any more. Not for more than six months now.

"In fact," the Commissionaire said, "I heard he left town and went to the States. Left his family and just took off. Not a very nice man. Not a very nice thing to do."

So that was why Chalmers wouldn't talk about him.

Poor Chalmers.

Then we went to the Français Theatre on Dalhousie Street to see the two o'clock show. It was twelve cents to get in.

We saw the guys ride horses. Ride up to an old mine site up in the rocks somewhere. There was a car parked outside a cabin. A car and some horses.

We saw the hero. He had a square face and his pants were high. He had a shirt on and his tie was undone.

He was fighting in some underground mine tunnel with three other guys who didn't have ties on and who were very ugly.

The fight lasted about half the show. They rolled around in the dirt and the music was loud and exciting.

A girl was standing with her back pressed against the wall of the tunnel, one hand in her mouth.

A gunpowder keg got knocked over and rolled along, leaving a trail which became a fuse when the girl knocked a flaming torch from the wall as she tried to help out the guy in the high pants. Girls were so useless. They were nice, though. You hated to see them get mutilated or shot or thrown in hot tubs of boiling lava or eaten by about forty crocodiles or blown up in some mine.

It wasn't a very good show, so I decided to leave.

I told Gerald and CoCo about my Richard Hudnut present for Margot Lane and how I'd be getting it Monday when the rest of my money came in. Then I left.

Money. Outside in the falling snow I decided to drop by the Union Station again to see if Red Cap meant it when he said for me to come back and he'd give me some more change. Every cent counted.

I found him at his usual spot and we talked about Christmas and money. I told him about all my jobs and he said that it was very good to have all those jobs.

Then he suggested another way of making money. He said he liked reading comics and if I had any that he hadn't read he'd buy them from me. Then he said that he knew other people who would buy them from me too. It would be a very good business to be in. In fact, some of the people who would buy them lived right near me on Cobourg Street.

One man specially.

He would buy all the comics I had.

Specially the war comics.

The violent ones.

"He lives right on your street. Works in the car b-b-b-barns there. Mechanic. Loves to read c-c-c-comics!"

The station was crowded and busy. All the Christmas travellers were going somewhere or coming from somewhere. There was Christmas music coming over the loud-speakers.

I could feel the back of my neck bristling.

I could feel gooseflesh on my arms.

I felt like I was standing near something very evil.

I felt terror.

I heard myself ask the question.

"What's this man's name?"

"L-L-L-L-Logg. M-M-M-Mister Logg."

All of a sudden the whole Union Station seemed to stop. Everything around me was like a picture. I walked up the wide stairs through the frozen crowds and the dead silence hearing only my own heart pounding in my ears.

L for Logg.

I went to Sammy's to see if there was anybody there. The apartment hall was dark and sad and nobody answered the door.

I went to the car barns and asked one of the drivers if he knew Mr. Logg.

"Sure, that's him over there," he said, pointing to a big man with his back to us, washing his hands in a sink.

I walked over to him as he was drying his hands. I stood behind him. I could smell evil.

"Mr. Logg?" I said.

He turned around.

He had little eyes and a big mouth.

Something ice cold ran up my back.

He looked down at me without saying a word.

"Would you like to buy some comics?"

"Maybe. Got any?"

"Yes."

"Bring them over to my place."

"Where do you live?"

"Thirty-two Cobourg Street, Apartment 406," he said, his little eyes burning.

At home Aunt Dottie was glaring at Dad's friend Frank. He had walked in with his army boots and tracked snow all over the place. They were talking about the Mock Duck and how there were definitely no turkeys or chickens because of the war that was over.

Frank was standing there picking his nose a little bit and Dad was asking him if he liked Mock Duck and would he like to come over on Christmas and have dinner with us.

Supper with us. Sipper with us.

Then Frank tried to go into the kitchen to get some water for his drink but he stepped on the cat and fell down before he got to the sink.

Then Dad asked him if maybe he'd like to come over Christmas Eve too and enjoy the tree since he was a bachelor and had no family to spend Christmas with.

My sister Pamela gave him a big hug after he got up and then he started to sing some army song and Aunt Dottie just kept glaring at him.

After supper (Aunt Dottie wouldn't pass him the butter when he asked for it and when he reached over to get it he spilled the jug of milk) I called on Gerald and we went over to CoCo's and had a meeting.

They were so excited they could hardly talk.

"It must be him," Gerald said. "We've got him! We've got him!"

"You're going over dere," CoCo said. "You must be very very careful, *tabarnac!*"

We went out into Lowertown and went to everybody's house we knew.

After a couple of hours we had collected almost fifty comics.

Many of them were just what Mr. Logg would enjoy.

6. BEYOND A SHADOW OF A DOUBT

Early Sunday morning I got up and made myself some Quaker. I looked at him and he looked at me as I ate. He looked pretty wise. He followed me around the kitchen.

Maybe he knew about Mr. Logg.

Aunt Dottie had left me a message to deliver before I went to church to do my six A.M. altar boy job. She left two Christmas cards to deliver next door to the McIntoshes' house. I would put them in their mailbox early. That way the McIntoshes wouldn't see me.

It would save paying for the stamps.

There were two cards. One for Mrs. McIntosh and one for Mr. McIntosh. There were two cards because Mr. and Mrs. McIntosh didn't like each other and never spoke to each other.

Mr. McIntosh had wired up the fence around his yard to keep the kids from climbing on it all the time. He had a switch in his cellar. He would wait until all the kids were on his fence and then he'd pull the switch and try to electrocute them all.

They'd all be screaming and diving off the fence and he'd be in his basement looking out the window with his hand on the switch and laughing. Mrs. McIntosh didn't like this. Whenever he did it, she would go into her cupboard and get out a whole lot of the homemade chocolates that she made all the time and go out and give them to all the kids.

Mr. McIntosh didn't like this.

While Mrs. McIntosh was handing out the chocolates, Mr. McIntosh would be in the cellar yelling and shaking his fist. You couldn't hear him yelling but you could see him.

That's why they never spoke to each other.

That's why Aunt Dottie sent over separate Christmas cards.

I put the cards quietly into the McIntoshes' mailbox and walked up St. Patrick Street to St. Brigit's Church through the dark and softly falling snow.

At ten to six I was in the sacristy with my surplice on, getting Father Foley ready for early mass.

It was interesting getting him ready for his show. He was a kind and gentle man with a nice face. Before I helped him get dressed up, he looked like any kind man you might see in a store or on the street or shovelling snow. But once he had his outfit on he became very special. He could have been in a movie.

While Father Foley was putting on his amice, I got his alb all smoothed out and ready. Then I put the alb on him, right sleeve first. Then I held the cincture for him, making sure the tassels were at my right. Then I gave him his maniple and he kissed it and hung it on his left arm. Then I gave him his long narrow stole for around his shoulders.

Finally I helped him on with his chasuble with all the gold and silver stitching.

He looked pretty nice. Pretty special.

Then we left the sacristy and went to the altar. I bowed a few times and went over to the credence table and fixed up the cruets of wine and water and the little wafers of bread.

There was a big crowd in church, everybody with their coats on, some coughing, a couple of babies crying a little bit. After "Alleluia" Father Foley read to us about what Jesus said on the hill.

I looked up at Jesus.

Jesus was up on his cross, blood on his forehead, in drops, dropping from his hands and his feet, some on his knees, and quite a bit coming out of his side.

Father Foley read: "How happy are the poor, happy the gentle; happy those who mourn; happy those who hunger; happy those who thirst for what is right; happy the merciful; happy the pure…happy… happy…happy."

It was a nice reading.

Later I went and got the wine cruet and the water cruet from the credence table. With my right hand I gave Father Foley the wine cruet after I kissed it. Then I gave him the water cruet with my right hand after I kissed it and got the wine cruet back in my left hand and kissed it again.

Then I got the plate and the towel and I helped Father Foley wash his hands.

Later, when Father Foley lifted up the chalice, with my right hand I rang the bell and with my thumb and finger of my left hand I held up his beautiful chasuble.

And I tried to whisper the mystery with Father Foley but I couldn't.

Then the people were lining up and kneeling along the rail and I was following Father Foley with the silver tray and the cloth, holding it under each chin of each person as each one took his bread and his wine.

The next chin raised up and a big furry tongue came out and over that the eyes opened and met my eyes.

I thought I heard somebody stab an organ somewhere.

Mr. Logg!

Mr. Logg in church with all these nice people.

And only two or three of us in church knew about what Mr. Logg had done.

Mr. Logg knew.

I knew.

And Jesus probably knew.

Then I got my idea.

More than the three of us should know about Mr. Logg and what he did. Many, many more.

After mass I got my pay (four dollars for eight Sundays) and I went home.

One shopping day until Christmas.

Tomorrow.

When I got home it was getting light and my sister Pamela was at her window and gave me a big welcome when I came in.

Aunt Dottie was up scrubbing and waxing everything for Christmas and Dad went out and got the *Star Weekly*, the Sunday paper.

I loved the smell of the *Star Weekly* and the cold feel of it when he brought it in. I smelled the ink of the funnies and lay down on the floor and read them.

They were all doing Christmas things in the funnies. Blondie and Popeye and Invisible Scarlet O'Neil and Dick Tracy and Andy Gump and Little Orphan Annie were all talking about Christmas.

Even Superman and Tarzan and Red Ryder were doing Christmas things.

The only one in the funnies who wasn't doing Christmas things was Alley Oop. Alley Oop was a caveman and didn't know anything about Christmas because Christmas wasn't invented yet in caveman days.

I helped Aunt Dottie wax the floor. I shook some ashes and I helped Dad put up the tree.

My sister Pamela was so excited that she started to howl and cry. We calmed her down with some shortbread that Aunt Dottie was just taking out of the oven.

I untangled the Christmas tree lights for Aunt Dottie and laid them out in a long string on the floor for her and then went to my room to sit on the bed and think.

It was time.

I got my pile of comics together and put them in a big brown paper bag so the snow wouldn't wet them.

I decided what I would charge Mr. Logg for them if he wanted them and then I headed up Cobourg Street to his place.

I went up the shaky little elevator in the building on the corner of

Clarence and Cobourg streets to Mr. Logg's apartment. I got off on the fourth floor and walked down the dark, dirty hallway to his door. The air was hot and lumpy. The radiators were clunking next to the garbage chute. I put my mitts on top of the radiator beside Mr. Logg's door and started knocking. He had a ratty-looking wreath nailed there with a cross-eyed Santa in the middle of it. Mr. Logg was probably asleep and I'd have to knock for quite a while before he'd get up and open the door. He'd be in his underwear and he'd be rubbing his little eyes. I just knew it.

And rubbing his huge unshaven face.

And scratching his big hairy arms.

I kept knocking and watching the steam come off my mitts.

The wreath fell off a couple of times and I had to hang it back up on the rusty nail each time.

I had war comics with covers that I knew he would like. They had pictures of Japs with big yellow buckteeth, about to shove red-hot pokers into girls' faces. The girls had on torn dresses. Or the covers had pictures of ugly German Krauts wearing big shiny black boots with nails in them, about to shove bayonets into girls' throats. The girls had on more ripped and torn dresses.

Mr. Logg opened the door and stood there scratching himself and rubbing his eyes.

"I was asleep," he said.

I checked to see if my mitts were on fire yet and then went into Mr. Logg's apartment. It smelled awful. It smelled like rotten meat or something.

His radiators were clanging so loudly I thought the whole place was going to blow up.

I showed him my *Crime* and *Cop Killer* comics first just to get him warmed up for the Japs and the Krauts.

The first one had a picture on the cover of a guy in an electric chair getting juiced and another guy in a black suit pulling a big switch. Mr. Logg sat down on the edge of his dirty bed and took a long look at the guy getting his reward for killing about a hundred cops. The guy in the electric chair was saying this:

"Aaaaaarrrrrgh!"

Mr. Logg studied it for quite a while. Then he looked up at me out of his little eyes.

"I seen this one," he said.

Brilliant man, Mr. Logg. Good idea to get him in with Blue Cheeks for a while to straighten out his grammar.

Mr. Logg scratched his armpits for a while and started studying the second one. It had on the cover a picture of some kind of ghoul with fangs and long fingernails and drool running out of his mouth, laughing and shutting this girl in a torn dress inside an iron maiden, the spikes just starting to stick into her chest and some drops of blood dropping.

Mr. Logg studied this one for quite a while too.

"Seen it," said Mr. Logg, and then he yawned, and his mouth opened wider and wider until he looked like a picture of a hippopotamus I once saw in *National Geographic*.

I was looking around Mr. Logg's room while he was grunting and breathing and trying to figure out which comics he'd read and which he hadn't.

His window was all weepy and stained and dirty. On his dresser he had a photograph of himself when he was young. He was just as ugly then as he was now. On his wall he had a big picture of Jesus with so much blood on it that you could hardly see his face.

He had pictures cut out of the paper, yellow and old-looking, of dead bodies and ambulances and executions.

And he had a big poster on the wall over his bed, a drawing of an evil-looking man in a raggedy cloak with hands like claws and burning eyes and a big hooked nose like a beak.

On the bottom of the poster it had the word JEW! in big black letters.

"Seen it," said Mr. Logg and he put down a *Crime Comic* with a guy shooting a policeman in the face on the cover.

He was getting down the pile. He was into the *Donald Duck* section. He was laughing.

Scrooge McDuck was eating a whole lot of money. Mr. Logg thought that was really funny. He laughed like he was choking.

When he got to the Japs and the red-hot pokers and Krauts and the big black boots he got really excited. He hadn't seen any of them. He started groaning and grunting as he put them in a different pile. He was going to buy those.

There were piles of dirty underwear and socks and rumpled pants sticking out from under his bed. And big fluffy balls of dust along the walls that moved a little bit each time Mr. Logg put a comic book down on one of the piles. The balls of dust rolled a little bit when the air moved. They looked like little tumbleweeds tumbling.

Mr. Logg was staring at a cover showing a soldier's boot crushing a Jap face with big buckteeth and another soldier throwing Japs over a cliff into a big fire.

While Mr. Logg was enjoying himself I felt something tugging at my mind. There was something awful in the room with Mr. Logg and me.

My eyes went back down to the mess under his saggy bed. There was something else there besides dirty clothes and dust balls. I could see the corner of something else there. Not clothes. Cloth. White cloth. White cloth with writing on it. The writing was partly showing. I leaned over a little to read the words. The words were: AND SEED.

My mind was whirling.

My stomach was upside-down.

"What're ya lookin' at?" I heard Mr. Logg's voice say.

I looked up and met his piggy eyes.

"What're ya lookin' at?"

"Nothing," I said in a whisper while his eyes burned me.

"Lookin' at nothin', eh?" Mr. Logg said and went back to his comics.

The pile he was going to buy was growing bigger. I figured there'd be around thirty comics he wanted.

"You think you're pretty smart, don't you?" Mr. Logg said.

I didn't answer. My eyes wanted to leave his but I wouldn't let them.

"How much for these comics here?"

"They're five cents each except the war ones. They're seven cents each," I said, trying not to swallow.

He stood up, and with his heel he kicked the mess under his bed and out of sight. He was smiling his rotten teeth at me as he took a handful of my curly hair in his big hand.

"Seven cents for the war ones, eh? Why seven cents for the war ones?"

He tightened his hold on my hair so that I had to stand on my toes.

"Because they're harder to get," I said.

"Why are they harder to get?" he said.

"Because people like to keep them, I guess," I said, not swallowing.

He tightened his grip. I was way up on my toes. I was hoping I wouldn't have to swallow. It's a sign of being scared when you swallow. Our cat did it all the time. When he was trapped, he'd look up at you and swallow.

I didn't want Mr. Logg to know how scared I was.

I hated him too much.

"Why do people like to keep them?" he said.

"Because they like them."

"But *you* don't like them!"

I didn't answer.

"Why don't you want to keep them?"

"I sell them because I need the money."

His foul breath in my face was going to make me sick.

"Christmas presents."

"Isn't that nice. The smart little business man. Seven cents for the war ones. Christmas presents. Who's gonna get the nicest present?"

I didn't answer.

"Who?" He jerked my head back.

"A beautiful girl," I said between my teeth.

"A beautiful girl! I thought only sissies had girlfriends! What's her name?"

I couldn't say the name. I couldn't say the name. He could have killed me but I would never have said that name in that room to that man.

"The name, sissy!" He jerked my head again. I was as far up on my toes as I could get.

"The name!"

"Fleurette Featherstone Fitchell!" I said.

"Who?"

"Fleurette Featherstone Fitchell!"

"What a stupid name!" said stupid Mr. Logg and let me go.

He laughed a big horse laugh and went into his bathroom but only closed the door part way.

I waited until I heard his water crashing into the bowl and then I dove under the bed and pulled out the pile of clothes. I spread out the piece with the writing on it. It was a cloth flour bag with eye-holes cut in it. And the writing.

RITCHIE'S FEED AND SEED, it said.

I heard the toilet flush. I shoved the stuff back under the bed and got up just in time and pretended I was looking out his dirty window.

He didn't say anything.

He was acting like I wasn't even there.

We counted the comics. The price came to a dollar seventy. He gave me the exact amount without saying a word. I picked up my leftover comics and quietly left. His face was buried in a war comic when I took a quick glance back. I shut his door quietly. When I shut the door his wreath fell on the floor. I left it there and got my mitts off the radiator.

When I got out on the street I sucked in big gulps of clean winter air.

Back home, under my bed, I had a big supply of paper for writing lines for people at school. I got out a stack of it and counted out two hundred sheets and put them in a neat pile.

I got out my best pencil and in big writing I wrote on the top sheet:

It was Mr. Logg of 32 Cobourg St., Apartment 406, who beat up Sammy Rosenberg's father of 102 Cobourg Street last week in the car barns. I have proof.
Signed
The Shadow
P.S. Merry Christmas.

Then, on the second sheet, I wrote out the same thing. And on the third.

I had finished sheet number fifty when my thumb got so sore I needed a rest. I went downstairs and had a little snack while my thumb was resting. My sister Pamela was at her window watching the snow and Aunt Dottie was finishing up the tree.

Dad was sitting back suggesting where to hang this and where to place that. Aunt Dottie paid no attention and put the decorations wherever she thought they should go. Each icicle was put on separately by Aunt Dottie and smoothed out straight so it would hang properly. Each ball was placed so at least two lights would reflect in it a certain way. Each little bell had to be just above and over to the left of each ball. Each little Santa faced out in one direction at a point on the other wall. Each little daub of fake snow was placed exactly where two branches forked together. Everything went into its own perfect place.

Aunt Dottie was the best tree decorator on the planet Earth.

"When that Frank person arrives here I want you to make sure he doesn't touch this tree," Aunt Dottie was saying.

"Don't worry," Dad said. "Frank never even notices things like that."

"As a matter of fact, I don't want him anywhere near this tree," Aunt Dottie was saying as she polished one of the reflectors with a little tissue.

"We could always lock him in the cellar until it's time for him to go home," Dad said.

"You know very well what I mean," Aunt Dottie said.

They kept talking about Frank while I went back upstairs and wrote the message fifty more times.

I went down again at six o'clock and listened to "Ozzie and Harriet." When "The Great Gildersleeve" came on I left for evensong at St. Albany's. I took fifty blank sheets with me under my coat and a couple of pencils. I could write a few sheets during Reverend Well's sermon.

During the processional the sheets almost slipped out from under my cassock but I caught them between my knees and pretended to almost drop my hymn book. After we sang a couple more hymns Reverend Well got up in his box and got going on his sermon.

There were a few empty seats where some people had stacked their coats. Because this church was very hot people liked to take their coats off. Not like the Dogan church where you had to keep your coat on because it was pretty cool.

Reverend Well's sermon was quite long and I had time to get fifty messages written out.

I looked up to see how the people were doing and I noticed that some of them had flopped onto their coats and were sleeping very heavily. You could hear some snoring and if you looked around you could see that practically everybody was nodding and jerking their heads back up before they hit the pews in front of them.

It must have been the heat.

I got my pay. I ran all the way home through the snowflakes and got there just in time to catch the last of Charlie McCarthy on the radio.

Then I listened to Fred Allen and went upstairs. But I didn't get undressed. I wrote out fifty more messages.

Waited until the tubes faded in the radio and everybody went to bed.

Then, very quietly, I got dressed warmly and went out to fix Mr. Logg. I had two hundred messages.

I started in Mr. Logg's apartment. I went up the fire escape by the garbage chute and got in the first floor hallway. I slipped one of my messages under each door.

Then I went to the second floor and did the same. And the third. And the fourth. Everybody got one but Mr. Logg. I passed by his door without breathing.

The cross-eyed Santa was hanging there, not following me.

Then I went to all the doors on all the streets around Mr. Logg's place. All of his neighbours got a message. All along Cobourg Street and Papineau and Augusta Street and Friel Street and Clarence Street and York Street until I had only one left.

Not one person saw me.

I was all by myself.

I was invisible.

I was Lamont Cranston. The Shadow.

I had one message left.

I walked down Cobourg Street, over Angel Square, across St. Patrick, and over onto Whitepath Street.

I walked down Whitepath Street to Margot Lane's house and up onto her little verandah.

I put my last message in the mailbox there.

Invisible.

The Shadow.

7. LONG PRAYER

Last shopping day till Christmas and Woolworth's on Rideau Street was an insane asylum.

I got there at seven in the morning before they opened and worked like a madman bringing stuff up from the basement and putting it on the shelves.

By nine o'clock we had everything stacked neatly in order and in the right place. My job was over at noon. Then I'd get my big pay and I'd be ready to pick up my presents.

They would pay me twelve dollars at noon for four Saturdays.

Our boss asked some of us to come and help him open the doors. There were thousands of people out there, standing in the falling snow. Some of the other workers said that our boss was afraid to open the doors by himself. They said that last year on the last shopping day till Christmas the people knocked our boss down and trampled him.

I noticed, as he put the key in the lock and as all the people's faces pressed up against the glass and breathed fog, that his face was very pale and his eyes were glazed over and he took a huge swallow so that his Adam's apple ran up his throat and back down like a little elevator. He was scared all right.

About an hour later when I saw him he was surrounded by about a hundred shoppers. They were all yelling at him and one of the sleeves was torn off his jacket.

About eleven o'clock, during my break, I got in line with all the little kids to talk to Ozzie O'Driscoll. Santa.

The kids were getting a little wild because it was the last shopping day till Christmas. Some of them were crying and others were pulling on Ozzie's beard. One of the arms of his throne was broken off and there was a big stain on his trousers. I guess one of the kids got too excited while sitting on his knee.

It was the turn of the kid ahead of me.

The one behind me was trying to shove me out of the way.

"You're too big to be here," he kept saying to me as he tried to push me out of line.

I could hear Ozzie O'Driscoll talking to the kid in front of me.

"You were here *twice* before," Ozzie said to the kid.

"No, I wasn't," the kid said. You could tell he was lying because his face was all twisted up like somebody had just made him eat a lemon.

"Yes, you were," Ozzie said. "I even remember what you wanted. A tank."

"A *real* tank," the kid said.

"I can't *get* a real tank in my *sleigh*, I told you. Real tanks are bigger than my sleigh. I told you that before."

"Get a bigger sleigh!" the kid said.

"I can't get a bigger sleigh. I've got only a few hours left before I take off. And I've got to get all the way up to the North Pole. I just haven't got the time."

"Tell Mrs. Claus to do it."

"Mrs. Claus is too busy. And anyway, even if she wasn't busy, she wouldn't do it."

"Why not?"

"Because she hates me. I'm never home."

"My dad says you're a fake," the kid said, with his chin stuck out.

"Well, ask your dad for the tank then!"

I knelt down beside Ozzie O'Driscoll's throne and put my mouth to his ear. His beard tickled me while I told him all about Mr. Logg. I told him about Sammy's father and about how I saw the hood under Mr. Logg's bed and how I put all the messages in everybody's place and how Mr. Logg pulled my hair and how he tried to make me say Margot Lane's name and how I wouldn't.

I told him everything.

Ozzie looked at me. His eyes got very serious. He told me I had done a very brave thing and he told me not to worry. He said he was going into the police station that night and he would get the Sergeant to send somebody over to Mr. Logg's to investigate. He said they might not be able to arrest him but they could put him under investigation and throw a good scare into him so that he wouldn't dare try to hurt anybody again.

Anyway, he would try.

At noon I got my pay and ran over to Freiman's.

I found the Virgin Mary lady and paid for the rest of Margot's Richard Hudnut Three Flower Gift Set.

I went up to Sparks Street to Laura Secord's and got Aunt Dottie her chocolates. The box said, "Old Time Home Made Laura Secord Candies."

Beside the writing on the white box was a picture of the crabbiest-looking lady I've ever seen. It was Laura Secord. Her mouth was turned down on each end and her eyes were narrow slits and her nose had a hook on it just like a parrot's. She had on a white hat pulled down over her head and tied so tight under her chin that she looked like she was choking. On the side of the box was a picture of her gravestone at Queenston Heights. The gravestone looked happier than she did.

But her chocolates were the best in the world, so she must have been a nice person.

I went to the Joke Shop on Bank Street and bought Gerald a big rubber cigar for when we played gangster movies.

I went down to Ogilvy's on Rideau Street and bought Sammy a repeater cap gun and two boxes of caps.

Then I went to Prevost on Cobourg Street and bought Coco Laframboise a private detective's badge. For his detecting.

I went in the house and my sister Pamela gave me a big hug and I put my finger to my lips and tried to make her understand that I had presents and that there were secrets and I sneaked up the stairs on my toes with my finger on my lips and she stood at the bottom of the stairs with her head on one side and her eyes shining and her face like a big question mark.

It was like when a puppy looks at you. Trying to understand. Almost understanding the mystery.

Dad was mixing up a big bowl of punch and another big jug of eggnog and Aunt Dottie was preparing the Mock Duck, tying it up with lots of strong string.

I wrapped my presents and put my sister Pamela's yellow duck and Aunt Dottie's chocolates and Dad's Flat Fifty under the tree and then I went out into the Lowertown Christmas Eve to CoCo's house.

Mrs. Laframboise let me in and I could smell pies baking and CoCo gave me a present and I gave him his. I opened mine. It was a picture of The Shadow in his cloak and his big black hat. It was autographed.

We had some Nesbitt Orange to celebrate and I wished everybody a Merry Christmas and CoCo put on his badge and I went out into the beautiful snow and all the warm windows glowing yellow along Cobourg Street and went over to Gerald Hickey's house and gave him his present and he gave me mine. It was a beautiful book of Shadow stories with a picture of The Shadow on the front in his black cloak and his big black hat with the brim down over his face and Margot Lane looking at him with her big eyes. And Gerald and I had some Honey Dew to celebrate and he put his rubber cigar in the corner of his mouth and shot me all the way out onto the street.

And we shouted Merry Christmas to each other and I went up to Sammy's apartment and knocked on the door.

I knocked again.

The hall was dark and there was some singing coming from another apartment down the hall and some laughing.

But nobody answered Sammy's door.

That night I went to bed early.

And I tried a prayer.

I had never tried a prayer before.

I prayed for a nice time.

A time when nobody thought some other person's face was funny to look at and nobody laughed at other people's parents and said they were stupid-looking and nobody made fun of the way they talked and nobody thought somebody else wore funny-looking clothes or hateful clothes.

And nobody got beat up because of the kind of hat they wore or because they were poor or because of the street they lived on.

And nobody got spit on because they had different kinds of food in their lunch or their father came to meet them after school with a long coat on and maybe a beard.

And nobody got their mitts stolen or got tripped in the snow because their names didn't sound right or they believed in some other kind of religion or read a different kind of bible or had freckles on their faces or had the wrong kind of hair or had to go home at a different time from school or didn't have skates or *did* have skates or weren't allowed to play alleys on Saturday or on Sunday or *were*, or got dunked in water at church or didn't swear or *did* swear or smelled funny or couldn't eat fish or *had* to eat fish or wore a hat in church or *didn't* wear a hat in church or said the Lord's Prayer different or *didn't* say the Lord's Prayer at all.

And nobody got punched in the mouth because they had clean fingernails or fat lips or couldn't understand English or couldn't speak French or couldn't pronounce Hebrew.

And there were no gangs waiting all the time, so nobody had to go down different streets just to get to the store or go to school.

And you could carry a book along with you or a mouth organ or something and people wouldn't take it from you and then tear it into pieces or grab it and smash it up against a wall.

A time when you maybe liked a girl and they wouldn't come along and twist your arm behind your back and try and make you say dirty things about her.

A nice time.

That's what I prayed for.

The prayer might work, I thought.

Or it might not.

It was a mystery.

8. HAPPY, HAPPY

Christmas morning we had the Quaker with brown sugar and cream instead of milk. My sister Pamela had trouble eating the brown sugar because she still didn't know what it was. She still wasn't used to it even though the war was over.

Then we went and sat around Aunt Dottie's perfect tree and opened up our presents. I opened up a new hat with fur on the forehead and fur ear flaps. My sister Pamela opened up her little yellow duck. We showed her how to squeeze it again, just like last year, to make it quack. It went quack for her just like last year. And she laughed and was happy all over again. Then I opened a present with new socks in it and a new sweater. Then Dad picked up his present from me and weighed it in his hands and felt the shape of it.

"I hope it's a Flat Fifty!" he said and ripped the paper off.

"It is! It is a Flat Fifty! Just what I wanted! Thank you very much!"

And while Aunt Dottie was taking such a long time to open hers (she wouldn't tear the paper) Dad said, "I wonder if it's chocolates!" And when she finally got it open, he shouted, "It is! It's chocolates! Let's have a couple!"

"You're not having any. I'm saving these for myself for a change this year," Aunt Dottie said. And she put them down beside her.

And then we all had a couple.

I got new boots and new breeks and new mitts and a new scarf. And Aunt Dottie got a book about poetry from Dad.

After Dad opened up some handkerchiefs and a tie and some socks and Aunt Dottie opened up some new rubber gloves and a new apron and some ribbon, there was only Sammy's present sitting under the tree all by itself.

Downstairs in the cellar while I was getting some shortbread with the half-cherry on each piece wrapped in the waxpaper, I could hear the sad sound of my sister's yellow duck quacking.

While we were having a little snack Dad turned on the radio and we listened to King George's Christmas message from England. It was quite static and his voice sounded very thin and lonely. He was so far away. Dad said that he sounded like that because he was very sick and he was going to die soon, he thought.

Not happy.

That afternoon I was sitting with my sister Pamela looking out her window. I was waiting for a feeling to come over me so I could take Margot's present over to her. I couldn't take it over there with the feeling I had on me. I wanted to feel like I did on the night of the moon eclipse. A good feeling.

Suddenly Sammy appeared out of the snow and knocked on our door. My sister Pamela and I got to the door at the same time and we nearly killed him with our hugs.

He told me that his father woke up in the hospital in Toronto and that he was going to be all right. His big brown eyes were full of water.

I gave Sammy his Christmas present even though it wasn't Christmas for him and he gave me mine. We both opened them at the same time. They were exactly the same thing.

Two repeater cap guns with two extra boxes of caps.

I told him all about Mr. Logg and the messages I sent and Ozzie O'Driscoll. I told him everything.

He said there were some people hanging around outside Mr. Logg's and that he saw a police car there when he came by to my place.

We ran up Cobourg Street and joined the crowd. Gerald was there and so was CoCo. And a big crowd of people. There was a police car parked along the snowbank and the people were looking at the car and looking up at Mr. Logg's window on the fourth floor. The snow was floating down.

"They say Mr. Logg didn't go to war because he's a coward," said a lady in a black hat.

"They say Mr. Logg kills little kids and he eats dem," said CoCo Laframboise.

"They say he reads comics all the time and his I.Q. is zero," said a man who was interested in measuring intelligence.

"They say The Shadow is going to get a medal," said Gerald. "Or at least a nice reward."

"Who *is* The Shadow, anyway?" said another lady.

"They say it's Tommy, down the street."

"You mean *this* Tommy?" said a man, pointing at me.

"It's not me," I said.

"They say people are putting in money to help Sammy's father pay the hospital," somebody else said.

"He's a Jew," somebody else said. "Nobody would do that for a Jew!"

"They say Mr. Logg has horns and a tail."

"They say he's afraid to come out."

Just then the apartment building door opened and the policeman came out.

"Aren't you going to arrest Mr. Logg?"

"No, I just came to ask him a few questions," the policeman said as he climbed over the snowbank and opened the door of his car.

"He's guilty as sin!" a lady shouted.

"No he's not," said somebody else.

"They say The Shadow found the evidence!"

The policeman shut his door and started his motor.

"Mr. Logg should be very careful," said a great big man about the size of Uncle Paddy. "Somebody might do the same thing to him someday!"

"Jews should be beat up," somebody said.

The police car pulled quietly away in the soft falling snow.

"Mr. Logg is a hog," said a small, quiet man.

Then everybody looked up at Mr. Logg's window.

It was opening.

And out came his ugly head.

"Come down you slimy coward!" said the man as big as Uncle Paddy.

"You're the one! You're the one who hit Sammy's father over the head, you filthy monster!" shouted the lady in the black hat.

"Get away from here! Get away from here! You have no proof!" said Mr. Logg's ugly mouth.

"We don't need proof, we know what you're like!" shouted another lady.

"He's innocent," said somebody else.

"It's true," said the quiet man, "there is no *real* proof. It's not right to accuse a person unless you have proof."

"The Shadow has proof," I said.

"How do *you* know?"

"Because he told me."

"He told you. You know this Shadow?"

"Yes."

"Who is he?"

"I can't tell. But he saw the Ritchie's Feed and Seed bag under Mr. Logg's bed."

"It's under your bed, the evidence is!" shouted the big man up at Mr. Logg.

Suddenly the window slammed shut. For a minute nobody said or did anything.

Then my best Pea Soup friend, CoCo Laframboise, detective, solved it.

"Round da back. He'll trow it in de garbage. It will come down de chute at de back!"

Everybody ran down the laneway of the apartment building to the back and crowded into the garbage room to watch the bottom of the chute.

Sure enough, we heard something slam away up above, and something came bumping and hissing down the metal chute.

Out came a brown paper bag. CoCo grabbed it almost before it hit the bin and tore it open. Egg shells, tea leaves, bean cans, garbage. Nothing but garbage.

But wait! Underneath it all, rolled up in a tight ball, was the Ritchie's Feed and Seed hood. Everybody let out a big cheer.

"His I.Q. must be *less* than zero," said the I.Q. man.

Around the front again, the big man as big as Uncle Paddy sent me up the hydro post about six rungs to tie the proof right where Mr. Logg would see it from his window.

"Hooray for The Shadow, whoever he is!" shouted the quiet man while I was still up the post. And everybody looked up at me and shouted, "Hooray for The Shadow, whoever he is!"

In the crowd I could see Fleurette Featherstone Fitchell. She was looking up at me.

"Thanks, Fitchy!" I shouted.

"Hooray for The Shadow!" shouted Fleurette Featherstone Fitchell. And she had a nice look on her face as she looked at me.

And I thought I saw Mr. Logg at his window but I wasn't sure. And I didn't care if he saw me there or not, because he couldn't hurt me now, there were too many neighbours who knew he was guilty.

Neighbours in Lowertown, Ottawa.

I said goodbye to CoCo and Gerald and Sammy. I said I had something important to do and I'd see them later. They said *they* had an important message to deliver and that they'd see *me* later. I wondered for a minute what they meant but I didn't think of it anymore and went right home for the Mock Duck.

Now I had the feeling.

Right after I got home Dad's friend Frank arrived. I was coming downstairs after making sure Margot's present was all right.

Frank was in the hall trying to take his army boots off so he wouldn't dirty Aunt Dottie's floors.

He was standing on one foot trying to undo the lace of his boot. Then he started hopping. Then he lost his balance totally. He leaned on the door that went into the front room and the door opened and Frank went running and falling sideways in there. There was a tall floor lamp there and Frank grabbed it by the skinny neck but it wouldn't hold him so he let it go and it crashed on the floor. Frank was falling near the window now and had his hands full of our curtains. When the curtains gave way he went for some pictures on the wall and a bowl of nuts on the fake mantelpiece. Things were crashing all over the place and Aunt Dottie, who was in the kitchen reading her book on poetry, came out to see Frank aiming himself backwards towards our big armchair.

Frank missed the chair and came quite fast into the little living room pulling down all the Christmas streamers and tipping our dish cabinet as he headed for the tree.

"Not the tree!" Aunt Dottie said and went back into the kitchen just as Frank stomped on the unwrapped presents. Then he turned around, out of control, and dove headfirst into the Christmas tree.

Only Frank's legs stuck out from the mess in the corner and some smoke came up from the lights because of short circuits.

After we got everything cleaned up and Dad got the lights to work on the tree again and got Frank straightened out and I helped Aunt Dottie set the table we sat down to eat our Christmas dinner (sipper).

I asked if it would be all right if I ate quickly and left because I had a present to deliver.

"Who's it for?" Aunt Dottie asked.

"A girl," I said.

"Isn't that nice," Aunt Dottie said. She was glaring at Frank.

"Isn't that nice," Dad said.

"Yes," Frank said, pulling a piece of string as long as his arm from his throat that he'd eaten with the Mock Duck. "Isn't that nice!"

I walked slowly across Angel Square and up Whitepath Street towards Margot Lane's house. The snow was falling like it does in one of those round glass balls that you shake. There was nobody on the street because it was supper time. The streetlight made the flakes around it look like little silver flies.

If I looked back I could see my tracks. There were no tracks up Margot's walk and no tracks on her steps. The verandah light was on and there was a wreath on the door.

I was the only boy in the world.

I stood on her verandah and rang the bell. I had the present in my hand.

She opened the door and the warm light knifed out across me. Some bells on the wreath on the door shook out a little tune. I could see the reflection of part of their Christmas tree in a mirror in the hall behind her.

I held out the present.

"This is a present for you for Christmas, Margot Lane," I said.

She took the present and slowly closed the door until it was only open a crack wide enough for her lips.

"Thank you, Shadow," she whispered.

"I'm not The Shadow," I said.

"Yes, you are. You are Lamont Cranston, The Shadow. And you did a very brave thing."

"How did you find out?"

"Your friends CoCo and Gerald and Sammy told me. That's how I know. Everybody knows."

"Would you come for a walk with me tomorrow?" I said, my voice sounding like Lamont's.

"Yes I would, Shadow," she whispered.

Then she softly closed the door.

I went down from her verandah and ran all the way home. Across Angel Square.

The snow had stopped. And the moon, peeking out, followed me as I ran.

Happy.

Happy!

Happy Christmas.

People in the Book

Sammy's father — An innocent man who was hurt because of hatred.

Dad — Dad.

Aunt Dottie — A very clean and nice woman.

Mr. Aubrey — A butcher who was lucky to still have his thumb.

Sammy — My best Jew friend.

Mr. Blue Cheeks — The worst teacher on the planet Earth.

The lovely Margot Lane — The Shadow's companion on the radio.

The Shadow — Alias Lamont Cranston, wealthy young man-about-town, fighter of crime and rooter-out of evil.

The Quaker — A man on a box of porridge who saw everywhere at once.

Toe-Jam Laframboise — The delivery man whose socks were on forever.

My sister Pamela — An angel who couldn't know anything.

The cat — Our cat.

Margot Lane herself — The only girl in the world.

Miss Strong — A teacher who laughed at people who wanted to be writers.

Miss Frack and Miss Eck — Two robins.

Albert Einstein — An inventor.

Melody Bleach — The worst writer in the class.

Ralph — A moose stole his camera.

Geranium Mayburger — Dumb.

CoCo Laframboise — My best Pea Soup friend.

Killer Bodnoff — The toughest Jew.

Manfred Mahoney — The toughest Dogan.

Denny Trail — A Protestant who moved.

Arnold Levinson — The sissiest Jew.

Telesphore Bourgignon — The sissiest Pea Soup.

Clary O'Mara — The sissiest Dogan.

Sherwood Ashbury — The sissiest Protestant.

Anita Pleet — The smartest girl.

Martha Banting — The nicest girl.

Fleurette Featherstone Fitchell — The hamburger bun artist.

Delbert Dilabio — A horseball head.

Mr. Maynard — The best teacher in the universe.

Steve Wilson and Loreli Kilbourne — They were on the radio in "Big Town".

Sir John A. Macdonald — The Father of Confederation.

Gerald Hickey — My best Dogan friend.

Father Francis — A teacher with long arms.

Arnie Sultzburger — Dad was going to kill him.

Lester Lister — A friend of mine I didn't like.

Uncle Paddy — My favourite uncle with the big feet.

Mr. and Mrs. Lister and Esther — People that rhyme.

Turkeys — Secret weapons.

Chalmers Lonnigan — A person who wanted to go to heaven early.

Morrison-Lamothe — Our breadman who smelled like bread.

Ozzie O'Driscoll — Santa Claus on his holidays.

Mrs. Claus — A fed-up wife.

Uncle Jim and Captain Marvel — Two of Santa's reindeer.

Mock Duck — A pretend turkey.

Laurel and Hardy — They eat socks.

Frank — Back from the war with poor balance.

Red Cap — Dad's cousin from up the Ga-Ga-Gatineau.

Bing Crosby — A singer who makes Christmas feel right.

Rita Hayworth — A model.

Richard Hudnut — A present manufacturer.

Virgin Mary — A saleslady.

Doll — An Imbro's waitress.

Louis — The owner of the place.

Tony Janero and Humberto Zavala — They stopped fighting because of the tubes.

Snowman — A practice torture victim.

Abbot and Costello — People who eat furniture.

U-Wanta Waitress — She thought Gerald was dead.

Buffalo — His eyes are made of glass.

Commissionaire — A quiet guard (sometimes).

The Art Expert — His hair was his main interest.

High-pants — The hero, blown up till next week.

The girl — Useless but nice.

Mr. Logg — A bad man.

Mr. and Mrs. McIntosh — They disagreed about electrocution.

Father Foley — A very elegant dresser.

Jesus —

Reverend Well — A long speaker.

Laura Secord — A nice lady, mean face.

Mrs. Laframboise — A detective's mother.

King George — A far-way and lonesome king.

A Crowd of Neighbours — Good for Angel Square.

EASY AVENUE

To Fay, John, Jo, Kelly,
Tobias, Eliza, John Peter,
Wylie and Gabriel

And to Mike, Jenny, Sarah,
Moira, Simon and Rowan

And to Jackie, Megan and Ryan

1. THE WORLD'S WORST GOLFER

My last name is O'Driscoll and my first name is Hulbert. When I was little I couldn't say the word Hulbert very well. The word Hulbert came out something like Hubbo, and everybody started calling me that. They still call me that. Hubbo. Hubbo O'Driscoll.

There were lots of O'Driscolls in Lowertown, Ottawa. There was the O'Driscoll who was a policeman who took his holidays around Christmas so he could work at playing Santa Claus at Woolworth's on Rideau Street.

He's not in this story.

There were other people in Lowertown that you might know. Tommy, I don't know his last name, who thought he was The Shadow. He's not in this story either. Well, maybe he is, once. And Killer Bodnoff.

And Fleurette Featherstone Fitchell. You might know her. You might have heard of her. She is in this story.

My first memory about moving from Lowertown to our new place to live at the Uplands Emergency Shelter is not about moving there or about the bus to get out there, but it is about a place right next to Uplands Emergency Shelter. The golf course. The Ottawa Hunt and Golf Club, where I got a job caddying just a few days after we moved near there in the summer.

And where something happened.

Everybody in the Uplands Emergency Shelter was poor, and of course everybody at the Ottawa Hunt and Golf Club was rich, except the caddies.

We made seventy-five cents for caddying eighteen holes. And maybe a tip. I was one of the lucky ones though; I made a dollar fifty for eighteen holes because I was Mr. Donald D. DonaldmcDonald's special caddy. Nobody wanted to caddy for Mr. Donald D. DonaldmcDonald because he was such a rotten golfer and he had such a vicious temper. His face would get red and his eyes would begin to bulge out when his ball would take off into the bush, which was practically every time he hit it. And he would often throw his club into the bush too. I would have to go and get it and also find his ball for him.

His ball would be so far into the bush that I'd either never find it or if I did it would be in a hopeless place and he'd get mad all over again.

I used to find a lot of other golf balls while I was in there looking for Mr. Donald D. DonaldmcDonald's ball, and when I'd find one that was his brand I'd keep it so that sometimes I'd be able to drop one in not a bad place alongside the fairway in the rough grass and tell him it was his so he'd have a shot at it without taking a penalty.

He always played alone and even though he yelled and screamed almost all the way over the eighteen holes I knew he wasn't mad at me; he was mad at the golf bag, the ball, the clubs, the golf course, the trees, the bunkers, the rocks, the bushes, the water, the greens, the tee, the pin and himself.

He didn't seem to have any friends. Except maybe me.

Sometimes when we'd be waiting for other golfers and there was nothing to do I would practice my handstand and my round-off back handspring. He used to like that. It even made him smile sometimes.

He played two rounds every Saturday and two rounds every Sunday. And I was his personal caddy.

He said he played to let off steam.

Letting off steam meant that all week steam would build up inside him (not real steam) and on the weekends he'd have to let it out or he would explode.

The last time I ever caddied for him something bad happened.

I came out of the bush with one of his golf clubs and got a funny feeling that something was wrong. I couldn't see him anywhere.

Then I saw two golf shoes, the toes pointing into the ground behind the ball washer. There were legs attached to the shoes.

When I got to him his fingers were clawing the grass and his mouth was sucking in dirt. The back of his neck and his ears were bluish grey.

His golf bag was lying a few steps away where he had been trying to tee off. That's why I didn't see him fall. I was in the bush looking for one of his golf clubs that he threw in there after his first bad shot.

I unzipped the pocket of the bag where I knew he kept those pills. I knew everything he had in his bag because he'd get me to try and tidy it up after the first nine holes each time while he went into the clubhouse for something to drink and to relax.

He had to go in to let off some more steam.

His bag was always a wreck because of all the things he did to it when he was mad, which was most of the time.

Jumping up and down on your golf bag with those spiked shoes isn't good for it. Jumping up and down with both feet scars and tears the leather of a golf bag. And kicking it along the fairway. And throwing your golf bag into creeks and mud holes is bad for it. And so is swinging your golf bag by the strap with both hands, beating it against rough pine-tree trunks. And throwing it into sand traps. And lifting very heavy rocks over your head and crushing your golf bag with those rocks.

Or using your golf club like an axe and chopping your golf bag. He did these things all the time.

He would hit his ball as hard as he could and the ball would head right for the bush, bounce off a tree, and disappear. Or he would try to hit the ball and it would dribble just a few yards away.

Then he would attack the bag.

Then I would pick it up and carry it to where his ball was (unless it was in the bush) and give him his next club and he would try again. Then he would probably hit the ball on the very top and it would fly straight up in the air and come back down almost in the same place and then he'd throw his club away over into the bush and while I ran to get it he would attack the bag again.

He never got mad at me. Usually the bag.

This was why I knew everything about his golf bag. Each time he went into the clubhouse to let off steam I would work on the bag. Get it back in shape. I would clean it off with a rag and soap and water and then while it was drying I would go through the pockets cleaning out the mud and sand and broken trees and stuff. And I'd rub the bag down with protective wax and maybe put some shellac I'd get from the pro shop on the gashes and cuts in the leather.

He had his name printed inside a little plastic window on the bag. Mr. Donald D. DonaldmcDonald. Sometimes I'd say it over like a little song:

Donald D. DonaldmcDonald,
Donald D. DonaldmcDonald,

Donald D. Donald,
Donald D. Donald,
Donald D. DonaldmcDonald.

I was pretty good at saying it. I was a much better pronouncer than I was when I was little and couldn't even say Hulbert.

And I always wanted to ask him what his initial D. stood for, but I never did.

As I was saying, I knew his golf bag very well. That's why I knew what those pills were and what they were for. It said so right on the bottle. He was lying there on his stomach with his face in the grass. His fingers were out like claws, clawing the grass like our cat used to claw the blanket on the bed down in Lowertown. The back of his neck and his cheeks were a bluish grey colour.

There was nobody around and the golf course was as quiet as a graveyard. A squirrel bounced up to us and stopped to watch. I got out the bottle of pills from the bag and twisted off the top. The little sign on the bottle said, "Place glycerine pill under tongue. If mouth dry moisten with drops of water."

There was a tap sticking up out of the grass down by the ladies' tee. I ran down there and turned on the tap and cupped my hands under it. The water was gushing out so fast I couldn't get much to stay in my hands. I ran back up to him holding my hands high out in front of me. There wasn't much left when I got there but there was enough to wet his mouth. I looked around on the grass where I left the pills. They weren't there. I crawled around slapping the grass looking for the bottle. I looked up and saw the squirrel hopping away with it in his mouth. I let out a yell and he dropped it and bounced away a few times and stopped. A bold little guy. I crawled over monkey style and got the bottle.

Mr. Donald D. DonaldmcDonald gave out a long groan to me as I shoved a pill under his tongue with my finger.

I got out some driver covers and made a little pillow for the side of his head so his mouth wouldn't roll back into the grass. I looked to see if anybody was around to help.

The squirrel was sitting up, still as a statue, watching. The heat bugs were singing.

I looked down the fairway to see how far I'd have to run to the club-house. He gave out another long groan and his throat muscles started working.

I ran as fast as I could down the fairway and cut across to the first tee. In the clubhouse I explained what happened between breaths. They called an ambulance and we jumped on the sod truck and drove right down the middle of the fairway to where he was. When we got there he was trying to sit up. His face was white but not bluish anymore, and his eyes were fuzzy and unfocused. We helped him onto some sod on the back of the truck and I threw his clubs on and we drove off.

We met the ambulance half way up the fairway and the men put him on their stretcher and slid him into the back of the ambulance.

I told them about the pill.

"Lucky for him you knew about the pills," one of the ambulance guys said. "Probably saved his life."

As they were putting him in the ambulance, tucking in his blanket, his eyes got a bit clear and he looked right at me. With his free arm Mr. Donald D. DonaldmcDonald reached over and weakly squeezed me on the shoulder.

Then they shut the door and drove off with the siren crying.

I reached up and touched my shoulder where Mr. Donald D. DonaldmcDonald squeezed it a bit to see what he had felt there. How it felt to him.

I never caddied again.

2. DROWNED IN THE WAR

My dad was run over by a streetcar. He lay down on the streetcar tracks for a rest during a snowstorm. The driver couldn't see very well because of the blowing snow and ran over him. I never knew him because that happened when I was just a baby.

My mom died when I was born.

I guess you could say I was kind of an orphan.

I lived with Mrs. O'Driscoll. She was married to a distant cousin of my dad's. I thought of her as my mother and I loved her and at school and everywhere I said she was my mother but at home I always called her

Mrs. O'Driscoll. It was a warm little joke we had between us.

After we moved to Uplands Emergency Shelter Mrs. O'Driscoll got a job as a cleaning lady at Glebe Collegiate Institute. Glebe Collegiate Institute was a big high school in the southern part of Ottawa. The high school where I would go that fall.

Mrs. O'Driscoll's husband, Mr. O'Driscoll, was drowned in the war. In the Pacific Ocean. Mr. O'Driscoll was a wild kind of man with red hair and freckles on the backs of his hands and on his neck. He laughed a lot and he liked making jokes. Bad jokes.

The day he drowned he was talking with a man, making jokes and rolling a cigarette in the front part of the ship, on the main deck. Suddenly there was a dull sort of a thud and the horns started going and the ship started sinking.

The man who was rolling the cigarette shook hands with Mr. O'Driscoll and they said goodbye, they'd see each other later, and they both jumped in the water. One over one side of the boat and one over the other side.

The man rolling the cigarette got saved and came around to our house after the war and told us all about it.

Mr. O'Driscoll didn't get saved.

Just before he jumped overboard, Mr. O'Driscoll yelled out to his friend, "If I don't see you in the spring, I'll see you in the mattress!"

As you can see, Mr. O'Driscoll was quite a funny guy.

It was a joke mixing up spring, the season, with the spring in a bed. I guess it would be something one bedbug would say to another bedbug. Maybe Mr. O'Driscoll mentioned the bedbugs but the wind was howling too loud or there were too many explosions and things and the man rolling the cigarette didn't hear that part.

I remember when the man came to see us and tell us about Mr. O'Driscoll's last moments. We already knew how drowned he was because of the letter Mrs. O'Driscoll got from the government. The letter said he was "missing."

After she opened it and read it she said, "He never was much of a swimmer." She said this the way she said everything. Out of the side of her mouth. Then she cried for about three days.

When the friend showed up a few months later he had trouble finding us.

We lived in Building Number Eight, Unit B, Uplands Emergency Shelter.

We had to move there from Lowertown because of the housing shortage after the war. The person who owned our house on St. Patrick Street in Lowertown sold it to somebody and we had to move out.

He came over to our house at the end of June on my last day of public school at York Street and told us. I came down St. Patrick Street with all my books and my report that said I passed, On Condition, and there he was, standing on the steps, talking to Mrs. O'Driscoll, telling her that we had to get out.

On Condition meant if you didn't do very well in grade nine, they'd send you back to grade eight. I wasn't a very good student.

"I suppose you know what you can do with your house," I heard Mrs. O'Driscoll say to the man out of the corner of her mouth. But she saved the very corner of her mouth for special occasions.

She looked around for another place to live in Lowertown, but there weren't any. Finally, in July, she told me.

"We're going to Uplands Emergency Shelter," she said. "It's an air force base about ten miles south of Ottawa. Uplands Emergency Shelter." She said "Emergency Shelter" out of such a tight corner of her mouth that I could hardly understand it at first.

But the tightest corner of her mouth I ever heard her use was the corner she used when I told her about the mysterious money I was getting from somewhere.

"Mysterious money?" she said.

But that was after school started.

3. FLEURETTE FEATHERSTONE FITCHELL

All summer, families with nowhere to live were moving into Uplands Emergency Shelter.

Families with screaming babies and piles of brothers and sisters and broken trucks and torn furniture and tubs full of junk and mop handles pointing out and pails with leftover food and blankets tied with rope and bent beds and stained mattresses and ice boxes with the doors hanging and bureaus stuck in passageways and fat tires and homemade shelves and cracked dishes and three-legged chairs and twisted curtain rods and coiled springs sticking out of ripped sofas and yelling and swearing.

The mother of the new family moving into our building had a black eye and a cast on her wrist. She wouldn't look at anybody.

I recognized the girl carrying in the broken lamp. I asked her if she wanted some help and she said no. She had black curly long hair tied at the back with a white rag. She had brown-black eyes and long black eyelashes and very white skin.

She didn't say no in a mean way but you knew that she meant it. She wasn't just being polite or shy or proud or anything like that. You could tell that she just meant no.

I remembered her from York Street School. I was never in her class but I remembered that Killer Bodnoff and some of the guys would sneak over into the girls' schoolyard and chase her and her friends and throw snow at them and try to kiss them. Killer used to say that she would even take guys into her back shed with her on Friel Street. He used to call it *Feel* Street. He used to say that she was dirty.

Her name was Fleurette Featherstone Fitchell.

Later that day I was lined up at the toilet with some of the other people in our building—Mr. Blank, his strange little dog Nerves, Mr. Yasso, Mrs. Quirk and her boy with no brain and, behind me, my new neighbour.

"Is this the only toilet?" she said. "For six families?"

"Eight," I said. "There are eight families. Two for each part of the H. You are the eighth family to move in," I said. She looked at me.

"You went to York Street School," she said. "Can you still stand on your hands?" She was looking right at me from out of her brown-black eyes.

I did a perfect handstand while the little dog, Nerves, came around and stared in my face so that I started to laugh and had to come down.

"Your name is Hulbert O'Driscoll," she said.

"Hubbo," I said.

"How did you know I could stand on my hands?" I said.

"We used to watch you after school in the gym. Some of the girls really liked you."

"Me?" I was so embarrassed that I did another handstand and hand-walked away down the hall so she wouldn't see my face. Nerves clicked down the hall with me, trying to do a paw-stand probably. When I got back and stood up again I said that I knew her too.

"Your name is Fleurette Featherstone Fitchell. Everybody knew you." As soon as I said that I knew I shouldn't have. All of a sudden I felt awful.

The toilet was free now and I was next.

"Would you like to go first?" I said, being a big gentleman.

"No." Not polite, not shy, not proud. Just no.

I went in and shut the door.

I didn't want her to hear me going so I turned on the tap.

When I came out Fleurette and Nerves were staring at each other. A staring match.

"Is this a real dog or what is it?" said Fleurette Featherstone Fitchell. Then she went in the toilet and shut the door.

She didn't turn on the tap. I went down the hall to my unit with Nerves, who walked along beside me taking little glances at me as we moved along. Nerves was a little dog that looked a lot like a rat. His tail was like a little black whip and his body was fat and pulpy-looking and his snout was pointed just like a rat's snout. And when he walked his claws made little clicking noises on the floor. And his little whiskers stuck out like a rat's whiskers. And his eyes were shiny and always darting around and he'd move along a few quick steps going click click and then stop and his ears would stiffen up and his nose would start to move around like a little eraser rubbing out something invisible in the air in front of him. Then he'd click click on a little more.

Whenever Mr. Blank came in the door, Nerves would wait to see what mood he was in and then get in the same mood right away. If Mr. Blank was grumpy or frowning, Nerves would kind of frown and show his pointy little rat's teeth. If Mr. Blank was happy, smiling and feeling good, Nerves would jump up and down and wag his ratty little tail and squeak like a rat laughing.

And if Mr. Blank was thinking about something hard or trying to figure out a crossword puzzle, Nerves would stand there beside him and look down at the floor and sort of study it as if he were studying a speck of dirt or trying to read something that was written there.

Mr. Blank hated Nerves. He hated to come home from work after a tiring day and as soon as he walked in the door have Nerves there, imitating him.

"Why can't we have a normal dog?" Mr. Blank would say to Mrs. Blank. "I hate this dog. Look at him. He's making fun of me. Nerves! Be yourself! Develop a personality of your own! Leave me out of it!"

And Nerves would glare right back at him, doing a perfect imitation of him.

Then Mr. Blank would sit down with the paper in his chair and let out a big sigh and Nerves would get on the other chair and sigh too. A rat's sigh.

And after a while Mr. Blank would look up over his paper and say, "I hate you, Nerves."

And Nerves would show him his little teeth.

And sometimes when Mr. Blank would try to kiss Mrs. Blank or cuddle up to her while she was making the supper, Nerves would be right there beside them with his front paws around Mr. Blank's leg, kissing Mr. Blank's pants with his ratty little tongue.

And then maybe Mr. Blank, just so that he could relax and eat his supper in peace, would put Nerves outside. Then he'd sit down and start to eat and he'd lift up his fork with the spaghetti hanging from it and the fork would stop right about at his open mouth because he'd suddenly see Nerves, outside, staring at him through the window, licking his rodenty little chops and nodding his head as if he were saying, "Good, eh? Is it good? Is it? Is it good? Go ahead. Eat it. It's good! Is it good?"

"I hate that dog," Mr. Blank would say, "I want to take it to the Humane Society and have it executed."

"Oh, don't be silly dear," Mrs. Blank would say. "It's only a little dog."

Nerves was almost like a mirror.

Before I went into my unit, Nerves and I looked at each other for a minute. I tried out a silly sentence on him. I said this: "I think I like you, Fleurette Featherstone Fitchell," I said.

Nerves tucked in his chin and looked down at his foot, being very cute and shy.

What a dog.

4. PICNIC

The next morning across the parade square in Uplands Emergency Shelter, at the rec hall where the store was, I met her again. She was buying bologna, macaroni and stale bread.

So was I. Except I had to get some eggs and peanut butter too.

Fleurette Featherstone Fitchell said she never tasted peanut butter. I told her it was best if you toasted the stale bread and then spread the peanut butter on the toasted bread and then if you had some honey...

Then I realized I was making her feel rotten because she was so poor. But I also felt kind of good and big because I was so rich. Compared to her. Then I hated myself for being so mean. Feeling rich because of peanut butter.

"Did you used to live on Friel Street in Lowertown?" I asked.

"Yes," she said. "I'm glad we moved. I hated it there."

We were walking back across the parade square towards Unit Number Eight. Our building. Our home.

"Killer Bodnoff used to call it Feel Street," I said laughing a bit. Fleurette Featherstone Fitchell didn't say anything. She just looked straight ahead.

Beside Building Number Eight was Building Number Nine. Somebody else's home. Then Number Ten. Eight more families in there maybe lined up at their toilet. There were many many buildings all the same. All shaped like an H lying flat. In the bar of the H were the tubs and the toilet. In each arm and each leg of the H were two families. Each family had four rooms with walls separating them that didn't reach the ceiling. The four rooms were called units. In the right leg of the lying down H were units A and B. In the right arm of the H were units C and D. Units E and F were in the left leg. G and H in the left arm.

Fleurette Featherstone Fitchell's address was Building Number Eight, Unit H, around the back.

I looked and saw that her eyes were full of tears.

Our square building was bouncing closer to us as we walked across the parade square. The whole peanut butter business was stuck in my mind. Feeling rich over peanut butter. How stupid. And *Feel* Street.

"I hate that stuff about Feel Street," said Fleurette Featherstone Fitchell. "I knew they were going around saying that. I'm glad I moved. Nobody will talk about me here. Because *hardly* anybody knows me here." She looked right at me while we were walking. She looked at me so long that I had to look away. The word "hardly" stayed there in the air like it was printed in a comic book. I almost did a handstand to get away from her eyes but I couldn't because of the eggs and peanut butter and stuff that I was carrying.

You could tell it was going to be a hot day the way the sun was heating up the pavement of the square and the way the air was starting to shimmer, making Building Eight and the other buildings bend like rubber a little bit as they bounced toward us. It was a very big parade square and we walked together with our groceries for a long time without saying anything. Then I said a very smart, a very intelligent thing for a person whose mind was clogged up with peanut butter and rubber buildings.

"Would you like to go on a picnic?" I said.

"Yes," said Fleurette Featherstone Fitchell. "But only if you promise never, ever, to tell anybody about *Feel* Street. Never, ever."

I promised.

I left Mrs. O'Driscoll a note saying I was going to the sandpits for a picnic with my new neighbour. While I was writing the note I laughed to myself a bit imagining her reading it when she got home. She would say "Picnic!" out of the side of her mouth. "Picnic!" Then she would say "Sandpits!" out of an even tighter corner of her mouth.

I packed half a loaf of bread, a knife, a bottle opener, the peanut butter, a small jar of honey, some matches and a blanket.

I knocked on Fleurette Featherstone Fitchell's door and she opened it right away and came out and closed it right away. She didn't want me to look inside.

We walked out the gate and down the road along the edge of the airport and ran a few times to try and get right under the big planes as they came in for a landing flying low across the road so that you could almost reach up and touch them.

Then we went past the Ottawa Hunt and Golf Club parking lot with all the new cars shining in the sun and the golfers chunking their car doors shut and opening and shutting their trunks and walking with their clubs clinking in their squeaky leather bags and the men and women laughing and diamonds flashing.

Further down the road we turned left at Kelly's Inn, a crooked old shack of a store on the edge of the sandpits, and I bought two bottles of cream soda from the old man in there with the cigarette dangling and his torn undershirt.

And behind Kelly's Inn a way, we ducked through some trees lining the old road and suddenly, stretched before us, all the way down to the river, the sandpits. The first pit was huge and I ran down the steep sliding slope, part sideways, part sliding, part stumbling, part flying with huge steps, the sand giving and pouring around my ankles like brown sugar.

At the bottom I looked up at Fleurette Featherstone Fitchell, standing, watching me, her hands on her hips, at the top of the hot sand cliff. I put up my hand to shade my eyes from the sun. She looked about as tall as my thumb away up there.

She untied the white rag from her black curly long hair and started striding, leaping, jumping down the long steep sand toward me, her hair floating and flying and falling around her as she got bigger and bigger.

We climbed up the steep other side, sliding back half a step for every step we took. At the top we sat down in the hot sand to rest. There was a sand gulley that wove around the next two pits down to the Rideau River. It would be cool down there by the water under the trees.

"I want to learn to walk on my hands," she said, after we got our breath.

"Your fingers are like toes," I said. "You press them and lift them just like standing on your own feet to keep your balance. I'll show you when we get down to the river where the ground is harder."

On the shore by the river I collected some dead twigs and sticks and set up the fire ready for a match.

Then I showed her how to get up on her hands against a tree so she wouldn't fall over like all beginners do. You put your hands on the ground near the tree and put one foot in back of the other. You kick your back foot up and lean your shoulders forward and your legs float up over top of you. You keep your legs straight and your toes pointed. Your toenails rest against the tree and you're in your first handstand. Most people can't get up the first few times because they don't remember to lean their shoulders forward.

Fleurette Featherstone Fitchell got it the first time.

Her dress fell down over her and her hair hung down to the ground. All I could see of her was her legs. Her legs were straight and her toes were pointed. The top of her toes pressed against the tree. A perfect first try. She looked like a strange creature, feet-like hands, no head, and long straight white antennae with toes.

Her pants were frayed and raggedy.

"That was the best I've ever seen a beginner do," I said.

While she tried a few more times I put out the blanket, put the match to the fire and sliced two slices of stale bread. Then I got a couple of green sticks and held her slice over the fire until it was brown. Then the other side. While the bread was hot I spread it thick with peanut butter and then poured honey on the top. When I looked back at her she was sitting, leaning against the tree, watching me.

I gave her her first ever peanut-butter-and-honey-roasted-open-sandwich and went back and started to make my own. I peeked up and watched her. She started slowly, tasting. Then her bites got a little bigger and she started to eat around the outside, saving the best part, the middle, for the last. I was enjoying watching her so much I didn't realize that my toast was on fire.

After we ate two more and the fire went out I washed the knife off in the river and cleaned up the honey jar and threw the small hard crust of bread that was left to the fish.

"I'm sweltering," Fleurette Featherstone Fitchell said, "I'm going for a swim."

She reached behind under her hair and unbuttoned the back of her dress and pulled it over her head. Her undershirt had a big hole in the back and the bottom of it was in strings.

When she stood up out of the water with her wet hair she looked like a drowned rat. She didn't really but everybody always says that.

"Do I look like a drowned rat?" she said.

"No," I said. "You don't. You look like a girl who just came out of the water."

"Aren't you coming in?" she said. I was sitting on a log cooling off my feet.

"No," I said. "I'm not that hot."

Actually that was a lie.

I didn't want her to see my underwear.

It had holes in it.

On the way home I asked her if she liked the peanut butter and honey thing. I knew she did like it but I asked her anyway. A question I knew the answer to.

"Yes," she said.

Just yes.

Further up the road I asked her what happened to her mother's wrist.

"It was an accident," she said.

At home, in Building Eight, Fleurette went into her unit and I went into the toilet. When I came out I heard her door slam and a man with black hair and dark eyes came down the hall and left the building.

5. HELP WANTED

One morning in September, a few days before school started, I was going into Ottawa to spend the day looking for a part-time job so we could have some extra money for stuff I might need for school. Mrs. O'Driscoll was heading out to her new cleaning job at Glebe Collegiate Institute and we were on the Uplands bus together.

She was talking again about the prime minister's house on Laurier Avenue. It used to be Sir Wilfrid Laurier's house. Prime Minister King was living there now. She'd been there earlier in the summer applying for a cleaning job but she didn't get the job. But she couldn't stop talking about it.

"If only O'Driscoll could see that house," said Mrs. O'Driscoll about her drowned husband. "He'd just love that house. O'Driscoll always wanted to be rich you know. Rich was what he wanted. But how he'd ever be rich is beyond me. He never had two cents to rub together. That house is just full of mahogany and oak and rugs and gold and silver and paintings and fancy lights and…"

The bus was passing Mooney's Bay and we were starting to pick up some of the rich people on the way.

We, the poor people from Uplands, were already on the bus, taking up half of all the seats, when the rich people started to get on. They had to come down the aisle, past us, to find places to sit. Some of them tried to stay standing by the driver but he told them to move along and sit down. They had to come and sit beside one of us. They were putting half of their rear ends onto the seat and trying to balance the other halves on their legs in the aisle. Then they got tired and had to shift over a bit closer to us. But they still tried not to touch us and kept their heads in the aisle as much as possible and their noses pointed upwards so they wouldn't be breathing our air.

"…and lovely plush sofas," Mrs. O'Driscoll was saying, "and silk cushions and dark stained chairs and rugs all up and down the stairs and carved knobs on the railings and ceiling-high drapes on the leaded windows…"

The bus was rocking on down the road and causing the rich people a lot of trouble. They were squeezing their eyes shut and hanging tight to the seat bars.

At Hog's Back some more rich ones got on and tried to stay near the front but the driver told them to move down the aisle too. The bus was getting pretty crowded.

Hog's Back. Not a very nice name for a place for rich people to live. Some of the Uplands people were saying that the *next* stop should be called "Hog's Arse." They were saying it loud just to annoy the rich ones.

Mrs. O'Driscoll was still talking about the Prime Minister's house.

"…and three bathrooms and huge big cupboards full of fancy clothes and a big screened-in verandah all around the house with striped awnings all around and a beautiful garden and inside, oh, if O'Driscoll could only see it, inside there's beautiful woven tapestries on the walls and in the bedroom a huge white rug made from a bear with the head still on it and a carved four-poster bed with draw curtains all around..."

When we finally got to the Uplands Bus Terminal in Ottawa South the rich people were pretty well trapped. They couldn't get off first because there were piles of people, poor people, falling down the aisle and tumbling out the door and shoving and swearing and clawing their way out.

And they couldn't wait and get off last because the poor people from Uplands who had taken all the window seats wanted to get out and were crawling over the rich people or shoving them into the aisle. Once they were in the aisle it was too late. Everybody was touching the rich people now, putting their sticky hands on their nice coats, tromping all over their nice shiny shoes, breathing bad teeth right into their nice faces, bodies rubbing against their nice bodies, shoulders hitting shoulders, bony knees touching the backs of their nice fat legs.

They were in a panic as they at last got out of the smelly bus and some of them had wide eyes and others were whispering that they had to get a second car because they couldn't stand this any longer.

I walked Mrs. O'Driscoll up to the corner of Grove and Bank Street and waited until her streetcar came to take her to her job. Then I walked up the west side of Bank Street looking for good places to ask for a job. I tried a few drug stores that needed delivery boys but you had to have your own bicycle and that left me out.

I went into the Avalon Theatre but they didn't need any ushers who couldn't afford to buy their own uniforms.

I went into a little restaurant called the Mirror Grill but they already had a dishwasher. The man who smoked a big cigar there, joked with me and bought me a free coke.

I was in the district they called the Glebe and there was a whole lot of Bank Street to go before I got all the way to the Parliament Buildings where it ended. If I stayed on Bank Street I thought I'd get a job for sure.

But I didn't stay. I turned.

I don't know what made me do it, but I turned left off Bank Street and started down First Avenue. The street was cool in the shade of the overhanging trees and it was quiet and cosy, everybody with their own house and their own verandah and their own lawn and their own laneway and balconies and flowers and garages and backyards. And the people seemed so happy fussing with their kids or reading on their verandahs or snipping away at their flower gardens or dragging a hose up the laneway or shining their cars.

And neighbours chatting politely with each other or waving across the street and laughing. And the breadman talking with the maid on the verandah, the breadman with his basket strapped around his neck, his hands resting in the basket. And the smell of the groceries in the back of Devine's green delivery truck, the delivery man whistling, carrying the groceries up to the lady.

And the freshly cut lawns that smelled like the greens at the Ottawa Hunt and Golf Club.

And further down First Avenue the big square red quiet building with the high steps, Carleton College.

And then further, the biggest building on the street. Glebe Collegiate Institute, where Mrs. O'Driscoll was inside, cleaning, and where I would soon go to school.

I passed the school and the huge schoolyard, a block long, and crossed Bronson Avenue down Carling Avenue hill to Preston Street.

I turned right on Preston Street and tried a store and a bakery but they didn't need anybody—at least I think that's what they said because it was in Italian. I tried the Pure Spring soft drink company but the man there asked me how much I weighed. I wasn't heavy enough to work there. He was a huge man and it would be a hundred years before I weighed as much as he did.

"Put on some pounds and come back and see us," he said, and gave out a big laugh that just about blew me out the door.

Further down Preston Street I saw a church with a sign that said Lutheran and some other things on it. In Lowertown it was mostly Catholic churches and synagogues. I had never heard of a Lutheran church before.

I turned off Preston and went right on Somerset Street. Half way up the hill I went into a pool hall that had a Help Wanted sign in the window. A French kid about my age was dusting the lampshades over a table.

I thought I recognized him from Lowertown. I think his name was CoCo.

"You're too late, my fren'. I jus' got de job one hour ago! Tough luck, eh?"

Further up Somerset I saw a sign in the window of the Cinderella Book Store. "Student Wanted—part time." A feeling of excitement came over me. My heart started to beat faster. I looked in the window for a while pretending I was looking at the books there. I was really looking at my reflection, thinking about what I was going to say. I had a feeling I was going to get this job.

The man inside had thick glasses and hardly any face. He had a face all right, but it was so round and big and flabby that you could hardly see where his nose and his mouth started and where his cheeks ended. It seemed like a blur. And his glasses were so thick you couldn't see his eyes at all. He seemed like a kind man and he spoke in a soft, understanding voice.

We talked about what experience I had working in book stores, which I lied about, the books I'd read, which I didn't lie about.

Then he took out an application form and got my name.

"Hubbo?" he said.

"Actually, it's Hulbert," I said.

"I bet when you were small you couldn't say Hulbert so you said Hubbo and then everybody started calling you Hubbo," he said.

I wondered how he knew that.

My address. Uplands Emergency Shelter, Building Eight, Unit B.

He looked at me a long time after he wrote it down.

Phone? No phone. He drew a dash in the space and looked at me a long time again. My feeling of excitement was gone. I was now feeling nervous. I couldn't think straight. There was panic in me.

Religion? Religion. My mind was a blank. His face was looking like a pudding. If I could only see his eyes. I was trying to think of a religion that he would like. He didn't like the address. He didn't like the blank phone number. He probably knew I lied about my age. I had no experience working in book stores. I had to please him. I concentrated so hard trying to think of a good religion, one that he'd like. I could feel my face getting red. I felt like I was sitting on the toilet.

Then it came to me. The church I had seen down on Preston Street. Maybe that was the church he went to. It was in his part of Ottawa. The sign came up in my imagination in front of me. It was a bit blurry but I thought I could see it. I would try it. I would tell him that was my religion.

"Lithuanian!" I said. I felt like I was on a radio quiz program and I just got the grand prize question. I could hear the bells going and the applause.

Lithuanian.

A Lithuanian is a guy from a country somewhere in Europe called Lithuania.

No wonder he said thank-you but that he didn't think he needed anybody right now.

I was all the way down to the corner of Somerset and Bank Street when I realized how stupid he must have thought I was.

I didn't blame him.

I wouldn't hire me either if I acted like that.

The rest of that side of Bank Street took me until noon. I listened to the big clock on the Peace Tower gong twelve times and then I walked out on Nepean Point to watch the Ottawa River from away up high. The tug boats working the logs down there looked like toys and the logs looked like matchsticks. I was feeling pretty lonesome and small so I went up to the statue of Champlain Holding His Astrolab and sat down at his feet and ate the lunch Mrs. O'Driscoll had made for me. Like I told Mrs. O'Driscoll later, I lunched with Sam Champlain. He's pretty good company for lunch, especially if you're feeling lonesome and small.

After lunch with Sam I worked my way all the way down the other side of Bank Street, asking in about a hundred places for a part-time job. By the time I got back down to Ottawa South and the Uplands Bus Terminal I was pretty discouraged.

Nobody wanted to hire me.

It was six o'clock and the bus terminal was pretty crowded. Soon I spotted Mrs. O'Driscoll pushing her way through the crowd towards me.

There were about fifteen rich people standing near the door of the bus terminal, trying to keep as far away from us poor people as they could. They had on their nice suits and good shoes and fancy hats and even summer gloves some of them. When I first went in the bus terminal and walked by where they were standing I could smell their perfume and the newness and the richness of their clothes and the leather of some of their purses.

They stood near the door so that when the bus came they could get on first, sit together near the front, and then get off at their rich houses first, without having to pass by or go near the rest of us. They were very quiet and they seemed to stare straight ahead. Now and then, if they said anything to each other, they said it in a kind of whisper through their teeth and without moving their lips very much or turning to look at each other with their eyes. It looked like what they said was really important.

And if they had parcels or bags or purses they hung onto them and hugged them to their bodies as tight as they could, and they stood with their feet tight together so that they took up as little room in the bus terminal as possible.

Mrs. O'Driscoll was telling me more about Prime Minister King's house.

"...and he's got a nice big painting of his mother up on the third floor in his study. He's got a light lit in front of it at all times—night and day. The lady in the painting is very beautiful. They say he talks to the painting sometimes. He talks to the picture of his mother. He calls her my lovely mother....And his dog Pat. They say he talks to him too. It's a terrier. Cute little thing. Sometimes he talks to his mother about Pat. Sometimes he'll say, Mother, Pat and I think this or Pat and I think that....And they say he visits with dead people at night. They sit around a table in the dark and he talks to dead President Roosevelt and dead Sir Wilfrid and his dead grandaddy the Lyon. And they told me that an old lady sometimes comes over in the middle of the night with a silver trumpet and voices of the dead speak through the trumpet....O'Driscoll would say that he's crazier than a bag of hammers but who's to know these days...."

On the bus some of the poor people were drunk and laughing very loud and throwing bottles out the windows onto the highway. Some of the women were screaming and fighting with other women and everybody was lighting up cigarettes.

Then the driver said to put out those cigarettes, there is no smoking on the bus, and then everything got very quiet but the cigarettes didn't go out and the rich people in the front of the bus sank down in their seats because they were afraid of what was coming and the driver said again to put out those cigarettes and there was some giggling from some of the women and then some man in a big deep rough voice full of gravel and phlegm said, "Come back here and make me!"

By this time the driver had stopped the bus in the middle of the highway and the rich people were saying oh please and the driver took up a bat from under his seat and went back to the back of the bus and there was an olympic swearing contest and I heard two or three whacks and a lot of screaming and clothes ripping and the rich people at the front were saying oh my god and the driver went back to his seat, wiped the juice off of his bat, checked his mirror to straighten his tie, and started the bus moving again along the highway until he stopped a few times to let the rich people off at their stops.

And the poor people were saying to them as they got off, "Goodnight now, and do have an *awfully* lovely eveninggggg!" and then they added some long dirty names that even Mrs. O'Driscoll had never heard before.

"I wish we were rich," I said to Mrs. O'Driscoll when things quietened down a bit.

"What on earth for?" said Mrs. O'Driscoll, out of the corner of her mouth. "This is fun!"

Then she looked at me and got a warm soft look on her face.

"You had a disappointing day, didn't you, Hubbo, my boy," she said.

"I guess so," I said.

"Well," said Mrs. O'Driscoll, "Maybe you *will* be rich someday. But I'm telling you, if you care too much about it, you won't be any happier than you are now."

6. BETRAYED AT THE GLEBE COLLEGIATE INSTITUTE

On the Uplands bus on our way to our first day at school one of the Uplands kids who smoked pushed a lit cigarette into a rich kid's sandwich in her lunch box when she wasn't looking. There was some crying and complaining and some of the older kids at the back were doing volcano burps just to make the people getting on at Mooney's Bay and Hog's Back more disgusted.

We got off the bus at the terminal in Ottawa South and were pretty excited as we walked up Bank Street and over the Bank Street Bridge. We stopped at the top of the bridge and leaned over to look down at the Rideau Canal and the cars on the driveway running along beside it. It was a beautiful September day, the morning sun making diamonds on the water down the canal a bit, and some early fallen leaves floating. The canal was curved away up towards Bronson Bridge one way, lined with trees hanging over and beautiful houses half showing behind them. The other way it curved down past Lansdowne Park and around towards the Parliament Buildings that you couldn't see. The football grandstand made a long shadow across the grass in the sun and the green wooden fence around the field looked shiny because of some of the light.

A boy named Denny, who was covered with pimples, and I and Fleurette walked together down the rest of the bridge while the other kids from Uplands came behind us in small groups.

The rich kids were ahead of us in one big group.

Denny and Fleurette and I walked up Bank Street past the Exhibition Grounds and the Avenues and turned left on First Avenue. We strolled down First, looking at the beautiful lawns and the trees and the fancy houses with the big verandahs and the windows with the fat cats sunning themselves and the shiny cars in the laneways.

At the school there was a big crowd of kids standing around waiting for the doors to open. Somebody told Fleurette that the High School of Commerce was at the other end, a long block away, and I said I'd see her later.

I walked up the sloping driveway to look at the front entrance. I stood back and looked at the wide steps and the huge doors. Above the doors carved in stone was a giant shield and a hand holding a flaming torch. There were words underneath.

Alere Flammam.

I walked up the steps and turned around with my back to the doors.

A feeling of excitement and great power filled me. I could feel the building behind me. Solid. Important.

I wondered what *Alere Flammam* meant.

I was alone. Everybody else was down the sloping driveway standing around on First Avenue. Many of them were looking up at me alone at the top of the wide steps. Some were pointing. For a minute I felt like an emperor, standing on the great entrance to my palace, surveying my subjects.

I put my hands down on the cool concrete and kicked up into a perfect stand.

I could hear the hooting and whistling from the crowd. I jammed my pointed toes together and secretly pressed and released my fingers on the concrete to keep my balance. I was still as a statue. Somewhere, way above me, was the shield and the flame. My eyes were on a leaf lying on the bottom step below me. I didn't dare look anywhere else in case I'd ruin my handstand. It was perfect. I could have held it for hours.

Suddenly something was wrong. The noise the crowd was making had changed. They weren't hooting and whistling and clapping any more. They were saying something else.

Then I heard a big door click shut and I felt someone behind me. Then my hair was grabbed and the back of my shirt. I was lifted right off my hands and the leaf disappeared and the trees spun around and the cement flame flew over like a great bird and I was in the air and then on my back at the bottom of the steps.

At the top I could see shoes and pants and hands hanging and a red floppy face and lips snarling.

"You jackass! Out of bounds! You bums will follow the rules around here! Right from the start! Out of bounds! Jackass!"

It was the vice-principal.

A while later, everybody went into the school.

After a few speeches in the auditorium and some Home Room teacher business, some older students came around and told us about some of the clubs we could join. And some of the teams we could try out for. One team I was interested in was the gymnastics team. Then a very handsome senior student came in and told us he was president of the Boys' Hi-Y. He had on beautiful clothes and his smile was happy and his teeth were white and even. He invited anyone who was interested to join his Hi-Y Club. A very special club.

After they gave us our lockers and we signed some forms we went down to the cafeteria and got our books issued to us. While they were issuing the books the teacher in charge read out a list of names of people who hadn't paid their class fees. Those people had to get out of line and wait until the end.

There were two names on the list.

Denny Dingle, the boy we walked to school with.

And Hulbert O'Driscoll.

We didn't know anything about these class fees.

While we were waiting we walked down the basement hall where our lockers were. Near my locker was a little shop that sold chocolate bars, school supplies, gym socks and stuff.

Serving behind the little counter was the handsome Hi-Y guy who had given us the talk about the special club. The sign over the counter said, "Tuck Shop."

Back in the cafeteria just about everybody was gone.

"There's a special form you fill out if you have no money to pay your fees," the teacher told us.

Denny Dingle and I signed the forms and got our books. *Junior Science for Secondary Schools*; *General Math Book I*; *Building the Canadian Nation*; *Good Health*; *Cours Premier de Français*; *Junior Guidance for Today*; *The Merchant of Venice*; *A Book of Good Stories*.

Back down around the Tuck Shop I was standing by my open locker putting my books in and I saw Mrs. O'Driscoll coming towards me down the hall with a mop and a pail. The pail was on wheels and the mop was stuck in it and she was pushing the pail along like it was a funny-looking round dog on a wooden leash. She had on a light blue charlady's dress, with wet stains on it, rubber gloves and a rag tied around her hair. There were two boys walking behind her, imitating her.

I was going to step out from behind my locker door and talk to her, but suddenly I didn't.

Instead, I slipped along the lockers to where the Tuck Shop was, and I leaned over the little counter pretending to ask the price of some pencil sets and math sets there. When I was sure she had gone by I went back and closed my locker.

The first day of school was very short and by noon we were finished and I met Fleurette outside.

We decided to show each other our new schools. Fleurette's school and my school were attached. They didn't look attached though. They looked like one huge building. I showed Fleurette the big wide steps and the wide cement railings that were big enough to put statues on. I told her what had happened about the handstand and how the vice-principal pushed me down the stairs.

"Why did he do that?" she said. She had her eyes open wide and they were turning black.

"I don't know," I said.

"He shouldn't have done that," she said, with a tight look on her face. I was sorry I told her about it because it seemed to scare her so much.

"Did he hurt you?" she said, searching my face with her eyes.

"No, it was nothing," I said. "How could he hurt me? Nobody can hurt me." Then I showed her the shield and the torch and the words carved underneath and then we went in one of the six heavy doors tall enough to fit giants, and inside the doors the smooth, wide marble steps and the gold railings going up to the huge lobby outside the assembly hall, with the curved ceilings carved and coming down like cement cloth to the tall fat pillars.

"Are you sure he didn't hurt you?" Fleurette said. She didn't seem to be paying much attention to what I was showing her.

Leaning against one of the pillars was a tall boy by himself who was watching us.

I showed Fleurette the two shields carved in iron on the wall with the names of all the students from Glebe Collegiate Institute who were dead because of the First World War and the Second World War. I looked back at the pillar and the boy was gone. I showed Fleurette the oak case with the glass top with the holy-looking book open in there, with the wide purple ribbon bookmark in it and the fancy lists of the names of the dead with the capital letters drawn with gargoyles and animals and vines and flowers and cherubs and angels peeking out. I wondered what it would be like to have your name in that book for everybody to see.

"Wouldn't you have to be dead first?" Fleurette said.

I felt like somebody was watching us. I looked over and the tall boy was behind another one of the pillars, peeking around. He was very skinny and had flat black hair with grease on it. His ears stuck out quite a bit and his face was long and pointed like a fox.

"Wouldn't you have to be dead first?" Fleurette said again.

"Let's go over to your school," I said.

"Why?" she said, "there's nothing to see there."

"I want to. Come on," I said.

We walked up the long block to the entrance of the High School of Commerce. It had ordinary doors, ordinary steps, small cement railings that maybe one person could sit on. Inside, there was a little sign carved in the wall saying when the school opened.

While we were reading the wall the guy with a face like a fox came up behind us and pretended to read it too. He had skinny arms with black hair on them and bony hands with long fingernails. His eyebrows were black and really thick and they joined in the middle over his nose.

Then we left and walked down to Ottawa South to get the Uplands bus. Denny Dingle was there.

Fleurette Featherstone Fitchell was telling Denny and me about how nice it was at the High School of Commerce and how everybody was excited about meeting everybody and about how pleasant and kind all the teachers were.

I told her how rotten I felt when they made us get out of line and sign a special paper before we got our books. Denny just laughed and pulled fifty cents out of his pocket.

"If they want to pay for us, let them pay," he said. Then he asked us if we wanted to get off at Kelly's Inn near the sandpits and he'd treat us. The way he talked he didn't seem to care about what they thought about him at the school.

We got off the bus and went into Kelly's Inn on the highway and Denny bought us a bottle of Kik and some chips with ketchup and vinegar and lots of salt.

While Denny was lashing more salt on his chips he asked us if we wanted to go over to his place down the road. We could meet his whole family, especially his sister. His sister was twenty years old and was married to a guy and had a baby who was not even one year old. Denny was saying he was trying to teach the baby to say "Uncle Denny." It was hard to believe that Denny was somebody's uncle.

How could somebody who was so skinny and who had so many pimples be somebody's uncle?

His house was in some trees in a gully and looked like it would fall down if you touched it. "We're not rich enough to live in Uplands Emergency Shelter," he said, laughing.

When we went in they were all sitting around the room sipping lemonade. Out the window you could see the sandpits in the distance.

Denny introduced me first to the baby who was asleep in a basket. "This is the baby," he said. "She is no year's old and her name is Doris." The baby had almost no hair and one of her little fists was stuck up in the air.

"And this is the baby's mother," said Denny. "She's twenty years old and her name is Doris." Doris looked just like Denny only she wasn't skinny and she didn't have any pimples and she was beautiful.

"And this is the baby's grandmother. She's forty years old and *her* name is Doris." This Doris looked just like the last Doris except her face was a little fatter and her hair was starting to go grey. She looked pretty proud of her son Denny—of how smooth an introducer he was.

"And this is the baby's great-grandmother. She's sixty years old and guess what? *Her* name is Doris." Doris had grey hair and was knitting. She made a sweet smile.

"And this is the baby's great-*great*-grandmother. She is eighty years old and her name is, of course, *Doris!*" Doris was rocking and sipping lemonade. Her hair was snow white. She laughed. She was enjoying the introductions.

"And this is the baby's great-great-*great*-grandmother. She is one hundred years old and she's the greatest Doris of them all!"

The oldest Doris was humped over in a little chair in the corner with a blanket around her, sipping her lemonade through a straw. She nodded at me. She had hardly any hair at all. She stuck her hard little fist in the air as if she had just won a big boxing match.

We all had some lemonade and then the baby woke up and Denny tried to make little Doris say "Uncle Denny" a few times but she wouldn't. She just smiled and blew some bubbles at him, and then we left.

We left all the Dorises and their lemonade and walked home past the Golf Club and the airplane runways to Building Number Eight, where we were richer than Denny and all the Dorises. Fleurette Featherstone Fitchell and I talked and laughed about how funny Denny and all the Dorises were, but Fleurette didn't know I was doing two things at once. I was laughing, but inside I felt sad and scared.

Sad and scared because of what I did to Mrs. O'Driscoll near my locker that day.

Outside Fleurette's door I said goodbye to her and sort of hung around to see if she'd invite me in.

She always seemed different when she was around her door. She opened it and slipped in so that I couldn't see anything. But for just a second I saw her mother at the kitchen table with her head down on her arms.

7. JOB!

In science, the guy sitting beside me at my table was the skinny guy with the black flat hair and the one eyebrow who was spying on Fleurette and me the day before. He told me that he was getting some special grade nine guys to join a club called the Junior Boys' Hi-Y. He said it was a very special club. He said that his older brother was the president of the Senior Boys' Hi-Y and that someday *he* would take his brother's place and be the president. His name was Doug. Then he asked me who the girl was I was hanging around with. What was her name? Was she my girlfriend? Then he showed me some other guys around the room who he might get into the special club.

"It's a very special club," he said. "And it's hard to get into. People who get into it become successes in later life," he said. "I could maybe get you in if you wanted." I was trying to figure out why he was being so nice to me.

In fact, I was trying to figure out almost everything about school.

It all seemed pretty confusing. In history we were studying our book, *Building the Canadian Nation*. Our history teacher read out how Henry Hudson was put in a little boat with his son and how the mutineers pushed the little rowboat out into the icy water and how they sailed away, and how Henry Hudson and his son were never seen again.

And all the way home on the Uplands bus I kept thinking about what Henry Hudson and his son talked about as they rowed and floated along looking for shore and hoping they'd maybe find a way to live somehow in the cold in Canada.

Denny Dingle told me to quit worrying about it.

Fleurette said she thought it was nice that I would worry about something like that.

And I kept thinking about how awful it would have been if they didn't say anything to each other. But that couldn't be. They must have said stuff to each other. They must have given up rowing after a while and the father must have asked the son if he was cold and if he wanted a drink of water and the son must have come up to the middle seat in the boat and sat inside the father's coat to keep warm. There was a picture of them in the book.

And they must have gone to sleep that way.

Saying things to each other.

Denny kept getting A's on his tests. I was getting D's and F's.

"All you have to do is remember the dates," Denny said, "never mind that other stuff."

And in history the teacher made us read about Canada and its native peoples.

He told us that the native Canadians had no animals except dogs. There were no horses, cows, pigs or sheep. The white man brought all those animals over with him and gave them to the Indians.

"They had animals," Denny said, "but they were all wild. It's common sense."

We read in the book how the Canadian Indians lived from hand to mouth and from place to place. And how some other Indians lived in a "longhouse" the book said. The longhouse was made of a wood frame covered with bark, and was divided on each side into several cubicles, each occupied by a family, while down the centre ran a common passageway in which the fires were built.

It was sort of like where I lived except for the bark and the fires.

Another A for Denny and an F for me.

And the Hi-Y guys all laughed when the teacher made us read in the book how the Indians never invented the wheel. Everybody else had the wheel. Everybody except the caveman. And he was pretty well just a monkey.

And then we tried to have a discussion.

"And now we'll have a discussion about that," the teacher said.

And a Hi-Y guy got up and said that he thought that because the Indians didn't invent the wheel they were the stupidest people on the planet Earth. They were very unsuccessful.

"And what do you have to say about that, Lawrence?" the teacher said to Broken Arrow, an Indian kid who sat at the back who was from Maniwaki with his big dark face.

"They had water and canoes. They didn't need wheels," said Broken Arrow.

And all the Hi-Y guys and the Welfare Club girls laughed and giggled and whispered things about Broken Arrow and the teacher stamped his foot and said that will be enough of that.

And the discussion was over.

That's the way all the history discussions wound up.

"That will be enough of that!"

And I kept wondering how these guys got to be Hi-Y guys so fast. They were new at the school, just like I was.

And Denny Dingle just laughed and told me to quit worrying about it.

We weren't allowed to go over to the Commerce side of the school between classes or at lunchtime so at noon I'd eat my lunch fast just standing around my locker and around the Tuck Shop and then I'd go down to the corner of Bronson and Carling and meet Fleurette and we'd walk around the block together a few times until the bell rang.

And in guidance we had a guidance book where there were a whole lot of questions and answers with little drawings beside them. One question was about applying for a job. It asked if you would apply for a job this way (a) or this way (b). Under (a) there was a picture of a guy applying for a job sitting in a chair in front of some big shot's desk. The big shot was there with his two phones and his pen set and his photograph of his family and his face, very interested, looking at the younger guy in the chair. The younger guy who was applying for the job was sitting up very straight with his legs crossed and his hands folded in his lap and his pants all pressed just like knives and his shoes shining with little windows of shininess in each one and his tie up nice and neat and straight and his suit jacket buttoned and his hair all slicked back and a big smile on him, but somebody had inked in his teeth and crossed his eyes. He looked like the guy who ran the Tuck Shop except for the inked-in part.

Under (b) it showed the same big shot at the same desk but this time with a really disgusted look on his face like he had just swallowed a piece of rotten fish or something. The younger guy who was applying for the job wasn't in the other chair, he was sitting on the big shot's desk. He had pushed over the pen set and the family picture to make room for himself and he was leaning over breathing in the big shot's face. His hair was all knotted and ratty and his face was dirty-looking and there was spray coming out between his scummy-looking teeth. He had on a tight T-shirt and you could see the hair sticking out from under his arms. His pants were filthy and the bottoms were in rags and his shoes were turned up at the toes and scuffed and untied. There were mud marks on the floor where he had walked in mud or something worse. There were little squiggly lines coming up from each footprint.

Was the answer (a) or (b)?

These were the kind of questions we got to answer in our guidance book.

You were supposed to pick which was the best way to apply for a job. Very confusing. Did this have something to do with why I didn't get all those jobs I applied for?

And most days after school I'd meet Fleurette and Denny and we'd walk down to the Uplands bus and talk and laugh about school. And Fleurette would try to help me figure out some of these confusing things about school and some of the subjects we took.

The thing I didn't tell them was this: that there was one thing I had figured out perfectly about school, and that was how not to see, ever to see, Mrs. O'Driscoll. I knew exactly where she'd be every minute of the day, and I was always somewhere else.

And in science we always seemed to be taking the grasshopper.

The Hi-Y guys had more fun there than anywhere.

One day they had a bushel basket of leaves tied out the window. Every time Mr. Tool, our science teacher, turned around to draw another tibia or a mandible on the grasshopper one of the Hi-Y guys closest to the window jumped up and grabbed a handful of leaves out of the basket and fired them up in the air over the class and then sat down and buried his head in his grasshopper drawing. Mr. Tool turned around again just in time to see the last few leaves falling.

"Where are those leaves coming from?" Mr. Tool asked.

"Probably blew in the window," the Hi-Y guys said.

"How can they blow in the third floor window, boys? Leaves don't fly around at this altitude."

"Must have been a hurricane or something," the Hi-Y guys said.

While all this was going on I had a little chat with Doug, the big shot in the Junior Hi-Y, who shared my table with me. His hand on my arm was cold and clammy and his eyebrow was moving up and down like a window blind.

"Why don't you put your name in to join the Junior Hi-Y?" said Doug.

"What *is* the Hi-Y, anyway?" I said. I wanted to hear him explain it some more.

"It's a very special club. We have meetings every Thursday night at the downtown YMCA and we organize a big dance once a year and executives get to sit on the stage sometimes to welcome important visitors to the school during assemblies. We also get trips. Last year the Senior Hi-Y went to New York City to the United Nations to encourage peace among all nations in this world of ours. The president and the vice-president get their pictures in the paper every year. Many former Hi-Y members are now big successes in the world. You have to be all-round to join. Are you all-round?"

"All-round what?" I said.

"All-round. You know. Be on a team and also get pretty good marks. And fool around a bit. Not be a goody-goody."

More leaves were floating down and Mr. Tool was looking at the ceiling to see where they were coming from.

"Here's an application form. Fill it out and I'll hand it in," said Doug. Then he said, "How's your girlfriend?"

I looked at the application form while leaves floated down to the floor.

NAME:

ADDRESS:

PHONE NUMBER:

AMBITION:

EXPERIENCE IN CLUBS:

AWARDS:

TEAMS:

FATHER'S OCCUPATION:

MAKE AND YEAR OF FATHER'S CAR:

RELIGION:

While I was looking at the application I noticed somebody at the classroom door. It was Chubby, the principal of Glebe Collegiate. He leaned in and asked Mr. Tool if there was an O'Driscoll boy in the class.

I went to the door and out into the hall and Chubby, who was puffing deep and hard, told me about a job that I could have. I wondered how he would even know my name. Chubby was a fat man with a wrinkly suit that seemed too small for him and he leaned hard on a cane. So hard that his knuckles were white.

"I have a part-time job for you O'Driscoll, if you want it. Two nights a week. You stay overnight at an elderly lady's house so she won't be alone. That's the two nights her nurse takes a holiday. Tuesday and Thursday. Every Tuesday and Thursday you go over after school and sleep over. She's old and sick. She needs somebody with her. She gets scared by herself."

"Why do I get to get the job?" I said to Chubby, hoping he'd get his breath.

Chubby looked right in my eyes and puffed a few times. Then his voice changed a little bit and he said, "I picked your name out of a hat."

For a minute I had a funny feeling that he was lying. Then I forgot about it.

"You get five dollars a night. She'll give it to you each morning before you leave."

Five dollars!

After he gave me the lady's name and the address I went back in the room and sat down and looked at it.

Miss L. Collar-Cuff,
210 Easy Avenue, Ottawa.

It was about two blocks from the school.

One of the richest streets in Ottawa.

Leaves were floating down in the room and Doug was squatting on our table pretending he was a grasshopper.

After school that day I tried out for the gym team. It was quite late when I got to the bus and for the first time I went home without Fleurette or Denny.

I sat in the empty seat beside one of my neighbours, Mr. Yasso.

Everybody called him that because that's just about all he ever said. If you met him in the hall or in the lineup for the toilet and you said, "Nice day," he'd say "Yeah, so?"

Mr. Yasso was a garbageman in Ottawa.

On the Uplands bus at night nobody wanted to sit with him because he was such a rotten conversationalist. And also he smelled like he had garbage in all of his pockets.

Mrs. O'Driscoll didn't like him. She would maybe be out in the hall at the tubs doing a washing and Mr. Yasso would be standing there. He often stood around there, leaning against the tubs or against the wall or looking out the window at the boy with no brain sitting out there.

"That poor child just sits there, day after day," Mrs. O'Driscoll might say, trying to make conversation.

"Yeah, so?" Mr. Yasso would say.

"Why does Mr. Yasso stand around out in the hall so much?" I said one time to Mrs. O'Driscoll. "He seems to be out there all the time."

"He's out there because he likes to talk to everybody. He's such a wonderful conversationalist," Mrs. O'Driscoll said out of the corner of her mouth. "He drives me crazy!"

"Yeah, so?" I said, making a little joke.

I sat down beside him on the bus.

He smelled pretty awful, but I tried to start a conversation with him because, after all, he lived in the same building I did. A conversation is two people speaking to each other. You take turns listening to the other person. You try to help the other person out so that you can each say things back and forward for a while. That way you can find out about each other, learn some things, maybe even have some fun.

On the bus I tried to start a conversation with Mr. Yasso.

"I'm coming home pretty late today because I'm trying out for the gym team at school," I said.

"Yeah, so?" said Mr. Yasso.

Although I was dying to tell somebody about my new job with Miss Collar-Cuff on Easy Avenue, I didn't bother even trying with Mr. Yasso.

8. LIGHT THE LIGHT

Just as I got in the back door of our building I saw a big man with red hair leaving Fleurette's place. He closed the door quietly. Then the hall was empty. At the other end there was a horrible noise coming from behind Mrs. Quirk's door where she lived with the boy with no brain. A sound I'd never heard from there before. A sort of snoring. I put my hand on her door to feel the vibrations. The door wasn't shaking but I could feel it trembling as I rested my hand lightly on it.

Fleurette was at our place and Mrs. O'Driscoll told us all about it as I looked in the pot she had on the stove. She was boiling some chicken and potatoes. I would wait until we sat down to eat to tell her about my job.

"Mrs. Quirk moved out late last night. Her poor child went into a kind of a coma and some people came in a truck and took her and her child and her stuff away in the quiet of the night. Mrs. Blank told me all about it today when I got home from work. And about an hour later, no more, no less, another family moved in. A wife and her man. Mr. and Mrs. Stentorian. That's him you hear snoring out there. They were living in a tent, can you imagine, waiting for a vacancy out here! And it being November! That poor woman. Listen to that! If O'Driscoll could only hear that. You know, I don't think he's drowned at all. He's out there somewhere! I wonder what he'd say about this man Stentorian and his snoring!"

She was piling chicken and potatoes on a plate for me. And talking away. Fleurette said she had to go and I went out in the hall with her and asked her who the man was who was at her place.

"I don't know," she said, and walked down the hall to her door.

When I went back in, Mrs. O'Driscoll was still talking.

"And Mrs. Blank told me that Mrs. Stentorian told her that in that tent where they were living he snored so bad one night that some of the people in the other tents around got together and called the police. Can you imagine? Calling the police for snoring. Isn't that a good one? O'Driscoll would like that one!" She was using the corner of her mouth when she mentioned O'Driscoll.

While I was eating, I told Mrs. O'Driscoll about my new job minding Miss Collar-Cuff on Easy Avenue.

"That's one fancy street, Hubbo, my boy," said Mrs. O'Driscoll. "Isn't that grand now! A job on Easy Avenue! Well, you'll do well by her. You're a nice boy and you're a thoughtful boy. Every Tuesday and Thursday is it? That's tomorrow! You'll have to have a set of pajamas or a nightshirt or something for going to bed. I know! I've got the very thing! One of O'Driscoll's nightshirts. I didn't have the heart to throw it out. I'll cut some off the bottom and hem it up and wash and starch it for you. You'll be slick as a button!"

While I finished the chicken and potatoes, Mrs. O'Driscoll got out the nightshirt and the scissors and the needle and thread.

"Now this job you got calls for a celebration. I've got a nice surprise for you. Chubby gave us all a nice gift today with our pay cheques because we did such a good job keeping his school clean for him. He's a grand man, so thoughtful and kind. And him with that pain that he's always in. My gift was this beautiful bottle of sherry!"

Mrs. O'Driscoll got out two glasses, one for me and one for her, and poured us each some sherry.

"Now I'd imagine, I might be wrong, but I'd imagine this is the first time you've ever had a drink of anything like this. Taste it. You'll like it. And here's to your new job. Imagine! Easy Avenue! Won't you be the fancy one every Tuesday and Thursday!"

I sipped the sherry. It was sweet and warm down my throat.

Mrs. O'Driscoll took a gulp of hers and sang a little song that she sometimes sang.

Pack up all my care and woe.
Here I go, singin' low.
Bye, bye, blackbird!
Where somebody waits for me,
Sugar's sweet, so is she.
Bye, bye, blackbird!
No one here can love and understand me.
Oh what hard luck stories they all hand me.
Make my bed, light the light.
I'll arrive, late tonight.
Black Birrrrd,
Bye, bye!

Then she wiped her eyes with O'Driscoll's nightshirt.

"O'Driscoll and I would sing that whenever we'd have a little nip together. Oh, he was a nice fella. I don't think he's drowned at all, you know!"

Mrs. O'Driscoll poured some more sherry.

While she was cutting off the nightshirt I started telling her about school and Chubby and the Hi-Y boys and how confusing some of my subjects were and guidance and science and history.

"It's grand that you're going to a fine school, my boy. Learning all those things about history and science will make you happy in the long run, no question about it! And that Chubby, what a grand man he is. I'm sure he's the one got you that job over on Easy Avenue. He had a long chat with me when I first went there to work in the summer. He knew you'd appreciate his help. He knows all about O'Driscoll and you and your parents and where we live and everything about us. What a grand man. I'm sure he's the one!

Pack up all my care and woe.
Here I go,
singing low.
Bye, bye, Blackbird!

"Tell me some more about school, Hubbo, my boy!"

Mrs. O'Driscoll poured some more sherry.

I told her all about our English class and how we were reading a story in our *Book of Good Stories* called "How Much Land Does A Man Need?" by Leo Tolstoy. In the story a man is offered, for a cheap price, all the land that he can circle around on foot in one day. He can leave at sunrise and go as far as he likes in a big circle and when he comes back to the same spot at sunset, all the land he has walked around will be his. If he doesn't get back by sunset he'll lose his deposit. Of course, the man wants so much that he starts running and although he gets back at sunset just in time, he is so exhausted he dies. So they bury him right there and that's all the land he needs. Six feet for his grave.

"Ain't it the truth!" said Mrs. O'Driscoll, and banged the table.

"I've read that story and I've read other stuff by Leo Tolstoy—a great, wise man he was! Do you remember in the story, the blood that came out of his mouth just before he died? That's a little more than exhausted."

"The teacher said 'exhausted'," I said quietly, but I guess I had a surprised look on my face because I never thought Mrs. O'Driscoll ever read any books.

"You're surprised that Mrs. O'Driscoll, only a cleaning lady, can read a book now and then, Hubbo, my boy! That's a grand writer! Wait till you read *War and Peace*! There's lots to happen yet for you and Leo Tolstoy! Don't worry your head about it. You didn't hurt my feelings. Here, give us a hug. That's it. Now, have some more sherry! Yes, a grand story!"

I was feeling a little bit dizzy because of the sherry.

Did she know how I was avoiding her at school?

"Oh, Hubbo," said Mrs. O'Driscoll, "life is so lovely!"

She was trying to thread her needle to hem up O'Driscoll's nightshirt for me.

Did she know what a traitor I was?

"And so short! Life I mean. Not the nightshirt!" Then she let out a big laugh.

Did she know what a sneaky rat I was?

"I'll do this in the morning," she said, putting down the needle and thread and pouring some more sherry for herself.

Later on, in bed, I could hear, over the wall, Mrs. O'Driscoll in her room, laughing a bit, then crying some, then snoring a little bit.

And then I went spinning to sleep.

9. EASY AVENUE

Thursday after gymnastics, at about 5:30, I climbed the wide front steps up to the huge curved verandah at 210 Easy Avenue for my first day on the job. The door was heavy and black and the knocker was shiny brass. Miss Collar-Cuff's nurse opened the door and introduced herself and brought me into the dining room while she put on her coat. There was a huge table there, set for one.

"See you next Tuesday," she said, "if you work out." Then she touched me on the arm and left.

Miss Collar-Cuff was sitting in a big plush chair in her living room beside the fireplace that had tall gold lions on each side guarding the fire. The reflection of the flames was flickering in the glass eyes of the lions, making them look like they were blinking.

I sat at the dining-room table and a lady dressed as a cook brought my supper to me. It was three fat, sizzling pork chops with mint sauce and potatoes and tiny carrots that looked like candies. I tried to move my plate a bit but I burnt my fingers.

"Don't touch the plate," said the lady. "It's hot."

And all the milk you wanted. And hot apple pie with cheese on it.

The napkin beside my plate was made of heavy white cloth and was rolled up in a silver ring. The ring and the napkin had fancy engraved letters on them. C.C.

Three glasses of milk. And the glass seemed just as heavy when it was empty as it did when it was full. The table was long and shiny and black. The salt and pepper shakers were tall silver statues of a king and queen.

After I finished eating the supper I took my dishes into the kitchen and the lady dressed as a cook in there told me I didn't have to do that anymore.

"Don't forget," she said, "when you come back on Tuesday, you leave the dishes right where they are. That's if you're back on Tuesday."

I went into the living room and sat down on the chesterfield and looked at Miss Collar-Cuff and the blinking lions. She was very thin and her skin looked like white silk. She had on a long black dress with white frills around her wrists and around her throat. She sat very straight and very stiff, and with her chin up she looked like she was looking down her own long face and then at me.

She sat so still, staring at me, that I had to look away. I looked down at my legs and then at my raggedy shoes, then over to the window, then down at the flowered pattern of the couch, then at some paintings on the wall. Then at the blinking lions. Then back at her.

The lions seemed to move around more than she did.

I was wondering what Nerves would do if he were sitting here. I put my head back and looked down my face at her the way Nerves might but I knew I couldn't last. I would have a better chance of winning a staring contest with one of the lions.

Suddenly she broke the spell.

"Are you a nice boy?" she said.

A nice boy. I didn't know what to say. What was a nice boy? What did she want to hear? What would Mrs. O'Driscoll say? She would just start talking. Say anything. Let the words fall out all over the couch and the rug and fill up the room until you were up to your knees in words about this and that and the other thing. Or what would Fleurette Featherstone Fitchell say? She'd probably pause, think about it, and then say *one* word. Yes, for instance. Just yes.

I tried a Fleurette answer.

"Yes," I said.

Miss Collar-Cuff seemed pleased with this. She waited for a long time while I watched the lions blinking away. Then she asked me another one.

"Are you handsome?" she asked.

Was I handsome? I almost got up and walked over to one of the mirrors in the hallway to look at myself. To get the answer. But I was glad I didn't. She probably would have thought I was just trying to be clever or something. Mrs. O'Driscoll once told me I was handsome but not to worry about it. I'd get over it soon enough, she said. Mr. O'Driscoll was handsome, she said. But he *never* got over it. Probably out there now somewhere, looking at himself in a mirror in some foreign country, she said.

"Mrs. O'Driscoll said I was handsome once, but that I'd get over it," I said.

"Mrs. O'Driscoll?"

"She's sort of my mother."

"I see," she said. She was smiling a little bit.

"And are you popular?"

This was getting to be about the worst conversation I ever had in my life. My mind was a blank. I felt like the boy with no brain. Sitting there empty. Then I felt my mouth stretch over like Mrs. O'Driscoll's did sometimes when she was being specially sarcastic. Out of the corner of my mouth came the answer. I could hardly believe it was me. I think even the lions were surprised.

"Well, people aren't exactly stopping me on the street to ask for my autograph." I even *sounded* like Mrs. O'Driscoll.

"Oh, witty," said Miss Collar-Cuff. "And are you intelligent in school?"

"Yes," I said. I was ready to tell her anything.

"And are you a good athlete?"

"Yes. Would you like me to show you a trick?" I was desperate.

I jumped up and went into the kitchen. The lady, who was now not dressed as a cook, was leaving by the back door. I brought out a wooden chair and set it on the deep rug in the middle of the living room.

I sat in the chair. I put one hand on the back of the chair and the other on the seat between my legs. Then I leaned forward and pressed up into a perfect handstand. I could hold it for as long as she wanted. I could have stayed there for an hour. I was locked in perfect position. I took a quick peek at her. Her eyes were shining with excitement. At least this way, I didn't have to talk.

Suddenly she started slapping her thin little hands together, giving me a big round of applause. Then I came down slowly to show how much control I had.

While I was in the kitchen putting the chair back she called to me.

"What book are you reading in school?"

"*A Book of Good Stories,*" I said.

"What story?" she said when I was back in the living room feeling the lions' glass eyes.

"How Much Land Does a Man Need?" I told her.

"Ah, Tolstoy," she said. "Go in the den and you'll find everything Tolstoy ever wrote under T. Bring a big book called *War and Peace Part One* to me." The den was lined with books to the ceiling. They were in alphabetical order and when I got to the T's there was half a shelf full of Leo Tolstoy. I got down the one called *War and Peace Part One* while I thought of what Mrs. O'Driscoll would have to say about this. The cover was black velvet and the lettering gold. The pages were thin and silky and the edges were dipped in silver.

"Have you read *War and Peace?*" asked Miss Collar-Cuff.

I gave her a Fleurette Featherstone Fitchell no.

"Then you may read it to me."

And so I sat down between the blinking lions by the fire and began to read.

"*Eh bien, mon prince,* so Genoa and Lucca are now no more than private estates of the Bonaparte family…" is the way the book starts.

Miss Collar-Cuff closed her eyes and sighed.

Later, in O'Driscoll's nightshirt, I was in the biggest bed in the world. There was room for just about everybody in Building Number Eight in there. Mr. and Mrs. Blank, Nerves, Mr. and Mrs. Stentorian, Mrs. Quirk and the boy with no brain, Mr. Yasso and Fleurette. Everybody. Put Chubby in there too. And Denny Dingle and all the Dorises if they wanted. And the Hi-Y guys. And Mrs. O'Driscoll. And

O'Driscoll who was supposed to be drowned. And Fleurette's mother. And the man with the black hair. And the man with the red hair too.

Now and then the lights of a car passed evenly over the ceiling, and the bed lit up a bit, and I could see the lump in the covers about half way down where my feet were pointing up. And I felt the silk of the comforter with my hands and pushed my head just a little into the feathers of the pillow.

And the light sometimes glittered off the gold doorknob of the door and the silver candlesticks in front of the mirror and the shiny brass posts of the bed and the copper statues of angels and eagles and the glittering mirrors.

And the oak and mahogany furniture sat there solid and heavy and quiet.

And sleep tried to come.

Sleep tried to come quietly and silently slipping over me so I could slide down the long slide of sleep.

Suddenly my eyes clicked open and I saw that the end of the bed was shaped differently in the dark. There was a shape between the posts. A person was standing there.

A car went by and the light passed evenly over the ceiling and flashed off the gold and the silver and the brass and the copper and for a second over the face of Miss Collar-Cuff. And off the tears on her cheeks.

"It's all right," she said, standing there. "It's all right. I'll go away in a minute. I just wanted to watch you sleeping. May I watch you sleeping?"

I closed my eyes and waited.

And then sleep came.

What a job.

A lot better than the Cinderella Book Store.

10. SUCCESS

Doug had his bony, hairy arms across my notebook in science class. His greasy hair was stuck right near my face and he was making me sick. Also making me sick was the smell of the stink perfume some of the Hi-Y guys were pouring on Mr. Tool's stuffed owl.

Doug leaned over because he saw me filling out part of the Hi-Y application form. I had put next to the word ADDRESS, the words 210 Easy Avenue. When I saw that he saw me, I tucked the form into my science notebook with all the pictures of the grasshopper. Then he put his bony, hairy arms across my book.

"Haven't you got that thing filled out yet?" he said. "Do you ever take your girlfriend Fleurette anywhere? Where does she live? What do you do when you take her somewhere?"

"None of your business, Doug," I said.

"Is she dirty?" Doug said. His eyebrow was moving up and down.

"Doug, get your arms off of my notebook!" I said. I was going to say, "or I'll punch your ugly face off!" but I didn't. I guess I didn't because I wanted to be in the Hi-Y and be a success. And Doug could get me in.

After school while we were waiting for the Uplands bus I told Fleurette all about my job with Miss Collar-Cuff—the lions and *War and Peace* and my sort of dream in the big bed and how she came in the room to watch me sleep.

"Oh, Hubbo," she said, "you're so good at things. Someday you're going to be somebody. You're going to be a big success."

On the bus we were snuggled up and I asked her if she wanted to go to the Mayfair Theatre on Saturday to see the movie *The Jolson Story*. I could pay our way.

At home, when I told Mrs. O'Driscoll about Miss Collar-Cuff crying beside the bed she shook her head and looked very sad.

"Poor thing," she said, "all that money and so lonely and unhappy. Isn't it awful? I wonder what O'Driscoll would say? I don't know what he'd maybe say but I know what he'd probably do. He'd probably move in with her as a handyman or something and then get her to give him her chequebook and help her spend all her money and get her to put him in her will and inherit every cent she's got and the house and the car...and that's probably what he's doing right now, sweet talking some rich old lady out of her vast fortune on some fancy ranch somewhere with oil wells and gold mines..."

On Saturday at the Mayfair Theatre during *The Jolson Story* Fleurette started to cry when they sang the Anniversary Waltz about his parents who were married for such a long time and who were so happy and who loved each other. Then she said that I was really lucky because Mrs. O'Driscoll loved me so much and always thought of me and was always nice to me and did things for me all the time and hugged me all the time. She put her head on my shoulder and I started asking her about her family, and I asked her who the man with the black hair and dark eyes was and she said that he was her father and that he was very kind and that he had to travel around all the time because of his job but he always came home whenever he could and brought her and her mother gifts and loved them very much, and how he was a wonderful man. I tried to see her face when she was saying these things but I couldn't because her chin was tucked in my neck. I asked her who the man with the red hair was and she told me that he was her uncle and that he would come over sometimes and bring gifts and see how they were and that he was kind and very funny and would tell them funny stories of things that happened to him in his travels. And her voice sounded different when she was telling all this and I tried to see her face but I couldn't.

We were talking so much that the people behind us told us to shut up and if we wanted to argue we should go somewhere else. Funny how sometimes when you are talking about private things people think you are arguing.

After the show we saw the handsome Hi-Y guy who ran the Tuck Shop. He was with his girlfriend with the fancy clothes. I said hello to them as they passed by but they didn't answer me.

"Do you know them?" Fleurette asked. "What are you saying hello to them for if you don't even know them?"

I didn't know what to tell her.

A few weeks later I had guidance again and Mr. Stubbs was telling us all about success.

He mumbled quite a bit and looked up at the ceiling and out the window and at his shoes a lot. He would start saying something about how to be a big success and then he'd mumble lower and lower until you could hardly hear him and then he'd be looking out the window and up at the sky and although his lips would still be moving there would be no sound coming out and all the kids would be saying "There he goes again," and "Goodbye Mr. Stubbs," and singing bits of songs like "Dream" and "Rock-a-bye Baby."

Then he would seem to wake up and look around the room at the blackboard and at his desk and at the students and at the door and at all the pictures on the walls of big successes like Napoleon and Prime Minister King and Shakespeare and Lassie, the famous movie star dog, and everybody. It seemed like he had just landed there from somewhere else, some other planet maybe, and was trying to figure out where he was. His shirt was always wrinkled and dirty-looking and his tie was tied so that the thin part was longer than the wide part and the shoulders of his suit were quite lumpy, as though there were golf balls or something stuffed in the lining. His fly was usually open part way, and there was always egg or soup or something on his pants.

He didn't look very successful.

Then when he found out where he was he'd walk over to another part of the room and try again, telling us about how to be a big success in life.

And the kids would be saying stuff like "He's back," or "He's okay," and singing parts of songs like "Hello, Everybody, Hello!" or "When the Lights Go On Again."

This day we had a test.

He gave everybody a little piece of paper and told us to open our guidance books.

There were two drawings.

One was a picture of a doctor in a nice white lab coat. He was holding a clipboard and he had a stethoscope around his neck and a round metal disk on his forehead. He was very handsome and was smiling with a row of perfect teeth at a beautiful lady who was lying in a bed and smiling right back at him. Her hair was done up like she was all better and would hop right out of bed any minute now and go right to the dance with the handsome doctor.

Beside it was a drawing of a garbageman carrying a big pail of stinking garbage over to a truck with another guy in the back standing there waiting to catch the pail up to his waist in garbage. The guy carrying the pail was bent over a bit with lines showing how sore his back was. There were flies swarming around his head and sitting on his lips.

There was a question under the two drawings: "Which would you rather be? A or B?"

The test wasn't too hard. We had to write down A or B on the little piece of paper and sign our name on it and hand it in.

A was for the doctor.

B was for the garbageman.

As a joke I put down B and signed my name and handed it in.

While we were reading a little story in our book about a crippled orphan who became a billionaire somehow, Mr. Stubbs was going over the pieces of paper we handed in. I saw him put one piece of paper aside. It turned out to be mine.

At the end of the class while everybody was crammed in the doorway and trampling on each other trying to get out, I heard the name O'Driscoll.

I stopped at his desk to see if I heard what I heard.

"Come after school so that we can have a guidance chat," Mr. Stubbs said.

"But I have to go to gymnastics practice," I said.

"It's compulsory," he said. "You failed your test. You said B, O'Driscoll. The answer is A. A for doctor."

"But I just did it as a joke," I said.

"No you didn't."

"No, really. I want to be a doctor. I only said garbageman as a kind of joke. For a bit of a laugh."

"Not funny. After school."

"I could change it. I could put A down. I want to be a doctor worse than anything. It's been my life-long ambition since I was about six months old to be a doctor. And not just an ordinary doctor. A brain surgeon. I want to cure everybody in Canada and be famous and rich and get the Nobel Prize for doctoring and have a statue of me in the park. And start my own hospital..."

It was no use.

Mr. Stubbs was already looking out the window again. His eyes were fogging over fast. He was gone on a long one this time.

Later that day I found out that just about everybody in the class had put down B for garbageman.

After school Mr. Stubbs and I started all over again.

"You put down B for garbageman," he said.

"But I only did it as a joke. I don't want to be a garbageman." I looked at the clock. The gym team was already warming up. Tonight after practice the coach would put up the list of the eight guys who would make the team. Four seniors and four juniors.

"What about all the others who put down B for garbageman?" I said. "What about them?"

"They were only fooling," he said. "Making a joke."

"So was I," I said.

"No you weren't," he said. He had his jacket buttoned wrong. He looked like he was going to fall apart.

"You see, I know where you come from. You come from Uplands Emergency Shelter. You people have got to think about your future. You've got to be more ambitious. Look at these pictures on the wall here. You could be like Shakespeare or Prime Minister King or Napoleon. Or Lassie."

"Lassie's a dog," I said, but he didn't hear me.

He was off on his success speech. I waited until he really got rolling about success, and sure enough, he started mumbling and murmuring and his eyes rolled up and he was looking out the window up at the sky and mumbling himself into a real hypnotic trance. He was heading out on a very long journey. I waited until he was really gone and then I slipped out and ran down to get changed for gymnastic practice.

After practice we all gathered around the bulletin board while the coach put up the list saying who made the team.

My name was on the list.

The next day in science class I secretly took out the Hi-Y application form.

Beside the word TEAMS I wrote "Glebe Gym Team."

Beside the word TELEPHONE I put Miss Collar-Cuff's number, and I put "Tuesdays and Thursdays only."

Beside the words MAKE AND YEAR OF FATHER'S CAR I put "Cadillac" because that's the kind of car Miss Collar-Cuff had in her locked garage.

Denny Dingle was first in our class in everything but English. But he was always near the top in that too because I used to explain everything to him that we read.

But suddenly something happened to him that made him come just about last in everything.

A new girl came to class.

And Denny started acting like the boy with no brain.

She had on a very frilly blouse that you could see through. She had on a tight red skirt with a slit up the side. She had on silk stockings with seams straight up the back. She had on red high-heeled shoes. She had a tiny chain around her left ankle. She had bracelets around her wrists. She had a silver tiara in her long blond straight silky hair. She had lipstick on her very curvy lips and she had long eyelashes and she had rouge on her cheeks. And a black beauty spot beside her mouth.

And big cold blue eyes.

She walked very slowly, carrying her books, her chin up, not looking at anybody.

Like a queen.

When she came in the room, she came in last. Everybody knew she would be last. She came in, walking slowly, her high heels clicking on the floor, click, click, as she walked, the little wind she made full of perfume when she went by you, the sound of her jingling bracelets as she slid into her desk, the room so silent, as if a tiger had just strolled in and sat down.

Her name was Melody Bleach.

I looked over at Denny Dingle as Melody took her seat. He had a funny look on his face.

The next day when Melody Bleach came clicking in, I watched Denny. He was looking at her, following her with his eyes. He looked like Melody had just hit him over the head with a big wet fish.

The next day when Melody Bleach came in, I watched Denny. He was watching her, his mouth hanging open, his eyes glazed over, as though he were being hypnotized by Dracula.

The next day, Denny wasn't there when Melody Bleach came in. I knew he was at school because he was on the bus with me that morning.

Something was wrong. Suddenly, just as we heard Melody's bracelets jangling on her desk as she sat down, in came Denny. He had been following her. He walked in the room like a zombie. If he had been wrapped in bandages he would have been a perfect mummy. You could have snapped your fingers in front of his face and he wouldn't have noticed.

On the bus that night he sat there staring straight ahead. I felt his head to see if he had a fever. A little while later he spoke. I couldn't hear him at first because of all the noise and arguing behind us. I put my ear up to his mouth.

"I know where her locker is," is what he said.

He sounded like he just confessed to a murder.

He sounded like he said, "I just murdered my whole family."

Poor Denny. He was in bad shape.

The next day before class I followed him. He walked from his locker in the basement near the gym, up to the first floor outside the auditorium where most of our class was hanging around waiting for the assembly doors to open.

He walked by while everybody stared at him and went up to the second floor and then to the third floor, to the lockers near the art room.

Melody was standing with her locker door open, using the mirror that hung on the inside of the door. She was touching up her beauty spot with a makeup pencil.

Denny stood behind her. She raised her eyes and looked at Denny's reflection. Her eyelashes, when they came up, just about knocked the mirror off the door.

"Do you like me?" she said.

Denny's lips moved, but nothing seemed to come out. His face was the colour of ashes, which made his pimples stand out like little red lights.

"Am I pretty?" said Melody Bleach, going back to work with her pencil.

She had her tongue stuck out a bit. Some people do that when they concentrate. Suddenly I remembered her. She used to go to York Street School. She used to stick her tongue out like that when she tried to write. Her parents must have gotten rich or something, because where would she get all the fancy clothes? I remembered everybody used to say that she wet herself sitting in her seat in grade three.

"Do you think I'm pretty?" she asked Denny again.

"Yes," Denny said, tearing his eyes away from her reflection and looking down at his feet.

"Come here," said Melody, pointing to the floor beside her. "You may carry my books." On the floor her books were piled in a neat stack, the math set and the pencil box on top.

Denny picked up her books and followed her down the hall.

But that afternoon, something happened to me that took my mind off Denny. And off almost everything.

We were in English class.

Chubby came to the door while the Hi-Y guys were doing their humming song. They were all staring at their books pretending to read but humming. Whenever the teacher came down the aisle to try and find out who was doing the humming, another Hi-Y guy would start on the other side of the room.

Chubby came to the door and said something to the teacher. Then the teacher looked down at me and nodded, and then came part way down the aisle and pointed at me and told me in a sort of a whisper that the principal wanted to see me.

The Hi-Y guys hummed a little tune to go with my walk to the door.

Chubby was out in the hall leaning a lot on his cane and puffing. He said that we had to go down to the office because there was something important. I thought it was because of the humming and that I was being blamed for it.

All the way down the stairs I was planning what I would say. I was going to tell Chubby about how we were taking the same story for months now, and how I'd read it so many times I almost knew it off by heart. So that he wouldn't think I was wasting my time humming.

I thought that if I made conversation with him, got him talking while we were going downstairs, it would take his mind off the pain. He was so crippled. And there was sweat on his lip.

"What do the words *Alere* and *Flammam* mean?" I asked Chubby.

Alere and *Flammam* were the two words written in stone on the shield over the front doors of the school.

"*Alere Flammam* is Latin," said Chubby as he struggled down each step. "It means 'Kindle the torch' or 'exalt the flame' or 'hold up the fire' ..." We were almost at the bottom of the stairs. "...or 'raise the torch' or 'brandish the spark' or 'ignite the lamp' or 'elevate the ember'...that sort of thing."

I was glad when he stopped. All those meanings were making me dizzy.

That night I told Mrs. O'Driscoll as many of the meanings as I could remember. She said that O'Driscoll would say that none of those meanings were quite right.

"He'd have a better one than those," said Mrs. O'Driscoll. "He'd say it meant 'Light the Light!'"

After I thought about it I thought she was right. Her translation was the best one. Light the Light. It had a nice ring to it. It was also a line from her favourite song.

> *Make my bed, light the light.*
> *I'll arrive, late tonight.*
> *Blackbird, Bye, bye.*

In his office Chubby got into his chair and made a face because it hurt him so much to sit down. He hung his cane over the arm of the chair and took a little while to get his breath while he opened a brown envelope and took out some papers.

"He shouldn't have pushed you off the front steps," he said to me, looking over his glasses. He was talking about my first day at school.

"Yes, sir."

"Did he hurt you?" He took his glasses off and slowed down his puffing.

"No, sir."

"He shouldn't have done that, you know. That wasn't fair."

"No, sir."

"You were doing a handstand." He put his glasses back on.

"Yes, sir."

"Did you make the gym team?"

"Yes, sir."

"Good for you," he said, and coughed a few times. "I have a happy thing to tell you. I have a very pleasant job to do here. I have something to say to you that you will be very pleased about. And your mother... your guardian, Mrs. O'Driscoll—she'll be very pleased about it too."

"Yes, sir," I said. I was getting sick of saying yes, sir, but that was all I could think of.

"He didn't hurt you when he pushed you down the stairs?"

"No, sir."

"I have a very pleasant duty to perform this morning. A legal matter. A person has asked me to deliver to you a cheque on this day, the last day of the month, a cheque for fifty dollars. I cannot give you the name of the person who directed me to give you this cheque. The only thing I can say to you is that for every month you stay in school, this school, you will receive a cheque for fifty dollars."

Chubby sighed as if he had just lifted a big weight and then passed over to me with his fat fingers a piece of paper.

"That is a cheque," he said, "for fifty dollars. On the last day of each month I'll be giving you a cheque for this amount. You will come into my office here and pick up the cheque on that day. It's not from me, you understand, although I sign it."

I couldn't stop thinking about the humming in the English teacher's room and the Hi-Y guys. The office was quiet except for a clock ticking. I got my mind away from the English teacher and the Hi-Y guys and looked at the cheque Chubby had pushed over his smooth desk at me.

The cheque said this:

Royal Bank of Canada
Pay to the order of Hulbert O'Driscoll
The sum of Fifty Dollars.

And then it said;

W.D.T. Atkinson (In Trust)

"What do I do with this?" I said.

"You go and cash it," said Chubby. "I'll give you a letter of identification, signed by me, that you keep with you to show to the bank so they will cash the cheque for you. And another letter to Mrs. O'Driscoll, explaining that she will be your adviser about how to handle this sudden windfall."

At the Royal Bank on Bank Street they read the letter, phoned Chubby at the school, talked to each other about it, pointed at me, had a little meeting, brought the manager out of his office, had another meeting, looked at my clothes, phoned somebody else, filled out some forms, stamped about ten pieces of paper, counted out the money in tens, started smiling, put the money in an envelope, licked the envelope, smiled some more, and gave it to me.

I folded the envelope in half, put it in my pocket, and walked down Bank Street, over the bridge, past the Mayfair Theatre, down the hill to the Uplands Bus Terminal, and got on the bus.

With my hand still in my pocket covering the envelope I sat down beside one of the rich people and rode home.

All I could think of the whole time was what Chubby had said.

"Sudden windfall," he said.

"Lord strike me dead," Mrs. O'Driscoll said. "Sudden windfall all right!"

We sat down at the kitchen table and forgot all about supper. Mrs. O'Driscoll got out the photograph album and we looked at some pictures of O'Driscoll. In all the pictures he was standing there, legs apart, hands on his hips, his shirt open, his hat tilted on one side.

We were talking about the money. Who could it be? Who was giving *us* this money?

Maybe it was Mr. O'Driscoll. It was just like him, Mrs. O'Driscoll was saying. Just like something he would do.

"That's just like something he would do. He probably didn't drown in the war after all. After he said, 'If I don't see you in the spring I'll see you in the mattress,' he jumped into the ocean and probably swam to some island or something and married the witchdoctor's daughter and became king and opened up a diamond mine and is a billionaire and feels so guilty that he's sending us fifty dollars every month. Just like something O'Driscoll would do. Swim to Africa or somewhere and move in with the Queen of the jungle and talk her out of all her gold and become a trillionaire and send us fifty dollars just to tease us. You can't fool me, O'Driscoll. I know it's you!"

Then she said some more about O'Driscoll and how he was probably living with the Queen of Sheba or somebody.

"Well, she can have him!" Mrs. O'Driscoll said. "She's welcome to him. And more power to her!"

Then Mrs. O'Driscoll said that O'Driscoll probably swam all the way to Hawaii or somewhere and moved in with some mermaid who had jewels in a chest sunk down in the ocean and convinced her to give him all her treasure, and he's now a multi-zillionaire and he's sending us fifty dollars.

"Is he sure he can spare it!" said Mrs. O'Driscoll out of the corner of her mouth.

But I stopped listening to Mrs. O'Driscoll because another idea was starting to come into my head. I started thinking about Miss Collar-Cuff. It was Miss Collar-Cuff who was giving me the money. Because of how sad she seemed to be. She probably wanted me to be her grandson, but she was afraid that I wouldn't and so she was giving me this money and keeping it a secret.

I was thinking that I might look right in her face next time and see if I could see in her eyes the secret she had. Or maybe I would tell her about getting the money and then watch her face to see if it said anything. To see if an expression came over her face that was different or if she looked away so I wouldn't be able to tell.

That's what I would do. I would tell her about Chubby giving me the cheque and see what she did. I would tell her maybe when she came in the room when I pretended to be asleep. When she came in to look for a long time at me when she thought I was asleep. Or when I was reading to her.

I went out in the hall to see if there was a lineup at the toilet. Mr. or Mrs. Blank must have been in there because Nerves was standing there staring at the door with his face all squeezed up.

I practiced on Nerves, pretending that Nerves was Miss Collar-Cuff.

"Somebody is giving me fifty dollars a month, but it's a secret," I said to Nerves. "Mrs. O'Driscoll thinks it's Mr. O'Driscoll, but it can't be. He was drowned in the war. It's not him. And it's not Chubby. It's somebody else. Do you know who it is?"

Nerves studied the floor for a while then raised his ratty little eyes slowly up to mine. His head was still down and his eyes were rolled up looking into mine. He was looking very mysterious.

Then he fell over and played dead.

What a dog.

Just then we both looked down the hall. A stranger was coming out of Mrs. Fitchell's unit. He didn't have black hair. He didn't have red hair. This one was bald.

12. UPPITY

"Somebody is giving me, us, fifty dollars a month, but it's a secret," I said to Miss Collar-Cuff.

"Mrs. O'Driscoll thinks it's Mr. O'Driscoll, but it can't be. He was drowned in the war. It's not him. It's somebody else. Chubby will give me a cheque for fifty dollars at the end of each month but he won't tell where it comes from."

I was reading to her from *War and Peace* when I said it. I stopped reading as I had planned, looked up over the book right at her eyes, and said it.

She looked at me for a long time before she answered.

"That's a wonderful thing, you and your mother receiving this money. The fact that you don't know where it's coming from might be a little disturbing, but, on the other hand, the source of this sudden windfall being anonymous might make this monthly allowance all the more pleasurable. What a fascinating mystery it is!"

What a sentence! It was just as long as some of the sentences in *War and Peace*. And she said "sudden windfall" just like Chubby did. And the sentence sounded like she had it planned. But her face showed nothing.

Then she said, "Now that you are a young man of means, do I assume that you will no longer remain in my employ and that I should begin searching for a replacement?"

"Oh, no, Miss," I said. "I have to stay at least until we finish *War and Peace*!"

"Ah, good, Hubbo, my friend. Although I doubt that we will last together *that* long. We will try our very best, won't we?"

The next Thursday from the big bed I tried again to get her to talk about the money but she just came out with a sentence even longer than before.

So I gave up.

One day Mrs. O'Driscoll and Fleurette and I discussed Denny's problem with Melody Bleach.

"Sounds like a hopeless case," said Mrs. O'Driscoll. "O'Driscoll used to be like that about me. Followed me around for about a year before I ever really noticed him. Wore out four pairs of shoes running after me, he told me later. I didn't believe him, though. He only had one pair of shoes as far as I ever knew. Of course, he was always exaggerating. You could never get the truth out of him. Denny will survive, though. Don't worry about him. Soon as his pimples go away, he'll be fine. And that Melody person. Really dumb, isn't she? Didn't you say she comes last in the class all the time?"

Mrs. O'Driscoll was right. Melody Bleach did always come in last. But what I didn't tell her was that Denny was coming second last. And he used to be so smart. Used to come at the top all the time.

What Mrs. O'Driscoll said about Denny's pimples gave me an idea. I would use some of the money to take Denny to a doctor and maybe get rid of his pimples. Make him feel better. More proud of himself.

On the way home a few days later I told Denny about the appointment I had made for him at the skin doctor. The dermatologist.

It wasn't hard to talk Denny into going to the appointment. He was in such a daze you could have told him to jump off the Bank Street Bridge into the canal and he would have.

Fleurette and I steered him down Fifth Avenue and into the doctor's waiting room. Everybody sitting around the waiting room was covered with pimples. We had never seen so many pimples.

"A lot of pimples in this room," whispered Fleurette.

They called Denny's name and he went in.

While we were waiting I started talking to Fleurette about the Boys' Hi-Y and my problems with the application.

"What do you want to join that stupid club for? Those morons keep walking through my school in their little gangs and their nice clothes making smart-alec remarks and bumping into the girls and laughing. They really think they're something but they're not. Everybody hates them. Except the girls who are really brainless. They like those Hi-Y guys because they have money. Take them out to restaurants and stuff. But you should hear what the Hi-Y guys say about the girls after, behind their backs. You're not going to be like that, are you?"

I didn't know what to say for a long time, so we sat in silence in the skin doctor's waiting room.

After a while, Denny came out with the doctor.

Fleurette and I looked at the doctor's face. He had more pimples than Denny. His face was a mess of scars and splotches.

"Now, apply this salve three times a day and take one of these pills every day after supper," the pimpled doctor was saying to Denny as I paid the nurse.

"It's sulphur," Denny told us later on the Uplands bus. Denny already had some of the salve on his face. It was skin-coloured and looked like makeup. As the bus got warm I could start to smell the stuff. It was sulphur all right. It smelled like rotten eggs. In fact, Denny smelled quite a bit like Mr. Tool's stuffed owl.

We got off with him to have a visit and see what the Dorises thought of our plan to get rid of Denny's pimples. The Dorises were all sitting around the kitchen watching the potatoes and the kettle boil for supper.

All the Dorises agreed that something had to be done and everybody talked about pimples for a while, the history of pimples, the effects of pimples, how pimples can't *ruin* your life but can do a pretty good job trying to spoil everything.

The smell of rotten eggs from Denny's salve was getting worse. One of the Dorises told him to move away from the stove and maybe he'd be more comfortable.

"To be a success in life, you can't have pimples," I said. I said it, but it didn't sound like me. I could feel Fleurette's eyes go dark on me. I was starting to sound more and more like the guidance book.

"I suppose you couldn't join the Boys' Hi-Y if you had pimples," Fleurette said to me. Her black eyes were narrow and her lip was curled up. She was pretty mad at me about this Hi-Y stuff, I could tell.

Everybody talked some more about Denny's disease, and just before Fleurette and I left the oldest Doris piped up with something new.

"If this sulphur doesn't work we'll try the sand."

Sand?

"A teaspoon of clean sand every Saturday night. Boil the sand, take a big teaspoon of it every Saturday night after your bath, with a glass of warm milk to wash it down. Cured all of those things in my day."

Everybody said that this would be worth a try, and then Fleurette and I left to walk home to Uplands Emergency Shelter.

"Why did you say that about success and pimples? You sounded like somebody in that stupid guidance book. And why are you trying to join that awful club with those awful people? And Mrs. O'Driscoll told me that you're getting pretty uppity since you started getting that money. Maybe *you* should go to the doctor and get some of that rotten egg salve to put on your brain."

She never said another word and when we got into Building Eight she slammed the door.

Only Nerves was there in the hall. With his nose up in the air. He was mad at me too.

13. FEEL STREET

It was coming up to Christmas and the teachers were getting us ready for exams. In science we were doing the grasshopper all over again.

I was drawing those hairs or whatever they are on the grasshopper's tibia or his femur or whatever that part of his leg is called, when I heard some pounding at the front of the room. When I looked to see what all the fuss was about I noticed that Mr. Tool had gone berserk. He was pounding his head on the blackboard. His forehead, bang-banging on the blackboard. Then he picked up the cage with the snake in it and fired it across the room. Then he started ripping his charts down off the rollers and throwing test tubes at the class and at the windows. The Hi-Y guys had driven him crazy.

Then he tore two or three spouts off the sinks, and the water gushed up to the ceiling.

"I hate you!" he was screaming at us. "I hate you!" he was screaming while he threw some of his little dead experimental pigs at the class.

Then he picked up his horse skull and threw it through the glass windows of the cabinet where his stinking owl was sitting there glassy-eyed, staring at him. Then he picked up the owl and started ripping the feathers out of it. Then he started throwing all his stuffed rodents and the little logs and tree limbs they were stuck to out the window.

Then the vice-principal came in and started talking to him and taking him out, and Mr. Tool was saying, "…how can I go now, the period isn't over. I have to teach them the grasshopper…they have to know the grasshopper for the exam. Did the bell ring? Where's the bell? They don't know their work…what am I going to do? I hate them. Don't you see? I hate these students. I want to kill them, kill them and put them in bottles on the window sill…put them in formaldehyde…cut them up in pieces and give them to my fish…kill…kill…!"

He was pretty mad at us.

School got out early because that day they had a sock hop, which was a little dance in the gym with your shoes off and just your socks on. We went and stood along the wall and sat along the wall on the long benches and leaned up against the wall where the mats were hanging, leaning on the mats at the sock hop against the wall.

Sliding our socks on the glistening floor.

In the middle of the floor the head boy and the head girl were dancing. The record that was playing was the song "Dream."

On the other side of the gym the girls were standing around talking in little bunches and leaning against the wall and the mats and standing there in their socks and laughing and covering their lips with their fingers.

The head of the Girls' Hi-Y turned the record over and played the song, "Golden Earrings."

The head girl and the head boy were out there dancing again.

One of the Hi-Y guys tried to shove me out on the floor and we had a bit of a wrestling match. There were quite a few wrestling matches along our wall.

Then we saw Melody Bleach walk in, not clicking, and stand by herself. She touched her hair a bit, pushed it a bit with her fingertips every few minutes. She didn't look so scary without her high heels on.

Then we saw Denny walking across the floor toward her. Everybody was watching Denny. He was walking all wrong. When his right leg went out, so did his right arm. And then his left leg went out at the same time as his left arm. Everybody waited to see what would happen to him. When he got to her, he must have asked her for a dance. We saw her shake her head.

No.

Then Denny walked all the way back across the floor. It was a long walk. The floor seemed as big as the parade square at Uplands. Right leg, right arm. Left leg, left arm.

Poor Denny.

I left the dance and went to meet Fleurette at the Commerce door.

I had talked it over with Mrs. O'Driscoll and she had said it was a good idea.

I was going to buy Fleurette a present with some of the mysterious money.

I had on new underwear and new pants and new socks and shoes and a new shirt. Spoiling everything, I had on my long old raggedy coat and my galoshes with the soles flapping and the missing buckles.

We walked down cold Rideau Street and went into A. J. Freiman's. The heat blasted us in the swinging doors. We went up to the third floor on the elevator. The elevator lady had on a braided uniform and a cute cap and she called out what was on each floor and then opened the two doors by pulling down the handle with her red-gloved hand and saying, "Watch your step, please," but we didn't have to watch our step because she hit it right on.

They kept the girls' clothes on the third floor.

Over in the shoe department Fleurette told the man she wanted to try on some blue and white saddle shoes.

I saw the mother of a guy named Eddie I used to go to York Street School with. She was working in the girls' dress department. She saw me coming over and came to meet me a bit. She asked me what I was doing in the girls' clothing department, and I told her that a friend and I were buying some new clothes for her.

"Isn't that nice," she said. "Clothes are expensive these days." I could tell that she was, in a kind way, really asking where we got the money.

"I saw you come in," she said. "I think I know your friend. Doesn't she live around Friel Street somewhere? Pretty girl. I've seen her."

"We don't live in Lowertown anymore," I said. "We moved to Uplands Emergency Shelter. We got some money from a man my aunt knows."

I knew it sounded strange when I said it. Eddie's mother raised her eyebrows a bit. I wouldn't have lied about it, but I didn't feel like trying to explain to her what I couldn't even explain to myself.

She was a nice lady, not too nosy, so we talked for a while about Lowertown and Uplands until Fleurette came over wearing her new shoes over her old woollen stockings and carrying her ripped galoshes and her coat. Then Eddie's mother took her over to look at some more things and they disappeared for a while. I felt sort of silly standing around in the girls' clothing department by myself. So I went over and played with the X-ray machine. I stuck my foot in and pushed the button. I looked through the glass. I could see the bones of my feet. They were a kind of green colour.

When Fleurette Featherstone Fitchell came back she had on new blue and white saddle shoes, new pink lisle stockings, a new blue skirt, a new pink angora sweater and a new blue ribbon in her long curly black hair.

She stood in front of one of the tall triple mirrors and opened one of them a bit so she could see her back. Then she pulled the other one towards her a little so that she could see me looking at her. I turned the first part of the mirror so that I could see reflections of a million Fleurettes in the other mirrors getting further and further and smaller away.

They all looked beautiful.

A little way up Rideau Street, in front of the Chateau Laurier, we met Victor, the guy who ran the Tuck Shop, and his girlfriend, Virginia. Victor had on a silky-silver new bomber jacket with the white fur collar turned up, a set of shiny black earmuffs, a white silk scarf showing where his jacket was half zipped up, a pair of fur-lined gloves turned down so you could see the fur, smooth, light-grey gabardine draped slacks with a special stitched seam down the side, and open flight boots with the fuzzy white wool lining flashing when he walked.

He showed us his shiny-white even teeth as he passed by with Virginia.

Virginia had on a brown mink hat with the fur just down to her eyes, a long beige camelhair coat open at the throat showing her shiny necklace; the split in her coat made her long high-heeled cowhide black soft leather boots swish out when she walked. Her silver earrings glistened in the lights from the Chateau Laurier and the twinkling snow.

She showed us a big row of shiny-white even teeth as she passed by with Victor.

"Oh, my," said Fleurette Featherstone Fitchell. "Oh, my!", after they'd passed by. "That's one of those dopes that comes over to our school and bumps into us and everything."

We walked up to Rideau Street a little more, crossing Rideau Street Bridge, and stopped by Sir Galahad's statue in front of the Parliament Buildings.

Fleurette was looking straight ahead.

"How do they get teeth like that?" she said. "Do they buy them or what do they do? Are they false teeth or what? Maybe they paint them on or something. Maybe they're drawn on. Or they buy them at the joke shop or something. Bill's Joke Shop." She was talking like Mrs. O'Driscoll. Not talking sense. "My mother says it's their diet," Fleurette said. "What do they do, eat pearls for breakfast or something? Maybe they feed them oysters and grains of sand or…maybe they're injected with something…maybe they get ground-up diamonds and put it in their food."

She was in one of her Hi-Y moods.

As we were leaving the statue I saw a guy I sort of knew in Lowertown. His name was Tommy and he was with his friend Sammy. Fleurette and Tommy had a little conversation about Christmas. Fleurette was being really nice to him.

We went down Sparks Street to Bank Street and waited for the streetcar.

"Or maybe they take those sequins, those shiny things, and eat them in their cereal in the morning."

The streetcar came along and it was jammed and we jammed on.

"Maybe they're in the chiclet business. Maybe those are just chiclets!"

Fleurette Featherstone Fitchell calmed down a bit and smiled at me with her black eyes and after a while made me smile too and she put our two dimes in.

People were crowding and pushing, trying to get on and off at each stop while we moved deeper and deeper into the back of the streetcar. By the time we got to the Avenues we got a seat. By the time we got to Sunnyside Avenue by the Mayfair Theatre in Ottawa South and got up to get off, the car was only half full.

We got off at Coulter's Drug Store and started walking down the rest of Bank Street towards the Uplands Bus Terminal. The running lights from the Mayfair Theatre made shadows move on the snowbanks.

The Uplands Bus Terminal windows were dripping with dirt. Inside, the rich people were near the door and the poor people were lying on the benches and standing around with their broken parcels and their bags.

As we were getting off the bus at Uplands I was telling her something about Doug and Mr. Tool and going berserk and everything, and suddenly Fleurette Featherstone Fitchell stopped and turned.

"Doug!" she said. "Doug is the name of one of those guys that come over to our school with all those dirty sayings and grabbing at us! Doug is that slimy-looking guy with the grease on his head. Doug! That's your Hi-Y friend? That skinny, ugly guy! Do you know what he shouted at me last week? *Feel* Street! Did you used to live on *Feel* Street! You told him that! Nobody else knows that but you! You promised never to tell that!" She was screaming at me now. "*You* told him about Feel Street. What they said about me in Lowertown!"

"I didn't!" I said. "I didn't tell him anything about you. He was always asking me but I never said one word about you. Never!"

"You're a liar!" she screamed. "Nobody else knows that but you. It must have been you!"

"I didn't!" I said. "Honest to God, I didn't!"

"And I'm a liar too," she shouted. "Did you know that? The man with the black hair? He's my father all right! But he's not like I said.

Remember the cast on my mother's wrist? And the man with the red hair? He's not my uncle! He's just a man. And there are other men who come over. And sometimes they bring presents or money. But I don't know who they are! They bring ribbons maybe! Like you!"

She was tearing the ribbon out of her hair.

"You told about Feel Street! You traitor!" she said between her teeth. Her eyes were black as coal. "You blabbed all over..."

She threw the ribbon down in the snow and stomped on it.

Then she hit me in the face. Then she ran to Building Eight.

"Is that what you do?" I yelled after her. "Hit people?"

That's all I could think of to say.

The next morning Mrs. O'Driscoll found all the new clothes in a pile in the hall outside our door.

14. SIXTY-FOUR PIECES

All through Christmas and January and February and March Fleurette wouldn't talk to me.

In science Doug and some of the other Hi-Y troublemakers were moved to another class. I only saw Doug a couple of times in the boys' dressing room selling chocolate bars. Mrs. O'Driscoll said once she thought there was something funny going on about those chocolate bars and the Tuck Shop, but I didn't pay much attention to what she said.

At Miss Collar-Cuffs we were up to Book One Part Two of *War and Peace*, where two thousand Russian soldiers marched seven hundred miles to Austria and wore out their boots. That was four thousand worn-out boots. We were on page one hundred and twenty-five. One thousand three hundred pages to go.

Quite a big book.

One day I joined the library club and they gave me a job, one day a week after school, putting books back on the shelves.

One day in English class I told the teacher I was reading *War and Peace* by Leo Tolstoy. He kept me after class and told me that being a liar would never make me a success in life.

One day Melody Bleach quit school and soon Denny's pimples got a little better and so did his marks.

One day in guidance class I finished filling out the Hi-Y application form. Here's what it said.

NAME: Hulbert O'Driscoll
ADDRESS: 210 Easy Avenue
PHONE NUMBER: Central 34141 (Tuesdays and Thursdays only)
AMBITION: Brain Surgeon
EXPERIENCE IN CLUBS: Library Club
AWARDS: Glebe Gymnastics Sweater
TEAMS: Gym Team
FATHER'S OCCUPATION: Doctor and Lawyer
MAKE AND YEAR OF FATHER'S CAR: Brand-New Cadillac
RELIGION: Lutheran

After gymnastics that night, Doug was in the boys' dressing room selling chocolate bars.

"I'll make a deal with you," he said. "If you get that girl Fleurette to talk to me and get her to go out with me, I'll get you into the Hi-Y even without an application form."

"How did you know about Feel Street?" I said. I hated looking at his face.

"I was selling chocolate bars over at Lisgar Collegiate. There's a guy there, my chocolate-bar partner over there, he knows her. He told me."

"What guy?"

"A guy from where she used to go to school."

"What's his name?"

"Killer Bodnoff is his name," said Doug. "Will you do it? Get her to talk to me and I'll get you into the Hi-Y. No application form. I know your application form is a fake. I saw you put down 210 Easy Avenue. I checked. You don't live there. An old lady lives there. Is it a deal? I can get you in."

"No, it's not a deal," I said. "You're stealing those chocolate bars, aren't you?"

"Prove it," said Doug, his eyebrow going up and down.

I had my application form in my pocket, and on the way home I stopped at the top of the Bank Street Bridge.

You can only tear a piece of paper in half six times. I took the Hi-Y application form out of my pocket and folded it in half. Then I tore it down the crease and put one piece exactly on the other. Then I tore them in half again. Now I had four pieces. Then I put the two pieces on top of the other two and tore again. Now I had eight. I did it again and had sixteen. Mrs. O'Driscoll once told me that no matter how big the piece of paper was, you could only tear it in half five or six times. If it was the size of Lansdowne Park or the size of Ottawa you could only tear it in half a half a dozen times or so. Then it would be too small to tear anymore.

I tore again and had thirty-two.

My fingers were hurting and I was swearing and crying, and I tore once more for sixty-four. That was all I could do. Mrs. O'Driscoll was right. Six times.

I threw the sixty-four pieces of the Hi-Y application form up in the air over the railing of the Bank Street Bridge.

They floated down like snowflakes and fluttered down on the broken black melting spring ice of the Rideau Canal.

15. URANUS

It was near the end of May.

The next day was a school holiday because of a teachers' convention so I was coming in on the Uplands bus in the afternoon to go to Miss Collar-Cuff's. It was a strange time of the day to be on the bus. It was very quiet. In fact, the only other person on the bus with me was Mrs. O'Driscoll, who was going shopping.

When we transferred to the streetcar in Ottawa South, Mrs. O'Driscoll suddenly said she had some extra time so she'd be able to get off at Easy Avenue and come down to Miss Collar-Cuff's with me for a short visit before she went ahead to do her shopping.

"Might as well have a look at her, see where my boy is spending a lot of his time," she said out of the corner of her mouth.

I had a feeling of terror that maybe Mrs. O'Driscoll would spoil everything. Maybe she'd go into one of her long speeches or something. Embarrass me. Start talking about O'Driscoll and the war or say something about the money. Or start singing.

"Maybe you haven't got time. Taking an extra streetcar might make you late for shopping," I said.

"I've got lots of time. Never been late for shopping in my life. Not gonna start now, Hubbo, I can tell you that for sure. How can you be late for shopping?"

"Maybe Miss Collar-Cuff will be asleep. You won't be able to see her," I said.

"Yasso?" said Mrs. O'Driscoll, making a joke. "Let me worry about that. At least I'll be able to have a look at this awful fancy house of hers. Give her some tips. Rearrange her furniture for her." She gave me an elbow in the ribs. She was in a very good mood.

"Sometimes she just sits there. She won't even talk," I said, still trying to discourage her. "She never has visitors," I said.

The streetcar was close now. Two stops to go before Easy Avenue.

Mrs. O'Driscoll was all of a sudden quiet and I could feel her stiffen up as I leaned over to ring the bell. She had an expression on her face that didn't look like her. A blank expression. Looking straight ahead. Her hat straight on her head. She was almost like a photograph. Her eyes looking at nothing. Sitting straight in her seat. Her hands folded in her lap.

"Please don't come," I heard myself say.

Then the photograph spoke.

"You're afraid you might be ashamed of me, is that it, Hubbo?" said the photograph.

"No! No, it's just that..."

"Well, don't you worry about it. I wouldn't do that to you. There'll be time to meet your Miss Collar-Cuff. Anyway, you're right. I might be late for shopping. You'd better get going. This is your stop, isn't it?"

The streetcar driver was looking at me in his mirror. Was I going to get off or what?

"Go on. I'll see you tomorrow," said Mrs. O'Driscoll.

I got off and watched the streetcar move along the track. I gave a little wave as Mrs. O'Driscoll's window went by. She didn't look. She was staring straight ahead with that expression I had never seen before.

I felt like diving under the wheels of the streetcar and getting crushed.

I walked slowly down Easy Avenue and went into her rich house there. Miss Collar-Cuff was sitting reading while I hung up my coat and then went into the kitchen to make her some tea.

After a few sips of tea she put down her cup and said something that made my heart jump.

"Well," she said, "one of these times you must bring your Mrs. O'Driscoll over for a little visit. I'd very much like to meet her."

"Yes, Miss," I said to Miss Collar-Cuff. "Would next Thursday be okay?"

After I read to her a little bit from *War and Peace* she fell asleep in her chair. I got up quietly and went into the den to spend some time with the books in there. About half an hour later I went back into the living room to see if she wanted more tea but she was still asleep. The fire was almost out so I went out to the garage to get some wood. I opened and closed the driver's door of the Cadillac a few times to hear it chunk and I sat behind the wheel for a while.

When I came back in she was standing up, leaning on the back of her big chair. Her face was very tight and her lips were pressed together. And her eyes were staring straight ahead and glassy, like the lion's eyes. I put my shoulder under her arm and my arm around her back and we went up the stairs together to her bedroom.

Then I went back downstairs and phoned her nurse.

I brought her some tea and cookies upstairs and then some juice and later some ice water but she didn't want any of it. She dozed off while I read to her some more, and I tucked her in a bit and turned out her light and went downstairs to answer the door. It was the nurse, and after she went up to see Miss Collar-Cuff she came down and told me I might as well go home. She was going to call the doctor and stay the night.

When I got home I told Mrs. O'Driscoll Miss Collar-Cuff was sick. Mrs. O'Driscoll didn't say much. She just gave me my supper and then went right to bed.

The next day in science we were reviewing the grasshopper for the final exam and also talking about the planet Uranus and how the days on Uranus are forty-two years long and so are the nights. It was pretty interesting. The new teacher was telling us how the planet turned so slowly that the days and nights were forty-two years long. The planet Earth was really spinning around quickly compared to Uranus. Here the days and nights were only about twelve hours each. I was thinking some crazy things about life on earth and how fast it was. Go to bed. Sleep. Get up. Live. Go to bed. Sleep. Get up. Live.

"No wonder nobody lives there," some of the leftover Hi-Y guys were saying. "What if you stayed up all night with your girlfriend? Your parents would probably be dead by the time you got home!"

"Shut up, you stupid boys," our new teacher was saying when the phone rang.

"O'Driscoll you're wanted in the main office," he said, while the leftover Hi-Y guys were trying to stab the fish in the aquarium with their compasses.

Chubby was sitting behind his desk with a sad look on his face.

"Hubbo, my boy," said Chubby, "I have some very sad news to report to you. Miss Collar-Cuff passed away in her sleep last night. Her nurse called me this morning and told me."

I guess some tears came to my eyes because Chubby got out of his chair in his rumpled old suit and came around the desk without his cane and with pain on his face and put his arm on my shoulder and gave me a few pats. I felt my shoulder where he had put his hand.

"You liked her, didn't you?" said Chubby.

"Yes," I said, "I did."

"She was a very lonely lady," said Chubby.

Chubby was a very kind-hearted man.

Then he looked at me for a long time as if he was going to tell me something more. But he didn't. After a little chat about death and how it's good to die peacefully, in your sleep, with no pain, he said, "Now I have another unpleasant duty to perform. I have to see about some stealing that's been going on down at the Tuck Shop. You'd better go back to class now."

Back in class, while the Hi-Y guys were firing fish around the room, I was thinking about how long the nights were on Uranus and how short they were here on earth and how much can happen in one short night. How one short night can change everything.

Sleep. Get up. Live. Go to bed. Sleep. Die.

No more.

During gymnastics that day I felt sick and told the coach I was leaving a bit early.

On the Uplands bus the seat beside Mr. Yasso was empty but I went right past it and stood at the back the whole way home. In Building Eight I went right to the toilet and locked the door. I was trying to be sick but I couldn't. I sat in there for a while until I heard somebody try the door. Then I heard some talking. It was Mrs. O'Driscoll and Fleurette.

They didn't know I was in there.

They were talking about me.

Fleurette was talking to Mrs. O'Driscoll about what a drip I'd been since we got the money. How mean I was being and how snooty I was getting and how I was hanging around with those dopey Hi-Y guys. And Mrs. O'Driscoll was saying that I was acting a little strange and hurtful and how if O'Driscoll was here he'd sit me down and give me a bit of a talking to and straighten me out. Then I heard Fleurette go down the hall and I heard her door shut.

I called through the door as the tears came.

"Miss Collar-Cuff died," I called, half choking.

Out in the hall there was dead silence.

"Hubbo, my boy," I heard Mrs. O'Driscoll say.

I opened the door.

We were staring at each other.

Suddenly we were both talking and putting our arms around each other and patting each other and saying how sorry we were and saying everything would be all right and there, there and that's okay now.

"Oh, Hubbo," Mrs. O'Driscoll was saying, "I'm so sorry that I acted the fool. I should have gone to see her yesterday. It was so mean of me and so childish of me to do what I did. Not going to see her like that. Oh, Hubbo, please forgive me. Oh, Hubbo, don't feel bad. You're a good boy. Everything will be all right."

And even Nerves was there, putting his paws on my leg.

In the paper the next day it said that Miss Collar-Cuff had deceased and that she had no relatives and that she would be cremated because that was what was in her will.

16. A DEAL WITH DOUG

After gymnastics a few days later I was alone at my locker and the hall was empty.

Suddenly Doug came running up and his ugly face looked sick. He fumbled around with his combination lock with his long bony fingers and then tore open his locker.

"Quick," he said. "I'll make a deal with you." He took out a box of forty-eight chocolate bars from his locker. "Put these in your locker and I'll get you into the Hi-Y for sure. No questions asked. My brother told me Chubby and the vice-principal are coming down right now to search my locker! If they find these I'm done for! Quick!"

"I'll make a deal with you," I said. "You tell Fleurette Featherstone Fitchell who told you about Feel Street and I'll do it. I don't want to be in your stupid club."

"It's a deal!" he said.

I grabbed the box and shoved it under my gymnastics stuff in the bottom of my locker. Doug locked his locker and ran into the boy's can to hide just as Chubby came puffing down the stairs and the vice-principal behind him. I left my locker open and started piling up some books to take home.

Chubby said hello to me and the vice-principal took out the combination number he had written down and checked the locker number and opened up Doug's locker. They searched all through his locker and then shook their heads and closed it up again.

"Somebody's been stealing from the Tuck Shop," Chubby told me. "We think it's this fellow but we can't prove it. Do you know anything about it, Hubbo?"

I looked straight in Chubby's face. The vice-principal was behind him, his face hanging there. He seemed even bigger than ever. He must have been still growing or something.

"No, I don't, sir," I said to Chubby. My face felt funny and my lips felt thick and rubbery.

Chubby looked at me for a minute and then they went back upstairs. When they were gone Doug came out of the can and I gave him the stolen box of chocolate bars.

"Now, you'll come home with me and you'll tell Fleurette."

"I'll tell her later," said Doug.

"No, now!" I said.

"Maybe I will, maybe I won't," said Doug. "It's your word against mine now anyway!"

"My mother knows Chubby. She has proof. She saw you. I'll squeal on you and so will she."

"Your mother?"

"My mother is Mrs. O'Driscoll, the cleaning lady. He'll believe her. They're friends."

"Who's going to believe you and a cleaning lady?" said Doug.

All I could see was Doug's eyebrow. I felt like my mouth was full of blood.

The next thing I knew he was on the floor, his nose gushing out red. I had punched him so hard my hand felt like it was broken. I had never hit anybody in my life before. It scared me so much I started to shake. I used to fight in Angel Square all the time, but that was just for fun. I never hit anybody. I reached down and grabbed him by the wrist and twisted his arm behind his back so that he had to stand up. I knew how to do it because I had watched the Uplands bus driver do that to some of the passengers who couldn't behave on his bus late at night.

I twisted his arm so far up his back that he had to walk. I walked him down First Avenue that way and down Bank Street. Over the Bank Street Bridge I felt like breaking his arm and throwing him in the canal.

At the bus terminal the bus was just leaving and I shoved him on and made him pay our fares.

"Got yourself a prisoner?" the driver said.

Mr. Yasso was on the bus and the seat beside him was empty. I pushed Doug into the seat and we took off. His shirt was covered with blood and he was crying.

"I'm taking this guy home with me to confess to something he did," I told Mr. Yasso.

"Yasso?" said Mr. Yasso. He smelled worse than he ever smelled before.

When we got to Building Eight, Mrs. O'Driscoll and Fleurette were standing outside.

"Well, well," said Mrs. O'Driscoll, "what have we here? It's our Hubbo with a friend with blood all over him. It's the snot who steals from the Tuck Shop, is it?"

Fleurette was standing there with her mouth open.

"Tell her," I said to Doug. "Tell her about Feel Street," I said, "or I'll break your arm!"

Mrs. O'Driscoll had her chin stuck out and she was standing close to Doug, staring him in the face. She had her hands on her hips. The look she had on her was going to turn Doug to stone.

Then Doug started blubbering and saying that it was Killer Bodnoff who told him about Feel Street and that I never said anything to him about Fleurette no matter how many times he tried to ask me, and please would Mrs. O'Driscoll not tell Chubby about what he did.

Then Mrs. O'Driscoll made a little speech as Fleurette slipped her hand inside mine.

"You young scalliwag, you're going to be leaving my home in the next thirty seconds, but before you go you're going to listen to this. I know you've been stealing stuff from the Tuck Shop and selling it because I've seen you. I'm a very good friend of Mr. Chubby and I'm going to decide tonight when I go to bed whether I'm going to tell him about that tomorrow or not. So you go home and think about that tonight. And think about this too. Think about why rich boys like you steal. Think about that. If O'Driscoll was here he'd kick you down the stairs. If we had any stairs! Now get your ugly face out of here!"

Then we went inside and left him standing there.

We watched out the window as Doug walked over with his head down to wait for the bus.

"I shouldn't have hit him," I said.

Fleurette was holding my hand. She said she hoped in her heart all along that I had never told Doug anything about her. Then she gave me a little kiss on the part of my face where she hit me. Her eyes were a soft brown colour.

Then Mrs. O'Driscoll sang a bit of "Bye, Bye, Blackbird," and then we went into the kitchen and had a meeting to organize a big picnic Mrs. O'Driscoll wanted us to have at the sandpits to celebrate the end of school.

17. JUST LIKE SOMETHING O'DRISCOLL WOULD DO

It was the end of June and there was one day of school left. I went to see Chubby to see if there was a cheque waiting for me as usual. I didn't really think there would be one because I was more and more sure that it was Miss Collar-Cuff who was the secret moneygiver the whole time and now that she was…I couldn't even say the word.

Chubby was sitting behind his desk. He looked better than usual. Except for his suit. His face seemed brighter and he wasn't puffing like he often did. I think it was because school was over and now he could go for a two month's rest all summer.

When I asked Chubby about the cheque he got a very serious look on his face.

"Due to recent circumstances, of which you are sadly aware, the arrangement concerning your monthly expectations, as it has been up to this point in time, has ceased," he said.

Whatever that meant. It was the kind of sentence Miss Collar-Cuff used every time I ever tried to ask her about the money. Anyway, I said goodbye to Chubby and told him I would miss him over the summer.

"You'll be back in the fall, I presume?" he asked.

"Yes, I will," I said.

"Good," he said. "That will make everything just fine then."

I had one more thing to do.

Everybody was crowded around the Tuck Shop and around the lockers getting packed up for the summer. Everybody was in a good mood. Laughing and singing and joking around.

I stayed by my locker, hiding behind the open door. I was waiting for Mrs. O'Driscoll to come by the same time she usually did.

Right on time, I saw her coming down the hall, pushing her pail in front of her with the mop in it like she always did.

When she got near my open locker I stepped out in front of her and stopped her.

I took the mop handle out of her hand and put my arms around her and gave her a big hug in front of everybody.

A big cheer went up and everybody started laughing and hugging each other and slapping us on the back.

Mrs. O'Driscoll's lips were on my ear.

"Oh, Hubbo," she whispered to me, "you're just like O'Driscoll. This is what he would have done too. This is exactly what he would have done!"

I felt good.

I walked out of Glebe Collegiate Institute, and all the way down First Avenue. I wondered why Chubby was acting a little strange. First the Miss Collar-Cuff sentence and then saying "Make everything just fine then," was bothering me a bit.

On the way over the Bank Street Bridge some of the Uplands kids were throwing their school books and papers in the canal. Some of them really hated school a lot.

After Mrs. O'Driscoll got home she and Fleurette started getting ready for the picnic. Mrs. O'Driscoll kept saying that it *wasn't* Miss Collar-Cuff that was giving us the money, it was O'Driscoll the whole time, and this *proved* it was O'Driscoll.

"*What* proves it was O'Driscoll?" I said.

"The fact that he *didn't* send it this month!" said Mrs. O'Driscoll. "Don't you see? That's just like something he'd do! That's just like him to start sending some money every month and then just as you start getting used to it—he forgets to send it! The whole idea! It's perfect O'Driscoll! Forget all about his responsibilities! Start something and then don't finish it! Probably gave the money to some floozy in New Zealand or some-where!"

"What's a floozy?" I asked. Fleurette and I were laughing.

"Never mind what a floozy is, but don't you see? It's exactly like something O'Driscoll would go and do! Start something and not finish it! Started in the war—couldn't even finish that—had to swim off somewhere! Well, she can have him, whoever she is, and the money too! Typical O'Driscoll. Oh, it's him all right! Probably too tied up with that Egyptian princess he was likely staying with to remember a small detail like sending us the fifty dollars. What he needs is a good swift kick!"

Mrs. O'Driscoll had to stop talking about this for a second so she could take a big breath and start saying some more about O'Driscoll.

She sure had a lot to say when it came to the subject of O'Driscoll.

In a little while Denny Dingle came in and said that on our way to the sandpits we could stop by and pick up some of the Dorises because they were coming with us too.

Then he helped us pack some of the picnic stuff: the homemade bread, the peanut butter and the honey, the weiners, the oranges, the butter, the pickles and the mustard and the grape juice and the blankets and the boiled eggs and the cups and the salt and pepper and some plates and a knife.

And Mrs. O'Driscoll's sherry.

And my *War and Peace*.

Then Fleurette and Denny went around to the other units and got Mr. and Mrs. Blank and Nerves and Mr. Yasso and Mrs. Stentorian.

And Mrs. Fitchell.

While we were all gathered around outside Building Eight, getting our stuff organized and getting ready to walk down to the sandpits, a big fancy car pulled up.

Out of the car got Mr. Donald D. DonaldmcDonald!

He came right over to me and put his hand on my shoulder just like he did one time before. It seemed so long ago.

Then I knew!

I knew it was him. I knew he was the one who was the secret money-giver.

And then he explained everything.

He was Miss Collar-Cuff's lawyer. He got me the job with her.

"I knew she would like you. She tried others but they didn't work out. But I knew you would. And the fifty dollars a month. That's for your education. To help you with it."

Then he handed me a cheque.

"Here's this month's cheque. It's signed by me now because it's not a secret anymore. Before, I had Miss Collar-Cuff to keep an eye on your schooling. But you'll do fine from now on. How's *War and Peace* going?"

He said a whole lot of other things about Chubby and about how I saved his life and how he quit playing golf to try and let off steam. And everybody was excited and Nerves was running around like he was on fire and Mrs. O'Driscoll was crying.

And I won't tell you what Mr. Yasso said when I got around to introducing him to Mr. Donald D. DonaldmcDonald.

We all walked out the gate with our stuff (Mr. Donald D. DonaldmcDonald left his car there and walked with us) and walked along the air strip and past the Ottawa Hunt and Golf Club where I was remembering how the early morning sun used to be on the wet putting green glistening silver off the dew. The green slopes down and the fairway rolls away down into the mist and then comes up again soft and green.

The little tin flags sticking up out of the holes on the putting green. And a spider string or two, beads of dew glistening down on them.

And maybe there's one golfer out there practicing his putting, the ball making little rainbows when it ploughs its little way, throwing up a spray in the early morning.

The smell of sweet-sweet-warm-plant-juice-cut-grass. And the smell of the pine all around and the chuckling of the chipmunks, and then the crunch of somebody coming around the corner from the pro shop, crunching on the crushed stone path with the golf spikes like hearing somebody eating corn flakes.

On the way to the sandpits we stopped and picked up a few of the Dorises.

At the sandpits the sun was high and hot now, and everything was clear as in a photograph.

All of us sitting and lying around the blankets. The pots and dishes and stuff spread around the little smouldering fire. The smoke floating, curling softly in graceful shapes. The sand cliff rising behind us, golden brown sugar. The top of the sandpit, so far up there and so clear. The fine edge of it like gold steel against the sky.

And Mrs. O'Driscoll, standing now, staring up there, pointing.

Pointing at a figure standing away up there, legs apart, hands on his hips, his shirt open, his sun hat tilted on one side.

Mrs. O'Driscoll's mouth opening, dropping her glass of sherry in the sand, trying to say these words.

Then saying these words:

"Lord strike me dead!"

And then these words:

"It's O'Driscoll!"

Some of the Characters

Hubbo — a boy with success on his mind

Mr. Donald D. DonaldmcDonald — the world's worst golfer

Mrs. O'Driscoll — a lady to whom life is just like a song

O'Driscoll — a man who is missing

Mrs. Fitchell — a mother with a cast on her wrist

Fleurette Featherstone Fitchell — a girl who is proud though she wears
   a rag in her long curly black hair

Nerves — a dog who should have been a mirror

Mr. and Mrs. Blank — people who see themselves in their pet's face

Denny Dingle — a boy who was the victim of pimples

The Dorises — one big happy family

Mr. Tool — a teacher driven berserk by his students

Doug — a sneaky Hi-Y guy

Chubby — a man in pain but kind at the same time

Mr. Yasso — a rotten conversationalist

Mr. Stentorian — a man on the night shift

Mrs. Stentorian — a woman living a life of constant thunder

Miss Collar-Cuff — a rich lady and alone

the grasshopper — an insect studied to death

Mr. Stubbs — a man who travels a lot

Lassie — a success

Melody Bleach — a hypnotist

the English teacher — he keeps you from reading too much

Victor and Virginia — people with award-winning teeth

the dermatologist — a doctor who can't cure himself

COVERED BRIDGE

Thanks Patsy Aldana, Fay Beale,
Stan Clark, Keith Clarke, Jackie Doyle,
Megan Doyle, Mike Doyle, Ryan Doyle,
Paul Kavanagh, Marilyn Kennedy,
Dorothy McConnery, Cathy McGregor,
Mike Paradis, Dr. Peter Premachuk,
Rita Premachuk, Gene Rheaume,
and Alan Wotherspoon,
for your expertise and support.

CRICKETS ACTUALLY ARGUE!

My dog Nerves and I stood in the almost dark inside the portal of the covered bridge. My eyes were squinting, trying to see what was coming slowly, floating through the bridge towards us from the other end. I could feel one of Nerves' knees knocking against the side of my shoe.

The moon put a patch of silver-yellow through the open wind space in the lattice onto the deck about halfway between us and the white thing gliding towards us. The rafters above were off in the dark. The carriageway under our feet was dark except for the patch of moon.

Mushrat Creek burbled and gurgled quietly under us. Nerves' teeth were grinding and chattering politely beside my ankle.

Somewhere else, two crickets were arguing.

The thing took more shape as it approached the wind space. The shape of a woman. And a voice, saying words.

"Please, Father, let me in? Please let me in, Father! May I please go in? Can't I please get in?"

She wore a moonlight-coloured dress and a wide-brimmed dark hat.

There was no face showing under the hat.

Nerves stopped knocking and went stiff against me.

Then the woman turned in the moonlight and hurtled through the space and disappeared into Mushrat Creek.

Then we heard a big splash.

That is, I heard a big splash.

Nerves didn't hear a thing.

He was passed out.

That was the first night of my new job on the covered bridge.

The next day I was fired.

But we're going too fast.

I'd better go back a bit.

CHIPWAGON BECOMES U.F.O.!

You probably heard about how my father was run over by a streetcar. How he lay down on the streetcar tracks for a rest during a snowstorm. I never knew him because that happened when I was just a baby.

My mom died when I was born. I lived with Mrs. O'Driscoll. She was married to a distant cousin of my dad's. I thought of her as my mother and I loved her. But I called her Mrs. O'Driscoll. It was a warm little joke we had between us.

And you probably heard about all that stuff that happened to me at Glebe Collegiate and at the Uplands Emergency Shelter where we lived and about Easy Avenue and my job with Miss Collar-Cuff and the mysterious money and about Mr. Donald D. DonaldmcDonald and about O'Driscoll showing up from the War almost five years late.

And about the fight I had with Fleurette Featherstone Fitchell and how we made up after and went on a picnic with everybody.

But I definitely didn't yet tell how I wound up on a little farm up the Gatineau at Mushrat Creek in charge of a covered bridge and what happened about the bridge.

But before any of *that* happened I guess I didn't tell you how Fleurette Featherstone Fitchell moved away in the middle of the night one night, and the next morning there was nothing left of her except a short note to me pinned to our door. It was in a sealed envelope.

The note said this:

Dear Hubbo:
My Dear Hubbo:

I will always, all my life, love you.
Dad is back and we're leaving now.
Right now.
Everything is going to be better from now on, he said.

xxxxx in the middle of the night.
F3

And I also didn't tell you about how I couldn't write her back because she didn't tell anybody where she was going. I asked all the neighbours if they knew, I asked the post office across the parade square, I phoned the office where we paid our rent. Nobody knew what Featherstone Fitchell's new address was. They were just gone. Vanished. Fleurette, into thin air.

There was so much I wanted to tell her, to talk to her about.

I started a letter to her that I couldn't send. Not now, anyway. But you never know. She might show up. O'Driscoll, he was supposed to be drowned, dead, vanished in the War, and he came back. So maybe I would find her address or maybe she would get in touch with us sometime. I guess, then, it was because of the miracle of O'Driscoll showing up that I started the letter to Fleurette.

I told her that I couldn't send it, which seemed to be a pretty stupid thing to say, because, if I couldn't send it, she wouldn't hear me say that, and if I could send it, I wouldn't have to say what I just said.

Then I asked her if she remembered that afternoon we had the picnic at the sand pits and how O'Driscoll came down the hill of sand and how he stopped in front of us? And how he took a look back over his shoulder? And how, then, he spoke? And, after nine years away, what was the first thing he said?

"Well, now," says O'Driscoll, "what were we talking about before this interruption? Where were we, anyway?"

Then I reminded her, in the letter, how Mrs. O'Driscoll never said a word, just took a step forward, stomping on her sherry glass lying in the sand, and fell against his chest and put her cheek on his shoulder and her nose in his neck and her arms around him, and closed her eyes, squeezed her eyes shut.

But O'Driscoll's eyes weren't shut. He was looking at me. I remembered him from his picture, not from real life.

"You're young Hubbo," he said over the top of Mrs. O'Driscoll's head. That made me feel good. He made me feel like he'd be disappointed if I wasn't young Hubbo. O'Driscoll was like that. He could make you feel good.

Then I told Fleurette all about O'Driscoll and the chipwagon. And how, after we'd had the wagon only three days, something awful happened. We were crossing the train tracks that crossed Ottawa along Scott Street. Right on the tracks, a wheel fell off our wagon. We got the horse unhitched just in time.

The Scott Street line is pretty straight so we had time to unbuckle the traces and get the horse out of the shafts. The train didn't even try to slow down at the last minute. It was in the morning and the train was coming in from the west so I guess the sun was in the engineer's eyes. At least that's what they said afterwards.

O'Driscoll said he thought they did it on purpose. He said he heard the old engineer saying to the fireman that he'd hit a lot of things in his long career—cows, buffalo, a truck full of turkeys, a tramp who'd frozen to death, a house on a trailer—but never a chipwagon, and he was glad he did because he always wanted to see what it was like. See how high the wagon would go.

He wasn't disappointed.

O'Driscoll said that it was probably the best hit that engineer ever had in his long years as a rotten train driver. The air was full of potato chips and paper plates and toothpicks for about a half an hour. It poured salt.

And it rained grease.

The main part of the wagon turned over and over in the air and the unpeeled potatoes were flying and bouncing around like hail the size of baseballs.

I told Fleurette some other stuff about O'Driscoll's insurance and how he put a down payment on a little farm up here in a place called Mushrat Creek. Then I told her about how the dog, Nerves, was ours now because his family didn't want him anymore.

Then I wrote a letter to the Uplands Emergency Shelter post office.

Dear Sir:

Please send me the address of Fleurette Featherstone Fitchell who moved out of Building Number Eight, Unit 3 at the end of June, 1950.
We don't know where she went.
Yours truly,
Hubbo O'Driscoll

P.S. My new address is:
Hubbo O'Driscoll,
Mushrat Creek,
c/o Brennan's Hill Post Office,
Gatineau County,
Quebec, Canada.

FISH JUMPS OUT OF FRYING PAN!

From my bedroom window I could hear the fish jumping in Mushrat Creek. You can't *hear* fish jumping, but you can hear the water take a double kind of a slurp. Sometimes the two slurps happen so fast together it sounds like only *one* nice delicious slurp. But it's really two. One when the trout comes out of the water with his mouth open and his gills stretched to get the bug he's after, and the other for when he flips his body and his tail hits the top of the water to get him back down into Mushrat Creek.

I suppose he thinks he's safe down there but you'd think he'd know everybody can see where he's going and what he's doing because the water's so clear you see right to the bottom. But I guess he does know because he likes to take his bug or his caterpillar or his fly or whatever he's caught and swim with it under the overhanging alders or beneath where the grassy bank juts out or into the weeds or under the wharf out of the light.

He's probably like everybody else. You go where it's dark, where it's private, then nobody can see you. You *think*.

It's like the covered bridge.

Sometimes people go in there to do things that they don't want anybody to see them doing because it's dark in there at certain times of the day and night and it seems private.

But you never know who might be watching.

It wasn't these thoughts, though, that woke me up that morning.

It was the sounds of the trout jumping in Mushrat Creek.

And our rooster crowing.

I got up and lit a small hot fire in the stove in the summer kitchen and put on a kettle of well-water. I put a dipper of creek water from the pail into the basin and washed up.

I stepped outside to dry my face.

The sun was already giving the white trunks of the birch trees across Mushrat Creek and up on the top of Rock Face a bit of a golden glow. Upstream, though, to the west, the red side of the covered bridge was still a grey shadow. And west of that, up at Ball's Falls and Lake Pizinadjih, it would still be dark.

It was O'Driscoll who told me how to watch a sunrise. He learned it when he was a sailor in the war. He said you watch not the sun where it is supposed to come up, but something else.

Watch the flag away above you on the ship to get the first flash of light. Because the flag is higher than you, it will see the sun first. Specially when the sea is calm.

So he told me to watch the white birch trees standing on the top of Rock Face across Mushrat Creek, because they'd get the sun before I would see it. Or, even better, watch Dizzy Peak to the north, if it was clear.

This morning I missed it.

But that was O.K. because the next flash of light would be on the covered bridge and the tops of the trees, which were both higher than our house.

The rooster gave another couple of crows because he was watching for the light too.

I went down the short hill and cut through the ice house and stepped out on the little wharf on Mushrat Creek. My fishing rod was lying right where I left it in the cattails beside the wharf.

I baited my hook with a small worm I got out of my worm can that I kept in the ice house between two blocks of ice to keep cool. Worms like the cool. They might as well be nice and cool and have a nice life for a while because what was going to happen to them pretty soon wasn't nice at all.

Three worms—three brook trout. I pulled three brook trout from where they were hiding. The worms helped me. Fish eat worms. The O'Driscolls eat fish. That's Nature!

I cut open the stomachs and left the heads on and cleaned the bodies slippery clean in the clear water of Mushrat Creek.

I took them through the ice house and up the short hill to the summer kitchen attached to the back of our house.

I liked to cut through the ice house whenever I had the chance. Because of the smell of the damp sawdust and the wooden floor and the cold smell of the ice mixed with the wood and the log walls and the oakum stuffed between the logs.

It reminded me of jumping on the backs of the ice wagons to grab an ice chip to chew on a hot August day in Lowertown when I lived there and was small.

In the summer kitchen I put an iron frying pan on the stove, got a slab of butter from the ice box, some flour out of the bin. I melted the butter in the pan, rolled the trout in the flour and placed them carefully in the sizzling butter.

One of the trout bodies twitched a bit. Jumped.

"Now that's fresh fish," O'Driscoll would say.

I cut two slabs of bread and clamped them in the wire toaster. I lifted one of the stove lids. I put on the toast. I turned over the trout. I poured the boiling water over the tea bags in the pot. I turned the toast.

I moved the trout a bit in the pan. No more jumping. Getting brown in the hot butter.

I shook the fire. I made other breakfast noises. I knew that upstairs they would like to hear the breakfast noises.

I turned the toast again and then took it off and plastered both pieces with homemade butter. I put the lid back on the hole and placed the toast on the rack to keep warm.

Then I called upstairs.

The first of the family to come downstairs was Nerves.

I told you about Nerves, who we got from our neighbour at Uplands Emergency Shelter when we lived there. Nerves was our little dog who looked a lot like a rat. His tail was a little black whip, and he clicked when he walked. This morning his little eraser of a nose was moving around, smelling breakfast. Then he yawned and stretched and went to the door. While he was waiting for me to shove open the screen door for him (he usually opened it himself but this morning he was too tired), he leaned his little head on the doorjamb and closed his eyes. Seeing the ghost had played him right out.

I let Nerves out and heard the stairs creak.

After breakfast I would tell them about what Nerves and I saw last night.

We sat down to breakfast and Mrs. O'Driscoll's eyes were shining. She loved this farm. She felt like she lived on it all her life and it was only our second week there.

The people before us, the what's-their-names, had kept it up pretty well, but there was still lots to do. The people before us were only leasing it to us while they went on a world tour that they won. They won it in a baking contest. Something they baked.

They would be back in a year.

Maybe. Who knows.

Look how long it took O'Driscoll to come back!

And Mrs. O'Driscoll got to work right away as soon as we got there. Before O'Driscoll was even unpacked, Mrs. O'Driscoll had filled a half a pail with gooseberries she picked out near the cedar trees behind the outhouse. And the next day she had six jars of gooseberry jam sitting down in a neat row in the cool root cellar behind the henhouse.

I never saw Mrs. O'Driscoll work so hard and be so happy. Jam and pie and jelly and cake and homemade bread; washing, ironing, sewing, weeding, milking, separating, churning, scrubbing, feeding, picking, singing and laughing.

And O'Driscoll and I were busy, too; cutting and carrying and chasing and fixing, and hoeing and harnessing, and shingling and wiring and talking...talking...

O'Driscoll was talking.

"Did you know that the first covered bridge ever built on this planet was over the Euphrates River in the year 783 Before Christ? And that bridge is still there? At least I think it's still there. I'm not sure if I saw it or not or maybe I'm imagining it because of the amnesia. Or I saw a drawing of it somewhere," O'Driscoll was saying as he finished up his trout breakfast.

"The Euphrates River is in Egypt somewhere, O'Driscoll. How could you get to Egypt if you were in the South Pacific?" Mrs. O'Driscoll asked. She didn't seem to care if she got an answer. She was too happy to bother with answers. She always liked questions better than answers.

"Amnesia is a peculiar thing," O'Driscoll said. "You never know whether what you say about yourself is true or what. Like that business about prospecting for uranium in Labrador. I was sure about that, but now it doesn't seem real."

"Well, O'Driscoll," said Mrs. O'Driscoll, "don't bother your head about it. You're here now. We're all three of us here now and that's all that counts. We'll just prove to the government you're not dead and you can get your veteran's money and it'll all be forgotten."

"And the *longest* covered bridge in the world is right here in Canada. It's in New Brunswick and it's over the Saint John River. It's 1,282 feet long. And it's there as large as life because I was there and I saw it with these two eyes. I remember that as well as I remember this beautiful trout breakfast you made for us this morning, Hubbo me boy!"

O'Driscoll was never the kind of person who didn't listen to what you were saying. That is, most of the time. But when it came to something that might be a little bit unbelievable, he might not listen very well. Maybe he'd think you were exaggerating a little bit. I wondered where he'd ever get an idea like that.

"Nerves and I went down to look over the job after dark. Didn't get anything done. Saw a ghost..."

"A ghost, eh?" said O'Driscoll. "Well, those old bridges are full of ghosts...anyway, if you do well your first month or so, you'll be full-time caretaker at least until the what's-their-names come back. We could use the $12 a month..."

"It was the shape of a woman...it jumped into the creek...Nerves passed out...I was saying..." But O'Driscoll kept talking.

"Our job is to keep the lights in shape, report any damage or accidents or suspicious happenings and oversee the painting of the bridge every two years. The two years is coming up a month or so from now. There's expenses. Oil, wicks, tools and, of course, the paint and the labour during paintin' time is what the expenses are for."

"There was a splash. She had on a whitish dress and a dark hat with a big brim," I said quietly.

O'Driscoll was looking at me with pride.

I was saying just the kind of things that he would say. When I mentioned the splash, Mrs. O'Driscoll put her hands across the table, one on mine and one on O'Driscoll's, and smiled.

Then she said this out of the far corner of her mouth: "I love it here. Ghosts and covered bridges and everything! Are we ever *lucky*! I hope that the what's-their-names fall off the edge of the earth on that world tour of theirs and that they're never heard from again."

"I'll drink to that," said O'Driscoll, and gulped down the rest of his tea. They weren't going to listen to me about the ghost.

I was starting to think that maybe it never happened.

If only Nerves could talk. He didn't think it was so *lucky*!

A knock came to our front door. I went through the parlour we only used on Sunday and opened the front door we hardly *ever* used. It was stuck and I had to give it an extra shove and a kick.

It was the county chairman.

In our kitchen, he told us we didn't need to caretake the covered bridge anymore. We were getting a new bridge. I was fired.

It was the shortest job I ever had.

BOOK CAUSES EARTHQUAKE!

O'Driscoll was talking about the construction going to start about a mile up Mushrat Creek. They were going to build a modern bridge over the creek so the highway would go straight through instead of circling down to the covered bridge like it always did. This would take a big bend out of the road.

He also said a couple of times that he heard some of the farmers up in the post office in Low talking about the highway getting paved.

"That'll keep the dust off the chokecherries begod!" O'Driscoll told us one of them said.

And everybody was saying how good it was going to be because there would be jobs for everybody that wanted to work and there'd be money galore around for everybody.

And O'Driscoll explained once while we were milking the cows that the farmers around there had a pretty good life even though they had to work pretty hard for it.

But the one thing they never had very much of was money.

All the money they ever had was from the cream they sold to the dairy or maybe they'd sell a pig or a steer or maybe even raise some chickens and sell them but not very often.

And once when we were in the general store in Brennan's Hill buying what we needed which was salt, flour, tea, sugar and molasses, we heard the owner of the store say that his hired man quit on him to go and work on the new highway that was to approach the new bridge.

We bought more molasses than other people, mostly because it was our dog Nerves' favourite food.

Nerves loved to eat a big chunk of bread soaked in molasses.

What a dog.

Then he'd go down to the creek and wash his hands and face.

Maybe take a swim.

One hot afternoon Mrs. O'Driscoll was sitting in her rocking chair out the front doorway in the shade of her two rowanwood trees. She looked nice rocking there a little bit in her bright yellow and blue dress and the purple combs in her hair and above her the clumps of red rowanwood berries hanging like tiny chandeliers. And her head resting back and a little smile on her face. She liked that yellow and blue dress because yellow and blue were the school colours of the school, Glebe Collegiate, where she worked as a cleaning lady before she became a farmer.

She had on the stove a great big pot of preserves simmering away in the summer kitchen.

The smell of the raspberries bubbling there in the sugary red syrup was reaching out through the screen door, past the woodpile, over the side road, around the walls of the barn and into the pig pen where the pigs were lying in the cool mud in the hot sun grunting and snorting and sighing every now and then and snuffling into their big nostrils, the sweetness and the pureness of Mrs. O'Driscoll's great big pot of preserves of raspberries simmering on the stove in her summer kitchen.

And upstairs, in the heat, the way O'Driscoll liked it (Mrs. O'Driscoll said out of the corner of her mouth he must have been in the North Pole all the time he was away and he's trying to make up for it now), O'Driscoll lay sleeping, grunting and snorting a little bit and breathing in the hot raspberry syrupy smell that floated into the house from the summer kitchen up through the vent in the ceiling and right around O'Driscoll's body and up around his head.

I went down to the ice house and sat in there on an old car seat in the cool corner in the sawdust. The smell of the oakum between the logs was almost like chloroform, and I dozed off a bit and let my book, *War and Peace*, fall to the floor.

The noise the book made when it hit the floor shook the whole building.

And the ground.

It was deep noise, a thud from the centre of the earth.

No, it wasn't the book! A book couldn't do that! I was awake now.

It was dynamite!

They were blasting about a mile up Mushrat Creek.

Construction for the new bridge was starting.

A while later, some dead trout floated by. They floated on their backs, their white stomachs shining in the sun, the dark pink of the inside of their gills like little ribbons around their necks.

GOOSEBERRY HAS FACE OF A BEAUTIFUL WOMAN

I was writing more stuff to Fleurette. Trying to explain about Mrs. O'Driscoll and how happy she seemed to be. Her face, it was, it looked, it seemed like she was just going to start smiling any minute now. How some people's faces look like they are just about to start crying and other people's faces look like they are just going to get mad and start shouting at somebody.

But Mrs. O'Driscoll, her face was so different from what it used to be like. When she was a cleaning lady at Glebe Collegiate Institute and we lived at Uplands Emergency Shelter her face was often like one of those faces that might start to sigh any minute or maybe even start to cry.

And I tried to tell Fleurette how maybe it was because O'Driscoll was lost in the war and how it was only when she had some of the sherry that she liked that she wore her face in a different way.

But now, here at Mushrat Creek with O'Driscoll, Mrs. O'Driscoll's face was the same whether she had the sherry or not.

And I tried to think of what to compare Mrs. O'Driscoll's face to, to put in Fleurette's letter.

Her face was calm like the covered bridge. It was content like Mushrat Creek. It was clear like Dizzy Peak. It was funny like a gooseberry on a gooseberry bush. And it was full of love like the Gatineau Hills.

And it was wise, like the Gatineau River.

Fleurette would like these ways that I tried to say what Mrs. O'Driscoll's face was like.

And I was writing how you get to like somebody's face. Like O'Driscoll's. At first I thought he was sort of funny-looking. Now I loved his face. What happened? It didn't look like the same face at all.

But mostly I was trying to explain how they were going to let the bridge get old and rotten. How you have to take care of things or they'll disappear.

Or maybe they would just let it get neglected until it got dangerous, and then they'd have to tear it down.

It didn't seem right.

MAILMAN ENTERS COVERED BRIDGE —DOES NOT EXIT!

The very first person I met around Mushrat Creek was Oscar McCracken.

Oscar McCracken's farm was the last farm on the road going south before you got into Brennan's Hill.

Oscar lived there with his mother and his younger brother. He worked hard on the farm and also delivered the mail twice a day in his little car with only a front seat.

It was a pretty old car. A 1929 Ford Coupe. You could open the windshield by winding a handle on the dashboard. You cranked the motor with a hand crank to start it. It had two narrow steps under each door called running boards.

The train came up in the evening and went down in the morning. Oscar met the train at ten to six in the evening in Brennan's Hill and picked up the mail and delivered it up along the road past our place as far as Low.

Then he drove back home.

He also met the train in the morning at ten after nine in Low and did his route again.

That meant he crossed the covered bridge four times a day.

About a week after we moved in I walked down our side road past the potato field on one side and the dusty chokecherry trees on the other side to our gate at the main gravel road and our mailbox. The entrance to the covered bridge was right there on the right.

I stood leaning on the gate because I wanted to find out something. I wanted to find out why it took so long for the mail car to go through the bridge. First you'd hear it stop at the house of Old Mickey Malarkey and you'd hear the mailbox squeak and the car door slam. Then you'd hear the car groan in first gear, hear it swallow, hear it whine in second gear, hear it swallow and just hear it start crying in third gear and then stop in front of our mailbox. After the mailman put in our mail (it was never for us at first, it was always for the farmers who were going to fall off the edge of the earth), you could hear the car door slam, the motor moan in first gear, swallow, whine in second gear...but then the car would be inside the bridge and you wouldn't be able to hear as well, except for the rumbling of the wheels on the carriageway...then silence.

Sometimes two or three minutes would pass by before you would hear even any rumbling and then the car would burst out the other side, whining in second gear.

You could hear the thunk of the ramp as the wheels left the deck. Then, swallow, high gear and gone.

I stood there leaning on our gate to see if I could see why it took the mailman so long to get through the covered bridge.

Along he came to Malarkey's. I followed him with my ears:

squeak (the mailbox),

slam (the car door),

first gear, groan, swallow (gearshift), second gear, whine,

swallow, third gear, cry...stop.

The mailman got out. He came over to me and told me his name. Oscar McCracken. He gave me a catalogue. He got back in the car. He drove into the covered bridge and stopped about half the way in. He shut off the motor. He sat there.

I could feel the silence he was in as I leaned over our gate to get a better look.

After a long while, Oscar McCracken got out, cranked his car started, got back in and drove out the other side of the bridge and up the road towards Low.

I walked into the bridge and stopped almost halfway over and waited. I listened to Mushrat Creek below and to the swallows twittering secretly in the mud nests in the rafters. I was standing beside the gap in the siding which was for air circulation and also for cutting down on wind obstruction.

And for letting in the moon some nights. And for ghosts to dive out of.

Up in the rafters near the eaves was a gap, left there also for circulation and wind.

Further up the rafters closer to the arch, near where the end of a tree-knee angle brace met on one of them, there was something written. Carved in the wood.

I crawled partway up the truss using the ventilation gaps and the timbers and braces for my hands and feet until I could make out the writing.

The catalogue I still had in my hand slipped between my fingers, bounced off my foot and through the gap and down into Mushrat Creek.

I didn't even know I had it in my hand until it dropped.

There were five letters printed deep and strong and perfect into the rafter. Printed with care. Loving care.

O LVS O

I got down and checked out the gap for the piece of mail. Gone. Down Mushrat Creek. Didn't matter. It wasn't for us anyway.

O LVS O

O for Oscar probably. Oscar loves O. Oscar loves Oscar? Oscar the mailman carved in a bridge that he loves himself?

So much that he'd climb up and sit in those rafters and carve a message to himself?

Ridiculous.

It must have been some other person named O.

I walked through our gooseberry shrubs up onto some rocks and sat under the huge butternut tree between the stand of pine and the cedar bush.

I was thinking about what I had written in the letter to Fleurette that I'd probably never send.

I wrote that if you don't take care of things they'll rust and rot away and die. Then I got an idea.

Sometimes if you write things down you get ideas you never knew you had.

Under the butternut tree I got an idea that I didn't have until that very minute.

I would be the covered bridge caretaker anyway! Maybe that way, people would notice and...

COVERED BRIDGE HAS TWO EXITS
—BUT NO ENTRANCE!

I was out caretaking my bridge. When I checked the lamps I worked at night.

I ran a rope from the lantern to a small pulley in the top of the portal of the bridge to another pulley between the truss and the rafters and down to a nail in one of the braces, high enough up so some little kids wouldn't untie it or fool with it and have the lamp come crashing down or set a fire or break one of their heads open.

The caretaker before me used a long wooden ladder to take care of his lamps, but it was pretty old and shaky from being out in the weather leaning on the side of the bridge for so long, so I cut it up for stovewood and installed my pulley system in its place.

I had a lantern at each end of the bridge. The North and the South Portal.

Each end would be lit but the middle would be dark.

Unless the moon was right; then you had the patch in the middle. And, if you were lucky, maybe a ghost.

What I noticed was that the people who lived on the north side of the bridge always called the North Portal the *entrance* and of course the other end the *exit*.

And the people on the south side of the bridge called the South Portal the *entrance* and the other end the *exit*.

To some people this could be a bit of a mix-up. For instance, one night somebody who lived on the south side of the bridge might drop in to our place and tell me that the lamp was out at the entrance of the bridge. And then a little later somebody who lived on the north side of the bridge would drop by and say that the same lamp was out at the exit of the bridge.

And if the first person stayed a bit to talk to Mrs. O'Driscoll or to O'Driscoll for a while and then the second person came along with the news about the lamp, you'd get a little argument start up because they'd both be there at once.

"It's the lamp at the exit."

"No it's not; it's the one at the entrance."

The same kind of argument that they'd maybe have over what you meant when you said *this* Sunday or if you said *next* Sunday.

"Next Sunday; is that the Sunday *coming* or is that *this* Sunday? Or is it the Sunday after next? Wait now. Is *next* Sunday the Sunday after *this* or is it *this* Sunday? Which is it?"

"The dance is next Saturday. Is that the Saturday coming or the Saturday after this?"

"It's this Saturday coming."

"Well, why didn't you say so?"

"I did. I said it was next Saturday!"

"It's *not next* Saturday then, it's this Saturday!"

On my very first Sunday working for free on the bridge, a report came that a lantern was out at one of the exits. I got my can of coal oil, my scissors and my cloth and strolled down our side road to the bridge.

It was a beautiful night, Mushrat Creek gurgling and babbling away like a baby full of milk and the Gatineau sky full of stars.

As I came up to the South Portal I could see that that light was on. It was bit sooty but it was burning.

It was the North Portal they must have said was out. I walked into the bridge and shaded my eyes from the light above me so I could see the other portal.

The moon wasn't quite right so there was no patch in the middle.

At the other end there was a light on but it wasn't in the right place. It was right close to the level of the carriageway, not up near the peak of the portal where it should have been hanging. Could it have slipped down? Broken pulley? Bad knot?

I decided to clean the South Portal light first, the one above me.

While I worked I glanced up from time to time to see the other end.

I reached up on tiptoe and untied the rope from the nail and lowered my lantern. I lifted the globe with the lever and blew out the flame. While I let the globe cool and my eyes got used to the dark, I realized the light at the other end was moving!

I pressed my back against the first timber of the truss of the bridge and let the light walk by me.

It was a man in a long robe carrying a big deer light. I knew who it was.

O'Driscoll had told me how Father Foley from our church would come over the bridge sometimes to visit the sick on Sunday nights on our side of Mushrat Creek.

I was embarrassed about hiding like that, so I said very pleasantly, "Good evening, Father Foley." But because I was trying to be so natural and friendly, it came out kind of slow and spooky.

Father Foley jumped up in the air so high that on his way down his robe puffed right out like the girls' dresses did outside the Fun House at the Ottawa Exhibition when they got over that air blaster.

"Holy Mary Mother of God! Don't come up sudden on a man like that, son! Do you not know any better?"

O'Driscoll also told me how jumpy Father Foley was.

"I'm sorry, Father Foley," I said. "I was tending the light when you came along and I thought you were...I couldn't see very well...you see, the other night..."

"Well, you shouldn't be out here at all hours of the night fiddlin' around this bridge! Do you not know it's condemned—or it's goin' to be? You know you're wastin' your time, don't you? This bridge is going to be torn down! It's commendable, I suppose, you workin' without pay—I know you're not gettin' paid—but to do any caretakin' work on this bridge is fritherin' away the precious minutes God gave us on this earth that He says should be spent in fruitful labour—a sin my boy, a sin— and don't be sneakin' up on innocent people in the dark like this…the Devil's work my boy—a sin!"

Father Foley and his light bobbed up the gravel road and round the bend and out of sight, now and then the long shadows of the plum trees darting out of the dark.

I turned up the wick in my lantern and by feeling with my fingers trimmed the burnt end square.

I shook the lantern and when I heard the slopping sound decided that there was enough coal oil in it for now and that it was too dark to pour oil anyway.

I wiped the inside of the globe which was cool enough to touch by now and lit the lamp again and raised it to its position.

I walked slowly into the gloom of the other end, my arms and my sides tight with gooseflesh.

The other lamp hung there, dark in the rafters.

I lowered it.

It was cold. It had been out for quite a while.

I filled it by the faint light from the other end and trimmed it and wiped it and lit it and raised it.

Back home in my bedroom I looked out the window up at my bridge.

It was a dark shape that cut a horizontal line across the star-filled sky.

I went to sleep and dreamed of Sin.

COVERED BRIDGE PLUGGED BY MANURE!

Trying to write the letter to Fleurette was getting harder and harder.

Every time I would try to tell her something, to explain something to her, I'd start to compare things to other things: I'd start to say that that thing was like this or that: or that other thing was like this.

The covered bridge is like a tunnel, I told her. But it isn't really because a tunnel goes under something and a bridge goes over. So how could you have a tunnel be like a bridge?

That's what always happened in my writing. I'd start saying one thing was like another thing but then I'd have to say that it wasn't really like that, not altogether like that, anyway, because there was always some part was maybe a little bit different.

Or the covered bridge is like a long barn with the front and the back missing and a road running through it. But there's no hay up in the loft, of course, and it's not quiet like a barn is because you can hear the water gurgling underneath and also it doesn't smell like a barn because there isn't a huge pile of cow shit out the back and I started imagining a manure pile out the South Portal with a car buried in it.

But if you're standing in the covered bridge looking out one of the vents and if it's raining and if you're watching the water passing underneath, you might feel like you're in a big tug boat on the river, but the sound of the rain on the shingles above you makes you feel like you're very cosy in a cabin somewhere in the bush beside a lake, but you have to close your eyes so you don't see the water moving under you or you'll still think it feels like a ship.

It seemed impossible to find something that was exactly like something else. Something that was exactly like a covered bridge.

In the world, there were many things that seemed to be a lot like many other things but not totally. There was always some small difference that would sort of spoil it.

Or make it not perfect.

Then I changed the subject.

I wrote to her about a habit O'Driscoll had.

O'Driscoll had a habit of turning around a bit and looking back over his shoulder just before he started to talk to you.

He didn't do it every time he said something, only when he first started to talk.

Or if he was walking up to you, meeting you on the road, just before he started to talk, he'd look behind himself, as though there might be somebody following him.

Even though he knew and the other person knew that there might not be anybody else come walking up or down that road for a half a day or more. Maybe the next person who'd come walking along that gravel road was just leaving Wakefield now and wouldn't be here until next Wednesday but O'Driscoll looked around anyway, just in case.

I don't think he knew he was doing it; it was just a habit.

He'd even do it in our kitchen when he came down for breakfast in the morning.

Mrs. O'Driscoll and I would be there and in he would come, look back over his shoulder and then start talking.

There definitely was nobody behind him because everybody who lived in the house was now in the kitchen.

Once, when O'Driscoll wasn't there, Mrs. O'Driscoll said that he probably got the habit after he was supposed to be drowned in the war and ran away and lived with that Indian Princess on Lake Pizinadjih.

She said this out of the corner of her mouth while the other half of her mouth was smiling.

I tried later to do it in the mirror; couldn't.

Didn't have the right mouth muscles, I guess.

Just then, O'Driscoll came marching into the kitchen, looked behind himself, and started talking.

"Here's how Lake Pizinadjih got its name.

"Years ago, the lake was then called Manitou, meaning Great Spirit, two Algonquin families lived across the water from each other. The son of one family fell in love with the daughter of the other family when, one evening, he heard the sound of her singing float across the sparkling moonlit surface of Manitou."

O'Driscoll was being very dramatic and Mrs. O'Driscoll was rolling her eyes which meant she'd heard this before.

O'Driscoll went ahead anyway.

"The two families hated each other for many generations and so, of course, the parents forbade the son to paddle his canoe across the water to be with his newfound love.

"The singing continued, however..."

"Of course," sighed Mrs. O'Driscoll.

"...however and after the fire died down and the family went to sleep, the son walked into the water, and began to swim, silent as a fish, to the other side and to his love.

"But it was late and the singing had stopped and the moon was now covered by cloud and the young man lost his way and swam until, exhausted, he sank and drowned."

Mrs. O'Driscoll looked at me. She had definitely heard this before.

"Days later, when they discovered his body stuck in the falls, and they figured out what happened, the two families patched up their differences and moved on together to a different place, far away, so they could forget.

"Before they left, in a carefully performed ceremony, they renamed the tragic water 'Pizinadjih.'"

Mrs. O'Driscoll—Pizinadjih. My, that's beautiful, O'Driscoll. What does it mean, exactly, Pizinadjih?

O'Driscoll—(Pause) It means…(O'Driscoll looks behind himself). It means *"LAKE STUPID"*!

So it was the first time I talked about love in my letter to Fleurette. I decided that maybe I'd try more of it.

I told her about the ghost and O LVS O in the bridge. I told her about the priest, Father Foley, and about Sin. And about Lake Stupid.

And I told her about Old Mac Gleason, who I will tell you about now.

And about how I started going to church.

ADOLF HITLER MAKES JOKE!

The person after Oscar McCracken that I met in Mushrat Creek was Old Mac Gleason. He sat on his verandah across from the church and sucked on his pipe. Sometimes we would talk to him in his chair on his broken verandah. Nerves and I sometimes took a walk past there after we started going to church.

Sometimes we first went home and changed into our old clothes and we separated the milk. Of course, Nerves didn't change his clothes; he wore the same furry little suit no matter what the occasion was. But he did go to church with us sometimes. On hot summer days when there was a bit of a breeze and not too many flies, Father Foley would get the altar boys to prop the big entrance doors to the church open so the breeze would circulate while he roasted us with his sermon. But no matter how much breeze there was, once Father Foley got going about Hell, he'd be sweating like a pig.

I don't know why people say that about pigs because I don't think pigs sweat. They grunt and drool and roll around in the mud but they don't sweat much. Not nearly as much as Father Foley, especially when he got very deep into the subject of Hell.

On those hot breezy days when the doors were propped open with two rocks, Nerves would walk in very quietly and respectfully and sit in the middle of the centre aisle near the back with his paws neatly in front of him and his head up, looking at Father Foley and the boys going about their business.

During Communion, when people started getting up and filling the aisle, Nerves would back himself out the doors and go over on the lawn and take a holy little snooze there under the lilac bushes.

Old Mac Gleason could see the church and the graveyard from his chair on the verandah. Everybody knew Mac never went to church. It was pretty obvious. Everybody in Mushrat Creek, everybody in Low and everybody in Brennan's Hill who went to church got a good look every Sunday at Old Mac Gleason sitting on his verandah, *not* going to church.

And people used to say that everybody up the River in Venosta and Farrellton and Kazabazua and everybody down the River in Alcove and Wakefield probably knew that Old Mac Gleason didn't go to church.

And Old Mac Gleason himself would often say, "I betcha there's people as far south as Ottawa who know I never been to church in my life and that there's people as far north as Maniwaki that know that I, Old Mac Gleason, have no intention of ever goin' to church in the future either.

"There's people who travel miles and miles to go to a church and here's me, livin' right across the road from one—and I never been inside it. Oh, I was inside it a couple a times to fix a door or a window for that Foolish Father Foley from Farrellton but I never prayed inside there and I never will!"

This Sunday, Father Foley was at the top of his sermon about Hell.

The altar boys had the doors propped wide open with the rocks, and Nerves was in his position in the aisle.

Father Foley was at the part about how thick the walls of Hell were and what a foul-smelling prison it was and the lost demons and the smoke and the sulphur and the fire and the never-ending storms of brimstone and stink of the putrid corpses and vomit and boiling brains and the screaming of the tortured and cursing victims and the puddles of pus that you had to lie in if you were bad.

Father Foley had a wild look in his eyes. He looked like he was scaring himself with his own sermon.

I took a look back at Nerves.

He was staring straight up at Father Foley with a look of hopeless terror in his eyes. Was there a Hell for dogs?

It was near the end of his speech. Father Foley was sweating so much that when he threw his head to one side and then the other to say NO! NO! to the Devil, the drops of sweat flew from one side of the church to the other. The heads of the people turned this way, then that, to watch the sweat fly across.

After Mass, Nerves and I crossed the road and strolled through the graveyard. The earliest dates on the gravestones were 1848 and 1850. According to Mrs. O'Driscoll, the first Irish settlers came here in 1847. "Some of them just made it in time," she said, out of the corner of her mouth.

Other gravestones were marked 1893 and the ages were all of babies and kids. There were whole groups of them, some all from one family.

There must have been a fire or a disease.

All the names were Irish.

We went to the edge of the graveyard near the fence.

Nerves and I stopped to look for a while at one interesting gravestone with flowers on it that were pretty fresh. Maybe put there just yesterday.

The name on it was Ophelia Brown.

Ophelia Brown
Lord Have Mercy on Her, the stone said.

All around the grave were special plants and perfectly cut grass.

But there was one thing wrong.

The grave was on the other side of the page wire fence. As if the graveyard was too crowded for Ophelia Brown and they had to put it outside the fence. But the strange thing was, there was lots of room in that part of the graveyard for Ophelia Brown.

In fact Ophelia Brown was outside the section of the graveyard with hardly any graves in it at all.

I heard a cowbell ding from a field nearby and somewhere, far off, a dog barked.

Nerves was looking like he was going to burst into tears and when he gave out a little whine I decided it was time to get out of there.

We walked by Old Mac Gleason's verandah to see if he'd invite us up for a chat and a drink of water.

He did.

He gave me the pail and the dipper and I pumped some ice-cold well-water for us from his well at the side of his house.

"That Foolish Father Foley was at it again this morning, was he?" said Old Mac Gleason. "I guess he knows that Hell speech off by heart by now."

"How did you know he was talking about Hell?" I said. "Were you at church today?"

"No, I was not," said Old Mac Gleason. "Nor will I ever set foot in that place as long as I live. I don't care if it is only just across the road! But I'll tell you, there's two ways you can tell a thing like that. First of all, you watch the people coming out. The looks on their faces. Some of them look like they've just dirtied their pants and some are kind of blue around the gills and some are so guilty-looking you'd think they just took an axe to their whole family."

I waited a little bit while we listened to a heat bug singing that one note about the heat.

"What's the other way you can tell?" I said.

"The other way you can tell," he said, leaning right over to Nerves and me, "is that you can hear the old fool from all the way over here!"

Then he looked up and over at the graveyard so steadily that Nerves and I looked over too.

There was a man at Ophelia Brown's grave, kneeling there, with flowers in his hands. He crossed himself and then he got up and replaced the flowers that were there with the new ones.

Then he knelt again and kissed the ground.

"Know who that is?" asked Old Mac Gleason.

It was too far away to make out the man's face but the way his back was humped over looked sort of familiar.

"You know the postman, don't you? Oscar McCracken? He's just finished the Sunday mail. He's also our grave-digger, did you know that?"

I could tell now it was Oscar McCracken the way he was walking now away from Ophelia Brown's grave with his head down, watching his shoes.

"Strange rig, that one. A queer duck, that's for sure," said Old Mac Gleason. "When you get to know Mushrat Creek a little better you'll find out more than you'll ever need to know about strange rigs like that Oscar McCracken and his grave outside the fence…you know you're the first strangers that have come in to live here for a good while now. You think you'll settle here? You could find a better spot than beside that old broken-down covered bridge…say, that's a funny lookin' dog—what kind of a dog is that anyway—or is it a dog at all—sure, it looks more like a—I don't know what the hell it looks like come to think of it…"

Just then, Mrs. O'Driscoll came along, calling to us from the road. She had been up a ways, visiting after church.

Mrs. O'Driscoll and I and Nerves walked across the covered bridge to our mailbox.

Was there a letter there from Fleurette Featherstone Fitchell? There wasn't, but there was a seed catalogue for Mrs. O'Driscoll and a Police Gazette for O'Driscoll.

At least some of our family was getting some mail.

O'Driscoll looked forward to getting his Police Gazette every two weeks or so. He would save it for Sunday and take it into the parlour after church and sit down in there and read it.

Nobody went in there very often unless maybe there was a visitor in the house. But O'Driscoll liked to go in there on Sunday when his shoes were shined and he had on his white shirt and tie. Sometimes I went in with my *War and Peace* and sat there with him and read silently there, sitting on the chair with the big sunflowers that matched the couch that O'Driscoll was on.

The parlour smelled of sweet dust and old bread dough. It was very quiet in there. Except for the ticking of the clock on the fake mantelpiece. There were two big old photographs in round frames on the walls, a yellowish colour, a man and a woman, stiff collars, sour faces. And one square photograph of a little kid who looked like he hated his clothes. There was something wrong with his face, though. I couldn't figure out what it was. Then O'Driscoll told me one time while we were having breakfast.

He told me that in the old days it took a long time to take a picture.

You had to stay perfectly still for quite a while to get your picture taken because of the way the first cameras were made.

You couldn't smile for that long because your face would get too sore.

That's why everybody in those old pictures looks so grumpy.

Even the little kids.

One Sunday, O'Driscoll was reading his Police Gazette and I was reading my *War and Peace*. I was reading the part where Prince Andrei was retreating from Napoleon in the War of 1812. He was leading his regiment through the dust in August in Russia. And they came along to a lake and all his men stripped off their clothes and jumped in the water. Then somebody yelled out that Prince Andrei might want to have a swim. So they all got out of the water to let their prince get in and take a swim. And Prince Andrei went in but he was embarrassed about taking off his clothes in front of his men.

It was in Book II, Part II, Chapter 5.

On the front page of O'Driscoll's Police Gazette there was a picture of Adolf Hitler, the German who started the war in 1939 that O'Driscoll got lost in. After the war was over they looked all over for Hitler but they couldn't find him. Most people said he committed suicide and his friends burned his body.

Nice to have friends. Even if you're Hitler.

But O'Driscoll's Police Gazette was saying that Hitler was still alive. On the front page there was a big picture of Hitler with his little moustache and a big headline saying the words, "Hitler Is Alive!" The story in the smaller print said that a barber in a country called Patagonia in South America said that Hitler came into his barber shop and got his moustache shaved off. The barber said that Hitler seemed to be a bit fatter than he was when he was losing the war that he started, but that he seemed quite cheerful and even made a few jokes.

"You can't win 'em all!" the barber said Hitler said.

O'Driscoll left the parlour to go out to the outhouse, and while he was gone I found out one of his secrets.

I was looking through his Police Gazette, taking a break from *War and Peace*, reading the stories in there. A story about a two-headed parrot. One head would tell a joke and the other head would laugh. Or one head would say, "Why did the parrot cross the road?" And the other head would say, "I dunno. Why did the parrot cross the road?" And the first head would say, "To get to the other side!" And then both heads would laugh their heads off.

And there was a story about a guy in Madagascar or somewhere who found an oyster with not a pearl in it but a whole pearl necklace. But when he took it to the jeweller's, they said the pearls were just imitation pearls, just fake.

Then on the next page there was a story about a drowning sailor being saved by a dolphin.

The sailor fell overboard and swam around for a long time and just as he was going to sink and drown because he was so tired a dolphin swam under him and with the sailor on its back, swam to a beautiful tropical island with the sailor. And the sailor got off there and got married to the Queen of the Amazons and became King of Paradise.

The thing about this story was that O'Driscoll told me and Mrs. O'Driscoll just the other day that that's what happened to him when he was supposed to be drowned in the War. That was the latest he told us. Then he said he *thought* that that was what must have happened because he lost his memory don't forget so he couldn't really be sure.

So O'Driscoll was stealing his stories from the Police Gazette. Telling me and Mrs. O'Driscoll stuff about when he was lost in the war. Getting the ideas from his Police Gazette.

No wonder he only half listened to my tale about a ghost.

But I had other things on my mind.

Things like initials.

O LVS O, for instance.

It had to be Oscar Loves Ophelia.

It had to be.

MAN DIGS A HOLE THEN CAN'T GET OUT!

I never went to church much when I lived in Lowertown or when I lived in Uplands Emergency Shelter but now that I was living on Mushrat Creek I was going to church almost every Sunday.

It was good to go and hear what everybody was saying about everything. And it felt good to get dressed up on Sunday morning after you did the milking and the separating and you fed the pigs and checked the henhouse for eggs.

At first O'Driscoll tried to get Mrs. O'Driscoll to polish our Sunday shoes and put them on the kitchen table so that when we slept in on Sunday morning we could come downstairs and jump right into these clean shiny shoes and head right out for church with no "delays."

O'Driscoll told her that all the other farmers' wives in Mushrat Creek did that for *their* husbands and their sons. He told her that it was a tradition. Then he told her more of what the other women did for their men on Sundays. They got up at five o'clock in the morning, made the fire, got the breakfast, heated up the iron, sponged and ironed the men's pants, ironed clean white shirts for the men, got out the tie they always wore on Sunday, went out and milked the cows, separated the milk, fed the pigs, checked for eggs in the henhouse, came back in, got out the good shoes, cleaned and polished them and then put them in a neat, side-by-side way, right beside the breakfast on the table.

While O'Driscoll was explaining this to Mrs. O'Driscoll, she just stared at him. She didn't really stare at him, she just calmly looked at him for the whole time he was telling her all this stuff about what she was supposed to do on Sunday morning for her *men*!

It was pretty cruel, really.

She didn't say a word, just looking at him, like maybe the way you'd look at a sunset or something.

And the whole time, you could tell, O'Driscoll was wishing she would say something, because if she started talking, then he could stop talking, but as long as she didn't talk at all, he had to keep talking. And the more he talked the worse everything got. It was like watching a cat play with a mouse.

Mrs. O'Driscoll used to call it "the silence." If O'Driscoll was getting a bit too "cocky," she would give him "the silence."

And it seemed to work every time.

O'Driscoll would get more and more excited and say things that got worse and worse.

Mrs. O'Driscoll said once that it was like watching a man dig himself into a deep hole. "You let them dig until they can't get out. Then you wait a while and then you help them get out," she said.

O'Driscoll was telling her about how it was a mortal sin not to shine your husband's Sunday shoes and that a lot of women up and down the Gatineau Valley were in Hell because they didn't shine their husband's Sunday shoes or if they weren't in Hell already, "they were definitely headed in that direction…"

Mrs. O'Driscoll waited a while and then she gave him a little tiny smile that you could hardly notice. This was the way she helped him out of the hole he was in.

Then she handed him the shoe polish.

He took the polish and gave me a big wink.

The wink was the way he helped himself the rest of the way out of the hole.

After church at home, Mrs. O'Driscoll was putting on her overalls which she never did on Sunday.

"Put on your workin' clothes, Hubbo me boy," she said. "We're goin' to do a little paintin'."

"Painting?" I said. "Painting what?"

"Your bridge, my boy," she said out of the corner of her mouth. "Your bridge."

"We can't paint that bridge. It's too big. You'd need dozens of cans of paint and scaffolds and rope and all kinds of things."

"We're only going to paint what we can reach, boy. I've been out gossiping. I heard the priest's housekeeper telling them all what Father Foley said to you that night about workin' on the bridge and Sin and all that.

That's wrong, Hubbo. Very wrong. You're not sinning to work for your beliefs. So just to show who's side I'm on, let them have a look at us paintin' this bridge, the both of us. Maybe by the example we set, others will join us and the bridge will be looked at as something worth saving!"

We got some painting done, but not much. Mrs. O'Driscoll only had a small can of red paint and one good brush, so we took turns.

"It's the thought that counts," Mrs. O'Driscoll was saying, as she hummed a little while I took my turn painting the tongue-in-groove sheeting on the outside of the trellis. I was leaning over the railing while standing on the abutment at our end of the bridge.

"I said I was out gossiping, Hubbo. But I've been doin' more than that. I've been listening."

"Listening?"

"Yes, my dear Hubbo. A tragic thing happened in this community over fifteen years ago. It involved the daughter of a poor woman I met up the road last Sunday, Mrs. Brown. Her daughter died. Her daughter, Ophelia, who was very young and full of hope, died."

"Ophelia Brown," I said. "I saw her gravestone. And Oscar Mc-Cracken..."

"Yes, Oscar the mailman was her betrothed."

"How did she die?" I asked.

"Brain tumour," she said.

Oscar McCracken and Ophelia Brown were lovers. This was almost twenty years ago. They were going to be married. Suddenly everything changed. Ophelia Brown started acting strange. She went kind of crazy. Looking around as though people were following her. Not talking to her friends. In the church three or four times a day. The tumour affected her brain. They found her in Mushrat Creek. She must have jumped out the ventilation window in the middle of the covered bridge. It was in the early spring. The water was roaring high almost over the centre pier. She must have hit her head. Anyway, she was drowned. Father Foley wouldn't give her a proper funeral. He was a young priest then. He had to follow the rules. His hands were tied. Wouldn't let her be buried in the church-yard. Against God's rules, he said. Oscar McCracken started going around watching his feet. Got a hump on his back from it. Ophelia wasn't allowed in the graveyard. She was buried just outside the fence.

We took a break from painting and I showed Mrs. O'Driscoll the initials up in the rafters.

We went in and put the rest of our little bit of paint on the outside boards around the vent where Ophelia Brown had jumped.

The paint lasted a tiny bit longer than it would have because Mrs. O'Driscoll watered it down with some of her tears.

"F"-WORD LINKED TO PRIEST!

My letter to Fleurette was getting fatter.

I was telling her about everything.

I was trying to tell Fleurette all about Father Foley and how Old Mac Gleason called him Foolish Father Foley and that Father Foley was from the town of Farrellton just north of Low up the road and how Old Mac Gleason called him Foolish Father Foley from Farrellton, which sounded funny because of all the F's.

And I wondered while I was writing to her about him what Foolish Father Foley from Farrellton would say to Fleurette Featherstone Fitchell about Hell and what she should do and what she shouldn't do.

Lucky that Father Foley couldn't read people's minds, because if he could and he read my mind in church when I was thinking about Fleurette, he'd probably blast me right straight to Hell for having such thoughts.

Funny part of it was that it was Father Foley who got me started thinking about Sin in the first place. If you yell and scream about Sin all the time, people are going to start thinking about things that they never thought of before.

Fortunately for Fleurette Featherstone Fitchell, Foolish Father Foley from Farrellton was far from fixing her with his fault-finding.

I put that sentence with all the F words in the letter.

Fleurette would like that one.

If I ever found her address.

I also told her as much as I could about Oscar McCracken.

Everybody loved Oscar McCracken.

One of the reasons was that he never missed the mail. He was always on time. He was as regular as the train. When you heard him pull up in his coupe car and when you heard your mailbox squeak (or whatever it did—some mailboxes squealed like little pigs, some groaned like cows, some went chunk like an axe hitting wood), then you knew just about what exact time it was, and you thought of what a nice man Oscar was.

Everybody also loved Oscar because most of the time, maybe all the time, the mail he brought them was nice mail—a letter from a relative from the States; a parcel from Sears or Eaton's, a notice saying pick up that sack of seeds you ordered. (Was I the only one that never got what he wanted from Oscar? A letter from Fleurette?)

And also, everybody loved Oscar because everybody knew what happened to Ophelia Brown and everybody knew how it changed Oscar forever. Everybody knew how he felt. How he got the hump on his back from watching his feet.

And everybody knew that whenever Oscar went through the covered bridge he would stay inside there for a while and have a little chat with Ophelia Brown.

But not very many people talked about what Oscar used to do four times a day inside the bridge. Everybody knew that he'd stop for a bit and have a little chat with his lost lover Ophelia, but because it seemed a little bit crazy they didn't like to mention it much. They didn't like to come right out and say that Oscar McCracken talked to a ghost four times a day.

And I didn't like to say that maybe I saw that ghost one night.

O LVS O. That's what the bridge said.

If they said that, then they'd have to say they believed there was a ghost there or say that Oscar was crazy. They couldn't say right out that they believed Ophelia's ghost was there in the covered bridge because if Foolish Father Foley got wind of the fact that they believed in ghosts, especially in Ophelia Brown's ghost, he would get pretty mad and go into a rage about Evil and everything. Father Foley already kept her out of the graveyard and anyway, Father Foley was in charge of things like ghosts and spirits and he'd be the one to decide about stuff like that. It wasn't the farmers who were going to decide about things like that. Farmers were in charge of cows and milk and manure and seeds and hay and homemade bread and chickens and things like that.

Foolish Father Foley from Farrellton was in charge of the other world.

That is why when people heard the covered bridge was going to be torn down everybody got very confused.

First of all nobody wanted to talk about Oscar McCracken and Ophelia Brown. If the bridge was torn down, what would happen to poor Oscar? Poor Oscar who everybody loved?

It was O'Driscoll who was one of the first ones to get into the mix-up.

"What was wrong with having two bridges?" O'Driscoll was saying to farmers in the store in Brennan's Hill. "One for the past, one for the future?"

Then I wrote about Oscar's goat to Fleurette.

After Mass one day when Mrs. Ball invited Mrs. O'Driscoll to walk back down the road with her and drop into her niece's place and have some tea, Mr. O'Driscoll and I and Nerves crossed the road for a stroll through the graveyard and then past Old Mac Gleason's house. I noticed from the graveyard that the sexton's cottage where Oscar kept the church equipment and graveyard tools had a pen and a small stable behind it that you couldn't see from the church. In the pen was a goat.

O'Driscoll started the conversation with Old Mac Gleason about the goat.

"You know goats are thought to have originated in China some ten million years ago." O'Driscoll sounded like he just read a sentence from a school book about goats.

"Well, sir," said Old Mac Gleason, "this goat originated here as a kid and belonged to poor Ophelia Brown. After she died, Oscar took the goat and still has it. As a matter of fact, Father Foley hired Oscar as the sexton so the goat would keep the grass cut. Shows you how much that Foolish Father Foley knows about goats! Goats aren't lawnmowers! Wasn't long until he had the pen built, though. One day the goat marched right down the aisle into the middle of Father Foley's sermon and started bleating away like she was saying what everybody else felt like saying—"Shut up, you old blatherskite Father Foley"—bleating away at him. The look on Father Foley's face! And the terror in the eyes! You'd think he was staring at the Devil himself!

"There's nothing Father Francis Foley from Farrellton hates worse than having his speeches about Sin interrupted. But that Oscar, he knows goats. Watch the way he feeds that thing. Nothing but the best. Goes out every now and then with that little car and loads it up with the kind of grub the goat loves. Pine branches, young bark, wild roses, clover. And milks her every twelve hours. I never seen a goat live so long. And keep givin' milk, too! Nice fresh goat's milk keeps that Father Foley nice and fat! I wonder, Mr. O'Driscoll, you being a man who has travelled widely and knowing a lot about a lot of things, do you think that too much goat's milk could affect a fat priest's brain? Make him crazy?"

"No, Mr. Gleason," said Mr. O'Driscoll. "I don't know anything about that, but I *do* know that the animal called the goat was always hooked up with Sin in the olden days. The old Hebrews in ancient times used to bring two goats to the altar. Then they'd draw lots. One goat went to the Lord and the other to the Devil. That one they called the scape-goat. Then the priest would confess all his sins and the sins of all the people. Then because all the sins were now with the scape-goat, they'd take it out in the bush and let it get away, let it escape."

Like everybody always was when O'Driscoll told one of his stories, Old Mac Gleason was silent and a bit amazed.

We listened for a while to the polite Sunday morning birds.

"Well, anyways," Old Mac Gleason said, "that Oscar, he is a queer duck himself since his lady did herself in. Rings the church bell, does the chores, takes the collection, delivers the mail, digs the graves. Never talks to anybody. Strangest package of a man I ever saw!"

I was starting not to like Old Mac Gleason.

O'Driscoll and Nerves and I crossed back over the road and cut in behind the church in back of the sexton's cottage where the goat pen was.

The goat was black with a white face and white legs and a white beard. She had two black tassles hanging from her throat and curved black horns. Her udder was swollen and her teats pointed straight and were stiff. She was full of milk.

She had a funny look on her face. She looked like a person looks who just pasted a "kick-me" sign on your back and is trying not to laugh while looking you right in the eye.

Suddenly she turned her eyes on Nerves and bleated once at him. Her eyes turned piercing and cold.

Nerves went roaring down the road in a little chuckwagon of dust.

O'Driscoll and I laughed all the way home. We laughed at the goat bleating at Father Foley and at the goat bleating at Nerves. And we laughed at Old Mac Gleason.

Fleurette would like this part of the letter.

DOG ATTACKED BY KILLER POTATO BUGS!

Father Foley was doing something to my mind.

For instance, even something that happened to Nerves made me think of Father Foley's sermons.

It was Nerves who first noticed that our potato field was being attacked by bugs. The potato plants were quite high when we took over the farm. Our field was outside our front door and across our side road. We had twelve rows of potatoes, twenty paces long. Since there are about four potato plants in every long pace, there must have been almost a thousand potato plants. More potatoes than we'd ever need. But we could use them for trading for other things we didn't have.

I saw Nerves come out of the potato field through the barbed wire gate. He was looking pretty disgusted. His skin was moving up and down his body. He was shuddering like someone in a restaurant who just found a cockroach crawling out of his spaghetti.

I went into the potato field to see what it was that made Nerves so nauseated.

On the first potato plant I inspected I counted fifty-six fat orange potato bugs with black spots, munching away on the leaves.

The next plant had even more.

Now I realized what was bothering Nerves.

Nerves hated bugs of all kinds. He always avoided flies, spiders, moths, butterflies, grasshoppers, ants, any kind of bug, whenever he could.

I guess he was just out for a stroll in the potato patch when he looked around and realized that he was surrounded by over 55,000 bugs. And all related to each other. Poor Nerves was outnumbered.

I got some empty Habitant Pea Soup cans that were piled on a shelf in our shed just next to the potato field.

By holding a Habitant Pea Soup can under the leaf of the potato plant and using a flat stick, you could knock the bugs into the can.

At first they made a pinging noise when they hit the bottom of the can, but then things got quieter and more disgusting as the can filled up.

I put the first full can on the gatepost and started a new one. I was starting to feel like Nerves must have felt, his skin crawling up and down his body.

Mrs. O'Driscoll came up to the gate with Nerves behind her.

She pulled on the gate but it stuck a bit, so she yanked a little harder. That caused the Habitant Pea Soup can, full to the top with potato bugs, to fall off the gatepost, dumping most of the bugs on top of Nerves.

Nerves was stunned. He stood still as a statue while the bugs spread over his body like bees. Nerves' eyes, which normally were kind of beady, were wider than Mrs. O'Driscoll or I had ever seen them. It didn't seem possible that his eyes could expand and bulge out like that.

Then his mouth opened wide like he was screaming, but no sound was coming out.

Then he took off as fast as his little legs could churn and kick up grass and dirt, down around the ice house, and we heard the splash as Nerves hit the water of Mushrat Creek.

"Well," said Mrs. O'Driscoll out of the corner of her mouth, "we'll find out now if potato bugs can swim or not."

We ended up with seven cans of potato bugs.

The stove in the summer kitchen was roaring hot, ready for baking bread.

Mrs. O'Driscoll and I dumped the bugs into the flames. What a stink for a while.

I couldn't help thinking about Father Foley.

The stink and the flames.

Of Hell.

Not long after we heard the first dynamite go off and saw the first dead fish float down Mushrat Creek, a poster went up in the store at Brennan's Hill.

MEN WANTED
BRIDGE CONSTRUCTION
MUSHRAT CREEK

Carpentry, Cement, Steel,
Labourers.
THE LAZY NEED NOT APPLY!

Madame Ovide Proulx
Proulx Construction

A lot of farmers were crowded around the poster. They read "Madame Ovide Proulx." *Madame* Proulx? A *woman*?

A *woman* building a bridge?

How could that *be*?

O'Driscoll and I went up to the place where the new bridge was going to be.

It was an ugly sight.

Blown-up trees and bulldozers and mud and big gashes out of the sides of beautiful Mushrat Creek.

O'Driscoll got in a line-up and got hired on as a carpenter. While he was signing his work card I saw him saying something to the woman in charge. She looked up at me. Then O'Driscoll waved for me to come over.

"Madame Proulx wants to hire you. She needs a nail puller. You get eighty cents an hour. You work from seven in the morning until six at night, one hour for lunch, only half days on Saturday."

Mrs. Proulx looked at me.

"Can you pull nails?" she said.

"Out of wood?" I said.

"Of course, out of wood. What did you tink, you pull dem hout of da hair?"

"Pardon?"

"Did you think you'll pull them out of the air?" O'Driscoll said, helping me out.

"Yes, I can pull nails," I said, ignoring her sarcasm.

"Sign ere!" said Mrs. Proulx.

I had a job.

I was already figuring out the money. Ten hours a day would be eight dollars. Five times eight. Four more dollars for Saturday. Forty-four dollars a week! I could buy more red paint with that. And other stuff for the bridge—lamp oil, wicks.

We started work the next day.

For the next few days, before I went to bed, I'd try to tell Fleurette about what it was like.

A farmer or two from almost every house along the road and by the river and up and down the valley were working on the new bridge.

There was rock and earth to be moved and holes to be dug and forms to be built and cement to be poured and steel to be laid.

The foreman of the job was French and he was from Maniwaki. His name was printed on the side of the truck and the end of the big generator. His name was Ovide Proulx (pronounced P R O O).

His wife, Mrs. Proulx (pronounced P R O O, too) was in charge of the Time, the Tools and Supplies and the Pay Envelopes.

All the farmers called her Prootoo.

On Fridays, Prootoo rang the bell at six o'clock sharp and the farmers lined up in their blue overalls and waited while she called out their names and made them step up for their envelope of money. She also sometimes searched the farmers for stolen tools or nails.

Sometimes there was money taken out of the farmers' pay envelopes for a tool they maybe lost or broke.

Everybody was afraid of Prootoo.

Except Mr. Proulx, the boss.

And everybody hated Prootoo.

Except Mr. Ovide Proulx. He loved Prootoo.

Whenever he went away in the truck he kissed her on the cheek and when he got back a little later, he kissed her again. And even while he was kissing her on the cheek, she turned her head so that she never took her eyes off the farmers as they slowly built the new bridge.

She never took her eyes off the farmers as they slowly built the bridge from seven o'clock in the morning to six o'clock at night except on Saturday, and then it was eight o'clock in the morning to twelve o'clock noon that she *never never* stopped watching.

Just before the twelve o'clock dinner bell one of the farmers who was swinging a sledge hammer let it go and it flew out and landed in the deep part of Mushrat Creek.

Prootoo was already marching over to where the farmer and I were standing even before the hammer hit the water.

"You go in and get it," said Prootoo, pointing at the farmer who let go the hammer. "Take off your overalls, jump in the creek, get the sledge 'ammer."

I could see the hammer down there, through the clear water, the hammer head on the bottom in the mud, the handle pointing straight up, floating.

I could see by the farmer's face, he wasn't going to take off his overalls for her or anybody else.

"You want to work?" she said to him. "Let's get in dat water!"

I knew the farmer was going to get fired.

I took a chance.

"I'll go," I said.

"O.K.," she said. "Fine. Let's go before it sinks in the mud!"

I was fiddling with the strap of my overalls, waiting to see if she would stop staring and look away. I got the strap undone and looked up again. Prootoo was still staring. She had the dinner bell in her hand. It was almost past twelve o'clock and all the hungry farmers were standing around staring at her, waiting for her to ring the bell.

My fingers went up to my other strap and I looked up again, wondering if she was going to turn her back while I took off my pants.

All the farmers stood around where the new bridge was going to be, all the farmers, still as statues, waiting for my pants to go down, waiting for the bell, waiting for their dinner, their stomachs groaning and rumbling.

I was thinking of Prince Andrei, how he felt.

If Prince Andrei could do it, so could I...

I couldn't write any more in Fleurette's letter. I was falling out of the chair I was so tired. I could finish it later. Working ten hours in a row every day makes you tired.

I lay down on the straw mattress that Mrs. O'Driscoll had fixed up and sank softly into it. I only had to move a couple of spikes of stubble sticking in me before I was comfortable. The mattress cover smelled clean like the breeze off Mushrat Creek. And because of the fresh straw, my whole bed had a smell of sweet dust and clover.

HORSEBALLS ROLL DOWN MAN'S CHEEKS!

On the first Sunday of my first week working on the new bridge, I went exploring.

Past the woodpile on the south side of our house, along the road between the barn and the stable, past the manure pile and the pig pen, past the strawberry patch and through the pine bush, down along our lower field and the ancient rail fence and onto the log road that led to the river, Nerves and I walked east.

It was called the log road because the lower swampy parts were made of logs, lying crossways, lodged in the clay and mud.

As the road moved up rocky hills and down into meadows and gullies and through pine and spruce bush, you could sometimes hear Mushrat Creek talking away as it wandered near us.

Further on, the tall thick sumac with the sickening blood-red fruit blocked off all sound except for the summer heat bugs.

And later, we edged sideways down the clay, and then passed through the dark bark and the white berries of the poison dogwood trees.

Then over the last rocky part to the water, feeling your feet squishing on the stinkhorn fungus until you and your totally disgusted dog reached the hemlock tree where the rowboat was pulled up and tied with a chain.

And then if you looked north up the Gatineau River, past where Mushrat Creek dumped in its pretty water, you would be able to see (but you couldn't, because the river turned there) Devil's Hole and the dam at Low.

I pulled the boat up a bit more, bailed it out with an old dented dipper that I found under the back seat.

I was thinking that if O'Driscoll and Mrs. O'Driscoll bought this farm, then this shoreline, these rocks, this boat, this hemlock tree that was supposed to be poisonous would all be ours.

I wondered if the water was ours too. Probably not.

Out in the middle of the river there were two people in a big rowboat.

You could hear them talking, and by the sounds they were making you could tell they were working at something, something heavy.

They were lifting something big and brown.

There was a man who had most of the weight and a boy, maybe his son, helping him.

What they were resting on the side of the boat now was a wood stove. It was about the size of our wood stove—four lids, an oven and a reservoir plus legs. The stove was very rusty and was breaking up a bit as they rested it on the gunwale of the boat.

Then Nerves and I heard the man count one, two, three, GO!

And over into the Gatineau River went the rusty stove.

A puff of red dust, probably rust, rose up, and the stove sank almost right away. A dirty little geyser of water shot up as the river swallowed.

Then there was some shouting and some crying.

Then the man and the boy both peered silently over the edge of the boat into the water.

Then they started tossing in the long, sausage, hollow pieces. The stove pipes. They were easy. And the lids.

I was imagining exactly what they could see. The stove lids taking longer to disappear because of the seesaw motion they made while they were sinking, like plates.

The rusty trail of large then smaller air pockets.

And I was imagining what they couldn't see.

The stove hitting bottom softly, bouncing over on its side, settling in.

To stay there for years.

But just *before* they dumped the stove, something happened.

There was some grunting caused by lifting.

Then the man was saying something like "lift your end, lift, lift!"
Then the stove went over.

But the boy must have hurt himself or cut himself or something because his both hands were down now holding his ankle and his head was a way back, his face facing the sky.

"Stop that! What happened? Let me see," the man was saying. "What are you crying for? What's this crying? Stop it! Be a man! Stop being a baby! Be a man! Don't cry! Be a man!"

I was remembering that only last year I cried. I cried about something I did that I was ashamed of and also because an old lady who was a friend of mine died. I cried and Mrs. O'Driscoll didn't say, "be a man!" She didn't say that. She put her arms around me and gave me a big long hug. I was wondering about Mrs. O'Driscoll when she was a little girl. Did she once cry and did somebody come along and say, "Stop that! Be a woman! Don't cry! Be a woman!"?

It seemed stupid to me. Why should the boy be a man? And what if he was a man? Men cry. I saw O'Driscoll cry. He cried the night he came home from being lost in the War. While he was crying, Mrs. O'Driscoll didn't run over to him and yell at him and tell him he shouldn't be crying because he was a man!

He cried and while we were watching him he started to laugh at the same time he was crying.

I heard him the other day telling one of the farmers at the bridge about it. "There I was," he said, "crying away, tears as big as horseballs rolling down my cheeks!"

In the parlour that afternoon, while we were reading, O'Driscoll looked up suddenly and said this: "I've got, I think, a good plan to save your bridge. You and Mrs. O'Driscoll have won over some of the people with your paintin' and your fixin'. Some of the farmers at the Brennan's Hill Hotel are sympathetic to the cause. But not all of them are, Hubbo. And when it comes down to the money, the few you've won over will give in. No sir, we need a stronger position. If it touches their pockets they'll buckle under."

"What are you going to do?" I said.

"Start a petition. Get a petition signed by every workin' man on the job is what I'm going to do, me lad! Get a list of names of everybody on the job saying they want the old bridge saved to show their children and their children's children how they used to live!"

BABY TELLS LIES BEFORE IT CAN TALK!

Prootoo and I were getting along fairly well. At least when she looked at me, her eyes seemed kinder than before. And the day that Mrs. O'Driscoll brought her the homemade black currant jam, she almost smiled at me.

There were farmers of all sizes working on the bridge. Small farmers, medium-sized farmers, big farmers.

The biggest farmer of them all looked like he was wearing shoulder pads under his shirt. He reminded me of a football player who played for the Ottawa Rough Riders named Tony Golab. We used to wait outside the little door in the green fence at half time for the players to come back on the field. There was a cement ledge you could stand on, and when Tony Golab came by I once jumped on his back and rode him into the park without paying.

"Hang on, kid!" he said while the security guard was trying to pull me off him. "Hang on, kid!" he said.

His sweater was covered with mud so you couldn't see his number. But I knew what it was. It was 72.

And there was blood on his cheek.

The biggest farmer of them all reminded me of Tony Golab.

Another one of the farmers liked to sing.

He had only one song but it had hundreds of verses. They were all about some ancient guy named Brian O'Lynn.

The verses sounded like this:

> *Oh, Brian O'Lynn and his wife and wife's mother*
> *Tried to go over the bridge together*
> *The storm it was howling, the bridge it fell in.*
> *"We'll go home by water," says Brian O'Lynn.*

But our most famous farmer was not working on the bridge at all.

He was a visitor who came over during our lunch hour and entertained us while we lay on the ground, sprawled out on the ground, full of food and resting.

Everybody said that Old Mickey Malarkey was the biggest liar on the Gatineau River. The Gatineau River runs from north of the town of Maniwaki right down to Ottawa. There are lots of little towns and villages in the Gatineau River Valley and lots of farms and houses along the river.

There were lots of liars living between Maniwaki and Ottawa. Maybe hundreds of liars. And so to be the biggest liar in the whole valley you had to be very good at it. There was quite a lot of competition.

Old Mickey Malarkey was the best.

He was also the one who had the most practice because he was the oldest. Old Mickey Malarkey was 112 years old and the farmers all said that he'd been lying since he was a little baby. Some of the farmers working on the new bridge said that Old Mickey Malarkey was lying before he learned to talk, if you can imagine that.

Old Mickey Malarkey was lying away back in the 1840's. Before Canada was even a country—before Confederation. Before the invention of the radio, the telephone, the car, before electricity. Old Mickey Malarkey was telling lies when my favourite writer, Leo Tolstoy, who wrote *War and Peace*, was only about twelve years old.

Whenever anybody asked Old Mickey Malarkey about being the biggest liar in the Gatineaus, he would say that he never told a lie in his life, which, of course, was one of the biggest big lies he ever told.

You could see the top of Old Mickey's house from where we were building the new bridge.

About a quarter to twelve Old Mickey would leave his house, and by the time Prootoo rang the bell at twelve noon, he was already shuffling along the road. By the time most of the farmers were finished eating, Mickey would finally arrive.

Most everybody would be sprawled out on their backs with their arms and legs spread out and their mouths open and their eyes half shut. And their stomachs swelling up and down, trying to digest all the food they ate and all the tea and water they drank.

It would take Old Mickey about forty-five minutes to walk that far.

I could probably walk from his house to where we had our dinner in about thirty seconds.

I told O'Driscoll one day that I could probably throw a stone that far.

"But, Hubbo, you're young. You know, he's pretty near a hundred years older than you. They tell me around here that fifty years ago, when your covered bridge was built, Old Mickey was sixty-two years of age. In fact, he was the foreman on the job. He's built many barns in his day, and so building a covered bridge is almost the same. Now, Hubbo, when you're—what is it he is, let's see—when *you're* one hundred and twelve years of age, I hope you can do as well!"

When Old Mickey finally got there he sat on a saw-horse or a bag of cement and got his breath and then he got up and walked around through the bodies of the farmers. He was bent over quite a bit and his hands were holding each other behind his back.

Then he started. It was a game they all knew. A conversation game.

"Went out last night after dark on the river. Stayed about an hour. *Filled* the boat with catfish!" said Old Mickey Malarkey.

"Filled the boat, Mickey?" said one farmer who was lying on his back with his arms out and his legs apart.

"Well, filled a *tub* and a couple of buckets."

"A *tub* and a couple of buckets, Mickey?" said another farmer, lying on his stomach with his face on his arm.

"O.K., a *tub* then. A *tub full*," said Mickey.

"A *tub full*, Mickey?" another farmer said, steam rising from him.

"Well, it was *half* full," said Mickey.

"*Half* full, Mickey?" another farmer said, pouring water over his head to cool off.

"Well, it was dark. But there were a *lot* of fish in there."

"A *lot* of fish, Mickey?" said the biggest farmer of them all.

"O.K. *Some* fish. *Some*."

"*Some* fish, Mickey?" said O'Driscoll.

"Well, say, half a *dozen* or so."

"Or *so*, Mickey?" said the first farmer.

"O.K. Two. Two nice big catfish."

"Two, Mickey?" said farmer number two.

"All right. One. One *huge* catfish. The biggest catfish I ever saw. Huge."

"Huge, Mickey?" said the wet farmer.

"A good size, a fair-sized fish."

"Fair size, Mickey?" said O'Driscoll.

"O.K. It was a small one. They weren't biting, it's the moon or something. I threw it back."

"Did you catch *any* fish Mickey?" I felt like saying, but the singing farmer beat me to it.

"No! I didn't catch one damn fish. Are you satisfied?"

"Did you even go fishing, Mickey?" somebody finally said.

"No! I didn't go fishing. I hate fishing. And I hate catfish. They're ugly and they scare me. As a matter of fact I've heard tell that they're poison. The Devil put them there in the river!"

"You're an awful liar, Mickey Malarkey. An awful liar!"

Just then Prootoo came along and announced that we were going to tear down the covered bridge as soon as one lane of the new bridge was laid.

It was in the contract.

It couldn't be helped.

The way she said that it couldn't be helped, you could tell she was sort of sorry.

But business was business.

BOY APPOINTED KING OF MUSHRAT CREEK!

I was learning a lot on my new job.

One of the first things I learned was that I wasn't going to earn forty-four dollars a week because I wasn't going to be able to work every day.

When I ran out of nails to pull, Prootoo would come up and say, "You're laid off. Come back tomorrow. We might 'ave some more cloux for you!" She would laugh when she said that. Then, I noticed that she was calling me "Cloux," which is the French word for nail. But it wasn't in a mean way.

"Hey, Cloux! You're laid off! Come back tomorrow. See if dere's any cloux for you!" I was the only one on the job she joked with.

Mrs. O'Driscoll said she didn't have any kids of her own and she liked me because I was adopted.

"How did she know I was adopted?" I asked Mrs. O'Driscoll.

"Why I told her, of course," said Mrs. O'Driscoll out of the corner of her mouth.

Another thing I learned was about whistling. One of the smaller farmers was helping with the pulling of the nails one day. Actually, he was banging the dried cement off the wood so I could get at the nails. He was whistling a song. He was whistling "I been workin' on the railroad." Just to be friendly, I started whistling the same song. Whistling "I been workin' on the railroad" right along with him. He stopped whistling and stopped banging the cement off his board and stared at me.

"You don't whistle the same song at the same time another person is whistling the song. Don't you know that?"

I apologized. I didn't know that.

You can learn a lot while you're building a bridge.

On one of my laid-off days (I called them cloux days), Mrs. O'Driscoll and I sat under her two rowanwood trees and watched a monarch butterfly chase Nerves around the yard. As soon as Nerves got settled down again and curled up for a snooze, the monarch was back right at his nose and Nerves was on his feet showing his teeth and being pretty ferocious. Then the monarch went out and came in again, this time not fluttering and playing but gliding and diving straight for Nerves, and Nerves took off across the sideroad until he realized he was heading right for the potato field and 10,000 potato bugs. He screeched to a stop and made a quick right and headed down towards the ice house and Mushrat Creek, and we waited for the splash.

I went again to the covered bridge to wait for Oscar to come by in his coupe. Lately I had gone part way with him. We even talked together a couple of times. He always seemed to be going to say something but he'd never say it.

If he didn't have stuff piled in the rumble seat I could sometimes ride back there. You felt like a king riding back there. Riding through your kingdom. Waving at the farmers along the road. The breeze flapping your shirt. You reach up sometimes, try to slap the leaves. You see a red-winged blackbird showing off his dive. You try to catch a handful of chokecherries when Oscar is rounding a curve close to the edge. Your hand is purple and sticky from the chokecherry juice. You watch the groundhogs praying in the fields, sitting up straight, just like in Foolish Father Foley's church. You are blinking at the sun flashing through the trees, following you along. Listening to the crows complaining about nothing. Smelling the sweetgrass and the clover. Hearing the heat bugs.

The King of Mushrat Creek.

Until you stop. Then the dust swirls up around you and you'd better hold your breath for a minute.

The trouble with riding outside like that though was that I wouldn't be able to talk to Oscar, find out more about his life, about his dead lover Ophelia, about what happened.

Ophelia dead.

Sometimes I walked down to Brennan's Hill for a small can of white paint maybe to touch up our milk separator shack. Past Old Mickey Malarkey's house, the road was lined with chokecherry trees and plum. Some of the plums were ripe enough to eat but were a bit hard, but the chokecherries were soft and juicy. Trouble was they turned your mouth purple and made you feel after like you just ate a cardboard box. I timed it so I would get to the General Store in Brennan's Hill at half past five. That gave me time to get the paint, talk for a while (this is where I learned to tell the different evergreen trees apart), and then walk over to meet the train from Ottawa at ten to six.

I stood beside Oscar McCracken's mail car and watched the train. The whistle echoed all over the valley between the hills and then the train rounded the curve out of the trees and roared and coughed and chuckled and burped and farted and screeched and stopped.

And the steam floating across the platform there tasted like metal.

Some people got off.

Nobody I knew, though.

One cloux day, Nerves and I strolled over to see if Old Mac Gleason had any news. It was fun watching Nerves try to stroll.

Old Mac sucked on his pipe for a while.

Then Nerves and Old Mac started a long staring contest.

Nerves often did this to people. Especially strangers. I never saw him lose one of those staring matches. I think that Nerves, in his other life, must have been a hypnotist. Old Mac looked away finally and Nerves lay down for a little snooze.

"And how's little Nerves today? You're looking well, Nerves. Keeping busy, are you?" Old Mac didn't like Nerves. Too much competition.

Nerves opened one eye. Then he wagged one ear as if to say, "I'm fine, Old Mac Gleason. And how are *you* this fine morning? How's your verandah doing? Do you think we'll get some rain? What do you hear about the new bridge? Are you in favour of tearing down the old one or leaving it there for posterity? Do you think the devil will get you for not going to church? Does living beside a graveyard bother you at night? Do you know everybody's business in Mushrat Creek? Do you think you'll go to hell for making fun of Father Foley? Is your pipe empty again? Is that why it makes that sucking noise? When you spit off the verandah, do you always spit in the same place? Or do you wait to see which way the wind is blowing? When you were young, did you ever cry? Did anybody ever say, 'be a man'? Does your rocking chair squeak the same way each time? When it was new, did it squeak? Did you ever write a letter to a girl when you didn't know her address?"

Nerves could say quite a bit with a little wag of his ear.

Cloux days came in handy.

I went for a walk up the road and talked for a minute to Mrs. Brown over the fence.

She was in her hollyhocks.

You could hardly see her.

You could hardly hear her.

She was Ophelia Brown's mother.

In my letter I tried to explain to F3 about Ophelia's mother, Mrs. Brown.

I said in the letter that Mrs. Brown looked like a cup and saucer that you only used on Sunday. Then I said she looked like meringue on the top of a lemon pie. That sounded even more silly than the cup and saucer one. But I left them both in anyway. Then I tried to say that Mrs.

Brown looked like a little glass statue of a ballet dancer. I liked the sound of that one so I left that in, too.

Later on I decided to try that she looked like a ripe milkweed pod. And, like ripe milkweed in a wind, if you blew on her, she'd come all apart and float away. And there'd be monarch butterflies all around you.

I smiled at Nerves while I thought about F3 reading this letter (if I ever found her address), and what a picture she would have of Ophelia Brown's mother: a cup and saucer, lemon pie, glass ballet dancer, milkweed with monarchs.

Then I told her in the letter how sad it was about Oscar and his dead lover Ophelia Brown, and I even tried to talk about F3 and me and about our love affair and how we were apart, sort of like Ophelia and Oscar. I knew I was getting a little too dramatic but I couldn't help it. Then I said our love affair was sort of like two potato bugs, one on one leaf at one end of the potato field and the other on a potato plant leaf way down at the other end of the field. I knew how dumb it all sounded so I read the whole thing out to Nerves. When I got to the part about the potato bugs, Nerves ran into the kitchen and hid behind the stove.

Then I wrote that F3 and I were like fire and wood. She was the fire and I was the wood and the flames were our love and the sparks were the love words we said to each other and the smoke was the fights we had. Then I wrote that *she* was the wood and I was the fire and that the heat from the flames was the ache in my heart and the ashes were the rest of the cruel world when we were apart and by this time I was so mixed up that I tried to change it all to where she was a squirrel and I was a nut.

But I didn't say in the letter what was on my mind all the time. About the bridge. And about Oscar McCracken.

And if they tore down the bridge, what would he do. Poor Oscar. If we could only help him!

But O'Driscoll had his petition ready.

Maybe something was going to happen.

TREE GROWS OUT OF BOY'S NOSE!

Everybody was talking and arguing about the covered bridge. Some wanted to keep it. Some wanted to tear it down. Some thought Prootoo was going to get a lot of profit from the contract for ripping it down. Some said maybe they should burn it down. Have a big corn roast!

Some didn't care. A job is a job.

Some wanted to leave it there for future generations. For Posterity.

"Future generations?" said the biggest farmer of them all. "What would you want to do that for? I suppose if you built a new barn, you'd leave the old barn there, all falling down and rotten so's future generations could stand around and admire it and say, My, look at the tumbled-down old shack they used for a barn in those days! I wonder why they bothered leavin' that there at all. Sure, it's only an eyesore!"

On our noon hour, one farmer, while he was eating a pig's leg for his dinner, gave us a little speech about the history of the bridge.

"Imagine them building our covered bridge in 1900! Everybody from all over the countryside coming with their picks and shovels and tools to work on the bridge. Just like building a barn! The walls, put up one big piece at a time, just like a barn, and the roof beam and the rafters and then lumber and the shingles—just like a barn and the hammers all hammering and the saws all sawing away and the men all shouting and then the big outdoor picnic at the church and the pies and cakes and beans and potatoes and bread and pork and tea and onions and cabbage and pickles and even tomatoes if it was the fall! Oh, it must have been lovely!

"And not one car came through the new covered bridge for a long long time. Only sleighs and wagons and carts!

"Will it fit a load of hay? Will it take a load of logs?

"Then it's all right!

"And after that, only a few cars a year came. And maybe a truck. Then a few more cars and trucks. And then more. And more.

"And then, in the last few years, it seemed like every day there was more cars and bigger trucks.

"So now we need a new bridge.

"Time to tear down the old bridge and build this nice new one like we're doing right now...it's progress!"

It was quite a speech. Specially while you're eating a pig's leg.

Then Mickey Malarkey tried to tell a story about a cousin of his who was told not to shove a bean in his nose and did. And how the bean took root and began to grow and how the leaves were hanging out of his nostrils. Mickey tried to say they had to get hedge-clippers to trim some of the foliage hanging out of his nose, so they could get at the root and dig it out—and did he ever learn a lesson about shovin' things up your nose, especially beans!

But even Old Mickey Malarkey couldn't keep the subject off the bridge for long.

Sometimes some people who lived in cottages up the river in Beer Bay and on Beer Point would drive up and get out of their cars and ask about the bridge.

"Are they going to tear down the old covered bridge?" they'd say.

Then the argument would start all over again.

And the farmers that came from up in around Low would always seem to wind up arguing with the farmers from down in around Brennan's Hill.

And even though they might both be on the same side of the argument, they'd argue anyway.

Then somebody started up about how hard it is to keep *up* a covered bridge! All the things that can happen to it. Trucks hitting it. Heavy loads. Porcupines. Bark beetles. Lichen. Moss. Wind. Rain. Ants. People carving initials. Kids. Drunks. Vandals. Suicides.

And then some other people would start talking about the good stuff about the covered bridge, about how school kids could meet there to wait for the sleigh to take them to school in the winter except there were no more sleighs. And also about in the summer how kids could swing on a rope attached to a lower cord or stringer under the bridge and flip into the creek to swim and cool off; or how a farmer could rest his horses in there, stay in the bridge for a while to cool off and get their breath before they went up the other side pulling their load of hay or logs; or the advertisements you could pin up inside the wooden portals about meetings or dances; or how you could hold your breath and make a wish while you're passing through; or how at night your girl would be afraid (she was only pretending) because of the dark and you put your arm around her; and how trout would sometimes leap right out of Mushrat Creek and fall through the windows into the bridge!

And how magic it was when the bridge creaked in the wind.

And how lovers could meet in there.

And the drumming of the hooves, and the rumble of the wheels.

And then some other people would spoil it and tell how a farmer once hanged himself in the bridge because his crops wouldn't grow. Was it true? Maybe. Maybe not. Maybe it was another covered bridge. What difference did it make?

And then everybody started thinking of Oscar McCracken, but nobody mentioned him. And Ophelia Brown. And nobody said her name, either.

On Friday of the week when the news came out that they were going to tear down the old covered bridge as soon as one lane of the new bridge was finished, O'Driscoll was ready.

The night before, I told Mrs. O'Driscoll and him about how Oscar would talk four times a day to his dead lover, Ophelia Brown.

"We have to save this bridge," said O'Driscoll. "Not only for Oscar, but for Posterity. In my travels I have learned that without a past, we have no future!"

Mrs. O'Driscoll rolled her eyes. "What a Romantic," she said.

"You'll get fired," I said.

"No, I won't," he said. "I'm on the side of right! The side of History!" O'Driscoll had a plan.

Everybody knew that on Friday, about half past one, Prootoo would go to Wakefield to get the money for our pay. The bank closed at three o'clock so she always left in the truck with her husband who loved her, Ovide, to drive down to Wakefield and get the money before the bank closed.

At 1:30, O'Driscoll started taking the petition around to the bridge workers asking them to sign if they were in favour of saving the covered bridge.

I was watching him.

The first person he talked to was the biggest farmer of them all, who was a pretty good mechanic and who was lying under the generator, working on it.

O'Driscoll lay there under the generator with him. Their legs, sticking out, were the very same.

They had on the same overalls and the same boots. Almost everybody wore the same-coloured overalls. Everybody bought them at the same store. There was only one kind.

The generator was right beside Prootoo's shack.

But the truck was gone. Everything was O.K. She wouldn't be back for quite a while.

We were sure Prootoo was gone in the truck to Wakefield to get the pay.

Suddenly the door of the shack opened and Prootoo stood there listening to O'Driscoll talking to the mechanic about signing the petition about saving the bridge. You could hear him explaining it.

You could tell that she didn't know *who* it was under there, but she could hear *what* it was he was saying.

She had a can of white paint in her hands. She began to lean away over to look under the generator to see who was talking about this petition about the bridge.

Some of us were watching.

We knew that if she got down on her hands and knees and looked under she would find out it was O'Driscoll doing the talking and fire him on the spot for trying to start a strike.

Just then Mr. Proulx's truck drove up in a cloud of dust. He said in French to her that they had to go. Right now! They were in a hurry! Wakefield. The bank closes at three! Tout d'suite!

Prootoo then got a very wise and crafty look on her face.

She didn't say a word to her husband as he gave her a little kiss on the cheek out the truck window. While he kissed her, she never took her eyes off O'Driscoll's pants. Then, as she walked around the front of the truck to get in, she deliberately spilled some white paint on the right leg of O'Driscoll's overalls.

Then she put the can of paint in the shack, got in the truck, and they took off.

O'Driscoll, on his back, worked his way out from under the generator.

"Thank you, Paddy," said O'Driscoll. "That's good enough for me."

"Did he sign his name?" I said.

"No, he didn't," said O'Driscoll, "but he said he liked the idea of going around and asking people. He said he thought that was fair."

I told O'Driscoll about what Prootoo did. The paint on the pants.

"I heard the truck taking off," said O'Driscoll as he looked at the right pant leg of his overalls. "Why do you think she did this?"

And then I thought. Then the more I thought, the more excited I got. I had a funny feeling that I was going to know the answer. The answer was right around the corner! Any minute now! Don't think too hard. It might go away. Why did she do that? She didn't know who it was. She didn't know who was saying these things about the bridge because all the legs of all the overalls looked the same.

But she put on the paint. On the pants.

This is payday!

Tonight at six, we line up.

For our pay.

All our pants will be together!

She'll pick the pants with the paint!

"That's it!" I said to O'Driscoll.

"What's it?" said O'Driscoll.

"Tonight. At six o'clock! In the pay line-up! She'll check the pants. She'll make a speech. She'll fire you! Just like teachers do in school sometimes. Make an example of you...fire you in front of everybody. That's what she's like!"

Before I was finished, O'Driscoll was looking in the supply shack.

I thought he was looking for paint remover.

But no. He came out with Prootoo's can of white paint.

"An old trick I learned in the navy," he said.

"What are you going to do?" I said.

"Follow me," said O'Driscoll as he took a quick look over his shoulder. "Follow me!"

WOMAN'S FACE SPROUTS PINE KNOTS!

I tried to explain in my letter to Fleurette the look on Prootoo's face when she came out of the shack at six o'clock and saw all the farmers lined up so straight, just like in school.

Every farmer had a splotch of white paint on the right leg of his overalls.

What a coincidence! Which worker was passing around the petition? Who knows!

Prootoo's face was like a crowbar, I said in Fleurette's letter. No, it was more like a bag of cement. No, it was like a one-by-six piece of pine lumber with too many knots, and full of bent nails.

It was like a flying sledge hammer.

It was fun writing it. But I didn't admit that I felt kind of bad. I felt a little sorry for Prootoo. She wasn't as bad as they thought. In fact, sometimes she was almost nice. Maybe it was because I knew she liked me. I don't know.

The farmers on the bridge had so much fun that day that they all signed the petition whether they agreed with it or not.

It said this:

"I, the undersigned, refuse to tear down the covered bridge.

I would rather save it for Posterity. For, without a past, we have no future."

Saturday at noon, while she was ringing the time-to-quit bell, Prootoo had the petition put in her hand by O'Driscoll himself.

GRAVEYARD FENCE MOVES DURING NIGHT!

The next day was Sunday, and it was a day that the people of Mushrat Creek would never forget.

Father Foley started in on his usual sermon and was scaring himself half to death about Hell. Then he paused and changed the subject a bit. He started talking about Obedience. About following the rules about doing as you're told. About how Satan was cast out of Heaven because of Pride and about how Adam and Eve, especially Eve, were kicked out of the Garden of Eden because they wouldn't do as they were told and how the Lord once sent a big flood to drown all the people who wouldn't do as they were told which was just about everybody and the way Father Foley told it, it looked like God could hardly get *anybody* to do what they were told.

Then Father Foley whipped out a long sheet of paper.

It was O'Driscoll's petition!

"It has come to my attention," shouted Father Foley, "that the workers who are working on our spanking new bridge are refusing to honour part of their contract. Their *Duty*. This, my parishioners, is a disgrace to this fine community. Mr. Proulx is a fine businessman and an excellent craftsman. He has been hired and is being paid by the provincial and local authorities to do his duty. He will do his duty. And you will do yours! As God is my witness, the covered bridge will be torn down when the time comes for it to be torn down! And this foolish petition is now null and void!"

Father Foley then tore the petition four or five times and threw it down at his feet in the pulpit.

The way Father Foley told it, it sounded sort of like God wanted the farmers to tear down their own bridge that their fathers had built.

Everybody was shocked.

But not as shocked as they were a few seconds later when a voice came from the back of the church.

"That bridge is none of your damn business, Father Foley!" the voice shouted.

Everybody turned around.

It was Oscar McCracken doing the shouting. Quiet Oscar McCracken was almost screaming in Father Foley's church!

"What happens to the covered bridge is none of your damned business, Father Foley!" Oscar was choking and crying.

Oscar McCracken, who never said boo to anybody, was yelling and *swearing* at Father Foley in Father Foley's church!

"I wish you were *dead*, Father Foley! I wish you were dead and burning in Hell!" screamed Oscar McCracken and ran out the open doors, knocking over the pile of collection baskets on the table there.

When I looked back up at Father Foley, everybody was looking down. Not looking at anything.

Ashamed of Oscar McCracken.

Afraid of Father Foley's rage.

For the rest of the service, nobody would look at Father Foley. Everybody looked down at their feet.

When we left, Father Foley wasn't at the door to wish us goodbye.

That evening, under the rowanwood trees, we were quiet. There wasn't much to say. Nobody spoke to anybody, it seemed, since Oscar stood up and swore at the priest in church that morning. People moved out of the church quietly, not speaking much of anything to anybody. Some of the mothers maybe told their kids to hush up or hurry up or don't do that, but that was about all anybody said.

And we were sad. Sad for Oscar and Oscar's family. Because now, for a while anyway, nobody was going to talk too much to Oscar, even though they liked him and everything. Now, when he'd deliver the mail and maybe they would be out at their mailboxes, they would maybe say good afternoon and then look down at their mail right away so as not to look into Oscar's shame in his eyes.

And we were worried. Now that the bridge was going to be torn down for sure, maybe everybody in Mushrat Creek would say to us, I told you so, I told you that old relic would be nothing but trouble, and maybe people would think we were strangers, poking into their business, especially O'Driscoll with his petition. Maybe they'd start to say he tricked them into signing it and that now they were in trouble because Father Foley saw every one of those names on the list and knew every one of them and had visited every one of them when they were sick and when their kids were sick or the old folks were dying and Father Foley prayed for all of them and loved them and now they turn around and do something like this? Be Disobedient? And maybe they'd say it was all because of those new people, the what-do-you-call-'ems, the O'Driscolls.

I tried to change the subject, maybe get O'Driscoll talking.

I asked him a question.

"What did you mean when you said you learned that trick about the paint on the pants in the navy?"

"Oh, that," said O'Driscoll, taking a quick look behind him at Nerves, who was walking by with one of our hens. "That was the way you could come in late at night, a way after you were supposed to, past curfew, run right past the Duty Officer, you roar right down into the mess where your hammock is already slung, give all the full hammocks a swing as you go by, then get into yours without even taking your clothes off. A few seconds later when the Duty Officer sticks his head in the hatch to get your number, *all* the hammocks are swinging! Get it? Who just came in late and got in their hammock? Just about everybody, sir!"

It was something but not the real O'Driscoll.

Mrs. O'Driscoll sighed.

The bridge would be gone. Nothing would be the same. Maybe we'd have to move again.

Hopeless.

Nerves was back from walking the hen to the henhouse and was sniffing some plants alongside the house.

I tried O'Driscoll again.

"What are those plants Nerves is so interested in over there?"

I knew that if O'Driscoll didn't know the answer he would make something up.

I hoped he didn't know the answer.

"Those plants? You didn't pull one up, did you? Because if you pull one up by hand, all alone, you'll die a horrible death by strangulation within the next twenty-four hours. Why would you want to pull one up? I'll tell you why."

You could tell O'Driscoll was glad to talk about something that would take his mind off his torn-up petition.

Mrs. O'Driscoll eased back in her chair to get comfortable. She was going to try to enjoy this one.

"Did you learn this in your travels?" she said and shut her eyes like she always did when she didn't expect an answer.

"They're called mandrake plants. People take the mandrake root and grind it up and make a powder and mix it with pig's blood and drink it. It can make a woman have as many babies as she wants and a little touch of it once and a while can make a man very handsome indeed. But too much of it has been known to drive a lad right around the corner and out of his mind. Julian, one of the emperors of the Roman Empire, took so much of it that he thought for a while he was turned into a goat and nearly died after he ate most of his blanket one night."

Mrs. O'Driscoll sighed.

"How do you pull it up without getting strangled within twenty-four hours?" O'Driscoll went on.

"I'm glad you asked that, Hubbo me boy. You *don't* pull it up. You get a small rope, tie one end of it to the base of the stem of the mandrake and tie the other end of the rope around the neck of a *dog*."

I looked down at Nerves, who was studying some ants in the sweet-grass.

He glanced up at us with a sarcastic look on his face.

"Then," said O'Driscoll, "you *chase* the dog!"

"Where did you say you learned all this, again?" said Mrs. O'Driscoll, trying to trap O'Driscoll. She kept her eyes closed this time, which meant she knew she wasn't going to get an answer and that she didn't really want one anyway.

"And when the mandrake is uprooted, you'll notice two remarkable things," O'Driscoll kept on. "One: you hear a small, blood-curdling scream. Two: you'll see that the root is shaped exactly like a little statue of a man!"

I was right. O'Driscoll didn't know what those plants were at all.

After dark, Nerves and I went out to trim the lamps on the covered bridge. The moonlight sparkled on the water of Mushrat Creek and pierced through the openings of the bridge, sending bars of softness onto the carriageway inside.

The moonlight turned the red side of the bridge into silver.

It was sad to think that the covered bridge would soon be gone forever.

After the lamps, Nerves and I took a walk. Behind the church in the sexton's cottage there was a light shining out the curtained window.

The door was open a bit. I politely opened it some more.

"Oscar?"

Oscar, sitting at the table, with his sad eyes.

"I can't go home. My family won't talk to me. I'll stay here tonight or with Mrs. Brown. Hello, Nerves. How are you tonight?"

Nerves sat with his head up and his paws together. Best behaviour. He liked Oscar McCracken. He liked riding in the rumble seat of Oscar McCracken's coupe car.

"I shouldn't have spoke like that in church. I shouldn't have shouted them things."

Oscar let out a long, long sigh.

"Everything's over," he said.

Then he looked at Nerves a while and smiled a little bit.

"I met you before you met me, you know," he said, leaning over to Nerves.

Nerves, sitting even straighter.

Oscar turned to me.

"You know, Hubbo, I never did in all my born days ever see a dog faint, so help me God, until that night."

My mouth must have fallen open, because there was a moth trying to fly into it.

"You?" I said. "That night?"

"Come out, I'll show you."

In the goat pen, on a little clothesline, hung a long white dress and a blue hat with a wide brim.

"I did it to try and make Father Foley move Ophelia's grave inside the graveyard fence. It was the second stupidest thing I ever did. This morning in church was the stupidest. Now she'll never get in."

"That was you?"

"That was me. I thought I'd meet Father Foley coming back from visiting the sick. Turned out it was you."

"I should have known it was no ghost," I said.

"Why?" said Oscar.

"The splash!" I said. "Ghosts don't splash when they hit the water. A big splash!"

"I know." Oscar was almost laughing. "I did a belly flop. Stupid me!"

Then we both laughed.

And then we stood for a while until the goat poked her head out of her little barn.

Nerves got around behind my legs.

"I'm goin' to leave this place forever," Oscar said quietly. "But there's one thing I got to do before I go. And that thing I got to do, I got to do tonight."

Oscar went into the sexton's cottage.

There was clanging and rattling around in there.

Oscar came out with a roll of page wire. And a post-hole digger. And a shovel. He had wire-cutters and a carpenter's belt full of tools and nails.

"Do you want to give me a hand?" he said.

Up in the graveyard Oscar already had a cedar post cut and hidden in the long grass a little away from Ophelia Brown's grave.

He was all ready. He knew exactly what to do. He had been thinking about it for years.

Ophelia's grave was just outside the fence right between two fence posts.

The first thing he did was cut the page wire away from the two posts and leave an open gateway in the fence.

Then we dug a hole on the other side of Ophelia Brown's grave and we sank the post and tamped it down with rocks and earth. This was a strong post.

Then we cinched the new page wire to the first original post, brought it out around the new post and stapled it there, then brought it back to the second original post.

We cleaned up around the job and walked back a bit to look.

The grave of Ophelia Brown, Oscar McCracken's lover, was now inside the graveyard fence.

In fact, it looked kind of special.

It looked like the fence went along and then said, whoops, let's jog out here a bit, we don't want to forget to include our Ophelia Brown, now do we?

Back at the sexton's cottage we sat on the grass and drank cold water. Nerves seemed glad to get out of the graveyard.

Oscar was calm now, and in a sort of a good mood.

"Maybe I'll wait a few days before I leave. See what happens. I'm not mad at Father Foley. It's not his fault. It's the rules."

Then, Oscar, just for a joke, pulled the wide-brimmed hat off the line and put it carefully over the goat's horns.

"This looks good on you, do you know that?"

We both laughed. The goat bleated.

Even Nerves looked at the goat without hiding because she looked so harmless in that hat that she wouldn't hurt a fly.

Oscar said he was tired and went in. I noticed he didn't shut the goat pen gate, but I was too tired to care. He could do it later when he went up to Mrs. Brown's to sleep.

Nerves and I went home.

I fell onto my straw mattress, mud and all. And I drifted and rode off into a sleep.

There was a big dance in the covered bridge.

I was dancing with the biggest farmer of them all. Fleurette was there, dancing with Father Foley. She was wearing a white dress with lace, blue shoes and a blue hat with a broad brim. She had a white rag tying up her black hair. Some of the farmers were tearing down the bridge during the dance. There was hammering, with the sound of little hammers like the hoofbeats of a goat. Oscar was up in the rafters trying to hang himself and underneath us Mushrat Creek was boiling, spurting red-hot lava. O'Driscoll came riding through the bridge on a dolphin while Mrs. O'Driscoll, floating, played the fiddle, her face the face of an angel.

Then the music gets faster and Old Mac Gleason has got Nerves and he's throwing him out the wind-vent and Mushrat Creek is full, like in the spring, but it's not water that fills the creek and lashes against the sides of the bridge, it's potato bugs! And Ophelia Brown is trying to stop Old Mac Gleason and my feet are nailed to the deck and I can't move! I've got my nail puller but I can't move! No...! No...! No...!

"Hubbo! Hubbo me boy! Wake up, lad! It's me, O'Driscoll. Get up. Get up. Quick!"

It was. It was O'Driscoll, shaking me awake.

"Come quick, boy! Something terrible has happened! It's Father Foley! They found him in the bridge! He's dead! They say somebody must have killed him. Get your pants on!"

MAN'S HEAD TURNS INTO PUMPKIN!

Everybody working on the new bridge was saying that Father Foley didn't just die, he was murdered. They weren't saying it very loud, mind you. Maybe only whispering it, or saying it without saying it at all.

For instance, you wouldn't actually hear somebody come right out and say, "I think so-and-so murdered Foolish Father Foley last night in the covered bridge." Oh, no, you wouldn't hear that. But you might hear somebody say this: "They say that there's rumours going around that some people have heard others say that they've been told that there's a suspicion that something bad that you wouldn't like to say out loud happened to Father Foley in the covered bridge last night."

And the other person would maybe say, "Well, he died in there, we all know *that* for sure."

And the first person might say, "Yes, we do know that for sure, but they say that maybe they know *how* or why he died."

And the other person would say, "Well, what *is* it that they say is what maybe happened?"

And then the person who started it all would probably say, "Oh, I wouldn't like to say."

And then some other people would stop working on the new bridge and put down a hammer and lean on a shovel and then start talking about who it was who maybe *killed* Foolish Father Foley from Farrellton in the covered bridge last night.

One might say, while he was leaning on his shovel, "They say that people have heard people say that somebody, who maybe even some of us *know*, might be the one to be the *cause* of Father Foley's death."

And the other, while he was putting down his hammer, "Yes, and they say, now don't get me wrong, I'm not saying this but they say that *that* person who was maybe *in* on the Father's horrible death the other night in the covered bridge was somebody we know that has something to do with delivering the mail around here in this part of the country."

We all carried steel rods for about three hours.

Before noon two policemen drove up with Oscar and Mrs. Brown in the back.

The policeman asking the questions had a big wart on his nose.

"This is the young gentleman here," said Mrs. Brown, showing me to the policeman. You could hardly hear Mrs. Brown.

The policeman with the wart on his nose was very quiet and polite and friendly. He asked where I was last night, what was I doing, what time was it, when did I last see Oscar?

I told him.

"And this graveyard business. What were you doing there?"

"We were fixing the fence."

The policeman's wart seemed to swell up a bit.

He got back in the car and they drove quietly away.

We carried steel rods until noon.

I was so tired I could hardly talk.

Lunch hour came at last.

"They're saying Oscar could have sneaked out of Mrs. Brown's after she was asleep and waited for Father Foley inside the bridge," O'Driscoll said. "And hit him over the head."

"I know," I said. "But it's not true. He couldn't have!"

"Pretty strange, all right, Hubbo me boy," O'Driscoll sighed. "Everybody heard Oscar threaten the Father. That's a very serious thing, Hubbo. Are you sure you didn't see Oscar do anything last night?"

Now O'Driscoll thought *I* was holding something back. That maybe *I* was a witness to something. I'd probably spend the rest of my life in jail.

Or be hanged by the neck until I was dead.

O'Driscoll all of a sudden gave me a hug.

He must have realized he made me feel bad.

"I'm sorry, Hubbo me boy. Listen now, don't worry. I know you're telling the truth, and when you tell the truth, everything always turns out fine!"

I wondered what Mrs. O'Driscoll would say if she heard O'Driscoll talk that way about the truth.

The rest of the hour we spent half listening to Mickey Malarkey telling us a pack of lies about his father and his ancestors.

It's hard to imagine, when your muscles are aching and your bones are sore and your eyes are full of dried sweat and your stomach is so full of food and tea that there's steam coming out of your mouth; it's hard to imagine somebody as old as Mickey Malarkey having a father.

He told us his father, Justin, *also* lived to be 114 years of age and had a head bigger than a large pumpkin. He said that his father Justin's great-*grandfather* whose name was Brendan and was born in the year 1695, the year before the discovery of *peppermint* also lived to be 114 years of age!

Later in the afternoon but long before quitting time, Prootoo rang her bell and when we all were around, Ovide Proulx made an announcement:

"Everybody will report to the church at five o'clock. The town council has got the coroner over dere from Wakefield because he wants to tell everybody personally what 'appened to da body of Poor Father Foley. Also, de police are dere too and dey want to question everybody about what dey can tell after dey hear what the coroner is going to tell. Work is finish for today."

Everybody was walking and packing up and asking questions and guessing what the coroner was going to say.

We headed up the road in small groups towards the church. It was going to seem funny being in there without Father Foley yelling about Hell.

The singing farmer sang part of his song behind us:

> *Brian O'Lynn and his wife and wife's mother*
> *All went up to the church together*
> *The church it was locked, and they couldn't get in*
> *"We'll pray to the Devil," says Brian O'Lynn!*

I ducked behind the church and took a look around the sexton's cottage.

The gate was open to the goat pen.

The dress hanging on the line was gone.

The goat was gone!

Could it be? Could that be what happened?

PRIESTS BLOOD SUCKED UP BY SPONGE!

News that the coroner was coming up from Wakefield spread fast, and when he arrived there was quite a crowd waiting for him in the church to hear what he had to say about Father Foley's death. Just about everybody was there. Even Oscar.

And beside him, the policeman with the wart.

Mrs. O'Driscoll slid in beside us in the pew we were in.

"Oscar's goat's gone!" I whispered to her.

"What do you mean?" she said.

"I think I know what happened," I said.

"Shh," she said.

"Ladies and gentlemen. The autopsy showed that Father Foley did not die of a blow to the head. That wound was superficial and probably was caused by his fall. Nor did he die of a heart attack or of a brain tumour or a blood clot or any other such normal causes of sudden death. No, the cause of death in this case is much more rare."

The coroner waited. He thought that everybody standing around would look at each other and say words like "rare" and "normal" and go "oooh" and "ahhh." But they didn't. They just sat there.

Then the coroner said some more.

"Father Foley died of a mysterious and sinister condition sometimes called Neurogenic Shock or Vasovagal Collapse. Vasovagal Collapse is due to a loss of peripheral arteriolar resistance resulting from reflex dilation in areas of skeletal muscle. The pooling of blood in peripheral vascular beds with loss of vascular tone results in inadequate venous return, a fall in cardiac output and subsequent reduction in arterial blood pressure. The heart has not sufficient fluid on which to contract. The lost blood of Father Foley did not pour out of him. It disappeared into his vastly dilated capillary bed and into his tissues.

"Something paralyzed the vast capillary bed of Father Foley's body, causing extreme dilation. His blood then disappeared into it as if sucked up by a sponge!" He waited again. He was waiting for people to start asking questions. They didn't. They just sat there.

"What could have paralyzed Father Foley's capillary bed, you ask? All he was doing was passing through the covered bridge." The coroner seemed mad. The audience was not co-operating.

"There is only one answer to that," said the coroner slowly. "And that answer is FEAR!"

"FEAR!" he repeated. Nobody moved.

"Yes, my friends. I have to conclude that Father Foley dropped dead because someone, or someTHING, SCARED him to DEATH!"

Now the audience co-operated.

This made sense! Now everybody started talking at once.

Of course Father Foley could have been scared to death!

Didn't he almost scare himself to death just about every Sunday during his sermon about Hell?

What about when he just about jumped out of his skin the time the goat came into the church that time?

"He certainly was the *jumpiest* priest we've had around here for a while," said Old Mickey Malarkey.

They were all talking now.

"I knew it!" I said to myself.

I knew it.

GOAT POSSESSED BY SATAN!

When the coroner was finished his report, the policeman and his wart took over and a discussion started.

I slipped out the small north door that Oscar always used. Nobody saw me.

I ran down the road, through the covered bridge, up our side road, under the red chandeliers of our rowanwood trees, around the house, past the woodpile and the summer kitchen, past the log stable and around by the manure pile and the pig pen, up through the pine bush and turned onto the old logging road towards the Gatineau River.

Beyond the corduroy there was a section of road where a purplish brown mat of dead pine needles stretched back as far as you could see into the bush.

This part of the road was damp clay and would show tracks.

I found what I thought I'd find.

Small cloven hoofprints!

I looked down the road. The evening light was slanting and filtering into the tunnel of tall sumac and poplar trees. The road turned and dipped into gloom.

I turned back and went home to wait.

I stuck my head in the big stone crock and pulled out a chunk of homemade bread.

O'Driscoll hit the door open and looked behind himself and said, "There's a lot of talk goin' about a missing goat Hubbo me boy. What's goin' on?"

"That's it!" I said. "That's what happened! I heard the hammering last night! I heard the hooves! I'm sure the goat got out! She ran through the bridge! Met Father Foley coming home from his rounds with the sick. The timing is perfect. I heard the goat hooves last night when I was half asleep! We left the gate open. The goat ate part of the dress off the line, got tangled up in it, ran out the gate and met Father Foley in the bridge. And she was wearing that hat! There's fresh tracks on the road. Let's go! The goat came down our road. I heard her!"

"Let's go and get the policeman to come with us," said O'Driscoll.

I guess everybody must have told the policeman with the wart on his nose what Father Foley was like because he seemed to enjoy the idea of coming with us to follow the goat tracks.

On our way, I explained to him about the hat and the dress and Oscar's ghost trick and the open gate.

"Quite a place, this Mushrat Creek," said the policeman with the wart. "Ghosts and goats and covered bridges and devils and dead priests."

His wart was starting to look kind of cute.

We were walking down the slope over the stinkhorn fungus and edging our way down the bank.

And there she was. Tangled up in some branches. Looking pretty lost. She gave a little bleat to us.

The hat was still over her horns.

The dress tangled over her body so that running through a covered bridge towards you in the dark, the dress flying and those eyes behind the hat brim and the thundering hooves could be pretty scary all right.

Specially if you were Father Foley with his light.

Poor Father Foley!

MAN LAUGHS FOR WHOLE WEEK!

Three weeks later, on one of my cloux days, I went up on Dizzy Peak to pick some blueberries. While I picked I spoke to Fleurette as though I was writing more of the letter. I tried to make it dramatic. I tried to make it sound like she was reading it.

From up here on Dizzy Peak you can see the whole world. To the east, the dam and the big flooded country above it and below it the narrow fast river the way it used to be when only the first Canadians lived here.

North there is the town of Low and then Venosta, and in the mist of the mountains, maybe, Farrellton.

West, rolling humpbacked mountains and lakes here and there like broken bits of mirrors.

And the covered bridge down there, with its new paint job.

And the new bridge just above it, a cement slab.

I could hear her voice reading it. And her sighing.

I already wrote in her letter how it was that the bridge didn't get torn down after all.

It was Mrs. O'Driscoll who figured it out. And Prootoo.

At a county council general meeting Mrs. O'Driscoll got Prootoo to get up and make a motion. Mrs. O'Driscoll told her to move that the covered bridge be dedicated as a monument to the late Father Foley. It was seconded by the biggest farmer of them all.

That way Ovide Proulx got the contract to paint the bridge instead of tearing it down.

How could anybody vote against that? Even Old Mac Gleason, who actually went to the meeting, had to put his hand up!

Business was business.

O'Driscoll laughed for almost a week about it until Mrs. O'Driscoll finally got sick of the whole story and shut him down by giving him the silence.

Now as Oscar McCracken travelled the bridge four times a day and paused each time inside, in the quiet there, he could, if he wanted to, read at each portal, a brass plaque.

The plaque said these words:

Let this covered bridge be dedicated to the memory of Father Francis Foley of Farrellton who gave his life herein for the people of his parish.

God Love Him

May He Rest Peacefully.

Up on Dizzy Peak, I pretended to write some more.

And here on Dizzy Peak, the sun beats on the rock and in between, the tough blueberry bushes growing in the moss, loaded with blueberries, powdered and fat, wait.

You lean over the edge, hanging by one hand to a ridge of rock a million years old and strip a handful of berries from a plant growing out of the side of the peak. Your pail on the ledge beside your hand is almost full, so you jam the handful of berries into your mouth instead.

The berries are hot and firm and sweet and you can feel them burst and pop in your mouth and the blue juice overflows down your chin.

You are eating the sun and the earth and the rain.

Fleurette would like that writing. If I could ever write it that way.

I got home with a pailful of blueberries, washed them and cleaned them, and put them on to simmer in some sugar for Mrs. O'Driscoll.

Later I met Oscar in the bridge, sat with him during his quiet time, and drove down with him to meet the train.

Sitting there on the fender of Oscar's car, my feet on the wooden station platform, my arms folded across my chest. I was feeling the muscles in my arms with my fingers. My muscles were hard and bulging from the work on the bridge.

My hands were rough and leathery from carrying the steel and the bags of cement. The fingers feeling my muscles that were strong and hard felt like steel hooks.

The train came howling around the bend in a cloud of soot and smoke and steam at exactly five to six and screamed and cried and moaned and chugged and grunted and sighed and farted and then stopped.

The bell was ringing and clanging and stabbing clean through the air and into the hills and up and down the track and off the station walls. The station master and his helper pulled a big red wagon by the tongue alongside the baggage car. I waited and watched Oscar sort his mail.

Some people were getting off the train carrying their bags and suitcases.

You could always tell when the last person was off the train because the conductor would pick up the little step and put it back inside between the cars where he kept it.

I watched the conductor pick up the little step and get up into the train with it.

The train belched and started to move.

I looked over at Oscar.
He was wearing a big smile.
He had a letter in his hand.
He gave it to me, turned upside down.
I flipped it over and right away, the handwriting!
It was from Fleurette Featherstone Fitchell.

UP TO LOW

Thanks to my wife Jackie, the classiest of ladies,
who teaches that to leave something of you behind
is your reason on earth.

PART I

We hadn't been up to Low since my mother died two years before. Aunt Dottie was living with us now so Dad and I were going to go up ahead to clean the cabin up and then she was going to come up later. You see, Aunt Dottie was very clean and Dad knew that she would be unhappy if there was dirt around or any germs or crud in the cabin.

Aunt Dottie always covered her face when she coughed and when anyone else coughed too. And she always wiped her feet three times each on the mat, and not on the same place on the mat either. And she never used anyone else's spoon or took a bite of anyone else's apple and she didn't like me to do these things either. And always put toilet paper on the seat if you're at somebody else's house. And never touch the toothpaste tube on your toothbrush when you're putting on toothpaste. And always rub the cucumber ends against the cucumber to get the poison out. And don't eat candy unless it's wrapped. And always wipe yourself three times.

And all that.

We were packing and Aunt Dottie was helping us. Dad was talking about Mean Hughie, one of his old rivals.

"They tell me Mean Hughie's going to die," he was saying as he rolled up a pair of pants and shoved them into his suitcase.

"And don't drink the water unless you boil it first," Aunt Dottie was saying as she took out the rolled up pants, folded them, wrapped them in sheets of tissue paper and put them carefully back in the suitcase.

"Yes," Dad was saying, "Mean Hughie's got the cancer, they tell me. I'll believe it when I see it. I think he's too mean to die." He was firing socks into a knapsack.

"And after you kill flies," Aunt Dottie was saying, "be sure you wrap them each in little tissues and burn them." She was taking the socks from the knapsack and spraying each of them with Lysol and placing them in little individual bags. "And the same if you blow your nose," she said. "Blow it in a little tissue and burn it right away."

"Mean Hughie is the meanest man in the Gatineau," Dad was saying, while Aunt Dottie was in the kitchen scrubbing the bottoms of our shoes with steel wool and Dutch Cleanser.

"And don't step in anything around that farm," she called over the sound of the taps running.

"Yesser," Dad was saying, "if Mean Hughie dies, he'll have to go somewhere, but I can't for the life of me guess where it is they'd send him. Heaven's out of the question and Hell's too nice a spot for him."

"And be sure when you pick berries to wash them in this Lysol before you eat them," Aunt Dottie said as she placed a large jar of Lysol in the big knapsack.

It was finally time to go.

We said goodbye to Aunt Dottie, and when I went to kiss her she turned her face away and I got her on the ear.

Germs, I guess.

She promised she'd see us in a couple of weeks.

"It'll take her a month to get ready," Dad was saying as we went down the stairs. "It'll be a month before she's clean enough to even leave the house!"

We had two army backpacks that Dad had brought back from the war and two old suitcases. We walked down to St. Patrick Street to wait for the streetcar.

There are two kinds of streetcars: tall and short. My favourite are the tall ones. They seem to me to be more intelligent looking. They have a serious look on their faces. And they rock side to side in an easy kind of way. A way that makes everybody lean together. The person you sit beside can lean on you a bit and you can hold a bit stiff until it is time to lean the other way and then he can do the same. This way you are always touching, back and forward, as though you are one person. It is very friendly. The short streetcars are different. They snap and whip and make people sitting together bump each other and crash around in the seat so that you can't think straight.

The streetcar we got on was a tall one and Dad and I put our back-packs and suitcases on one seat and sat in another. We were rocking from side to side down St. Patrick Street, nice and even and easy, and I was thinking about Mean Hughie.

Mean Hughie and his big, poor family and the farmhouse they lived in with the daylight coming through between the logs and the crooked floor and the broken furniture. I had only been there once, when I was a kid. My mother sent me over to buy some raisin bread from Mean Hughie's wife, Poor Bridget. That was her name. Poor Bridget. Everybody called her that because of what she had to put up with. Poor Bridget was standing at her kitchen table, up to her elbows in flour, punching a big lump of bread dough and sprinkling raisins on it while about a million flies buzzed around competing with the raisins. And everywhere you'd look there was a kid peeking, very shy, from behind something or from under something. Kids under Poor Bridget's dress, behind chairs, under the table, behind the stove, peeking out the cellar door, behind the butter churn, and from under an old bed in the corner where their grandfather was lying like a corpse with his mouth open.

The bread that was already baked was stacked, hot, at the end of the table. Poor Bridget swept the flies off the stack with her hand and gave me three loaves. They were too hot to hold, and since she had no paper or bags or anything I took off my shirt and wrapped the bread in it.

Just as I was handing her the fifty cents for the bread I felt the room get dark. It was Mean Hughie at the open door behind me. He filled the whole doorway blocking out most of the light. I could hear him breathing. Suddenly every kid's face disappeared. Like a dozen groundhogs ducking down in an open field.

"I'll take that fifty cents. That way it'll be nice and safe!" says Mean Hughie.

I dropped the five dimes in his big lumpy hand while Mean Hughie nailed me with his eyes and let a big slow grin open up the bottom of his face.

"How's your father!"

"Fine thank you, sir," I said, extra polite.

"Good," says Mean Hughie. "Let's hope he stays that way!"

I tied the sleeves of my shirt in a knot and slung the bread over my shoulder. On my way out of the yard I heard Mean Hughie growl something and I heard a slap.

As I turned the corner around the barn I almost bumped into the oldest of the kids. She was about my age and she was carrying a tin pan of chicken feed in her right hand. Her left arm was missing from the elbow down. Her dress was raggedy and her feet were bare. We stood there staring at each other until I heard her mother call from the house. There was a sad sort of crack in her voice.

"Baby Bridget, Baby Bridget," she called.

Baby Bridget looked quickly at the house, back at me, and then stepped around me without saying a word.

Sitting there on the streetcar, swaying from side to side against my dad, I was seeing the whole thing again. And especially one thing above all else. More than the hot bread against my back and the sound of the slap and the flies and raisins and all the dirty-faced little kids and Mean Hughie's ugly grin. More than all that. More than all that was the colour and the shape of Baby Bridget's eyes. They were eyes that were deep green. The deep green of the Gatineau hills. The eyes that took me in and made my tongue thick so I couldn't speak. The greenest green. And their shape was the shape of the petals of the trillium.

◆

Right on the corner of Dalhousie and St. Patrick the trolley pole came off the wire and the streetcar went dead. I was beside the open window so I had a good look as the driver walked along outside the car to put the pole back on. He was taking his time and he had a nice look on his face. Everything else was stopped. All the pedestrians with their parcels or their push carts or their canes stopped to watch. All the cars were stopped and the people were leaning out the windows to watch. A streetcar behind us and one coming on the opposite track were stopped and all the people were hanging out the windows to watch. The storekeepers along both sides of St. Patrick and Dalhousie came to their doors or stood in their windows. Upstairs the people in the apartments over the shops, older people, in dressing gowns and underwear tops, leaned on their windowsills and watched.

Everybody was taking a break. Taking a break on a nice day in late June at the corner of St. Patrick and Dalhousie about one o'clock in the afternoon. They all wanted to watch the sparks when the driver put the pole back on the wire.

When the pole sparked, the generators came back on, and everybody gave the driver a little bit of applause and some car horns.

Before we got off at York and Dalhousie, Dad slipped the bottle of Lysol out of the big knapsack and left it under the seat.

"Ruins the taste of the berries," he said, and gave me a big wink.

There were some things you just didn't let on to Aunt Dottie. Like leaving the Lysol on the streetcar. There would be no use trying to tell her that we didn't want to lug a big jar of disinfectant around just because she thought all berries were infested with germs. It was easier just to leave it on the streetcar.

And another thing we didn't mention to Aunt Dottie was that we were taking Dad's friend Frank with us.

She'd have a fit if she knew that Frank was going to be there. She couldn't stand Frank. One of the reasons she couldn't stand him was that he used to pick his nose a bit when he was over at our place for supper. Not much. Just a bit. Most people wouldn't notice. But you'd have to be some great magician like Houdini or somebody to get away with picking your nose when Aunt Dottie was around. And he also put his beer bottle on her white doilies on the arm of the chesterfield.

And he didn't flush the toilet.

And last Christmas he fell head first into our Christmas tree and broke everything and nearly electrocuted himself on the lights.

So we didn't tell Aunt Dottie that Frank was coming. Dad said that by the time she got there, he'd be gone, anyway.

"The train leaves at two, so we'll have time to go to the liquor store, get Frank out of the hotel, pick up some meat at the market, and be on our way," Dad was saying.

We went into the liquor store.

"Haven't seen Frank in a couple of weeks. Wonder what he's been up to," said Dad.

"Is he going to stay with us the whole time?" I asked.

"He's going to pitch a tent at the top of the hill behind the cabin. He'll be with us but he won't be with us if you know what I mean."

I knew what Dad meant. Frank was a nice guy, but sometimes his boozing would get you down.

Dad bought a bottle of gin and we headed down to York Street and into the Dominion Hotel where we were supposed to meet Frank.

I waited in a little back room and had a coke while Dad sat out with the men to wait for Frank. I was only half way through the coke when Dad came in and said the waiters told him that Frank was meeting us at the Union Station.

"It must be something horrible important to drag him out of this place," Dad said and we strapped on our packs and headed across to Aubrey's Meat Market.

We were standing in the sawdust on Hector Aubrey's floor and there was old Hector. He looked like a side of beef dressed in a white apron. He was chopping something very close to his thumb with a big flashing cleaver.

Dad was getting a ten pound chunk of corned beef and some other stuff from one of the other butchers, and old Hector, who knew everybody, spilled the news about Frank.

"I hear Frank bought a car," he said, as he wiped blood from his hands onto his huge apron. "Who's he goin' to get to drive it for him? You gonna be his driver, Tommy?" He was talking to Dad.

Everybody in the shop knew what he was talking about. Frank would be too drunk most of the time to drive a car, and the butchers and the customers were all talking and laughing about it. As we were leaving, old Hector said: "You could always get Young Tommy here to run ahead of the car and warn the innocent people along the Gatineau highway what it is that's in store for them!"

Everybody laughed at that too, and then we left.

Just as we got to the pillars of the Union Station a new car came staggering around the War Memorial, cut right across Confederation Square, rode up on the sidewalk in front of the station, and crunched into a lamp post right in front of us. Behind the wheel was Frank.

"It's true," said Dad under his breath, "he *did* buy a car."

It was a brand new 1950 Buick Special with Dynaflow transmission, eight cylinder engine, vertical grille bars and bomb-shaped parking lights mounted on the front bumper. It had three air vents on each side of the hood, whitewall tires and an aerial in the middle of the windshield pointing back with the wind, four door, wraparound bumpers, and teeth— nine big long teeth, chrome teeth, for a grille!

We threw our stuff in the back and Dad shoved Frank over into the passenger seat and backed the car off the post. We left two of Frank's new chrome teeth on the road beside the post. We eased nice and easy out into the traffic, turned on Sussex Street and headed over the Interprovincial Bridge.

"Frank, why didn't you tell us you bought a car?" Dad said, after he got used to the feel of her.

"I wanted to surprise you," Frank said. "It'll be faster than the train. And we can go anywhere we want once we get there."

"Surprise us! You pretty near ran us down!"

"She got away on me," said Frank. Then he let out a long beer burp.

It was a good thing Aunt Dottie wasn't there.

Away down below us, on the water, the huge log booms sat like pancakes.

A couple of tugs were churning away, looking like they'd never get anywhere. If you look at a tug hauling logs, then look away for a while, then look back, you can see that it's moved a bit. But if you just stare right at it, you'd think it wasn't moving at all.

"They tell me Mean Hughie's going to die," Dad was saying. "He's supposed to have the cancer."

"Believe it when I see it," said Frank. Then he went into a coughing fit.

The loose boards on the Interprovincial Bridge were slapping on the steel under our wheels and the black girders with the rivets were zipping by.

Frank coughed all the way over the bridge and most of the way through Hull until we stopped at Romanuk's for groceries.

They sold everything in Romanuk's: naptha for the Coleman lamp, minnows for bait, vegetables, beer, rubber boots, overalls, tools, candy, hats, egg lifters, bottle openers, spinners, canned potatoes, rosaries, lamps shaped like naked women, joke books, yoyos, seeds, shotgun shells, blood pudding, pork hocks, head cheese.

There was a deer head on the wall with a beer bottle stuck upside down on one of the points of his rack.

Mr. Romanuk gave Dad and Frank a shot of whisky from underneath the counter while they talked about Mean Hughie.

I had two more cokes.

"Is dat the guy you hit with the shovel years ago, Tommy?"

"That's the lad, all right," said Dad. "Hit him a two-hander right over the forehead with a long-handled gravel shovel and they say he didn't even blink. Snapped his braces clean off. Got a head like a rock!"

I had heard the story many times before. I could picture it as though I'd been there, even though it happened before I was born.

Mean Hughie blinked all right, but he only blinked once, and then his eyes got narrower and narrower and he got staring out over the river and up to where the mountain meets the sky. Then he turned around and set out for home. I could see his big back and the blue shirt marked with the X where his braces were before Dad's blast with the shovel snapped them.

Dad was still talking. Dad loved to talk.

"He had a notion he was goin' to set fire to my cabin. I tried to explain to him, when I caught him, that he'd better not do that. Had to slap him with the shovel to get his attention. It cured him of that notion, anyway. I told him that if I ever came up the Gatineau and found my cabin burned, I wouldn't even ask any questions, I'd just take a gun and go over to his place…"

While Dad was talking I was thinking about Baby Bridget. When we got up to Low I was going to go over to her place again for some bread. I wondered what she'd be like. Three years. I wondered if her eyes were the same.

We got back in Frank's new car with the two missing teeth. Frank was driving again.

"Go nice and slow, Frank," Dad said and we took off up the road. Frank had one eye closed and he was aiming the car along our side of the road. There were black tracks where the tires made marks in the tar. Frank was trying to follow these tracks. There was no traffic for a while and Frank had the road to himself.

Dad was humming and singing his favourite song:

> *"The place where me heart was*
> *You could easy roll a turnip in…"*

It was a song about an Irish guy who lost his heart.

Up ahead, a truck pulled onto the road and headed our way.

"Can you get by this truck, Frank?"

Frank was hugging the right. The closer the truck got the more Frank hugged the right. Soon our right wheels were on the mud shoulder. He was giving the truck a lot of room. He had one eye closed and he was looking through the steering wheel. I guess he thought that if he closed one eye he could aim the car better. He looked like a guy trying to fire a rifle for the first time.

Frank was the worst driver on the whole Gatineau.

The truck was so close now that I could see the driver. He was looking at Frank like you would look at a rare, tropical, one-eyed fish in an aquarium. Our car was down to about ten miles an hour. Then all our wheels were in the soft grass and mud and we stopped very quietly against a pretty big rock. I heard another one of the Buick's teeth go.

We were leaning away over to our right so we had to get out Frank's side. That was hard because Frank had to get out first. And Frank was just sitting there and still steering.

The truck turned around and parked in front of us.

"Hello Frank!" said the driver as he opened our door and helped Frank out. "See you got a new car!"

"Good day, Baz" said Dad. "Got a chain in your truck?" Baz got out the chain and hooked us up.

"Heading up to Low?" said Baz. "Guess it's a lot handier with the car, eh Frank? No more waitin' on the train?"

"Yep," said Frank, "go anywhere we want to; freer'n birds." Then Frank played a little patt-i-cake with both hands on his pot. He always did this when he felt sort of proud of himself. Pitti-pat, pitti-pat, with the fingers of both hands, on his pot.

As Baz pulled Frank's new Buick out of the ditch, I could hear the train whistling down in the gully along the bank of the Gatineau. It was half-past-two.

We would've been on that train if Frank hadn't bought that car.

"I hear Mean Hughie's got the cancer and he's threatening to die," Baz was saying as we helped Frank to get back behind the wheel and Baz gave him a little drink of gin.

"I'll believe it when I see it," said Dad and we pulled away.

About a mile up the road we wheeled into the Avalon Hotel. Frank crunched his left fender a bit against the corner of the hotel as he tried to park.

I didn't hear any of the Buick's teeth fall this time.

It was going to take a long time to go the forty miles up to Low the way we were going.

◆

Inside the Avalon it was damp and dark. The ceiling was low, and Dad had to duck his head a bit walking around in there. We sat at a table with some guys that Frank and Dad knew. Everybody had a quart of beer. I had another coke.

They were talking about Mean Hughie.

"Is it true he has the cancer and isn't long for this world?" said a guy with a big wart on his nose.

"That's what they say," another guy said. He had a great big face, red as blood. "But I'll believe it when I see it."

"He could never twist you Tommy, could he? I heard he twisted you, but I never believed it. I'd bet real money he never twisted you." It was the guy with the wart talking, who had wrists and arms almost as big as Dad's.

"He's put both my arms down at one time or another. But not in one sitting. Don't forget we been going at it since we worked breakin' rocks at the dam when we were only about fifteen years of age. So we've twisted many times. As of now I'd say we're about even. We were only about the age of Young Tommy here when we got started. We been feudin' since first we ever run into each other. I think it was because I was so handsome and good looking and he was so ugly and horrible looking…"

Dad, when he got started, was a pretty good talker. Most guys, when they talk, can only say a little bit and then they have to take a rest. But Dad, he could say a lot and pretty well keep everybody's attention.

He was talking about Mean Hughie and how every time anything bad or stupid happened to him he seemed to get uglier and meaner.

You could tell that Dad felt a little sorry for Mean Hughie because when he told about the worst thing that ever happened to him, he got quite serious and stopped making fun of him.

The worst thing that ever happened to Mean Hughie was there was an accident with his binder and his oldest kid had half her arm cut off. She was their first baby; Bridget her name was. Baby Bridget.

When we got back in the car I asked Dad what happened.

"They say the binder was stuck on a rock and Mean Hughie got off the binder to beat the horses and they reared up and ran a few steps and the little girl was in front of the knives to pick up a flower—clover, I guess. And the knives took her arm. It was a sad day for Mean Hughie. And they say he hit her for being in the way. It was a mean thing to do. And a sad day for both of them."

Frank was trying to back the car away from the corner of the hotel. He put a big rip in the left fender and tore out the headlight. It was hanging out and springing up and down like the eyes you get with those joke-shop glasses.

We passed Ironsides and the Alonzo Wright Bridge and started to climb the mile hill into the mountains.

The train was long gone, following up the river. Too bad we weren't on it.

I was wishing Dad would drive.

"I'll take over later," he said. "It's a new car. He should drive it the first part of the trip. I'll take over at Wakefield." He was talking quietly to me out of the side of his mouth. Frank was concentrating on all the curves the road took to get up to Chelsea.

Frank, the worst driver on the Gatineau.

Luckily there was no traffic coming against us. Frank was going about fifteen miles an hour. He was in the middle of a long coughing and sneezing fit. In the middle of the hill, after the fourth turn, he dropped his cigarette between his legs. For the rest of the hill and the three worst turns he coughed, steered from one side of the road to the other, sneezed, and had one hand underneath himself looking for his lit cigarette. You could smell burning. I wondered what Aunt Dottie would have said.

At the top of the hill was Hendrick's farm where everybody in that huge family was red-headed. You knew you were done climbing when you started to see some red-headed people along the side of the road or leaning on a fence.

"Watch you don't run down a Hendrick," Dad was saying, "you know it's unlucky."

Chelsea was coming up and Dad decided to try and get Frank into King's gas station near there for some gas and a rest. More for the rest than the gas.

We were about six miles from home. Thirty-four to go. It was almost half past three. Dad and I left our place around one. Two and a half hours to go six miles. I was figuring that to be about three miles an hour. A person can *walk* faster than three miles an hour! Just then, Frank turned into King's Station and knocked over a pyramid of motor oil cans near the pumps.

King came running out laughing. "Frank! I heard you bought a new car! Is this it? She ever a beaut! Look at the nice big teeth! Did you hear about Mean Hughie! I'll believe it when I see it! Come on in the back! I'll get a couple of Hendricks to service your nice new car! Come on Tommy! Come on Frank! Bring young Tommy with you! Would you like a coke? No, no, never mind those cans! I'll get some Hendricks to pick them up! Come on! Come on around the back and have a snort…!"

Around behind King's, in Chelsea, Dad got talking more about Mean Hughie. We were sitting on some barrels. I was having another coke. Dad, Frank and King had some snorts of gin.

I was listening carefully to Dad's stuff about Mean Hughie. I was trying to fit Baby Bridget into it all. Frank wasn't listening. He had both eyes closed. He was resting. He must have been pretty tired! Six miles is a long drive!

Specially if you're Frank.

"We were both workin' on the dam," Dad was saying. "Mean Hughie and me, shovelling and pickin' and mixing cement and hammering up forms. And breaking rock. No bellies like now, no flab. Stomachs hard and flat as boards. Six days a week, ten hours a day. And twisting wrists at smoke break. I'd win with the right. Mean Hughie with the left. He was awful powerful in those days. He was about six foot four and weighed around two hundred and twenty pounds and he had a great big head on him and shoulders about this wide. And I remember dinner time with big chunks of homemade raisin bread and green onions big as apples and lots of salt and slabs of fat pork and cold buttermilk from the icehouse. And the dam taking so long and goin' up so slow and everybody on the river above Low, their life going to change forever. They knew it but they didn't really know it. And Mean Hughie living by himself in a cabin he built for himself before he was flooded out and squatted over on the farm where he is now. And his shack, his cabin, was about two hundred yards from the bank of the river. And that's plenty, says Mean Hughie, the water won't come up that far when they slam that dam closed for good. But everybody disagrees with Mean Hughie. Everybody said the water would come way up past his shack. Even the dam man, he came around two or three times and told Mean Hughie that he'd have to move and even offered him money. They took more than five years to put up that dam, so Mean Hughie was about twenty-two then when the dam man made his last visit. Mean Hughie laid him on the sawhorse and rested the bucksaw blade on the dam man's neck and put his left boot up on the dam man's bellybutton and made him say that the water would *not* come up or he would saw off his head.

"No, the water, I promise you, will *not* come up and flood away your nice cabin, Mean Hughie!" says the dam man.

"That's better," says Mean Hughie. "Now you can go."

Dad stopped talking and let everybody laugh for a while.

Even Frank was laughing a bit, in his sleep, about how mean Mean Hughie was and after Dad told some more stuff we woke Frank up and we all got back in the car.

Dad started talking again after we waved goodbye to a whole bunch of red-headed Hendricks and Frank got the car back out on the highway without hitting anything.

Dad didn't know I was interested in Baby Bridget, but he knew I liked his stories so he kept going.

"Now, Mean Hughie's cabin was on deceiving ground. It looked like it was above and back enough from the river, but it wasn't. Most people try to tell Mean Hughie this just about every other day but Mean Hughie isn't listening. He says his shack was there long before they started building the dam and it's a long walk to the water and it's just not going to come up that far. Yes it is, everybody says, you're going to wake up one morning and your bed'll be floating! But they don't like to say it too often to Mean Hughie, or at least not too loud or bold or sarcastic or in a mean way, because they know Hughie will bounce them around the rock pile for a while or deliver them a backhander on the ear which would set your head ringing for about a week. Or worse! Like what happened to Buck O'Connor. Old Buck was acting a bit too frisky around Mean Hughie, talking about his house floating down the river and asking him if his windows were closed and stuff like that. Buck paid for that with one of his ears. Buck was in the middle of saying that Mean Hughie should quit helping to build the dam at Low and go home and build his *own* dam around his house, or take swimming lessons, when Mean Hughie decided to kneel on his chest and cut off a big part of one of his ears with a rusty jack-knife. They say that Buck went right home, looked in the mirror, took a big pair of scissors and snipped off most of his *other* ear just so's he'd look *even*! Anyway old Buck went out West for the harvest that year and never came back."

Just as Dad finished his story about Buck O'Connor's ear, Frank swerved off the road a bit and clipped off a mailbox at the end of somebody's laneway and put a big crack in the right side of our windshield. We were passing the town of Tenaga.

I was thinking that when we got up to Low, if we ever did, Crazy Mickey, my great-grandfather, would be right where he always sat, on the two-seater swing, with my great-grandmother, Minnie, holding hands. She was ninety-nine.

He was a hundred.

I was wishing we were on the train. We'd be almost there by now.

Between Gleneagle and Kirk's Ferry, Frank had a race with a big fat cow with a bell on.

The cow stopped and Frank won the race.

Going past the golf course at Larrimac there was a golfer crossing the road pulling a golf cart.

Frank chased the golfer right up onto the grass on the other side of the road, hit a rock coming down and took our muffler partly off.

The pavement ended around Burnett and instead of following the old road through Cascades and along the river bank, we took the new highway overland through the rock cuts and all that dust and loose grav-el and machinery.

We were creeping along about fifteen miles an hour and Dad was singing that turnip song. It was his favourite song. And mine too.

We were about halfway down the mountain into Wakefield and I was wondering if Frank was going to drive into the water and take the river for a while just to get some of the dust off. That would be nice, it seemed to me, to be floating along the Gatineau River in our new Buick with the missing teeth, to trail our hands out the window in the water and cool off, maybe throw in a line and do a little fishing.

But instead of going in the river, we took the turn into Wakefield just as nice as pie. The sun was making diamonds on the Gatineau River water and Dad let out a cheer and took a big suck on his gin bottle and started singing. I'd heard the song a hundred times. And I could hear it a hundred more.

> *"The place where me heart was*
> *You could easy roll a turnip in;*
> *It was as broad as all Dublin*
> *And from Dublin to the Divil's Glin;*
> *And when she took another sure*
> *She could'a put mine back agin';*
> *Ah Molly's gone and left me here*
> *Alone for to die!*
> *Oh mum dear did ya never hear*
> *Of pretty Molly Brannigan?*
> *Since she's gone and left me, mum,*
> *I'll never be a man agin';*
> *There's not a spot on me hide*
> *That the summer sun will tan agin',*
> *Since Molly's gone and left me here*
> *Alone for to die!"*

It was the song about the Irish guy who lost his heart.

◆

The car was making a ticking sound. The fan began pinging on a part of the hood that was bent in.

We drove down the street in Wakefield a bit, beside the empty train tracks and the river and then turned into the yard of the Wakefield Inn. Frank parked the car without running into anything, and we went in.

Another coke!

We talked for a while with some guys about Mean Hughie's cancer and Frank's new car. Some guys went to the window to look at the car and laughed quite a bit.

"We're going to have to do something about Frank's drinkin'," Dad was saying when Frank was gone to the toilet.

"Take him in and make him take the pledge at the church in Martindale," a big farmer said. He was drinking a quart of Black Horse Ale.

"We might just do that, because his drinkin' is gettin' out of hand altogether," Dad said, and a little later we went into the toilet to get Frank who was asleep in there and then we left.

We drove down the street in Wakefield a bit more and turned into the Chateau Diotte Hotel to find a guy with a crowbar to pry the fan away from the hood of the car.

I had another coke. I went into the bathroom to look in the mirror to see if I was starting to *look* like a coke. Frank and Dad had a large Black Horse each. I took my coke outside and watched a guy with a crowbar pry the hood away from the fan.

"I hear Frank's going to Father Sullivan to take the pledge," the man said, "I'll believe it when I see it!"

"What's the pledge?" I asked.

"It's when you go into the priest's office behind the church and sign a paper swearing to God and the Virgin Mary you'll never touch beer, liquor or wine again, so help you," the man told me.

"I'll believe it when I see it," I said.

Back in the car Dad asked Frank if he'd take the pledge.

"Would you go into the priest's office and take the pledge, Frank?" Dad said to the back seat.

Frank said something about a leak. He was lying down in the back seat with his cheek on his hands.

"We better stop for a leak," Dad said. "Can you wait 'till we get to Alcove? We'll go into 'Chicks' there and have a leak and a bite."

At "Chicks" we had hot chicken sandwiches, a coke and two more large Black Horse Ales. The sandwich made Frank wake up a bit and he started singing "Goodnight Irene" to our waitress. That was his favourite song. Then he fell over backwards off his chair.

It was six o'clock.

"Yes, we definitely have to try and get Frank to take the pledge," Dad said and we left.

We passed right by Farrellton, waved at Father Farrell and didn't stop until we got to Brennan's Hill. We stopped at Monette's Hotel and bought a pail of minnows and some worms.

In Low, we only stopped at two hotels, Doyle's Inn and the Paugan Inn. We were making very good time.

We passed Father Sullivan's church in Martindale with his little bit of paved road outside and got back on the dirt again. We were certainly making very good time. It only took us around six hours in a brand new 1950 car to go about forty miles. A world's record!

Six point six miles an hour!

Could have walked!

◆

Along the road small pigs were walking on tiptoe.

The clouds were like kindergarten cut-outs pasted up there on the blue sky and all piled up like my great-grandma Minnie's white hair on Sunday—and the cows were standing there like wooden statues on somebody's huge lawn and the horses were warm and brown and set up in twos so their heads and tails were together.

It was half past eight when we turned into my grandfather's farmyard.

It was like a photograph, only coloured. Or a painting. For a second everything and everybody was still. All the people were there, in their places, all with their faces turned looking at us in our car. Like a big crowded beautiful coloured painting in a museum.

At the back of the painting was the sky and the humpy green mountain. A little closer, there was the river. In the middle was the rolling field. In the front was the farmhouse and the yard and the shed and the big poplar trees and the butternut tree with the evening sun making shade and bright pools of golden light in the yard. And in the yard, the people.

There was Crazy Mickey, my great-grandfather, and his wife Minnie, on their swing. Crazy Mickey, born in 1850. One hundred years old. And Minnie, ninety-nine.

There was Old Tommy, carrying a pail. That was my grandfather, seventy years old, born in 1880.

There was my dad's sisters: Leona, forty-four, at a table washing dishes; Monica, forty-three, drying; Martina, forty-two, pulling wool; Ursula, forty-one, sharpening a knife; Lena, forty, feeding slops to chickens.

There was my dad's brothers: Gerald, thirty-nine, lying on his elbow, smoking; Vincent, thirty-eight, lying on his back, smoking; Joseph, thirty-seven, lying on his side, smoking; Sarsfield, thirty-six, on his stomach, smoking; Armstrong, thirty-five, leaning on the house, lighting up.

And in the very front of the painting, a big crow, flying across, caught for a second, perfectly still.

We got out of the car and Frank leaned on the gate so he wouldn't fall over and everybody was talking at once about Mean Hughie and the cancer and maybe taking Frank to the priest and the weather, but I had my mind on something else.

I was thinking about Baby Bridget.

Soon we would go down to Dad's cabin and set Frank's tent up on the top of the hill and get settled in for the night and then it would be tomorrow and I'd find an excuse to go over to Mean Hughie's farm and see Baby Bridget.

Then I heard somebody say the word "disappeared." Somebody disappeared. Who? Mean Hughie! Mean Hughie has disappeared! About three weeks ago. Gone. Vanished. Just like that. Nobody knows where. Damndest thing.

Mean Hughie.

Gone!

PART II

My excuse came the very next day.

Dad and I got up early and went up the hill behind the cabin to see how Frank was doing. His tent didn't look as good as it did last night in the dark when we put it up. He must have knocked the main pole out during the night because the tent was flat on the ground and we could see Frank lumping around underneath the canvas.

The trunk of Frank's new Buick was open beside the tent.

"Looks like he took his beer and his outboard motor into the tent with him last night and knocked down the pole," Dad said. "Let's go down and cook up some bacon and eggs. He'll be all right."

Dad and I lit up the outside stove and I went down to the well and got some water. When I got back there was bacon frying. I loved to see the smoke from the chimney of the outside stove moving up through the pine trees and to smell the bacon and the wood.

I put the kettle on.

Dad moved the bacon over and broke four eggs in the deep grease and then moved the pan over to a cool part of the stove and started splashing grease on the eggs with the egg lifter. I took one of the lids off the stove and cooked some toast in the flames with a fork.

I poured the tea and Dad took the hot plates out of the oven.

Then we sat down on the little verandah and had a great big breakfast.

I was mopping up the last of my eggs with some toast when I heard Frank coming down the hill behind us. I knew it was Frank by the thumping. Everybody thumps when they come down the hill, but only Frank would thump like somebody who didn't know if he was walking or running. He thumped right past us and headed down to the river. He was carrying his outboard motor. We watched him go by, but we didn't say anything. We figured Frank didn't want any breakfast. He disappeared for a while and then we could see him again at the shore.

"Have to get that fella to Father Sullivan to take the pledge," Dad said.

We stood up on the little verandah of the cabin to watch Frank down at the river try to put his outboard motor on our boat.

"How about running over to Poor Bridget's and see if she's doing any baking today? Get us a few loaves of nice fresh bread?"

I was thinking about Mean Hughie disappearing and where he might be hiding.

"I'm going to cook up a great big roast of corned beef," Dad was saying, "and we'll have a great big feed of cabbage and corned beef and some nice fresh homemade bread with it for supper."

Frank, down at the river, had his motor in one hand and was holding out his other hand to keep his balance. He stepped into the rowboat. Now he had both feet in the boat. It was rocking from side to side.

"I'll clean out that great big iron pot and we'll do it all on the outside stove here. I'll pick a great big pail of raspberries when you're gone and get some fresh cream from them up at the farm. And we'll have a great big feed."

Frank was high stepping it now, and the boat was rocking worse. Now he was towards the back of the boat sort of running.

Now he was over the end of the boat, head first, with the motor in one hand, into the water.

Dad was shaking his head.

"We've got to get him in to talk to Father Sullivan about the pledge," Dad said.

"I'll go for the bread," I said.

I ran up the hill, passed Frank's tent, cut across Old Tommy's hay field and picked my way carefully through Mean Hughie's slash fence.

A slash fence is made of fallen trees, unlimbed. They're the sloppiest, worst fences in the Gatineau. To make one you just cut down a big tree and leave it there. Then cut another one and leave it there. Do this all the way along and there's your fence. Old Tommy's cows were always getting caught in Hughie's slash fences and sometimes breaking their legs or cutting their stomachs and tearing their bags on the sharp sticks and broken branches in the slash.

I was over on Mean Hughie's land.

I was a bit scared so I started whistling. Mean Hughie has disappeared. Almost three weeks now. Sure. What if he's hiding out in this bush? He could shoot me or jump on me from behind.

The thicker the bush got the more I whistled.

By the time I got to the old logging road, that I remembered from three years before, I was all whistled out. I turned the corner around the barn where I first met Baby Bridget and headed across the yard.

Poor Bridget was baking all right. I could smell it before I knocked on her broken door.

"Young Tommy!" Poor Bridget said, "Holy Mary Mother of God, you've grown like some kind of a lovely weed you have—look at you now. Jesus Mary and Joseph, you're here for bread now and I have lovely bread for you to take home to your father, Tommy. You haven't been here for years, but you're here now and I guess you and your father are stayin' at the cabin and will you be up for a while? Holy bald-headed, here's a chair for you to sit on and rest yourself..."

While she was talking and offering me raisins and water a whole lot of kids came peeking and falling into the kitchen through windows and doors and giggling and shoving each other and taking looks at me.

I don't remember what I said when Baby Bridget came in. I think I said hello, but I was trying to swallow at the same time and I sort of choked.

She was hiding her poor arm and looking out through her hair at me with her green eyes. Her mother was still talking.

"...and Baby Bridget here often asked me about you, the poor darlin' with her poor arm and she..."

Baby Bridget turned around to the stove and used the bottom of her dress to open the hot oven door and check on the bread in there.

"...and you'll stay and wait for this next batch of bread to come out, not this one, for God's sake, but the next one, and you'll sit down with us and have your dinner before you go back to your lovely father with the bread...Baby Bridget, get two pails, one for you and one for Young Tommy here and take him down to the berry patch, for the love of God, and get us some berries for dinner while I finish punchin' up this dough ..."

Baby Bridget and I went to the berry patch across a creek behind the house. Some of her brothers and sisters tried to follow us, but she gave them a look and they disappeared.

Baby Bridget could pick raspberries faster than I could even though she only had one hand. She'd lean over and hold the berry stem against her stomach with her short arm and pry the berries off the bush with her hand so they'd fall into the pail tied around her waist. She used her fingers on the berries sort of the way you'd tickle a cat underneath the chin.

And her hair fell down like a curtain covering her face when she leaned over.

"It's easier if you tie the pail around your waist," said Baby Bridget.

"What with, a piece of string or something?" I said.

"Binder twine is fine," she said, and then she laughed a bit because of the rhyme she made.

"What's binder twine?" I said.

"It's twine you use in a binder."

She leaned over to start on another bush and then looked up through her hair at me.

"You can't pick berries when you're watchin' somebody else pick berries," she said. I started picking berries like mad.

When my pail was half full I looked up to see how her pail was.

It was full. She was standing there eating what she picked.

Then, I don't know why, but I said this:

"My Aunt Dottie says berries have germs on them."

"Your Aunt Dottie's crazy," said Baby Bridget, and then we went back to her house for dinner.

I felt pretty stupid about the picking berries, but as soon as I got back into the kitchen and all the berries got poured into one bowl I started to forget about it. Then, when Poor Bridget brought out the pot of steaming potatoes and told us all to sit down and the kids started coming out from behind everything to grab the best seats and Baby Bridget kept her hand on the seat beside her to save it for me and told me to sit there, I felt smart again.

I was wondering if they were going to talk about Mean Hughie and all the stuff people were saying about him when Poor Bridget got out the rest of the dinner.

A big bowl of boiled potatoes from the garden with the skins still on,

steam coming off them, some of them split, the white showing; a heap
of green onions, lying sideways on a plate, the onion part washed but the
long green part with mud still on; a platter full of curly pieces of fried
pork, the rind still on, the pieces curled up like ears; a loaf of bread and
a knife beside it; a big bowl of butter; lots of salt. Plaster the potatoes
with butter, put a pile of salt on the oilcloth covering the table beside you
to dip your onions in. Pick up the pork with your fingers, one piece at a
time, and with your front teeth bite the meat and fat off the rind. Put
the rinds in a little pile on the oilcloth on the opposite side of your plate
from where the pile of salt is. Get Poor Bridget to cut the bread you want
while she holds the loaf against her chest. Eat your crusts.

Eat about four or five potatoes, eight or nine onions, five or six pieces
of pork, two slices of bread, lots of salt, lots of butter and leave enough
room for two cups of tea and you'll feel good after.

Get your hands sticky with mud and butter and your face covered
with pork fat and potatoes. Then burp politely.

Oh, Aunt Dottie! If only you were here to see this!

Poor Bridget didn't sit down at the table with the rest of us. She ate
her dinner off the kids' plates and at the stove. She would take a piece of
fried pork out of the pan and nibble on it and then come over and feed
the rest of it to one of the younger kids. Then she'd take an onion or a
piece of potato from one of the other kid's plates who wouldn't eat anything and take a bit of that and then jam the rest of it in that kid's
mouth. Then, when she saw another kid eating more than his share,
she'd grab whatever he was shoving in his mouth and eat that. And when
another kid would slide off his chair under the table, she'd pick up an
onion or something, take a bite of it and hand the rest of it under the
table to that kid.

And every now and then she'd charge over to the table and flap her
apron to get the flies back up in the air.

She was talking about Mean Hughie.

"Their father is gone, did you know? They say they last saw him in
the store in Low. Last seen there. Three weeks ago or so. Doctor said he
had the cancer. God only knows where he's gone to! Have another potato. How's your father? Is he well? Not sick or anything? Fine man. Their

father's gone somewhere. He was a troubled man. God knows he had his troubles. Eat up that pork. There's lots. Have yourself an onion. Yes, he went and disappeared. Just vanished. Gone. A troubled man..."

Outside, after dinner, Baby Bridget was standing with me while I wrapped the bread in my shirt.

"Want to see some binder twine before you go?" she said, and took me over to an old falling-down machine shed on the other side of the house.

Inside the door that was hanging on one hinge I could hear pigeons gulping and I could smell machine oil and straw. The sun was rodding through the walls in the gaps between the logs.

The binder sat there like a giant toad. Baby Bridget ducked underneath the raised knives and opened a greasy lid on the side of the machine. Inside there was a big spool of thick string.

"That's binder twine," she said. "It's strong. It comes out of here, through the machine and ties up the oats into sheaves. You can use it for anything. It's very strong. Almost nobody could break that with their bare hands."

"*Almost* nobody?"

She didn't answer. She just looked at me with her green eyes burning.

◆

That night after we had the corned beef and cabbage I asked Dad if it would be all right if I invited Baby Bridget over for supper some night. We were watching Frank trying to clean up the dishes. It seemed like the place got dirtier the more he cleaned.

"Sure," Dad said, "bring her over for supper and I'll make a great big stew and I'll cook a great big raspberry and gooseberry pie. Then we can play cards. Does she like to play cards?"

"I don't know."

"Are you worried about her only having one hand?"

"No. I guess I was wondering if they even *had* cards at her place. They're awful poor. Maybe she's never played cards."

"That's all right. We'll show her."

Frank was trying to dump some slops out the window. But he didn't open the window first so you could say that quite a bit of it wound up on the glass.

"We've gotta get that fella in to see Father Sullivan to take the pledge and quit drinkin'," Dad said.

"I'll believe it when I see it," I said.

◆

A couple of days later Baby Bridget came over for supper. We had the stew and cleared off the table to play cards. We didn't get much cards played because we couldn't concentrate.

Frank was cleaning up again.

The floor was covered with soapy dishwater and Frank was slipping and stumbling all over the place and breaking dishes and losing forks under the stove.

It was just as well that Frank was interrupting our game. Baby Bridget was a little shy about the cards because, as she told me later, she'd never played cards before.

Frank was trying to heave out the leftover stew from the big iron pot. Since Dad had cleaned up the window from the last time, Frank decided he'd do it properly and use the door. He gave the screen door a shove so it swung right out and then grabbed the big iron pot and tried to heave out the stew before the door closed. The door was a little faster than Frank was and a lot of the stew got caught in the screen and on the wooden frame. Then Frank looked back to see if anybody was watching (of course we weren't; we were playing cards) and then started to try to clean off the door with the egg lifter. He pushed his face right up close to the stew on the screen and was using the egg lifter to flick off the carrots and peas and stuff. Because Frank was such a good housekeeper, he was opening the screen each time so that what he'd flick would land outside. This made him lean forward. He was concentrating pretty hard on a small chunk of beef or something and leaning further and further forward. Then gravity took over and out the door he went onto his hands and knees. We couldn't see him now, but we could hear him out there grunting and talking to himself and falling down and sliding around on gravy and potatoes on the grass.

"I never put long celery in my stew anymore," Dad was saying, "because there's nothing slipperier than long cooked celery on grass or floors and I also hesitate to put those real small peas in the stew because they stick to a screen door worse than anything."

But later we found out that something sticks to a screen door even worse than small peas and stew. Coffee grounds. Coffee grounds get right in the little holes in the screen and they're almost impossible to get out. And when they're way up near the top it's even worse.

You see, Frank emptied coffee pots overhand. That's how the grounds got so high on the door. Dad told Baby Bridget that Frank used to be a great baseball player before his head was run over by a tank in the war.

That was the first time I ever heard Baby Bridget laugh out loud.

Suddenly we heard a car horn and Frank started yelling, "Visitors! Visitors!"

Baby Bridget and I went out, stepping over Frank and the stew and ran up the hill to see who it was. It was Gerald driving, Vincent and Joseph in the back, Sarsfield and Armstrong on the running boards, all smoking cigarettes. And it was Aunt Dottie in the front seat! We certainly didn't expect her this soon.

I went over and kissed her ear and told her I was glad to see her. She was sitting on a sheet of white paper in case the seat was dirty. Gerald, Vincent, Joseph, Sarsfield and Armstrong were making a big fuss over her and jabbering away, but she wasn't paying any attention. She was staring at Frank's tent.

"Whose tent is that?" she asked, pointing at it as if it was a big turd or something.

"It's Frank's," I said.

Aunt Dottie got out of the car and asked somebody to get her suitcases out of the trunk. Gerald, Vincent, Joseph, Sarsfield and Armstrong got her suitcases out and piled them around the hood of the car. Aunt Dottie opened one and took out a long pair of rubber gloves and a doctor's mask. Then she took out a pretty big pump spray full of fly tox and some kind of disinfectant.

Then she ordered the boys to go in the tent and throw everything out. Out came Frank's sleeping bag, some shorts, a sweater, a pillow and a bunch of dirty socks. Then his fishing box, and about a hundred bottles of beer and some empty gin bottles.

When it was all out she sprayed everything with her pump gun and then started firing the beer, one bottle at a time, in every direction, as far as she could, down and over the hill into the deepest, thickest wild raspberry bushes.

It took her quite a while, and she was quite puffed out when she was finished.

Then she packed her gloves and her gun and her mask, put a new sheet of white paper on the seat, had the boys put her suitcases back in the trunk and got in the car.

"I will not stay here when that horrible Frank is here! I'll stay at the farm. Drive off!" And away they went.

We looked down the hill where Frank was already crawling around looking for his beer. You could see the bushes moving and hear Frank saying "Ow!" and grunting a bit and talking to himself.

Dad was sitting on the sawhorse.

I said goodbye to Baby Bridget and watched her go up the road and cut through the slash fence.

Later Frank stood up out of the bushes in the evening light. His clothes were torn into long thin strips. He was covered with blood. But he was smiling.

He picked up some bottles in his arms from the pile he made on the grass and headed up the hill to his tent. He had found every single one of his beers.

I went in and got ready for bed. I could hear Frank popping a beer now and then. And I could hear the crickets.

Later the moon came out and Frank was snoring. I went out and looked up the hill. I could see Frank's tent in the moonlight. I thought I could see the sides of the tent moving with the snoring.

The snoring sounded as though someone very cruel was slowly torturing a huge pig.

◆

A few days later I took Baby Bridget fishing. She wasn't as good at fishing as she was at berries.

I put on my bait just right so my hook didn't show and straightened out my leader and checked my spinner and let my line out nice and even and slow until it touched bottom and then raised it up gently a couple of feet and moved it up and down very gently and quietly and then I looked up over the water to the mountain across the river and out of the side of my eye I saw that Baby Bridget was watching me and I laughed and soon after I got a bite and hauled in a nice pickerel. You can't win at fishing when you spend most of the time watching the other guy.

We pulled the boat up on a small sandbar and cleaned our fish on a big white log. Baby Bridget couldn't clean fish because of her arm. But she was good at washing them after they were cleaned. Except the first time. She was swishing our biggest one around in the water and it squirted out of her hand and slid out into the deep water and disappeared.

The sun was hot and the fish blood was bright red on the white log and Baby Bridget was looking at me as though I was going to hit her or something. She was still crouching in the sand with her hand still in the water and she was looking at me as though I was going to go over to her and slap her across the face. Then her eyes filled up with water and the water spilled out and poured down her cheeks.

I told her never mind, it was just an old fish, but it didn't do any good. She just crouched there crying as if she was waiting for me to go over and hit her.

All of a sudden the sun went in and it started to hail. It does that in the mountains around Low, especially on some hot summer days. Before you know it, it's not sunny any more, the wind comes up, a lot of hail is dumped on you and then, all of a sudden, it's over, and the sun is back again.

We waited under a tree and didn't say a word. When it stopped we got in the boat and headed home.

Baby Bridget only said one thing all the way home.

She said this: "Sometimes the hailstones come down as big as walnuts."

I was worried about her, so later I told Dad about it and Dad said that it was probably because Mean Hughie hit her bad one time. He told me that when she had her accident and lost part of her arm, Mean Hughie hit her for getting in the road of the binder. He hit her while the blood was pouring out of her poor arm. I asked Dad how he knew what happened and he said that one of the kids was there and told Gerald, Vincent, Joseph, Sarsfield and Armstrong about it. And they told Old Tommy and Old Tommy told Dad.

And also he said that Mean Hughie broke off a piece of binder twine, with his bare hands, from the machine, and tied Baby Bridget's arm with it so she would not bleed to death.

When I was getting dressed for bed Dad asked if I wanted a little late snack. He had set out some cheese and tea and maybe some pie if I liked. I must have eaten too much because I had a terrible dream.

A man is standing beside a horse. It is Mean Hughie. Mean Hughie is beating the horse with a long black whip. Beating the horse across the back. The horse's eyes are glittering, glistening, shining white and wet, rolling white, flashing, rolling back. Mean Hughie picks a long piece of two-by-four from the wagon and smashes the horse over the back and the skin breaks and the blood comes and the horse pumps his iron back feet, pounds his steel boots into the grey ground and the chains on the traces are jingling and clattering like broken bells.

Someone is yelling.

This is what they're yelling.

"They say Mean Hughie's got the cancer. There's something wrong—Hughie would fill up the whole doorway. But now there's something wrong. What's wrong? The Gatineau's gone. They damned the water. They'd twist wrists 'till their chairs broke. He could drink ten quarts in a night if he had the money. Ten quarts of Black Horse; and eat pickled eggs for a half an hour. One after another steady and then sneeze and blow pickled egg out his nose all over his hands on the table. Pickled eggs and froth and snot all over his sleeves and the back of his big hands on the table. Wait till Aunt Dottie hears about this!"

◆

The next afternoon Baby Bridget and I were all set to take a swim when we realized that Frank's tent was surrounded by cows. Somebody left a gate open and the cows were having quite a time licking the tent and eating Frank's socks and shirts that he hung on the front of the Buick to dry.

Baby Bridget and I chased them away and rounded them up to

where they were supposed to be in Old Tommy's other field. It took us about an hour and as we were walking past Old Tommy's barn we thought we heard somebody crying inside.

We stopped to listen and sure enough, it was somebody whimpering and crying.

We were still talking about who it might be when we got back to Frank's tent. We stopped to check what the cows had done.

His socks and things he had hung out were lying around and looked like short thick green ropes. The cows had eaten them and then spit them out. They had licked all the windows of his Buick and dropped about a hundred fresh pies all around the tent.

Could make for hazardous footing. Specially if you're stepping out of a tent. Specially if you're Frank stepping out of a tent!

We heard the sound of rustling around inside the tent and then beer opening and some grunting.

We waited to see him come out. Baby Bridget hooked her hand in my arm and we stood there like friends in line for a movie.

Frank stepped out. He had on bare feet and the bright sun closed his eyes. He hit the first cow pie and his leg shot out sideways. His other foot came down to get his balance and hit the second pie. He was running sideways now and pretty well out of control. You could see he was trying to steer himself onto the path through the bushes that went down the hill to the cabin. He was holding his beer up trying not to spill it.

The next two pies did it.

Both feet went straight up in the air and he let out a holler and disappeared, back first, into the raspberry bushes.

Just then, a short distance away, in another part of the berry patch, someone stood up. I could tell by the helmet and all the bug-netting hanging around her face and shoulders and the rubber gloves that it was Aunt Dottie.

She was dumping out the pail of berries she had picked.

"I will not keep berries from the same patch that that horrible Frank has been near! Poisoned! All poisoned!" She picked her way carefully out of the bushes and headed towards the farm.

Then Baby Bridget and I went swimming.

◆

About a week later I sort of told her that I loved her. It came from something Dad told me about Crazy Mickey and Great-grandma Minnie and their swing.

I was sitting on the two-holer with Dad, looking out over the river and the mountain on the other side. When you're in the two-holer you leave the door open so you'll get the breeze. When you're finished you close the door to keep the cows from going in there to lick the seat for the salt and wreck the place. It's opposite from at home. At home when you go into the bathroom, you close the door. Here, you leave it open when you're in there and close it when you leave.

"I heard someone crying in the barn. Someone was sobbing and crying in the barn the other afternoon," I said to Dad.

"It was Crazy Mickey. Every day in the early afternoon he goes in there and has himself a good cry," Dad said.

"What's he crying about?"

"Most days after dinner Great-grandma Minnie has a little lie down upstairs and Crazy Mickey thinks she's gone away and died somewhere so he goes to the barn and has a good cry. Then he has a snooze and by the time he gets back to the swing, Great-grandma Minnie is all rested and is there on the swing waiting for him. Then he figures she's back from the dead and it's a real miracle and he's so happy to see her he has another good cry."

"This happens every day?"

"Not every day."

"How many times, then?"

"Every day but Sunday. Sunday Great-grandma Minnie doesn't have a snooze after dinner. She doesn't have any dinner. Stays in church all day. Crazy Mickey waits for her outside on the bench."

"Every day but Sunday he thinks his wife died and he feels awful?"

"And every day she comes back and he feels just great."

"Why does he go way over to the barn to cry?"

"Because it was around there that he went to cry when his mother died. He was just a kid then. That'd be about ninety years ago. When they first got here from Ireland."

"How do you know all this?"

"Because Old Tommy told me."

"How does Old Tommy know?"

"Because Crazy Mickey told *him*. Hand me some of that paper."

"When did people start calling him crazy?"

"He was always called that. Hand me some more of that paper."

"How do you know that?"

"Because Old Tommy told me. Hand me some more of that paper."

"And Crazy Mickey told him?"

"Yep."

"Can you believe someone who's called crazy?"

"Have to."

"Why?"

"Because he's all we've got. I'm going now. Shut the door when you're done."

Anyway, I told Baby Bridget all about it and I said that I thought it was beautiful that they loved each other so much for such a long time.

She didn't say anything, but I could tell what she was thinking. She was thinking it could be us.

Us for that long.

We were out in the boat when I told her that.

It was quiet and clean and slow—just trolling—letting the shore stay just the length of your oar away, chipmunks sitting on the bank watching you slide by, sometimes a porcupine's bum heading up, in a big hurry, going nowhere, waddling away…

And rowing, quiet, don't splash the oars, put them in the water each time so there's no splash—watch the little whirlpool that the oar makes run by you, maybe there's a water spider spinning in it, wondering what's happening. And all you can hear is the gurgle sometimes—and maybe a wasp or a dragonfly goes by and makes a small racket, and a bird sings, and you're right under the mountain, in the shade of the mountain there, and you look up, and the mountain and the clouds are moving slowly by, sliding by, and you are still, perfectly still in your little rowboat that doesn't need a motor.

We were trolling down river. I was rowing and Baby Bridget was fishing with a hand line on a stick, a June bug and worms.

We were farther down river than I'd ever been.

We rounded a point, sticking close to the shore. It was evening. I asked Baby Bridget if she wanted to turn back.

"We can go a little more," she said.

We could see the dam in the distance. She had caught two pike. They were lying in the bottom of the boat, their gills pumping a little bit.

We were getting closer to the dam. Baby Bridget pointed to a little log stable sitting right on the edge of the water near the dam.

"That's where Old Willy the Hummer lives. He's a healer. Some say he's crazy, but he isn't. That's all that's left of his farm. That old stable. He lives there. There's no road to it. You have to go by water."

In the distance you could hear the generators humming.

"Those big cables go right over his shack. It's so noisy there you have to shout."

"You've been there?"

"Yes."

"Why did you go there?"

"He's a healer."

"What were you doing there?"

"I wanted to see if he could make my arm grow back. It was a dumb thing to do."

"What did he do?"

"He said he would heal me someday but in a different way."

"A different way?"

"Yes, a different way, but he wouldn't say any more. He said I'd know when. And I'd come to him and he'd make me right again."

"Make you right?"

"Yes, but he wouldn't say any more. Just started humming."

"Humming?"

"He hums with the humming of the generators. He makes the same sound. I'll take you there sometime. Father Sullivan doesn't like him. He says he's sinning against the church."

◆

The next day Baby Bridget came over in the late afternoon and we had the cabin all to ourselves. Dad and Frank were gone to Low to the hotel.

I didn't want to play cards and since it didn't look like they'd be back from the hotel until quite late I decided to get out Dad's cookbook and make something fancy for me and Baby Bridget to eat.

We read each other some of the recipes. They were very old.

Then it got dark and I lit the Coleman lamp and we read some more recipes.

Baby Bridget was a good reader. She read me this one twice. It was one of her favourites.

My Mother's Bread Pudding
4 or 5 slices of day-old bread
milk
raisins
brown sugar
Dice up the bread in diced sizes the size of dice.
Put them in a large soup bowl and sort of pat them with the pads of your fingers.
Pour boiling milk over.
Sprinkle with raisins and brown sugar.
With a tablespoon, up in your room, try and eat it, while, downstairs, they're all eating roast beef and laughing.

The one I liked best was this one:

My Father's Fried Potatoes and Eggs
10 potatoes
5 onions
some butter
a bunch of black pepper
lots of salt
Boil the potatoes until they're not quite done.
Let them sit in a bowl in a cool place all night with their coats on.
The next morning, Sunday, when nobody's around, undress them and cut them in irregular shaped, half-a-biteful-sized pieces.
Cut five onions in chunks about the size of dice.

Cover the bottom of a great big black iron pan with 1/4 inch of simmering butter.

Throw in some of the onions.

After a while, throw in some more onions and darken the whole surface with a thick dark mist of pepper.

After another while throw in the potatoes and the rest of the onions.

Lash the salt to it and crank up the heat.

For quite a while keep turning the whole thing with an egg flipper or something. Clang the side of the pan with the egg flipper, violently, making the pan ring, if you can, like a church bell. Do this until everything is brown.

Turn off the heat; cover for the time it takes you to drink one pint.

Forget the eggs.

But the one we made was this one:

My Father's Onion Sandwich
2 huge Spanish onions
fresh bread
butter
salt
beer
mayonnaise

Cut the middle slice (1/2" thick) out of each onion. Throw the rest of both onions out in the yard.

Get a big loaf of fresh, hot, homemade bread from some farmer's wife whose dress smells like milk.

Cut 2 slices (2" thick) from the centre of the loaf.

Save the rest of the bread for tomorrow's bread pudding.

Plaster the bread with butter.

Put on the onion slices.

Pour salt to her.

Get a beer and some mayonnaise.

Put lots of mayonnaise on the onion slices.

Close the sandwich and with the heel of your hand, press.

Eat.

It was quite a romantic evening.

♦

A couple of nights later we were up at the farm, all sitting around Old Tommy's kitchen talking about Mean Hughie. There was Crazy Mickey and his wife Minnie in their rockers in the corner by the stove. There was Old Tommy, fixing a pail at the table. There was Leona shucking peas in a big dish. There was Monica throwing the shucks out the screen door for the chickens in the morning. There was Martina pulling wool. There was Ursula sharpening a knife. There was Lena, sewing.

There was Gerald at the door, smoking; there was Vincent having a smoke at the table with Joseph who was doing the same; there was Sarsfield with his feet up on a stool, smoking; and there was Armstrong, scratching a match on his boot, lighting up.

And there was Aunt Dottie in front of the stove with one of the lids opened part way. You could see the fire glowing a bit through the space.

A little fire at night, just to take the chill off.

Aunt Dottie was wearing a gauze mask over her nose and mouth, tied behind her head with a snow-white lace.

On a stool in front of her there was a little saucer of honey. She was holding a very dainty, pretty little pink flyswatter in one hand and a tissue all ready in the other.

When a fly would light on the stool to investigate the saucer of honey, she would snick it with her little swatter, wrap it in the tissue and it would wind up in the fire just slick as a button.

What a way to go!

Baby Bridget and I were listening to what they were all saying about Mean Hughie. We were sitting in the corner on a bench.

Dad was down in the cabin having a snooze and Frank was gone out to Low in his car.

"They say they saw Mean Hughie at the store in Low charging up a lot of flour, salt, sugar, lard, baking powder and shotgun shells," Old Tommy was saying. "He bought it all right, but he never came home with it. Poor Bridget never saw him again. That was over a month ago. Nobody's seen him since."

"They say he's gone somewhere to die of his cancer," Leona said. She was handing Monica some shucks. Monica opened the screen door and threw the shucks out in the yard. Not one of them hit the screen. When the door closed I noticed something I had never noticed before. When the moon shines through a screen and you're looking through the screen at the moon you can sometimes see a cross. When you take away the screen the cross is gone.

"Mean Hughie's vanished," said Gerald.

"Gone," said Vincent.

"Disappeared," said Joseph.

"Thin air," said Sarsfield.

"Melted away," said Armstrong.

"There's quite a cross on the moon tonight," Crazy Mickey was saying to Minnie.

"Mother of God," said Minnie, "Mother of God."

"Did you see there's quite a cross on the moon tonight?" Crazy Mickey said. "They say when the cross is on the moon, our Holy Mother is nearby."

"Jesus Mary and Joseph," said Minnie.

"He thinks the cross on the screen is real," I said right close to Baby Bridget's ear.

"Shh," said Baby Bridget.

"Mean Hughie's gone and disappeared," said Gerald.

"Up and gone," said Vincent and Joseph.

"Vanished into thin air," said Sarsfield.

"Nowhere to be found," said Armstrong. "They say Mean Hughie is nowhere to be found!"

We were all quiet for a while just listening to the boys smoking and the peas being shucked and the knife being sharpened and the rockers rocking.

And the flies dying.

Then we heard a crunching sound outside. The sound of Frank coming up nice and easy in his car into a tree.

Frank was back from Low.

Gerald, Vincent, Joseph, Sarsfield, Armstrong, Baby Bridget and I went out to see.

Frank's car was up against Old Tommy's big butternut tree. There was some steam floating up. It looked pretty in the moonlight.

Baby Bridget walked me part way home and then cut across the slash fence to her place.

I called to her before she disappeared out of the moonlight into the bush.

"They say they're soon going to take Frank in to Father Sullivan to take the pledge!" I called.

I heard her laugh a very nice laugh from the bush where she had just disappeared. I think I heard her say, "I'll believe it when I see it."

I went home to the cabin and went to sleep.

◆

The next day we went swimming early and then lay down on the big rock beside where the boat was tied up. The sun was nice and warm and I had my chin on my hands and I was watching the water on my eyelashes making rainbow colours in the light.

All of a sudden I noticed, right in front of my face on the rock, that a dragonfly was just starting to stick his head out of the bug he was living inside of. He had crawled up from under the water and picked a warm place on the rock right where I was lying to dry himself out and crawl out of his skin and then take off. His head was out and I could see him moving his shoulders to come out farther. Next, I knew, he'd spring his long tail out and dry off his big wings. Then he'd leave.

It would take a long time.

Baby Bridget and I lay on the rock on our stomachs facing each other and watched him working his way out.

The dragonfly was between our faces.

Everything was quiet until I heard some thumping on the hill.

It was Frank coming down with his motor again. My mind started working. I knew he was going to come down and ruin everything. I knew he was going to come up on the rock to see what we were doing and probably drop his motor in the water or step on our dragonfly or make so much noise trying to get in the boat that a thunderstorm would come up and our fly would think it was the end of the world and quit right there.

Or he'd sit down with his legs apart and let his testicles hang out of his bathing suit and embarrass everybody and ruin everything.

I knew it.

But I was wrong.

He did something even worse.

Part way down the hill he stopped and put down the motor right in a gooseberry bush. Then he stood there, with his hand over his eyes, watching us. He was swaying quite a bit and I thought he was going to fall all the way down the hill and we'd have to get up and help him all the way up and by that time everything would be spoiled.

But he didn't.

What he did was he started shouting.

"Love!" he shouted.

He was shouting "love!" standing there, shouting "love!" and you could hear it echo all over the Gatineau River from the mountain and back again.

"Love! There's love here! Love!"

Then he turned around and staggered back up the hill to tell Dad.

"Love!" he shouted and the echo came back. "Love. Come and see it! There's love here! Love! Love!"

I heard the screen door slam and I knew that it was Dad, coming out to see what all the racket was. Then we heard Frank start his song.

"Irene Goodnight,
Irene Goodnight,
Goodnight Irene,
Goodnight Irene,
I'll see you in my dreams."

Frank was doing his pitti-pat, pitti-pat on his pot.

Dad had him by the arm. They were standing there looking at us looking at the dragonfly.

Then Dad shouted down the hill.

"Today's the day. Today's the day we go to see Father Sullivan with you know who!"

"I'll believe it when I see it!" I said. "I'll believe it when I see it!"

◆

We waited around for a while, but the sun went in and the dragonfly decided to wait so we went up the hill to see what was going on.

Dad was dragging Frank up to the car.

"We'll pick up some of the boys at the farm to give us a hand!" Dad said and we helped him get Frank into the car.

We picked up Gerald, Vincent, Joseph, Sarsfield and Armstrong, and the car was so full of people and cigarette smoke by the time we got to the church at Martindale that when we opened the doors to get out, I'm sure the people around, if they were watching, thought the car was on fire.

We got Frank out of the car and everything was pretty smooth until we got to the door of Father Sullivan's office at the back of the church.

Frank was holding on to the door frame with one hand. He had a pretty good grip on it and it looked like we weren't going to get him in there.

Father Sullivan was yelling at us, telling us what to do.

"Push his arse, lads! Push his arse!" shouted Father Sullivan.

Gerald, Vincent, Joseph, Sarsfield and Armstrong were pushing Frank pretty hard and Frank was starting to lose. Then all of a sudden he reached back with his other arm and grabbed the other side of the door frame. Now he had a good grip with both hands and it was starting to look like Frank just wasn't going in there.

Then Father Sullivan solved the problem. He went around the side of the church and came back with two big rocks. One for me and one for him.

"We'll hit him on the knuckles with these rocks," said Father Sullivan. "You hit him on *that* hand, Young Tommy, at the same time as I rap him one on this hand. Nice and hard now. It'll be good for him. And don't worry. We do this all the time."

Father Sullivan had his rock right over his head in both hands so he must have brought it down on Frank's knuckles a lot harder than I did.

Anyway, Frank let go in a hurry and Gerald, Vincent, Joseph and Armstrong (there was no room for Sarsfield) ran him into the priest's little office and into the chair.

We waited outside for about fifteen minutes and by the time Frank came out, quite a little crowd had gathered. When Frank appeared carrying his piece of paper that Father Sullivan made him sign saying he would never touch Beer, Liquor or Wine again so help him God and the Virgin, everybody started to clap and cheer a bit.

Frank was studying the paper and swaying there in the sunlight.

"He's lookin' for loopholes," Dad said and we helped Frank into the car and drove back to the cabin.

PART III

That night after Dad and I had some leftover stew (he gave me the last carrot), we went to bed and I went right to sleep thinking about the dragonfly.

But I didn't dream of the dragonfly.

I dreamt of Mean Hughie. It wasn't like the dream I had before.

◆

Mean Hughie is very small and away down in a well or a hole and I am looking down to him and he is crying out for help, but there is no voice, no sound, just his mouth opening and closing.

Then, away across the river, I can see two hands, gripping the top of the huge mountain like somebody's hands on a fence. I know they are Mean Hughie's hands. I can see the hair standing up on the knuckles and the scars and the black fingernails. The hairs on his knuckles are like pine trees. Then the top of his greasy hat rises slow over the mountain, blocking out the sun, and then Mean Hughie's huge face, the forehead, eyes and nose of Mean Hughie, looking at me between his hands, staring right at me from up over there, over the mountain, about a mile away!

I am screaming but I can't hear myself because of the wind that comes up, making the river black, and because of the thunder rolling around. My mouth opens and shuts, opens and shuts, but no sound comes. Only the wind screaming through the pine trees and the thunder rolling.

What if Mean Hughie's shoulders and his chest come next and then one knee, as he climbs over the mountain and steps into the river? Then up to his thighs in water he takes two wading steps and wades deeper until the water is up to his chin and then over his head, just his hat showing? Then, what if suddenly the water bursts open and up our hill comes Mean Hughie, water running from his clothes and slime and weeds and fishing lines and wagon wheels and farm wreckage left from the flood sticking to his pants and boots and grabs me like you'd grab a bird with a broken wing and tears the legs off my body like I once tore the legs off a grasshopper? I scream and scream but my mouth is only opening and nothing is coming out...

◆

When I woke up Dad was holding me in his arms.

I was yelling something about Mean Hughie.

"It's all right. It's all right," Dad was saying patting me and holding me in his big arms.

"Everything's all right. Everything's all right."

"I saw Mean Hughie come over the mountain!"

"Just a bit of a dream," Dad was saying and then he went and got me a cup of water.

I lay there for a long time staring up at the rafters of the cabin.

Then I got up and got dressed.

I went outside.

Dad was asleep and Frank was snoring up a storm in his tent up the hill. Across the river, the moon was sitting there over the mountain like a cut fingernail. The clouds were moving heavy past it, silver and black. There was a steady wind.

I had the feeling that something was going to happen. I could feel it in my stomach. I went up the hill, past Frank's tent, and looked out over the field towards the farmhouse and the road. The moon was spilling a little light from between the black mountain onto the field and the dirt road.

Then I saw a figure coming down the road towards me. I knew right away it was Baby Bridget. I walked up the road to meet her halfway. Before we reached each other she started talking.

"I've got to see the Hummer. The time is now. I can feel it. Will you take me? He's going to heal me. I know it."

"Now? Tonight?"

"Now."

"Row down there in the dark?"

"There's just enough moon."

There was a silence while two crickets talked to each other out in the field.

I got two old sweaters out of the cabin without waking Dad and we picked our way down the hill, through the raspberry bushes and the moonlight, to the boat.

I rowed. Baby Bridget sat sideways, the way she always did when she trolled, but this time there was no trolling. She was thinking and thinking hard.

It's funny, but if you like somebody, a girl say, you can tell what they're doing, even if you can hardly see them. I knew Baby Bridget had a lot on her mind.

My right oar had one squeak in it each time I pulled it back. It was the only sound except for the gurgling of the water. The steady breeze was warm and going with us. The mountains on each side of us moved by as slow as boats, huge and black.

I started to sing in time with my friend the squeak. I sang Dad's favourite.

> *"The place where me heart was*
> *You could easy roll a turnip in;*
> *'Twas as broad as all Dublin*
> *And from Dublin to the Divil's glin;*
> *And when she took another sure*
> *She could'a put mine back again;*
> *Oh Molly's gone and left me here,*
> *Alone for to die."*

My hands were getting a little stiff by the time we rounded the point. It was a long row. We could see the lights of the dam and the power plant twinkling up ahead. They looked pretty.

You couldn't hear the generators humming yet.

"When you came here before, how did you get here?" I was wondering how she could have rowed with her arm the way it was.

"I walked in from Low. I walked over the mountain and climbed down the cliff beside the dam. But it's a bad way to go. It's too hard. I almost fell. Hummer took me back out by boat."

We could hear the generators now. The lights weren't twinkling any more. They were staring. Beady little eyes. Not pretty any more.

We tied up to Hummer's little broken-down dock. His door was only a few feet from the water. The humming was so loud now that when I asked Baby Bridget one more question I couldn't hear my own voice. My mouth moved, but the humming swallowed up what I said.

Baby Bridget pushed open his door and we went in. It was an old stable fixed up inside. The breeze from the open door flickered the candles and made the whole place move. There were candles all over the room. In the corner there was a statue of the Virgin Mary with a candle burning before it. In the other corner there was a small altar with a crucifix and about a dozen candles that you pay a quarter to light for people's souls in church. There was a table in the middle of the room covered with candles in different shapes, the flames all burning and flickering, making the whole room dance with many shapes of shadows. There were candles on the stove and on an old barrel in the other corner. There were candles burning in the small window. Hanging from chains from the ceiling there were candle pots, all their candles burning, making the ceiling move with lights and shadows.

The humming from the dam was so deep and strong you could feel it in your feet and up your legs.

On one side of the room there was a ladder, leading up to a loft.

Coming backwards down the ladder, there was a man. A little wee man with a voice like thunder.

"BABY BRIDGET! BABY BRIDGET! YOU'RE NOT TOO LATE! GO TO MEAN HUGHIE TONIGHT! TONIGHT!"

He was bent over and wizened. He was standing beside me feeling my arm. He was bony and humpbacked. His teeth were black and his mouth wrinkled and his little ears were full of hair. He was feeling my arm with his skinny hand.

"YOUR FRIEND IS STRONG! HE'LL TAKE YOU TO MEAN HUGHIE! UP RIVER AT THE OLD RAMSAY PLACE! HE'S THERE! THERE YOU WILL BE HEALED! HEALED! YOUR FRIEND IS STRONG! HE WILL TAKE YOU!"

Then old Willy the Hummer started moving around his room. Humming.

If you're standing beside a machine, a furnace or a fridge or a motor or something, and you hum the same note the machine is humming, you can feel the vibrations; you feel like the machine and you are the same. The sound fills your whole head.

He was kneeling in front of the statue of the Virgin, humming with the dam.

"M M M M M M M M M M M M M M M M M M M M M M! HOLY MARY MOTHER OF CHRIST! M M M M M M M M M M M M M M M M M M M M M M!"

The sound filled the room, my whole body, the world. I put my hands over my ears. But it didn't do any good. It was just the same inside me as out.

"M M M M M M M M M M M M M M M M M M M M M M!"

He was sprinkling holy water around the room from a small bowl.

"M M M M M M M M M M M M M M M M M M M M M M! EVERYTHING CHANGES! EVERYTHING CHANGES! YOU CAN'T STEP INTO THE SAME RIVER TWICE! MEAN HUGHIE IS CHANGING! CHANGING VERY FAST! YOU HAVEN'T MUCH TIME! HUM M M M M M M M M M M M M! HUM! HUM WITH THE POWER! EVERYTHING CHANGES! YOU CAN'T STEP IN THE SAME RIVER TWICE! GO TO HIM BRIDGET! GO TO MEAN HUGHIE! THERE IS HEALING THERE! AT THE OLD RAMSAY PLACE!"

He was putting oil on our foreheads with his thumb. Crosses of oil on our foreheads.

◆

Next thing I knew we were outside. We were looking up at the power cables swinging over Hummer's place across the moon. They were buzzing and humming right in tune with old Willy.

I was feeling strange and dizzy, and Baby Bridget had me by the hand.

The Hummer held the nose of the boat while we got in. His voice blended with the dam and we pulled away.

I was rowing like mad.

The lights stopped staring and started twinkling again.

The sound faded.

We were back to the squeak of the oar when I stopped rowing to get my breath. I put on one of the old sweaters and Baby Bridget draped the other one over her shoulders.

She looked beautiful in the moonlight.

I asked her the question that she didn't hear me ask before at Old Willy's dock.

"How did he get to live there? There's no road. Why is he there?"

"He's there because that's what's left of his farm. A long time ago, before the water came up, he had a nice farm there. My mother told me. Old Tommy told *her*. Hummer stayed. His whole farm was flooded and washed away except his upper stable at the top of his last field. The road, everything. He stood at his last door and prayed the water would stop. It did. He stopped the water."

"Why did you go to him in the first place?"

"Because he's Mean Hughie's half brother. He's sort of my uncle. He knows all about Mean Hughie."

I was leaning on my oars and staring at the shadow of Baby Bridget. My mind was spinning. I was thinking of all her sadness.

"Can you start rowing soon? We have to hurry. Old Willy said there wasn't much time," she said softly to me.

I knew where the old Ramsay place was. It was about two miles farther up river than Dad's cabin. I'd been there a few times hunting blueberries with Dad. There were some abandoned farm buildings and some dead machinery. It was on the other side of the river. It was the loneliest place I'd ever been. Dad said there were ancestors of the farm animals there, gone wild. Wild pigs and cats and chickens and dogs. Ancestors.

But I never saw any.

I could feel my strength bulging.

I started rowing.

Not fast but long and hard.

The breeze was against us and so was the water. The moon was most of the way across the sky now. I could feel the blisters starting on my hands. We were passing Dad's cabin. We couldn't see it because there was no light on but I could tell where it was by the shape of the shore and the mountains.

I was thinking about Mean Hughie. Was he really there like old Hummer said?

The breeze was now more like a small wind.

I started humming the Heart Song.

"What's that song mean? That song you were singing. About the heart?" Baby Bridget asked.

"The place where me heart was
You could easy roll a turnip in?"

"It's Dad's song. He got it from old Tommy. Old Tommy got it from Crazy Mickey," I told her.

"Where did Crazy Mickey get it from?"

"From Ireland. He came here when he was ten. That was ninety years ago."

"Way before the dam came."

"Must have been nice here then."

"People must have been happy then," said Baby Bridget.

My hands were getting pretty sore. Baby Bridget put her feet against mine for support to make my rowing easier. It was good to talk and take my mind off the pain.

"The song is about a man who lost his heart. The hole where his heart used to be was so big you could roll a turnip in it. And the hole got bigger. It was as big as the city of Dublin. Even bigger. It was as big as the space between Dublin and Hell. It's a sad song. Dad sings it when he's drinking. He sings it a lot around Christmas, too. It's not a Christmas song, but he seems to sing it around Christmas anyway."

I stopped talking and I could tell Baby Bridget wasn't in the mood for a story because she didn't laugh or say anything or even sigh. She just pressed her feet harder against mine to help me row.

The only noise now was the oar squeaking and the water slurping around the boat. We were getting close to Ramsay's Point. I looked behind me and I could see the shadow of the point humping out into the water. The light from the little moon made a needle in the water right against our boat.

The moon and the needle followed and watched every move we made.

◆

We rounded the point and rowed into the bay. Just before the moon went behind the point we saw the shadow of the broken dock at Ramsay's Landing. It looked like a giant grasshopper that had come to the water to drink, and drowned there, his back legs and part of his body still on the shore, his head under water.

We ran the boat up on the grasshopper's back and tied the rope on one of his jumping legs.

We walked up the clay bank and followed the trail into the black tunnel the trees made. We had no moon now and Baby Bridget took my hand and we felt along the road with our feet.

The steeper the path got the more we stumbled and felt our way. I was just going to say something about being lost when I could see a grey hole up above us. Some light. We headed for it and soon we could almost see the road we were on.

We could hear some pig noises and some running in the bush. Wild ancestors of the Ramsay pigs.

We came out of the tunnel into a clearing. Maybe the sun was somewhere. It was coming on morning.

Everything was getting grey as we followed the path across the clearing.

Soon we could see some buildings, small against a rock cliff, outlines of buildings, falling down slowly. The Ramsay buildings, dead buildings, falling over, and machinery, lying there in the tall grass, wheels up, curving rusty iron, pain in the grass, dead bodies of machinery, a binder upside down, in the tall grass, a rusted hayrake in the grass.

Close to the buildings now.

There's dew on the path grass.

We see, beside one of the buildings, a long box.

And maybe something or somebody getting into the box.

The sky gets lighter.

We see that the box is like a coffin.

A coffin, not falling down like the buildings, but straight and strong. It's made of old wood, but it's not falling over. It's straight and strong.

We reach the coffin and look in.

It's Mean Hughie in there.

Poor Mean Hughie. He looked so pitiful. His eyes were big and his face was bony and his hair was almost gone except for little patches every now and then. His cheeks were sucked right in and his teeth were showing like he was grinning, but he wasn't.

He put his hand on the side of the coffin to pull himself up. He wanted to lean on one elbow. His shirt was open down the front and coming off his shoulders. His arms were like sticks and his shoulders were smooth as driftwood.

He had one knee raised; it was a smooth white ball showing through the rip in his pant leg. His hand, holding on to the side of the coffin, was like a claw.

His chest was bumpy and glistening white and you could almost see through him. The veins in his neck were pumping with his heart.

He had made his own coffin and then climbed into it.

He was trying to die.

His coffin was made of slab wood and barn boards. The frame was made of grey two-by-fours from the rack of the old hay wagon. It was away too big for him now. He made it to fit himself before the cancer got going faster in him and made him so small and light and thin.

I had the feeling that I could have reached down and lifted him out like a long bony baby.

And when he spoke his voice was so small it sounded as if he was talking over a telephone while you were holding the receiver away from your ear.

"I shouldn't have hit you that time you lost your poor arm," he said with his tiny voice.

His voice was so small that he sounded as if he were away down in the bottom of a well somewhere. Away down in the bottom of a mine shaft somewhere.

"I shouldn't have hit you that time you lost your poor arm," the voice said.

Then, like somebody way inside a cave somewhere or someone on the other side of a dam, the voice, again.

"I'm sorry, Baby Bridget."

Baby Bridget put her ear closer to Mean Hughie's lips to make sure she heard.

"I'm sorry, Baby Bridget, I was so mean."

Baby Bridget looked at me through her hair. She was asking me with her eyes if I was listening. Did I hear what Mean Hughie was saying? Did I hear the same thing that she heard?

I leaned over the side of the coffin a little more. Mean Hughie was too weak to hang on to the side with his claw anymore. He let his head back down.

"I'm sorry for what I done to you, Baby Bridget." His voice was as thin as paper. Baby Bridget leaned over and put the stub of her short arm near her father's hand. His fingers felt it and they curled around it and he groaned. He closed his eyes and stroked her arm, petted her arm with his fingers.

Then, Baby Bridget, in the nicest, most gentle, soft voice I ever heard, the kindest voice, the most forgiving voice I ever heard, answered.

"It's all right, Pa," she said, she whispered, she breathed the words close to her father's ear.

"It's all right, Pa.

"It's all right, Pa."

I got up and moved over to a stump quite a ways away so they could be alone. It was getting to be a beautiful morning. The sun was shining right through the cracks between the logs of Ramsay's old house. A couple of chipmunks were chasing each other somewhere in the bush.

Old Hummer had said there was healing here. Old Hummer said Baby Bridget's friend was strong. I was the friend.

Strong?

What could I do? I knew her arm wouldn't come back. I knew she would be disappointed. I knew she would get up off her knees after a while and turn around and her arm would be exactly the same.

Strong?

There was nothing strong I could do. All I could do was sit there and watch. A big crow called out from the top of one of the knotty pines. I looked up and spotted him. He called again. How lucky he is, I thought. Up there, away from everything, fly away whenever he wants.

"I know, old crow," I said up to the crow, "that there'll be no healing going on here." I must have been pretty exhausted, talking to
crows.

I looked down again and saw Baby Bridget standing up beside Mean
Hughie's coffin. Everything was quite hazy because my eyes were full of
the bright blue sky behind the crow.

She was walking towards me.

I could tell that Mean Hughie was dead.

I was trying to focus my eyes to see if her arm had grown back. I
knew it was a stupid hope to have, but I couldn't help having it. I was
feeling more sorry for her than I ever felt about anything before.

Her arm came into focus.

It was the same as before.

I was trying to think of something smart to say. Something that
would make her feel good. Tell her a Frank story maybe. No. Sing a little bit to her maybe. No. Throw a rock at the crow. No.

"He said he was sorry he was so mean," she said to me, looking right
at me, her eyes full of water.

"He said he loved me and he was sorry." Her eyes were big with
water, but she looked good. She had a nice look on her. It wasn't a happy
look. But it was a kind of nice look.

Then all of a sudden I knew. I knew what that crazy old Hummer
meant. Healing.

Healing. There was healing. But it wasn't her arm that got the healing. No. Not the arm.

It was the heart.

The heart got healed.

Baby Bridget's *heart*!

◆

We went down into the gully in the shade where the creek ran through
the Ramsay place and picked a lot of cool green ferns and brought them
up and put them quietly on top of Baby Bridget's pa in his coffin. Then
we went down into the gully and got some more.

Baby Bridget picked some daisies and some barley from Ramsay's old
front field and sprinkled them over the ferns to make it pretty.

I saw a wild ancestor chicken run out of the bush and run back in again.

The crow called from his lookout and then flew off.

"We'll take Pa home," Baby Bridget said.

I was already looking around for some way to get the coffin down the steep old road to the river. Behind the house I found the Ramsay's wooden stoneboat. It was a big wooden sleigh they used to pile rocks on. They'd pile rocks on it and the horses would pull it out of the field. Then when they used their mowers and binders their fields would be clean and the wheels wouldn't get caught in the rocks.

They worked hard, those Ramsays, so they could live.

I found a length of rusty chain beside a dead plough and lashed it onto the iron bar across the front of the stoneboat and towed the stoneboat over to the coffin.

The wood that Hughie made his coffin out of was very old and very dry but it was still pretty heavy.

I lifted one end of the coffin on to the stoneboat and then the other end.

"Your friend is strong. He will help you!" I could almost hear the Hummer saying it. I could feel my muscles in my arms and legs. Baby Bridget was watching me.

I stepped inside the chain so that it was around my waist and started to pull.

I was strong.

Strong as a horse.

I dragged the stoneboat with the coffin on it across the long grass of the meadow to the place where the old road took off down the mountain.

It didn't look like a tunnel now. Everything was bright. The sun was making quick shadows on the old road and the drop didn't look so steep.

And all the birds were singing their beaks off.

And Baby Bridget with the healed heart held Mean Hughie's coffin with her hand.

Half way down I had to get out of the chain, turn around and hold the load so it would slide easy and not get out of control.

We came down the clay bank to the grasshopper's back and sat down to rest.

Baby Bridget put her feet in the water.

I studied our next job.

We had to put the coffin in the boat and row Mean Hughie down the river. The coffin wasn't as long as the boat, but it was too long to fit any other way except across the gunnels in front of me, leaving enough room for me to row and balance the weight a bit.

I got back in the chain and waded into the water up to my waist, pulling the coffin until the end was wet. Then I pulled the boat alongside the end of the coffin and got Baby Bridget to go into the water and put her weight on the middle of the boat with her armpits.

I lifted one end of the coffin onto the side of the boat and slowly nudged it over until it was balanced nice and even across the back half with enough room for me to row. Then I swung the boat around so the bow was on shore and I got in and sat at the oars. Baby Bridget got in behind me and sat on the little bow seat. It was enough balance.

I backed off the shore and turned around and headed out of the bay into the main channel. The daisies and barley and ferns on top of Mean Hughie were moving a bit in the breeze.

I could hear a small plane buzzing above us somewhere. I looked up, but I couldn't find him. We must have looked strange to him. We were shaped like a cross. A cross rowing down the big river. I wondered what Crazy Mickey would think. A cross rowing down the river!

We rounded the point and came into the main channel. The wind there was bigger and I concentrated on keeping the boat balanced, using the coffin as a kind of sail. We were moving pretty fast now and I was working hard with the oars so we wouldn't get out of control. As long as the wind was right behind us, blowing the way we were going, we were all right. We were starting to get some whitecaps and I looked back to see if Baby Bridget was all right, when I heard a popping noise. It was a noise like someone had dropped a walnut from away up, and it hit the boat and bounced out again. I turned back and heard another one. Then I saw what it was.

_____

They weren't walnuts dropping into the boat. They were hailstones. The sun had gone out and there was a big deep black cloud sitting right over us. Up ahead I could see the water go dark and I could hear a hissing sound.

Then it hit us. The hailstones were bouncing off the boat and off our heads straight back up in the air.

I looked back. Baby Bridget had her arms over her head and her head down between her knees.

It was like someone was dumping buckets and barrels of walnuts on us. They were zinging into the water and bouncing off the bottom of the boat and the seats and thumping into the daisies and barley and ferns on top of Mean Hughie.

The boat started to swing and the wind was acting crazy. I knew it would only last a few minutes. I didn't want to fight the wind, just go with it until it settled down again.

We started turning.

We started turning, spinning, and I worked the oars so we would do just what the wind wanted.

We were spinning faster and faster and the coffin started to slide off and pull the boat over to one side. I shifted my weight to try to hold on, but we were out of control.

I knew we were going over and I looked back at Baby Bridget. She still had her head on her arms.

The next thing I knew we were in the water.

I came up and grabbed on to the side of the coffin. I couldn't see the boat or Baby Bridget anywhere.

I worked my way around the other side of the coffin.

Then I saw her arm come out of the water and I heard some shouting.

I helped Baby Bridget grab on to the coffin with her good arm. She was coughing a bit, but she was all right. Then I heard the shouting again. There was a boat somewhere. It sounded like Dad.

The hail quit as fast as it started and I could see a couple of boats and I could hear some oars squeaking.

It was Dad and Gerald in one boat, and Vincent and Joseph in another boat, and Sarsfield and Armstrong in another one.

I pushed Baby Bridget up into Dad's boat and Joseph helped me into his boat.

Sarsfield and Armstrong tied a rope to the coffin. They both had wet cigarettes in their mouths.

The wind settled down and the clouds disappeared.

"Hummer told us where you went," Dad was saying. "He told us you went to find Mean Hughie. So we took off to find you."

I looked at Baby Bridget. She was watching Mean Hughie's coffin being towed behind the other boat.

The ferns and barley and daisies were all gone and Mean Hughie was floating nice as pie inside his coffin. Each time the oars pulled, his head would hit the end of the coffin a little bit.

It wasn't funny. I wouldn't say it was funny. But it wasn't sad or horrible either. It was just kind of peaceful and restful looking.

We rounded the point and pulled in beside the big rock at Dad's cabin where we had watched the dragonfly. The day was being nice again and there was a bit of a crowd on the shore.

There was also a fire with a tub boiling on it. Aunt Dottie was poking in the tub with a stick, and there was lots of steam.

We got on shore.

Everybody was talking about what happened. Crazy Mickey and Minnie were there holding on to each other and Father Sullivan walked into the water and kneeled beside Mean Hughie's coffin. Hummer was there shouting something to the sky and Leona and Monica were knitting and Martina and Ursula and Lena were spreading some clothes on bushes to dry.

Gerald, Vincent, Joseph, Sarsfield and Armstrong went up the hill to get a wagon to take Mean Hughie to the churchyard at Martindale.

And Frank was there.

Frank was there in his bathing suit with the usual hanging out, drinking some very green stuff out of a bottle. He was singing "Irene Goodnight" and drinking this green liquor out of a bottle with a long neck and a fat bottom.

"What about the pledge?" I said to Dad. "Didn't he promise not to drink beer, liquor or wine ever again?"

"Yes he did," said Dad. "But that's not beer, liquor or wine. That's Creme de Menthe. That's not beer, liquor or wine. That's what you call a *liqueur*. I told you he'd find a loophole. He went into Low this morning and bought a case of it!"

"And what's Aunt Dottie doing?" I asked.

"She's boiling clothes."

"Boiling clothes?"

"Frank's clothes. She's boiling them."

PART IV

Later that day I ended up at Baby Bridget's. There was nobody else around. Just Baby Bridget and me.

She said she wanted to show me something in the machine shed.

I was shaking inside like a poplar leaf. We were standing in the machine shed beside the same binder that cut off her arm. The shed was dark with rods of sunlight stabbing through the gaps between the logs. It smelled of machine oil and straw. She was fiddling with a long piece of binder twine, showing it to me, wrapping it and unwrapping it around a nail in the wall.

It was the piece of twine Mean Hughie had used to save her life.

We could hear the pigeons gulping up on the beams.

I said I wanted to kiss her and would it be all right.

Her eyes were green in a rod of sunlight.

And they were open wide, and they were full of water and she said yes, it would be all right.

Cast of Characters

Young Tommy — the hero
Baby Bridget — his friend with her poor arm
Dad — the hero's father, Tommy, a good singer and talker
Mean Hughie — a mean and troubled man
Aunt Dottie — the cleanest aunt a hero ever had
Frank — Dad's friend, one of the worst drivers in Canada
Poor Bridget — Baby Bridget's mom
Hector Aubrey — a huge butcher
Romanuk — owner of a store that sells everything
A turnip — what you could roll in the space where your heart was
Baz — a helpful truck driver
A bunch of Hendricks — a red-headed family
King — a gas station owner who gives you gin
A dam man — a man with a very scary job
Buck O'Connor — a man who lost a part of his ear
Irene — the girl in Frank's favourite song
Father Farrell — a waving priest
Crazy Mickey — the hero's great-grandfather from Ireland
Great Grandma Minnie — his wife for so many, many years
Old Tommy — the hero's grandfather, the farmer
Leona — older sister to Monica, Martina, Ursula, Lena
Monica — second sister to etc.
Martina — third sister
Ursula — fourth sister
Lena — youngest sister to Leona, Monica, Martina and Ursula
Gerald — older brother to Vincent, Joseph, Sarsfield and Armstrong
Vincent — second brother to etc.
Joseph — third brother
Sarsfield — fourth brother
Armstrong— kid brother to Gerald, Vincent, Joseph and Sarsfield
Father Sullivan — a determined and practical priest
The Hummer — a flood victim
Mr. Dragonfly — a love bug
and others, all, by the way, made up